TRIAL OF ICE:
Elf Queen of Kiirajanna
(volume 2)

STEPHEN H. KING

(TOSK)

ISBN-13: 978-0-9989355-4-6

CONTENTS

ACKNOWLEDGMENTS

It's amazing to me, still, after all these pages written, how much goes into writing a single novel, and also how much help is needed to accomplish this feat.

To my beloved bride, Heide, for all the lonely hours you put up with while I'm banging away at the keyboard, and for all the times you've listened to drafts and had the wisdom and the tact to tell me how it could sound better, I give my utmost of thanks. I couldn't do this without you.

To my friends who read my words before they ever get released into the world, giving me stark but always valuable feedback, thank you also.

To Shelly, my Alaskan photographer friend who captured the beautiful Northern Lights in all their glory and then gave me permission to use her amazing image on the cover of my book, I say thank you, and, though it may pain me (but only a little) to add: Go Seahawks!

A Mission

Some say it's bad to show off. Usually, I'd agree.

thwack

The arrow stood, vibrating a little from its force of impact, embedded right smack in the center of the red dot in the middle of the archery target. I grinned and continued showing off.

thwack *thwack* *thwack*

Three more arrows quivered, their points deep in the same dot, the shaft of each rubbing against the first one. With each perfect hit I smiled, but I held back the *whoop*. Too much showing off is too much, right?

I continued sending arrows whooshing to the target. Each hit pretty much right where I aimed it. When I got tired of abusing the little circle in the middle, I targeted other spots out and around the concentric colored wheels. Those places soon sprouted arrows, too. Then I improved the picture into a clock face with a quintet of arrows at what would've been each number's position, one through twelve. With the remaining arrows from the hundred, I lined in the clock hands, the long one toward the twelve and the short hand toward the five. That finished, I nodded in satisfaction.

"Hey, it's five o'clock somewhere, right?" I asked the empty archery range. It wasn't, at least not at Cysegredig. The early morning sun still struggled to climb over the treetops. I couldn't resist the joke, though.

I'd been practicing archery for what seemed like years, though it had really only been a few months. Still, under Prince Charming's tutelage, and his requirement that I shoot a hundred arrows a day, I'd gotten pretty good at it pretty quickly. Oh, I'd grumbled at first. I'd grumbled a lot. It hadn't been long, though, till I'd actually needed that skill in order to survive, and after that I'd been much happier to practice it as long and as often as I had the time.

Go figure.

"Very nice, Princess. Do you do portraits, too?" a smoothly sarcastic voice sounded from behind me, announcing Charming's presence.

Technically, his name was Keion, though my habit of calling him Prince Charming was catching on among my small circle of friends. He was, too. Charming, that is. Tall and exceedingly well-muscled, he was considered the poster-child for Handsome throughout the realm. It didn't hurt that he boasted a thick black mane on his head that glimmered in the sunlight, especially when he chose to flip it around handsomely for us ladies' pleasure. He chose to do that an awful lot. He was the queen's son, too, so of course he had all the finest attire as well as all of the best teachers. That, and he was the male grandson of one of the finest athletes who'd ever graced the elf lands, and as such he'd inherited a legendary prowess in most things physical.

It didn't faze me. Not one bit.

Okay, well.... So, maybe it fazed me just a little bit. Still, considering his ever-sharp sarcastic wit, I wasn't about to let that show.

"Would you like me to do *your* portrait, Keion?" I jabbed, turning a grin his way.

"How well do you do *cythruddedig*?" he asked.

Now, I'd caught on to the language of Kiirajanna pretty quickly; apparently speaking the language fluently for my earliest years of life went a long way toward the schooling I'd received upon arrival that summer. I now spoke elf pretty much all the time, and pretty well too, but there were still some words that stumped me.

"I don't know what that means," I finally admitted.

"I'm sure you've seen the expression frequently." He demonstrated, wrapping his face up into the most exasperated look I've ever seen. That's saying something, too, since I saw a lot of exasperated expressions through my years of attendance in a Mississippi public high school.

Now, I should point out that the way native elves smile had brought me up short when I first got to Kiirajanna. It's not just a grin. No, they use their whole face, every muscle in it, and everything from chin to hairline lights up. It's absolutely spectacular, in an angels-singing sort of way. Apparently they do exasperated the same, only it's not anywhere near as beautiful, and especially not on a face that I'd graced with a kiss not too long ago.

Then again, I'd been trying to just forget that kiss part, and the exasperated purse of Prince Charming's lips just brought it right back to mind and irritated me all over again.

"I'd rather not," was all I could come up with. Frustrated with my own sudden inability to verbally joust, and angry that the boy still held the power to make me angry in the first place, I slung the bow across my back and took off toward the castle, loping along across the lawn on strong, sleek legs that definitely showed the benefit of my recent, often-outdoor life with the elves.

I think he followed me. I didn't check. I didn't really care, or at least that was my thought as my long paces brought me quickly around and into the castle.

"Alyssa," a familiar voice boomed my direction as I crossed the main entry. I stopped and looked through the grand dining hall into the throne room that stood beyond where three elves sat, obviously interrupted in their discussion. Each beckoned me over.

I stopped, one foot on the stairs leading up to the second floor and the relative safety of my bedroom. The call by all three was pretty significant. I waved meekly, and then wrapped up my courage in all the irritation I'd felt toward the prince and walked across the dining room in to the chamber that served as the ruling center for all of Kiirajanna, my bow still draped insolently over my shoulder. I nodded to the ebony-haired male elf, whose long frame and wide shoulders made the golden throne he sat in look small. His purple velvet robe and white tabard, as well as the royal insignia bearing the stag and raven on a huge medallion, labeled him the king of the elves.

"Hi, Dad," I chirped after tossing him the most basic of nods. "And greetings, Your Majesty, and to you as well, High Priestess," I added, addressing the other two occupants of the throne room a little, but not much, more formally. It occurred to me, a little too late, that I really should be worried about why I was being summoned. It was pretty rare for me to spend any time in there, other than the occasional talk with Dad by himself. I'd had audience with the queen a couple of times, and both of those were incredibly formal occasions. To be summoned by the full trio would've probably terrified me on any regular day. After the way the day had started, though, I just didn't care.

"Bad day at the range?" my father asked, his eyebrows drawing up in a show of surprise. By custom I should have genuflected with my right hand held high for both the king and the queen, since they each firmly and completely outranked me, and then given at least a token gesture of respect to the high priestess. Dad didn't usually expect much from me in the way of honorific gestures, but when the royal pair were together in the throne room it should have been a different matter entirely. I would have cared a lot more about the different matter entirely if I hadn't just dealt with Prince Smugpants, though.

I shrugged and replied, "Keion," the tone of my voice saying everything that needed saying about the encounter.

"At some point, my dear, you and my son must need get over yourselves and start attending both seriously and urgently to the business of learning to rule this land," the queen launched her words at me with a biting tone. "You are, after all, slated to be the heralded one who not only fills my shoes but also rises to the heights set for you so long ago by an entire volume of our prophetic works. At the same time, my son will most likely become the king who faces the challenges of your era, laid out in that same prophetic work, while ruling by your side. The future of Kiirajanna is too important for you to keep acting like a pair of love-struck teenagers with nothing better to do." The queen's beauty, her porcelain, fragile-featured face framed with blond hair done perfectly in little ringlets interwoven with tiny pearls, cream-colored dress covering from neck to toe in satin and lace, set the heat in her tone out of place.

The high queen of the elves flashed an expression my way that, I swear, would've frozen a pot of boiling water in an instant. My father, who tradition said could be her co-ruler but not her mate, still managed to flash me an identical expression. Luckily he could only hold it for a brief second; his glare seemed so much more powerful than hers did.

If the queen's gaze could've frozen a pot of boiling water, the high priestess's could've thawed it right back out again. Then again, that expression was normal for her, and it was the reason I'd been calling her Sternyface in the first place. Naissa was her real name, and I actually cherished that at least we had an open and honest relationship going on. She, bless her cold little heart, didn't like me, and I didn't like her, and we both knew, accepted, and appreciated each other's position.

Sternyface cleared her throat and intoned, "Admittedly, her lapses in judgment and protocol do her little credit, yet Crown Princess Alyssa has little time to review studies already completed. She must continue her education toward becoming Queen Talaith's successor. That next step in her education is, if I may remind His and Her Majesties, what we have summoned her here to discuss."

Relieved to learn why I'd been summoned, I was still shocked by her manner of speech. Talk about double standards. What I'd done was, basically, a little bit flippant in blowing off the proper level of genuflection. What she'd just done, though, was downright disrespectful for someone who wasn't a member of the royal peerage. I can't imagine anyone else getting away with forcibly reminding the ruling pair of business at hand and, in doing so, verbally glumping them both into one unit.

Still, the high priestess had some sort of relationship with the two of them that I didn't quite understand yet. Instead of being offended, the elf king and the elf queen nodded agreeably and sat forward, obviously intent on getting on to the business at hand directly, as, apparently, the high priestess desired. It took all of my self-discipline to hold back the frown I felt like showing.

"That is correct, Naissa, and thank you," Dad said. He and the high priestess were old friends; I already knew that. When I'd committed the apparently unforgivable act of using magic, he was the one who'd intervened on my behalf with her in order to prevent my exile back to Earth. Not that returning to Momma had sounded like a bad idea at the time; matter of fact, I still thought the idea sounded pretty good sometimes.

"Alyssa, it is time that you journeyed to the four clans, in order to learn their ways and earn their friendship as well as their respect," the queen said in a formal intonation, and I saw my father fail at hiding a wince when she said it. I tucked it away to ask him more later on. His reaction was a surprise, but the task wasn't. The queen had already prepared me for it, through the intervention and ministrations of the queen's Lady, whose official position had something to do with ensuring all things related to Her Majesty were done properly. My queen-to-be lessons had recently shifted away from basic history, geography, and language to hours spent listening to the queen's Lady discussing everything that could be known about every other part of the realm.

I'd known this time would come, and so, I knew, did Dad. It was one of the major steps in anointing the new queen, the first being to take a girl from Earth and teach her the language and basic diplomacy. The next, still to come, step was to have the crown princess—me!—become an official elf adult by going on what was effectively a vision quest into a sparse and unknown part of the world to survive on my own. Honestly, I'd been looking forward to getting away from the castle and its occupants, especially Keion, for some time.

My father nodded and picked up the line. "It is rapidly heading toward the autumn season, and so going north before that land is gripped by a blanket of snow makes the most sense. Assuming you pick up Padrig's approval quickly, which I doubt will be a problem for you, then you will be able to travel for the remainder of the winter within warmer climates."

I'd met Padrig, the *bennaeth* of the northern clans, and he'd seemed impressed by me. I was looking forward to seeing him again, truth be told.

"They are also the closest," my father continued, "which is a good thing, but they are also the region in which the Cult of the Wyrm has reportedly been the most active. We must keep in mind, my daughter, that the Cult, and the danger it represents to you, is still out there."

I nodded, hiding my surprise. The Cult was the group who'd tried to kill me rather than see the prophecies come true, but I thought we'd beaten them down at the Library of Alecsanddrha.

He continued, "So I will be sending a small contingent of my own guards–not too many as to offend Padrig, of course–in addition to Sephaline, Keion, and Aerona along with you."

I started to object at the same time the elf queen did, and we both closed our mouths at once. She would be objecting that her son was needed, which was exactly what I was going to say except that I wanted to add Aerona to my list of unneededs.

Now, Aerona is the best bodyguard in all of Kiirajanna. I haven't met the other bodyguards to be certain, but I believe it. The woman can stare even the darkest corner in a room into admitting its part in a plot, and then giving up every other corner as a member of the cabal to boot. She makes Sternyface look downright gleeful in comparison.

She's just really not all that much fun to be around.

I couldn't object, though. In truth, Aerona had spent more hours glaring over my shoulder at perceived dangers than anybody else in the realm. When I'd snuck off to investigate–and, um, burn down, but that's a whole different story–the main library, she'd actually seemed hurt by the subterfuge. In fact, she was the one elf in all of Kiirajanna besides my father for whom I could say I knew exactly, unequivocally, which side she was on, and that was mine.

Aerona would die, I was sure, rather than see me hurt. That brought a lump of joy to my throat at the same time it chafed at my adventure-loving self. Besides, if the ill-fated trip to the library had taught me nothing else, it was that I would rarely, if ever, get my way in matters of elf affairs. Well, that, and my foretold place in the whole dang prophecy thing, whether I wanted that place or not.

No, I realized, I couldn't object, nor did I even dare try. It would be annoying, but the simple fact was that the sooner we got there and back, the better. Plus, with this first trip going safely as it had to with that many guards and guardians along, Dad might let me do the rest with fewer guardians.

Finally I nodded. "Well, okay, then. So, Keion, Aerona, Seph, and me. Six of your finest guards, also, and northward ho. Sounds like more fun than a greased pig race, so when do we leave?" I asked.

"Soon," Dad said, ignoring the sarcasm completely. "And I will brief Aerona, Alyssa, so you do not need to."

"All right," I agreed, though it wasn't. Not really.

DRAIG

a dragon, a wyrm.

Preparations

"A road trip with you, me, and Prince Keion! It will be just like old times," Sephaline said, earning one of my best glowers. She actually sounded excited.

"You, me, the prince, Aerona, and six of my father's best guards," I corrected her. "Not quite the same as that last road trip."

A gentle whoosh and a thump sounded from the corner of my room. We both ignored it.

"True, but it will still be lots of fun," my cousin observed, turning a huge grin my way before looking back to the hump of clothes spread out on my bed. She finished rolling up one of my tunics and handed it to me to put in my travel pack. "When will we be depart?"

I ignored another whoosh and thump while wondering if I should correct her grammar, but then I decided not to. She had trouble with English verb tense pretty often, and I was becoming convinced that she just wasn't going to get it. That was okay, really. We were speaking a language that was only spoken on Kiirajanna when the nobles or the scholars chose to. Seph being my cousin, she had a spot in the lower rungs of the first group, and so she always wanted to practice English when we were alone. At that moment, we were as alone as we ever could be with Aerona standing guard.

Well, and the whoosh and another couple of light thumps in the corner, but I kept ignoring it.

Oh, and Booboo, also. Booboo was snoring at Seph's feet. Seph's familiar, a rottweiler-sized killing machine that looked like a bear but was actually a wolverine, weirded me out when it acted like a regular pet and just curled up at her feet. I'd seen the monster take down a dire wolf, and then more than one Cult member at a time, all by itself. The killing image was stuck firmly in my mind, and its peaceful snores made me wonder if it didn't have some diabolical plan in mind.

"Tomorrow morning," I answered, ignoring an even louder whoosh and thump combination. A look of glee flashed across her face; Seph was a ranger by trade and training, and so she always preferred the woods to the stuffy castle walls. We'd spent at least a small part of every day together since I came to the elf realm, so I knew her gleeful expression well. The thought of hitting the trail within a day had just made her very, very happy.

"Have you been to the northern clan's lands much?" I asked, still carefully rolling up clothing to make it all fit in the pack. I only had the one pack, after all, and I had to take enough clothing to be prepared for nearly anything Padrig's household could throw at me. One of Seph's lessons for me was how much more could be fit into a pack if you rolled the clothes tightly instead of folding them, and in between ignoring the thumps and whooshes from the corner we were demonstrating that fact.

"No." The sudden, small change in her expression was the only indicator as she rolled another tunic, but I caught it anyway.

"But you've wanted to, haven't you?" I guessed.

She shook her head tightly and answered, "Not particularly."

"I'm confused, then. I thought you were excited to be going."

"Oh, I am, Cousin. I can't wait to get out on the trail again, and I'm looking forward to seeing the lands up north."

"So why the long face?"

Seph sighed and raised her eyes to meet mine. "I didn't mean much by what you call the long face. The northern clan is strange, that is all. Though we always seek permission to enter any other clan's territory as a matter of politeness, theirs is the only one that requires it. More often than not, the answer is negative, which is unheard of in the remainder of the realm. Very few of my fellow rangers from Cysegredig have ever seen those lands."

Cysegredig was the name for the central region we were in, the part of Kiirajanna that was ruled directly by the king and queen's castle and by the main elf cathedral. Though there wasn't really a clan structure, the region still contained the most rangers by far, according to other talks Seph and I had enjoyed. That made her statement even more startling.

"Has Master Owain been there?" I asked. Master Owain was an elderly, plain-looking man we'd met on our earlier jaunt. I'd been shocked to learn later that he was actually the head of the entire class, as well as Seph's personal mentor. I mean, he'd certainly seemed old enough to be in charge, with the weathered age lines criss-crossing his face as they did, but he was also completely unassuming–just a regular guy type.

"Master Owain has been everywhere," Aerona butted in from her traditional station standing in the corner, and Seph showed her support with a vigorous nod.

"How do you–*would you stop that noise?*" I redirected my words toward the small elm tree in the corner. I had been able to ignore the rhythmic beating of its branches against the wall for a while, but that just made it whack them louder, and the thumping and whooshing had finally gotten to me. I was close to coming unglued at the poor thing.

"We have settled this. You cannot go with us," I said, and then turned back toward Seph. "And why are you laughing?"

"You have such a good singing voice, Cousin," she said, hiding her giggle behind her hand.

"Stop laughing at me over it, then," I growled back, and my mood apparently made the elm sapling even more insistent on going as its branches beat a steady rhythm against the nearest wall: *whap* *whap* *whap*

"I'm not laughing *at* you, Cousin."

"Well, you're sure not laughing *with* me, because I'm not laughing, now am I? *Little Treebeard, that's enough!*" I screamed, losing my patience to frustration.

Blessed silence filled the room for a moment. It didn't bring me the peace I'd hoped for, though. Every little leaf on the elm tree's meager branches wilted downward in a pout, and as funny as it would have been otherwise, it actually made me sad that I'd yelled at the poor thing. I couldn't help it; I rolled my eyes upward to the ceiling, appealing to the–the great gods of the ceiling tiles, if nothing else. For sanity–yes, that's it. Sanity, and a peaceful period of quiet, bless all their little hearts.

I sighed and went back to the sing-song voice that had proven to be my best way of communicating with my–well, my tree. I hated to call it–her, technically–a familiar, because– well, because it's–she's–a tree. I hate to say *just* a tree, but trees where I come from don't have feelings, don't get angry over being left behind, and they sure don't beat their arms–branches–whatever–against the wall. At least, not on purpose.

I took a deep, calming breath, and then went back into my lilting tree-speak voice. "We will be traveling long, traveling hard, out in the weather. That is no place for a young elm sapling. You must stay here, keeping this room warm for me. I will not be gone for long, I promise. Please stay. Please accept. Please do not be upset," I brought the impromptu melody to an end on the lowest note I could hit.

"Your cousin is correct, Alyssa. You do have an excellent singing voice," a voice interrupted from the door, surprising me so much that my butt completely left the bed as I jumped.

"Dad, what are you doing here?" I asked defensively, though it was pretty obvious that the king was stepping in to see how his daughter was doing.

"I had to see what all the yelling was about, my daughter. You do realize that you were screaming at a tree?"

I sighed again, this time in exasperation. "Yes, I do realize. L.T. has been upset since I told her she wouldn't be going on the trail with me, and the way she was beating her branches against the wall finally wore through my ability to deal with it."

"Hmm. If a small elm sapling can drive you to screaming, I wonder what our friends to the north will be able to do," he observed, and then he ducked out and closed the door before I had a chance to retort.

"He has a point, Cousin."

"Oh, hush up," I snarled at Seph, and then I stuck my tongue out at her to make it clear I was joking. Mostly joking, anyway. It worked; Seph and I fell back into our old routine of laughing and giggling, and even L.T. relaxed.

We finished putting my pack together after the window had darkened. It had taken some time for me to get used to the fact that darkness here in Cysegredig wasn't necessarily all that late. It was farther north, one of my teachers had explained, than what I was used to in the southern United States, and that made summer days longer, winter days shorter, and the transition between them that much more dramatic.

Still, I'd sent Seph, and consequently Booboo, away to put her own pack together, and so it was just Aerona, L.T., and me. A knock sounded at the door, and I knew who it was by the rhythm. I jumped to the door to open it before Aerona could. "Hi, Dad."

"Alyssa, I was wondering if I could tear you away from your room and your guardian—and your tree—for a brief evening walk."

I smiled, knowing what that meant. He'd already taken me on several brief evening walks, and each time they ended up in a session of father-daughter conversation and bonding. As angry as I'd been at him at first for leaving me alone growing up, the bonding sessions were something I looked forward to more and more. Dad really was a cool guy to be around, in spite of his being an old man and all.

"You can. It would be my pleasure to accompany you."

"That is very good, as I fear that I shall not see you for a while after tonight. Come, please." I smiled at his choice of language; even in the elf tongue he spoke very formally. It was a choice, too, I'd learned. Unlike the queen who'd grown up in the very tippy-top of the British upper crust, Dad had grown up in a small elf village without the benefit of anything royal at all around him. I'd seen him and his brother, Seph's father, get together, and when the pair started talking, all formality of wording in the complex, multi-level elf tongue zipped right out the window. The speech of the king, then, was an act, a fancy hat that he'd worn for so long he just naturally put it on whenever he went out in public.

"To what do I owe the pleasure of this evening, my father?" I mimicked his formal tone once we'd passed through the heavy black velvet curtains that hid the opening behind his throne into the king's private man-cave.

Dad walked over to the bar, put a couple of pieces of ice into each of two glasses, and poured a honey brown liquor that just covered the ice. He presented one to me, and then we silently toasted each other with glasses lightly clinking together. His eyes twinkled merrily as he sipped from his drink.

He said, "Who said you owe anyone anything, my daughter? I am merely guilty of cherishing my time with you."

"Here in this room where none but the king himself is permitted."

"The very room, yes. I do enjoy the privacy it provides, and so I am willing to risk being joined by you."

"Well, then, may I ask a question?"

"Anything."

"Anything?" I asked, turning my voice up at the end in what I hoped was a playful tone.

He took the question more seriously than I'd hoped he would. "Yes," he nodded gravely, his face firming up into the same kingly expression I saw when he sat the throne. "Anything."

I could tell I had him, so I leaned in closer. He leaned in too, and I was glad for the opaque drink to hide my grin.

"Who fills the ice bucket?" I whispered, trying to put as much conspiracy into my voice as possible.

I was rewarded as the king of all of Kiirajanna stopped, went totally deadpan, and blinked in confusion. Finally he found his sense of humor and laughed, and then he found his voice and asked, "Why do you ask, Alyssa?"

"Well, you said I could ask anything, so I asked what was troubling me most at the moment. I noticed that each time we're here the bucket seems to be filled with fresh ice. Now, the whole 'it's not really magic, we just use earth energy to freeze large vats of water' possible argument aside, your ice bucket isn't big enough for that method, and besides, I could sense it if you were using magic. But you're not, and I doubt you fill the bucket, and yet you've said nobody but you is allowed in here. Except for me, of course, but I know I haven't filled it either. So either you have the great ice poltergeist running around in here, or somebody else comes in here sometimes."

"I wish you would stop conflating magic with earth energy, Alyssa."

I sighed. I knew I wouldn't win the argument. To the elves, the use of magic had been forbidden for eons due to the destruction they'd wrought with it. Meanwhile, the elves, or at least those trained in it like the priests and the rangers, used earth energy every single day for its benign utility. What I could see, and what drove me nuts that I couldn't get anybody else to see, was that the two were the same thing. It wasn't the power that was bad, but rather its use, but trying to convince even the most reasonable of elves of that was like trying to tell a mockingbird not to sing.

"Okay, fine. I will if you'll tell me who fills the ice bucket, Dad."

"I do not know who fills the ice bucket, Alyssa."

"What do you mean you don't know who fills the ice bucket?"

"I believe that is pretty clear. It is simply one of the servants."

"So servants are allowed in here, then."

"Well, yes, of course, Alyssa."

"But then why would you say no one but you is allowed in here? Are the servants no one?"

My father, who was widely regarded as one of the most egalitarian elf kings ever, the man who regularly jumped down off his royal carriage to dance with commoners every time we rode into a village, blew my mind by nodding.

"Well, yes, Alyssa. That is the way of the world." He spread his hands, smoothingly rather than apologetically, as though accepting that servants were beneath our status was something I'd just have to do eventually.

"It's not the way my world will be when I'm queen."

He gulped down the rest of his drink, nodded, and refilled both our glasses. "I—am glad to hear of such lofty goals as you have, my daughter. Perhaps, though, you might consider changing aspects of elf life that have *not* been part of our custom for thousands of years, at least not at first. You know, tackle the little things, and then move on and up from there." He stopped briefly to examine the determined expression on my face. "Oh, who am I kidding? You are my daughter," he paused again to raise his glass in a salute. "And the dragon queen, too, the mighty one prophesied to change the very bedrock upon which our society stands."

"Are you okay, Dad?" I asked, a little worried. He'd gone melodramatic on me, and that wasn't something I'd ever seen in him before.

He laughed, his good-natured smile returning. "I am fine, Alyssa. Sometimes I worry that you will not be. Perhaps that is just the overprotective father in me. But yes, I do worry. Your youthful fire wants to change the world, while my experienced, thickened hide knows how hard that can be. Meanwhile, you face challenges that I never had. You have strong powers, and strong allies, yet I fear those gathered against you are even stronger than we currently realize. You—"

"Dad, you're scaring me," I objected with a half-grin. In truth, he was, but I wanted to get off of the uncomfortable topic and back to the normal talks we'd had the couple of times we'd come to his chamber before.

"I am sorry, Alyssa. Father I am, you know. So, are you ready for the beginning of your next journey tomorrow?"

I nodded. "Yes."

"Just like that? Truly ready?"

"Well, my clothes are all rolled up into my pack, and from what I've been told the kitchen is preparing us a fairly large food supply. The guards have been notified. I think I'm ready."

"I am not talking about clothing and food, Alyssa."

"The queen's Lady has prepared me—"

"I know well what the queen's Lady has prepared you for. I have no doubt that you are quite knowledgeable on what to do should Padrig introduce his son instead of his wife first, or if you are treated to a meeting of the bens. That is not what I am asking, either."

"So, what are you asking?"

"You know your mission." It wasn't a question as he said it, actually, so all I could do was nod. "The script is simple. Padrig already likes you, both as a person and as a potential queen, and he and I have a strong relationship. He will play with you a little to ensure your knowledge of our customs, and then he will pleasantly and happily give his blessing upon your coronation."

"You seem sure of that."

"I am sure of two things, Alyssa. I am sure that you are my daughter, and in part because of that, I am sure that you will find a way to succeed."

"If I don't, I don't get a second chance, do I?"

"No one ever has."

"So some have failed before?"

Dad sighed. "Yes, some have. That is not for you to worry about, though."

"I'm not worried. At least, not terribly. But what might happen if, let's say, I were to fail?"

"Exiled to Earth. But that will not happen. You will go up there and be your strong, lovable self. Padrig will see that you will make an excellent queen, and he will give you his blessings and send you back to me." I nodded as he swallowed the rest of his whiskey and poured us both some more. Once done, he looked me directly in the eyes and said, "And all that I have described will come true, unless the Cult of the Wyrm has their way."

"Dad, we beat the Cult at the library."

"We handed them a defeat, yes, but it was only in the aftermath of that victory that I learned how deeply those roots have been allowed to run."

"Oh. How deeply is that?"

"Very deeply, it seems. Those who talk tend to say very little that is specific, of course. We have some names, and we are looking for the right opportunity to bring those in for – for questioning."

"Names in the north?"

"Names everywhere, Alyssa. Some in the north, yes."

"Can you give me a list so I can look for those people up there?"

"No. Your mission, Alyssa, does not involve scouting out the Cult. Your mission is to gain Padrig's acceptance while staying out of trouble. Leave the hunt to me and my men."

"So what should I be looking for to stay out of trouble, then?"

"If I knew that, Alyssa, I would not be concerned over your trip."

"You're no help," I said, the alcohol warming my insides and making me a little more jocular than I would've been otherwise.

"Alyssa, you know I would move the moon and stars if—" Dad started in defensively, misinterpreting my attempt at humor. I cut him off.

"I know you would, Dad. I was only joking. But I'm strong, and I'm smart, and you're sending me up there with the strongest and smartest companions in the realm. I'll be fine, trust me."

"Says the girl who quite recently burned down the Library of Alecsanddrha," Dad chided, but at least this time I could tell he was joking. Tiny wrinkle lines beside his eyes gave it away.

"I suppose you're going to ask me to avoid burning anything down this time, too, aren't you? What a spoilsport you can be."

"I would never ask that, Alyssa. You are quite capable of making burning decisions for yourself. I would only suggest that you might wish to seek the bennaeth's permission first."

"Ask permission first, gotcha." I gave him a thumbs-up signal with both hands, and then realized that I still had some whiskey in the glass I'd set down. I remedied that, and then asked, "So what other wisdom do you have to give me regarding this trip?"

"Two things. First, limit your drinking up there, as I am certain they will be delighted to get my daughter inebriated on their strong variety of ale and see what kinds of mistakes she makes. Second, you need to get to bed now so that you can rise early and begin the trip."

"Fine," I said, and realized I really was slurring my words more than I should have been. "Hey, Dad, have you ever been there?"

"Ganolog? Yes, I have been to Padrig's hold a time or two. Not very often, mind you, because he and his clan enjoy their privacy. Still, I have enjoyed the warmth of his hearth on a couple of occasions. I believe that you will enjoy your time up there as well. Just–be cautious."

"I shall," I promised as grandly as I could manage with the whiskey gnawing away at my sensibilities, and then I let him lead me back to my bedroom for that night's sleep he'd mentioned.

I slept most of the night, but I woke with memories of really strange dreams. A dragon attacked us as we rode, killing one of the king's guards by breaking his body up into a mangled glop, and then seducing the rest of the party to take up the fight amongst ourselves. Its vivid clarity made me wonder if it represented something more than just a bad dream.

TAITH

a journey.

Departure

Our departure the next morning embarrassed me. It was embarrassment in a good way, I guess, if there is such a thing, but still....

Now, I'd gotten used to being clapped and cheered over. I'd gotten used to being fawned over as the Crown Princess. I'd even gotten used to the bowing and scraping of the servants in the castle, though my father's suggestion that they counted as nobodies had shaken that up a little. Yes, I'd gotten over my consternation over the fact that I was to be the queen of the realm, and the dragon queen to boot. I had accepted that the normal people looked up to me the same way we looked up to superheroes on Earth. I still wondered why in the heck I deserved all the brouhaha, but I'd nevertheless gotten used to it.

No matter how much fawning and clapping and cheering I'd gotten used to, though, it didn't prepare me for a gosh dang parade. At least, it didn't prepare me for one in which I was the star.

"Relax, Princess. The people are gathered because they love you and are excited for a chance to see you off on your journey," Keion whispered as the front guards' horses began picking their way through the crowd.

I turned and searched his face for the sarcasm that was normally there, but I didn't find any. Instead, he pulled his cheeks and lips up into a broad smile and gestured ahead grandly. I nodded, turned back to the front and smiled as he'd suggested, and urged Awel to step forward. Believe it or not, that earned me a tumultuous cheer from the elves gathered all around us.

I fixed the smile to my face and held a hand up, waving to my people—my subjects?—just as I'd been taught. We started out to the south. The road from the castle only went that direction at first, and then it turned to the left to pass around the massive hill that, though many referred incorrectly to the ruling province by the name, was truly identified as *Cysegredig*, or "sacred place" in the elf tongue. As the trail spun around the prominence and shot toward the north, we paraded through the largest village in the region. As we rode, we passed by the main entrance to the cathedral, which sprouted out from the east side of the hill at exactly the opposite point from the west-facing castle. Sternyface and her scarlet-robed minions stood in observance there, watching me leave with silent but mostly-approving stares.

Dad accompanied us on his great war charger, and he brought along his own private retinue of guards in addition to the six he'd assigned to travel the whole way with us. There were forty-three of them in all: our six, his thirty-six, and the king's standard-bearer, all riding along in a double-wide file.

There were several elves I'd met on Dad's travels interspersed through the cheering section. Most were village elders, and some were the kids I'd taken a liking to. I saw Gwyn toward the end of the crowd. I smiled and waved, but his smile, when he caught me looking, quickly reshaped itself into an expression of terror as he shrank back into the crowd. I glanced over to see if either Keion or Dad had noticed, but neither gave any indication. I snickered, wondering what the first elf boy I'd danced with was up to. Undoubtedly it was nothing good, as my father had assured me acerbically after our night of dancing. I made a mental note to visit Gwyn's village after all the travel was done and over with, in the hopes of seeing just how much no-good the boy who looked exactly like Legolas could possibly be up to. Life's a dance you learn as you go, the old song had told me many times over the radio, and since Keion had made it clear that he and I couldn't ever dance together, then I might as well give it a whirl with somebody else, right?

Dad seemed to know everybody, calling out names often and pointing to people as he did. He'd taken me on several rides around the countryside over the summer, and while I'd enjoyed them, it had always surprised me how many people Dad had a friendly relationship with. He'd explained that the relationships were his favorite part of being king, and looking at the bright gleam of happiness on his face as we rode, I believed it.

I kept trying to be more like Dad. He told me that his trick to remembering names was imagining bins or buckets for each letter, and whenever he met a new person he'd make a mental image of putting the name and a portrait of the face together into the bucket. For most, Dad said, he used to add some sort of mnemonic device, generally a rhyme. For Gwyn, for example, he'd probably have imagined a question mark with the word "when," because when rhymes with Gwyn. Except that it really doesn't, because when isn't a word in the elf language, but you get the basic idea. He'd also explained that after a few years of going through the discipline of this technique, he'd been able to drop the mnemonic part most of the time.

I'd been practicing the technique, but it wasn't sticking. Most of the reason for the slow pick-up was probably that I didn't get out and meet people anywhere near as often as I had during the summer. Probably, anyway—I hoped that I'd eventually be able to do as well as my father with it.

It seemed like hours of yelling and clapping and cheering and hearing "Crown Princess Alyssa" over and over again, but it was really only a mile or so before the crowd finally thinned out. Soon we rode along in silence, the occasional snort from a horse the only interruption. Awel, the mare Seph had recommended to me on the first day of riding lessons, was feeling feisty. She pulled several times against the reins, wanting to take off, but I managed to hold her back as Dad urged.

"It is a long trip ahead of you, Alyssa," he said once. "You do not have any spare horses, so you should take your time."

It was fine by me; I didn't want to rush toward my fate in the great elf northlands, anyway. Keion wasn't as happy, though. He did a good job not showing his impatience in front of my father, but I caught his furtive glances downward and forward. He and I both knew that my father was right that we couldn't run the horses the whole way, but I could read on his face that he was ready to run the horses at least a little bit of it.

Lunch was the old elf traveling standard of dried sausage, cheese hunks, and bread. Seph was proud to have brought a few apples out on the road, having snatched them from the kitchen that morning, but I didn't like the idea of eating such a delicacy in front of Dad and all the king's men. With a sigh, she stowed them away again.

After lunch was done, Dad enveloped me in a firm hug and kept me close to him for longer than normal. Finally he let me loose, looking me in the eyes as I slipped back and away from him. I saw a single tear rim the bottom of each eye as I did, but he quickly hid them under a smile.

"Good luck, my daughter. It is not that you will need luck, of course. I am certain that you will do well in impressing Padrig and earning his trust, his approval, and his recommendation. Be careful whom you befriend in his region, though. I challenge you and all your companions to remain wary of the Cult of the Wyrm and its members."

Assurances were passed all around, and formal farewells were shared between Keion and my father. Apparently none of the others, being only minor nobility in Seph's case and commoners for the rest, owed the king a gesture of goodbye; sometimes elf custom is strange. Finally my small party rose into our saddles and pushed our horses back onto the trail heading northward.

Seph disappeared first, darting her horse ahead with Booboo running right behind in order to do her scouting job. Soon the rest of the security detail fanned out, leaving just Keion and Aerona clopping along with me down the narrow road.

"How long of a trip is it?" I asked, not really caring about the answer. It felt a little weird, going from raucous cheering to a chatty company of about four dozen people and then down to the awkward silence of a trio.

"Far too long at this pace," Keion growled.

"You were the one who first told me that you can't push horses too far, too fast, on the road, Keion. What's different now?"

After several long moments of surly silence from the prince, Aerona decided to answer my question. "I believe that it is three days at a full ride. As we are riding, though, with more effort given to security than to speed, it is likely to be closer to four full days before we see the gates of Ganolog."

"And is Prince Keion going to be this grumpy for all four full days?" I asked her with my eyes directed toward Charming's face.

He ignored me. So did Aerona.

I let out a big sigh and let my mind relax itself into the plodding rhythm of Awel's walk. It was going to be an annoyingly boring trip, I predicted.

If only I knew how wrong that prediction was going to be.

On The Trail

"Oh, what glad tidings you bear, Sephaline. I was just, this afternoon, hoping and praying that we might be allowed to enjoy more of your ranger *stew*," Keion growled into the steaming bowl my cousin had just handed him. He'd finally explained his grumpiness; he wasn't happy to learn that he was coming with me in the first place. It had something to do with some sports season starting up soon, and Mr. Athlete having to be there for the practices. His mood had actually deteriorated over the couple of days we'd been on the road. He was starting to make even glowering Aerona look downright giddily cheerful.

"Oh, I get it now!" I said from across the plain hewn log table inside the even plainer ranger cabin we'd stopped at for the night. Granted, most of the ranger cabins I'd seen—and by that, I mean the three we'd stopped in along the way to the library and the one the night before that was still in Cysegredig territory—were plain, but this one seemed to serve as a tribute to severely rustic settings. The others had at least had linens and a tablecloth dyed in the multi-colored manner that the elves all seemed to love, but this one's linens were sparse, thin, and white, and the tablecloth was nonexistent. There weren't any curtains, either, just hunks of wood that could be put up into the windows to block excessive moonlight if desired.

"What is this exciting tidbit that you now get?" Keion asked me, his tone not improving from his earlier growl.

"Your expressions, Keion. I've gotten to where I can read your happy face, your angry face, your irritated face, and several others, but I hadn't figured out your sarcastic face yet. I just did. It's been hiding in plain sight as your 'normal' expression this whole time."

Sephaline snickered, earning her a glare from Keion. Aerona snorted, too, but apparently Prince Charming didn't have the guts to glare at the tempered battle ax who walked around disguised in female elf form.

"With all due respect, Prince and Princess, you two behave more like an old married couple than most of the old married couples I've ever known," Aerona said just before making a happy slurping sound of her own. Apparently she, at least, liked Sephaline's ranger stew. I did, too, now that my cousin had learned the use of foraged herbs.

That had been our first trip, in fact. As we rode to the library, she had shown me how a ranger always traveled with a large pan and some dried meat and veggies, all of which could be combined with water—the stream water being kept unpolluted here in Kiirajanna—to make a stew that was filling, if entirely bland and chewy. At our last stop, though, we'd run into Owain, who had demonstrated to her what some of the non-healing herbs of Kiirajanna looked and tasted like. She'd been knocking it out of the park with her cooking ever since.

I really liked the new culinary style, and Seph liked it, too. Aerona and the small squad of troops Dad had sent all seemed to approve. It seemed like it was just the Prince's palate that was finicky, and, to be honest, we'd all realized that it wasn't just his palate that was annoying. No matter how few beds were placed in the ranger cabins, he, the prince, was set on having one to himself. Similarly, when it came to guard duty—well, according to Prince Charming, that was why my father had sent commoners along.

Speaking of the commoners, the six of Dad's finest warriors all lounged and ate outside. I wanted to feel bad about that, but Aerona suggested that that was where she would be most comfortable, too, if she were not personally entrusted to look over my sleeping form. It was just what elf warriors do, how they live.

Even though Dad had explained that he had to send six guards along as a show of respect for my status as crown princess, he hadn't explained that the quantity six was not just a nice, even number. I learned by talking to them that six soldiers allowed for three shifts of two for the night watch, in part so that nobody would need to consider entertaining the suggestion that the princess's party members actually lower themselves to pulling guard detail. Meanwhile, those three shifts, being three to four hours each, allowed for each guard to get six to eight hours of sleep while still doing his duty. The six to eight hours of sleep were important, too, because that's what the warriors needed to recharge themselves for another day of duty.

See, that's the stuff they don't teach you growing up in a small town in Mississippi. To be fair, there's a lot about being an elf queen that they don't teach you growing up in a small town in Mississippi. Oh, maybe they teach it in Wales, where the original connection between Kiirajanna and Earth has been maintained for millennia. Still, the current queen was from England, which I'd gathered was very different from Wales, and she'd been telling me how difficult it had been to step from her own childhood into the top ruling position in Kiirajanna. It made me wonder what kind of psycho had come up with the idea of a half-elf girl raised outside of the kingdom becoming its queen. Dad had explained it in clinical terms, of course, talking about varying genetics and diversifying the ruling family's background. That all made sense, but in the larger picture, it still didn't make any sense to me that I, Alyssa, a gangly and entirely unexceptional girl from a similarly unexceptional place on Earth was going to be the next queen of Kiirajanna.

No sense at all, right?

As for the challenge ahead of me, I'd been working on it all day. As much fun as it was pestering Keion, I'd stopped that in favor of asking politely for information because, for the most part, he'd been full of good information. Granted, I didn't know how I was going to use it yet, but it seemed like it had to eventually be useful. As we rode through the day I'd asked, and he'd told me, all he knew about the political structure of the northern elves. For example, there are four main clans up there, each one following their own *ben*, or chief, who in turn reported to their *bennaeth*, or chieftain, who was Padrig.

"While they all respect strength above all other virtues, each tribe defines strength differently from the others," Keion lectured from horseback as I watched two of Dad's men riding up ahead of us, their crimson uniforms brightening the autumn colors. It was pretty, but I couldn't help thinking about a certain science fiction thing involving crewmen wearing red shirts. I mean, it was Earth-based science fiction, but then again, we all knew that wearing a red shirt on away missions meant certain death.

"Aren't you going to ask how they're different?" the prince prodded after I'd been lost in my own thoughts for longer than his limited patience would allow.

"What?" I'd already moved on from that line of conversation, focused as I was on the odds of crewmen in red shirts dying.

"I said that each tribe defines strength differently from the others. Aren't you curious how?"

"Oh. Sure. How are they all different?" I asked, trying to keep my voice neutral. As much as I wanted to learn everything I could, just talking to the prince could be exasperating. That, and after a full day in the saddle my butt hurt.

The prince let out a sigh. "Alyssa, you should be more concerned with coming to know all you can of the people whose approval you will need in the near future. You never know what detail, great or minor, will make the difference."

I shrugged. "Fine. You're correct, mighty prince. So please, tell me how they're all different."

"You don't even remember what we're talking about being different, do you?"

I leveled the darkest glare at him that I could muster and held it firm against the steady walking pace of Awel.

The glare took a little while to work on Keion, but it finally did. He shrugged and said, "Okay. So, the four northern tribes of elves are as different as tribes of the same clan can be, and that is in large part due to the geography of their home regions. They're different, and they're very strong rivals, too. You're just as likely to see them raiding each other as fighting side by side."

"Kinda like the clans in Braveheart, then," I mused.

"In what?"

"Oh, sorry. Movie reference. I keep forgetting y'all haven't had the chance to see many Earth movies. So if the tribes hate each other, why are they all together in one clan?"

"They don't hate each other. Far from it, in fact. If an outsider makes a rude comment about one, he's in for a fight with all four. But the one consistent thread that ties all four tribes together is a respect for might and power. Their bennaeth, or chieftain, who is Padrig currently, is always chosen from among the strongest warriors."

"Wait," I interjected. "You said each tribe defines strength differently, and then you just said they define strength the same."

"*Du du!*" Keion exclaimed so sharply that I almost fell off Awel. It's an elf phrase that I really can't translate directly into English, but it's similar to "Oh, my God!" in English high school speak. "You actually were listening to me, weren't you, Princess?" he asked, his face registering fake shock.

"Yes, Prince, I really was listening to you, especially after you repeated yourself. So, can you put away your ego for long enough to tell me the answer before you hyperventilate?"

He stayed silent for a while, staring off into the distance, and then shook his head. "I'm not sure I can do it justice, Alyssa. It's a key, but complex, differentiation. One clan values pure, brute strength, while another values that strength used in the act of protection. The clan to the west values a kind of strength used for providing for others, while the clan to the far north values strength used for pure survival."

"What do you mean strength used for pure survival?"

"The northlands are said to be harsher than anything you could ever experience anywhere else, Cousin," Seph's voice cut in as she rode up to us from the side. I looked over in surprise, but it wasn't the first time she'd completed a scouting circuit by sweeping in from one side or the other only to ride off toward the front again.

"I've never been there, so I wouldn't know," Prince Charming said, his nose rising a little into the air.

"I've never been there either, but I have listened to the tales brought back by other rangers," Seph answered in an even voice, as if she hadn't caught the testiness of the prince's reply. "The extreme northern reaches of the realm are dominated by a near impossibleness of life. There are no trees, no bushes, only a constant and killing wind. It seldom becomes warm enough for any plants to grow. Even something as straightforward as fresh water can be difficult to come by on the frozen tundra. Survival in those circumstances requires not just a physical strength, but also a mental stamina that is unheard of elsewhere. That, I believe, is what Prince Keion was referring to."

He nodded, and my cousin rode off toward the north once again.

"It does sound like a subtle matter of differentiation," I said.

"It is. But it boils down to a respect for strength. For example, according to their reasoning, any village—even one belonging to their fellow northern clans—that can be raided, deserves to be raided."

"But doesn't that result in a lot of needless death?"

"Death? Not really. They'll usually knock each other out instead of delivering a killing blow, and those they take are eventually allowed to return. Not that many do, from what I've heard. The women reason, and rightfully so, that they were taken by a stronger, and thus more desirable, man, and because of that many of them remain with their new village by choice."

"That's barbaric," I said, thinking of what I'd heard of the ancient times on Earth.

"Perhaps. Perhaps, though, instead of judging, you should pay attention to the attitudes and the rationales for those attitudes while you are there. That is, I suppose, the main reason to send you around to visit the four clans."

"Didn't your mother find them barbaric?" I couldn't imagine Keion's mother taking kindly to such behavior.

"If she did, she never informed me, or anyone else, of that judgment. A queen must never have favorites, Alyssa, nor, on the other end of that, use terms such as barbaric to describe any of her people. You should know that."

"I do." I really did; he and his sisters had provided me with plenty of lectures about proper royal decorum. I just didn't care, since we were out on the trail in the middle of the woods. "I was just curious if she's ever confided."

"She has not," Keion bit off the end of that topic as he returned us to the other. "So, if we can get back to the matter of the tribes, please? The elves of the central north, through whose lands we will first be passing, know themselves as the Y'arth'gwych. Their current chief, Ben Madog, is without equal in strength, probably in all of Kiirajanna. He stands nearly as tall as your father, has a lot more bulk across the shoulders and chest, and wins the wrestling tournament every midwinter. His favorite pastime is not wrestling other people, though. What he is said to enjoy even more than that is hunting the wild game of the north armed with nothing but a rough club."

"He sounds tough," I said, trying to sound impressed. The tribe called themselves Y'arth'gwych—the people of the great bear—and so you wouldn't expect them to be led by the chess club president, would you?

Keion nodded and continued, "You've seen a map of the continent in the library at the abbey, right?" I nodded. "So the second tribe of the northern clan resides along the northern seaboard, where the cliffs swoop down from the great mountain range of the north and curve east and then back to the north. In the past, that region has looked like a good route for invasion, with some easy paths to use to climb up onto the shelf.

The invaders were proven wrong every time, though, by the ferocity of the Amddiffyn tribe."

"Amddiffyn is a good name," I agreed, still trying to keep Keion happily engaged in his explanation. Amddiffyn means protector, in a mighty fortress kind of way. Those elves obviously thought pretty highly of themselves.

A grunt was the only acknowledgment I got before Keion surged on with the lesson. "Their chief is Ben Rhodri, a man who stands every bit as tall and carries all the same heft as Ben Madog."

"Is he a good wrestler, too?"

"He might have been in his younger years. Now, his body has seen its share of battles. His face bears the truth of it in a scar that goes from here to here," Keion motioned as he spoke, pointing to his right temple and running his finger all the way down to the point of his chin.

"Easy to recognize, then?" I asked.

"You'll never forget him once you see him, and not just because of the scar. I remember him most for the thick, coarse, black hair he wears all over. His beard probably hasn't been trimmed, or even combed, for decades. With the hair sticking out from the creases in his clothes you might think he actually was the great bear the central tribe has named themselves after. And, don't tell him I said this, but to be honest he usually smells that way, too."

"Sounds like a real nice guy."

"Oh, he's nice enough, I suppose, at least as the northern tribes recognize niceness. That is, unless you have the misfortune to challenge him. He doesn't wrestle, at least not anymore, but I have seen him split an oak cask with an ax thrown from one end of Padrig's main hall all the way to the other. Once when I was young he visited Cysegredig and showed me everything I know about wielding the battle ax. There is not a more proficient instructor on that class of weapons in all of Kii-rajanna."

"So one tribe leader prefers a club, and another the ax. Does that mean one of the other tribe leaders prefers the staff?"

"It does, indeed, though I don't really see the logical flow in your assumption. There are an awful lot of weapons. But you are correct; the northern portion of the west coast of Kiirajanna, from the Hcillo mountains that set off the desert region of the extreme west, up to the Dalen range, is a scene of prime fishing. That's where a majority of the salt-water fish eaten in Kiirajanna come from. The Digonol tribe there is led by Ben Merfyn, an old but spry fisherman who prefers, as you surmised, to fight with a gysarm. It's a staff about the same length and breadth as a deep sea fishing rod with a hooked blade attached at one end," he explained when I looked confused. "He's particularly good with it."

"I don't suppose he'd be the ben without being good with it."

"Very likely correct, but like I said before, his people honor strength in providing for others rather than that displayed in direct combat, so he might have won the title more through hard work with fishing equipment than through his gysarm. It is not a question I have ever asked."

"Their name—the tribe of plenty—does that come from their fishing?"

"For the most part, yes. But their fields in the north of the continent are not only vast, but also particularly fertile for certain colder-weather crops, and their tribe includes some who are masters of agriculture."

"That makes sense. What's the last tribe?"

"The Pobl'yrhew"—people of the ice—"are led by Ben Iolyn. They're a quiet, secretive tribe, living in the ice fields north of the Dalen range. Few outsiders ever venture there, as the mountain passes are treacherous even in good weather. Your cousin has already told you more of them than I know."

"And they value strength in mere survival of the extremes of weather?"

"They must," he agreed. "They do very little else of a competitive nature. Pobl'yrhew are seldom seen outside of the great white north. All I know on that topic is based on what I have been told of them."

"So the ax and the club and the staff have been taken. How does Ben Iolyn prefer to fight?"

"I have no idea. I've never met him. There aren't even any rumors, because nobody who's not involved in matters of governance even know that his tribe, or he, for that matter, exists. He, and his clan, are a huge question mark in the lore of Kiirajanna."

"He wasn't at my coronation?" I'd thought that all the leaders of all the clans had been there the day I'd been accepted by the queen as the one to succeed her, but I hadn't had the time or the knowledge to take all the names and tribes down.

"No, and that wasn't surprising to any of us who knew better. Ben Iolyn never attends any of our organized festivities."

"Were the other bens there?" I didn't remember meeting anybody but Padrig and his son Llew, a lack of observation that should probably be seen as a fault in a future queen.

Keion echoed my thoughts as he said drily, "You should know the answer to that question yourself, Crown Princess, but no. What is most troubling to your father, to my mother, and to me is that *none* of the bens were at your coronation. It was a bit of an insult, honestly, and not merely to you, but also to the crown of Kiirajanna. That is why the trio decided to send you a little bit early; a quick acceptance from and alliance with Padrig might deter whatever is going on with his subordinate leaders. Of course, were you to ask Padrig directly about it, you would offend his leadership, but you should nevertheless go into this meeting with that fact in the back of your mind."

"Okay, I'll do that. But, just to play devil's advocate, they might have just been preparing for the winter, right?"

"It is possible," Keion said in a voice that told me he thought that it wasn't very likely.

"So, back to Ben Iolyn. Your mother has never told you of him?"

"If she ever met the chief of the great white north, she has never had occasion to describe such a meeting to me."

"Wonderful."

"What is?"

"Sorry, I forgot my sarcasm expression."

"Of course you did," Keion said with his own sarcasm expression out for all to see.

The rest of that day's ride proved relatively sarcasm-free. Which is, I should add, another way of saying silent, bless Keion's little heart.

Slipping Off

That night, I had trouble sleeping. It wasn't the accommodations; the cabin was comfortable enough for all of us. It actually held two separate beds, one for Keion and one for me, and another sleeping pad for Seph. Anytime my cousin and I didn't have to share a bed on the road rated excellent in my book. Despite the relative comfort of a bed to myself, and despite being tired from the road, though, I laid there in my bed for a long time, eyes closed but mind wide open. I just couldn't get it to shut down, filled as it was by so many various thoughts and feelings. On one hand, I was so excited to get started on the next phase of this ascension thing that I could hardly stand it. On the other, I was terrified, and not just over the obvious stuff.

"What if Padrig says no?" was the obvious stuff. For the not-as-obvious stuff, my brain invented complications like "what if we get snowed in all winter?" and "what if we run right into the Cult up there?" I tried telling my brain that the first was ridiculous because we'd planned meticulously to be there and gone before even the first hint of snowfall, and the second because I still wanted to believe, despite my father's warnings, that we'd delivered a knock-out punch to the Cult at the battle of the Library. No matter how scary the black-robed murderers were, they were gone now, or, at the very least, they were too hurt to threaten me.

It didn't seem to matter what I wanted to believe; my mind was convinced that it needed to keep me up to go through all the various deadly possibilities. Finally I got tired of pretending to sleep and rose quietly. I draped the light cloak that my father had given me over my shoulders and stole out into the night.

I moved silently. Granted, it wasn't like I was trying to sneak past the orc army to Mount Doom or anything; I was just getting some air and I didn't have any great desire to wake up the party or the guards in doing so. It was a test, really. I listened carefully to the slow, steady breathing of the other inhabitants as I padded across the age-smoothed wood floor of the cabin, and then I grinned when I managed to cross over the threshold without hearing the pattern of sound changing. One guard on the early shift–the captain, I thought–nodded to me as I padded by. I heard him shift position a little as I disappeared into the woods behind him, and figured he was turning to watch my departure path. I didn't pay too much attention. I was walking just for me, and I didn't care whether the guard followed me or not.

He didn't. I can usually tell, though I'm not sure how. I was born with a sixth sense–I called it a "spidey-sense" growing up– that lets me know when people are behind me. I'd thought everybody had it until my friend convinced me otherwise. A very few people, one being my father, have been able to slip through it, but most people coming up behind me set off alarm bells in my head. I don't know how it works; I just get this feeling, a sort of vibration in the air, when someone approaches. Since I'd been in Kiirajanna it had gotten stronger, and whenever I put my hand on the pendant Momma gave me–Draignerthol, a relic from the magical era of Kiirajanna–the spidey-sense expanded, stretching outward and becoming richer till I could tell not only where others were but also who they were, even from several yards away.

The forests of Kiirajanna are like no woods I've heard of or seen back on Earth. It's more like the fancy gardens rich people have at their mansions, only much bigger. On the travels with my father to meet the villagers, I'd gotten used to the pristine beauty of the manicured woodlands, where every tree has its place and every blade of grass grows as planned. So used to it that I'd stopped seeing it, I realized as I strolled along in the dim moonlight. Walking through the night as I was, seeing the forest through a different lens, was like hitting a refresh button. I marveled as I noticed how the trees played with the deep shadows, their trunks and limbs throwing geometrical designs onto the patterns inscribed by the shaped grass on the ground.

It was like walking on a living stained glass window made entirely of black, white, and hundreds of different shades of grey.

I stopped for a moment to raise my gaze to the sky. As often as I'd been out at night, it was always on some mission, this training or some other, and I'd never taken the time to just stop and look up. Part of me expected to see a completely different field of stars than what I'd seen in the woods on Earth, but that part was disappointed. I quickly found the Big Dipper partway up in the sky, right where Momma taught me it would be, and then I followed its bucket edge to the North Star. Looking to the right I saw the Three Sisters, as Momma had called them, though I'd also been told that the three bright stars were often called Orion's Belt.

What Momma called them was good enough for me.

It hit me that, on Earth, I usually saw the Three Sisters to the left, not the right, of the North Star. I wondered what that could mean. My first idea was that I was actually in the southern hemisphere, but that couldn't be, since if it were true then I wouldn't be seeing the North Star. After a few moments of pondering and coming up with nothing, I shook my head and pushed the mystery back, burying it in thoughts of how beautiful the nightscape around me was.

I continued walking.

After a bit, I changed course. Well ahead on my new path I saw the shadow patterns change, becoming lighter and thinning out substantially, but that wasn't what prompted the turn. Instead, Draignerthol tugged me in that direction, and not very gently either. It felt like a piece of steel being drawn to a magnet.

As my quiet footsteps brought me up to the clearing, I saw what Draignerthol was pulling me to. I could hear it, too, once I got close enough. In the center a single granite stone stood upright, waist-high and about the same distance wide. It was placed precisely, carefully carved into perfectly rectangular dimensions. It looked like it had been intended as an altar of some sort, but by whom?

I admit, I didn't put too much energy into wondering. I was completely enchanted by the action above the altar as little tylwyth teg, Kiirajanna's native fairy folk, danced in the moonlight. There were hundreds of them, each only a few inches tall with iridescent wings that glistened brightly. Their dance formed itself in concentric circles above the obelisk. Each circle spun one way, opposite the one next to it, for several moments and then, at some cue I could neither see nor hear, stopped and switched direction.

They were singing, too. Their tiny voices didn't carry far, and the rhythm was so quick that I couldn't pick out any words, but the melody was bright, cheerful, and beautiful. It was simple and repetitive, but it captivated me.

I sat down on a log to watch the dance. The log should have surprised me by its very presence, since trees don't just fall in the forests of Kiirajanna, but I was captivated otherwise. The tylwyth teg seemed to actually be playing, cavorting, and even from the edge of the clearing I could make out the gleeful expressions on their tiny, sharp-featured faces. As I watched, I even noticed one or two occasionally miss the cue to stop, a mistake that caused sharp, mirthful laughter to ripple down the line.

It looked like one heck of a party I'd stumbled across.

They noticed my presence, too. Draignerthol was glowing brightly, and even seemed to be humming its own little counter-tune, so I doubt they could have missed me. Soon two of them detached themselves from the outer circle and, gossamer wings flapping, flew over to me with smiles on their faces as their companions just closed ranks and kept dancing.

Now, the tylwyth teg have a language all their own, one that even the best elven scholars have failed to figure out, probably thanks to the fairies' interest in trickery. The two who came over tried to get their message across in that language, but their words ran together into squeaks I couldn't make out. Their wild gestures, though, made their intent clear. They wanted me to step into the clearing and dance with them.

I didn't want to, though. It wasn't that I didn't want to dance. I'd learned, through the series of trips with Dad to the villages, to relish the elves' wild manner of dancing, but the dance of the tylwyth teg seemed special that night. Sacred, even.

I shook my head. "No," I said, hoping the pair could understand the elf language. "Thank you, but your dancing is so beautiful, and I don't wish to disrupt it with my own plodding along. Please, go back and join your friends, and grant me the honor of being allowed to watch from the sidelines for a while."

The pair didn't take no easily, both gesturing with a *come on* look on their faces, but I replied by shaking my head again and shooing them back with a smile. One turned back to the festivities without comment, but the other gave me the cutest little *oh, shucks* gesture, smacking his open palm on his tiny little knee and looking sad for the length of a heartbeat before grinning again and following his fellow.

I giggled. I don't do that often, but I couldn't help it then. The whole scene washed over me, leaving me feeling happy and contented.

Despite all the noise in the clearing and Draignerthol's complementary humming, I still sensed the elf gliding up behind me a little while later.

"Isn't this the most beautiful thing ever, Cousin?" I asked over my shoulder without turning my head away from the dancing fairies.

"It's quite a show," Seph agreed. "Could you sense it from inside the cabin?" She sat beside me on the log.

"No. I just needed a walk to clear my head and get to sleep. After a bit, Draignerthol dragged me here," I murmured. Speech, even in the elves' lilting tongue that I normally found so beautiful, seemed staccato and brash against the scene to our front.

"Ah. That makes sense."

"I'm surprised you followed me all the way here just to ask that."

Seph snorted. "I didn't follow you, Cousin. I tracked you. You did a good job in leaving silently, I must say."

"Booboo?" I asked. It had been silly of me to ignore the wolverine when I left; he'd always been right on top of everything before.

"Believe it or not, even Booboo didn't notice you leaving. Not his fault; he was apparently investigating something else on the opposite side of the cabin from you when you left."

"I wasn't looking to blame him," I said. I actually felt honored to have evaded the little tracking monster.

"I figured that," she said, and settled in to watch for a while.

"You do know that the tylwyth teg do this for the entire full moon cycle, right?" Seph asked.

"Yeah."

"Your cloak is burning."

"Okay," I acknowledged whatever it was she had said, trying to get her to be quiet so I could continue enjoying the fascinating dance of the fairies.

"You're not listening, are you?"

"Sure."

"There's a dragon about to eat you."

"Uh huh."

A shadow slid between me and the dance in the clearing. I started to protest, but then I realized I was looking into my cousin's face, right where a concerned expression rested. "You're. Not. Listening. To. Me," she said, punctuating each word as its own sentence, her tone urgent and forceful.

Her words knocked around in my brain till the meaning touched down. "What?" I asked defensively as I came back to my senses. "Of course I'm listening, Cousin. At least, I am now. What were you saying?"

Still standing in front of me, Seph looked me directly in the eyes and related in a cold, flat voice, "I was telling you a story of many years ago, when a ranger initiate named Iain sat down on a log much like the one you're sitting on now to watch a dance exactly like the one that just mesmerized you. They discovered his dehydrated corpse many days later." Her gaze grew more intense as she measured my attentiveness, and then, satisfied, it lightened just a little as she continued, "The theory is that he became so engrossed in watching the play of the tylwyth teg that he lost track of himself in so doing. It is a dangerously addictive sport you were participating in, Cousin."

"Oh, I wasn't addicted," I argued. "I was just–"

"Engrossed. Yes. I could have set your cloak ablaze, and you probably wouldn't have noticed. Hey, it's not a bad thing to appreciate such beauty; it's just–" Seph said, but she was cut off by a member of the fairy folk who flew over to us, stamped its little foot down on an imaginary surface in mid-air, and shushed us with an indignant expression.

It was all I could do to not laugh at the poor little creature. I looked over at Seph's face and saw that my mirth was mirrored there. I nodded, and she nodded, too, and the fairy flew back to rejoin the dance with a *harrumph*.

"How long does this go on for?" I whispered.

Seph sighed. I looked over at her, asking for the reason behind the sigh with my eyes, but she just grinned and shook her head. "The entire full moon cycle, Cousin," she whispered back.

"A couple of days, then?"

"More like four or five. They start when the moon first appears full, and end once the circle begins diminishing."

"Hence the dehydration of the entranced ranger."

She nodded and said, "Ah, so you were listening to that."

"Of course I was."

"Uh, huh."

I looked over at my cousin again, suspicious this time. She just grinned sweetly, shrugged, and turned back toward the middle of the clearing. She was, I realized, becoming extremely adept at sarcasm.

"You seem to have come into your own, Seph," I whispered after a bit.

"What do you mean?"

"When I first met you this summer–seems so long ago now, doesn't it?–but back then you seemed kinda timid. Now–"

"Timid?" Seph looked at me, eyebrows raised.

"No, no, not timid. Sorry, wrong word. It's just that when I got here, you seemed–unsure of yourself. Like when we met the royals on the stairs and you jumped backward. Remember that?"

"Oh, right," Seph said, her lips curling into a wry grin. "That was funny, wasn't it?"

Yes, it was funny. We were on our way down to the dining area together, and the queen's three children had met us on the stairs. I'd immediately formed a dislike for them thanks to their haughty expressions. That feeling just made me want to stand up to them, but Seph had actually *meeped* and jumped backward to stand behind me.

"That was inside, though," she continued. "I'm a ranger, Alyssa. I belong out here among the trees, not in a huge bastion of stone. Of course I was out of sorts on the main stairs of the castle."

"Sure. There was the arrow incident, though, and that was outside." The first I'd learned of the Cult, we were out walking and an arrow barely missed getting itself embedded in me. Seph had recovered quickly enough, but at first she'd leaped backward just like on the stairs of the castle.

Her face darkened as she retorted, "I'd prefer not to be reminded of one of the most embarrassing moments of my life, Cousin. I reacted poorly, and your father disciplined me for it, if you'll recall."

"No, I don't recall. He disciplined you?"

"Not him, personally. He reported my error to Master Owain, who made me run–novice exercises–over and over again till I was certain not to react that way in the future."

"Oh." I'd seen Master Owain as a kind and gentle old man who Seph looked up to like a second father. I couldn't imagine him being cruel. "What kind of novice exercises?"

"I couldn't tell you if I wanted to, and I certainly do not want to. Can we just drop it, Princess?" Her use of the title startled me; she'd only called me Princess a couple of times before, and that on the first day we'd met.

"Okay, sorry," I said, shrugging. "So, do they ever vary this dance they're doing, or is it always ring around the big stone thing?"

She relaxed a little and followed my gaze back to the center, where the fairies were still dancing. "The lore is unclear, Alyssa. Anyone who's ever watched for any length of time hasn't lived to report on it. We should probably be getting back, ourselves, as the next watch will be rising already and we don't want them out searching for us."

"The next watch? We've been here–" I started, and she finished for me.

"Several hours, yes. You have, anyway. See what I mean?"

I rose from the log, surprised to feel my legs sore and stiff. They protesting the march back to the cabin at first.

"I wonder what would've happened if I'd taken them up on the invitation to dance."

Seph looked sideways at me. "They invited you to dance with them?" I nodded. She whistled and said, "Now, that's rare."

"How rare?"

"Rare enough that I've never heard of it happening. They must really have a thing for you."

I nodded. They had seemed to warm up to me, riding along part of the way to the library and even making fun of Prince Charming for me. "So why," I asked, "would they try to kill me like they just did?"

"Who says they were trying to kill you? Maybe having you dance with them would've refreshed you. Maybe they don't know the effect sitting and watching their dance has on an elf. Besides, they weren't the ones who called you to the clearing; that was Draignerthol's doing. Right?"

"Right," I agreed. It still seemed an awfully dangerous thing to do, mesmerizing me as thoroughly as they had.

"So back to our conversation earlier, you said I seem to have come into my own. Does that mean what I think it means?"

I searched her face to make sure I wasn't walking into a trap, but she seemed sincere. "I'm not sure what you think it means, but I meant it as a compliment. You're great out here, Cousin, and you always seem so confident in what you're doing. Dad's guards seem to look up to you, and Keion even defers to you in ranger matters. It's honestly rather shocking that he'd defer to anybody in any matters."

"Well, thank you," she said, her smile radiating even in the darkness. "As much as I appreciate your noticing, though, it is not surprising. The ranger code is something I've trained to live by all my life. It seems natural that I should possess some talent in that regards."

"I thought you–didn't you tell me that you didn't–elves don't become–well, whatever their profession is going to be–till after the vision quest?" I asked, stumbling over the words and what I wanted to say.

"Well, yes, that's correct." She gave me a look and a shrug, so I explained further.

"How can you have studied all your life if you didn't know what you were going to be till after the vision quest?"

"Oh. Semantics, Alyssa. We consider the time since our vision quests to be 'all our lives.' It's all of our adult lives, anyway. We go from playing with hoops and balls to doing what we're meant to do, and that's—well, it's becoming an adult."

"So how does everybody look at me, when I haven't done that yet? I mean, they respect me enough to my face, but I'm not technically an adult yet, right?"

"Well, you're a special case. You didn't grow up here, and so you didn't have an opportunity to make the transition at the same time most of us did. You will do one, of course, and that's all that really matters to us. Well, that, and we all hope that you don't stink at being a princess."

I glanced over to see that she was grinning, so I felt better about the last bit she'd added. "Hopefully I don't," I agreed. "But I want to go on my vision quest soon, so I can catch up to y'all."

"Y'all?" Seph asked, and I realized I'd switched back into English for that word. I was flat exhausted after watching the fairy show for hours, and the language came out as it had been for most of my life. At least Seph, being the cousin to the future queen, had been taught English at a young age so she understood most of what I tried to say.

When I grinned back, she said in English, "Well, the process of elevation from princess to crown princess to queen isn't something I am asked for advice on, so you'll have to take your desires up with those who matter. I'm just here to keep you from wandering off of the trail and into the woods."

"Like I did tonight?" I asked.

"Yes, pretty much," she said, and then waved at a tree. "Just returning our princess to her bed. You can stand down now."

The shape of one of my father's guards detached itself from the darkness of the tree trunk. "Ranger Sephaline, I did not receive a report that you had departed. I will investigate."

"No need," she said. "The day a ranger who has come *into her own*, as the crown princess says, cannot by herself slip past guards at their duty post is a bad day for the ranger class."

"I disagree, ranger," he said, coming out into the moonlight so we could see the gentle smile on his face. "The day anyone can slip past a member of the king's guards is a bad day for the guard class."

Seph chortled. "Point made and accepted. In the morning I will show you the path I took so that you'll be more prepared next time. For now, there's no harm done, so let's all get some rest. Well, all except for–well, you–I guess." She chuckled again, this time a little weakly.

"It is and will continue to be my pleasure to keep the crown princess and her party safe, ranger," the guard responded, his voice still polite and friendly in spite of Seph's slip-up. "May I help you through the darkness to find your way to the cabin door?"

"Uh, thanks, but no," she said, still sounding a little embarrassed. "I can help the crown princess back to the cabin all by myself."

"As you wish," the guard replied, and then he faded back into the shadows. Sort of, anyway. I'd seen Seph *actually* fade into shadows, and watching a warrior in armor try to do the same was a little bit funny. I wanted to call out, "I can still see you," which would've been the truth. He hadn't gotten back into the shadow far enough to keep his eyes from glinting, and the bulkiness of his armor gave him away now that I knew where to look. I decided instead to just smile and follow Seph silently. There wasn't anything to be gained by antagonizing the guards over the whole warrior versus ranger conflict.

"Where's Booboo, by the way?" I asked, realizing I hadn't seen the little bundle of tooth and claws the entire evening.

"Back there," Seph said, pointing to a spot a little behind and off to our right. Staring that direction, I thought I could see the wolverine's eyes glowing back at us. "He's been watching over us, but he and the tylwyth teg aren't on the best of terms, as you know, and he's content just staying out there by himself."

"I don't suppose I could scratch him behind his ears before we go to bed, could I?" I asked. I hadn't known that Booboo and the tylwyth teg were on any sort of terms at all, but I added it to my mental notes anyway. The wolverine was such a strangely dichotomous animal, savagely fierce one moment but enjoying a good head scratch or a spot curled up on the floor the next.

"You know he hates that, don't you?"

"I know no such thing," I argued. "He obviously enjoyed it when I've done it before."

"Well, no promises, but I will ask," Seph said, her voice sounding doubtful. She reached out over whatever link she had to the wolverine and then grunted softly as a brownish-grey furry lump leaped from the shadows and raced to my side to be scratched behind the ears.

While I scratched, I looked over at Seph and was rewarded with another smile.

"He likes it, doesn't he?" I asked.

"Apparently so, Alyssa. At least, after a long day on the trail followed by a long evening watching over us in the forest, he's enjoying your kind ministrations. He asks me to express appreciation."

I shrugged and let up on the scratching, letting the wolverine free to bound back out to the nearby shadows. "He saved my life," I reminded Seph. "He gets an ear scratching whenever he wants an ear scratching."

Ganolog

Pacing ourselves as we were, we didn't make it to Ganolog till the late afternoon a couple of days later. It was a good long ride that would've taken a few days even at a hard pace, but nobody was in any real hurry to get there. Nobody but Keion, anyway, and he finally gave up on his bristling. Besides, Dad's guards, Aerona, and Seph all said that going at a slower pace gave them more time to scout and guard and do all the things they needed to do to keep the crown princess safe.

Yay, me.

I'm sure the horses were glad for the slower pace, considering the strain of the physical path we followed. As we rode, we climbed. The upward movement wasn't obvious as first, though they'd briefed me ahead of time that the overall change in altitude from Cysegredig up to Ganolog was drastic. That was the reason for the major difference in climates, they'd said. The elf capital and most of the rest of the kingdom sat somewhere within a thousand feet or so of sea level, plus or sometimes even minus, but the entire north part of the continent sloped upward to create what they called, kind of unimaginatively, the

Rim. This northern rim was several thousand feet higher and, as a result, remained significantly colder than the rest of the land.

While we climbed up onto the Rim the forests changed in two major ways. The first, and most obvious, was in the orderliness of the woods, or lack of it. Seph was very proud to be part of the class who maintained the grounds of the central Kiirajanna forest as a park-like setting. All the trees when we'd started out were in rows, all the flowers blooming, and all color coordinated. There wasn't a single leaf out of place near the capital, a fact that everyone found perfectly normal. Above the Rim, though, it became obvious that the northern rangers thought they had better things to do than keeping the forest floor looking pretty. The trees lost their rows and grew like normal trees, randomly spaced about. The grounds weren't tended to, either; gone were the conspicuously lovely patterns in the grass I'd enjoyed near the capital. In their place were the variations I'd seen back home, with rocks here, moss there, and bushes over yonder. It was kind of weird, going back to unsculpted forest after becoming used to the well-tended woods of Cysegredig.

The second change was in the turning of the seasons, and though this one shouldn't have surprised me, it did. We had started out from the capital down a path that wound through tall trees and late-blooming flowers, the greens competing against the blues and the yellows. As we climbed, though, everything turned pretty quickly to brown, the spent leaves every bit as dull as the tree trunks, the dirt, and even the dying moss.

It had been spectacular for a little while. Somewhere around halfway up, the trees suddenly decided hey, it's autumn, and the resulting colors exploded across the landscape. Leaves took on hues that ranged from red to orange to bright yellow, combining into a massive landscape of pigmentation. It was the most beautiful fall day I've ever seen.

Well, it was the most beautiful fall half-day, anyway. A few hours was all it lasted. Quickly, the signs of autumn petered out, and over the course of a few leagues we rode straight into winter. The path that had started with tall, green trees and blooming flowers ended flanked by short, stout, leafless trees and no colors but brown everywhere. It became obvious that the cold season really was coming, and rapidly.

It wasn't all brown, actually. Here and there we saw occasional clumps of green stalks that had small, vibrant, fuchsia flowers growing in a cluster at the very tip of each stalk. It looked like the flowers had begun blooming from the bottom and then shot up their stalks in a pattern that by that point was nearly done, leaving a strip of cottony tufts behind. Seph nodded when I pointed it out; she had been taught to use those flowers as a seasonal gauge if she were ever in the northlands. Six weeks from when the opening reddish-purple blossoms reached the top of the stalk, she explained, you could expect snow to blanket the land.

It looked to me like that six week period had started some time ago, an observation that Seph confirmed at one of our rest stops. "Yes," she said, "the snow's going to fall—though if I recall correctly, the northern clans say that the snow flies—any time now."

"The snow flies?" Keion mused. "That seems so much more—descriptive. Dangerously so. Before the snow starts flying at us, I would hope that we can be back down the mountain and safely tucked into our castle."

"I am certain that your hope has nothing to do with the upcoming sports season, correct?" I asked. Keion just *harrumphed* and ignored the question otherwise.

Finally, after days of bickering while riding the trail, we hit a flat, straight part that was the last bit in to Ganolog. The forest around us came alive. I sat up from my dozing slump in the saddle and watched Keion and Aerona quickly arm themselves. Their action made me think to do the same, but as I was reaching for my bow our assailant crashed out of the tree line.

I'd never seen a moose before, other than in pictures, and pictures don't do the size of the beast justice. This bull was bigger than Awel, and very nearly as tall as the prince's war charger, only instead of a barrel-shaped body it had a little bitty butt end attached to a round, muscular chest. Its horns—antlers—whatever you call those things—spread out at least four feet wide on either side of its huge head, which by the time it cleared the tree line was horizontal with antlers leading and ears flared back.

The moose snorted in anger, its hooves raising a thunderous ruckus. It sounded like we were being attacked by the Cult aided by a wyvern or two. Before I could get too nervous, though, my ears picked up high-pitched squeals of glee. My eyes caught sight of flutters of iridescent wings perched between the points of the wide antlers, and I realized that it was probably going to be okay.

One of the tylwyth teg rode square in the middle of the moose's head, and another two were each holding onto an ear like they were reins. Others were holding onto the points of his antlers. One more, apparently the leader of the merry band, stood perched on the angled snout of the enraged animal. He sniggered and chirped in glee and squeaked out little snippets of their own special fairy language, all while holding a stripped stick out, angled up, in the classic *charge* pose.

We all stopped and watched incredulously as the mischievous fairy band guided the moose across the path directly ahead of me, each of us doing our best to calm our terrified steeds.

The leader touched the handle of his stick to his nose in a salute to me as he passed, while the entire rest of his squad stuck out their tongues and blew raspberries that were obviously intended for Keion, who watched sullenly and released the draw he'd held on an arrow.

The incident was over in seconds, the moose disappearing into the underbrush on the other side and the tiny, shiny wings reappearing on the bare branches above us. Their shrill snickers were drowned out as thundering hooves rode up from the front and rear, and soon the other guardsmen pairs were with us.

"Is all okay, Princess?" the captain asked.

I looked around. Keion was visibly furious, but he obviously couldn't figure out who should be the target of his foul mood. Aerona, meanwhile, just sat quietly in her saddle looking amused as she slowly inserted several daggers back into their sheaths one at a time. Seph, as usual, was out scouting somewhere and had missed the whole comic scene.

I was going to have fun relating this one to her later.

"We're fine. That was a very large moose," I said, not really sure what else to report.

"*Bengarw*," Keion corrected, his tone a little sharper than it needed to be. I didn't get angry, though. I had spoken the word in English; I hadn't been taught the elf word for moose. So sue me. It wasn't a word that was either taught or used in the capital very often.

I breathed in and then thanked him for the correction as politely as I could. There was nothing to be gained by incivility, after all. Hey, the next time I saw a moose, I would know what to call it in elven.

Yay, me.

"Just the tylwyth playing their usual games. No danger," Keion said to dismiss the guards back to their places. They all turned their horses about with a sigh.

We didn't see any more moose—mooses?—on the way. The switching between one language that had a plural and another that didn't threw me off, and that filled my thoughts through the last half hour of quiet ride till Seph and Booboo bounded back toward us, my cousin excitedly pointing out that the capital city of the north was just over the next hill.

Ganolog looked more like a wild west fortress than an elf town, at least based on the other elf towns I'd seen. The villages my father had taken me to were all open, inviting concentrations of population with little elf homes scattered about at random among the trees. I'd fallen in love with the rambling nature of towns as well as the not-quite-rectangular unevenness of their construction.

Ganolog, on the other hand, was pretty much the opposite of all that. The northern elf fortress-capital backed up against one of the taller cliffs overlooking the northern ocean, and on each of the other three sides its occupants had raised a high wall of thick vertical logs. The walls were strength-enhanced by the "earth energy" that the elves were still refusing to call magic. I could easily see the blue glow surrounding the timbers from across the half mile or so of open space that surrounded it, so I knew it had to be pretty strong. Idly, I wondered who had the ability to cast such a strong protective spell, and how they'd managed to spin the characterization of magic as earth energy while doing it.

The town was impressive, though. It looked exactly like I imagined the frontier fortresses in the twenty-sided dice-rolling game we'd played back on Earth. Only, it was real.

We caused a heck of a stir at the gate. I guess that shouldn't have surprised me, since the party was made up of six guards bearing the king's livery, the prince, and the crown princess. The captain of the guard huffed about and then offered us a place to sit, rest our bones, and shake off some dust before presenting ourselves to the great Bennaeth Padrig, while his guardsmen scurried to find a few presentable chairs. Keion refused for us, though, and so we rode on into town still dusty and bone-tired.

"Surely we could've spared a minute," I complained in a whisper.

"For what?" Keion returned just as quietly.

"So that we don't crawl off our horses filthy."

"I guarantee, you wouldn't have gotten much cleaner in the guard house. Besides, Padrig isn't one to stand on cleanliness and freshness of new arrivals. He'll probably respect you even more thanks to that dirt smudge on your forehead."

I reached up to draw a hand across the accused area. Suddenly I found myself wishing I had a pocket mirror like the one Momma always had in her purse.

Keion watched me out of the corner of his eye, snickered quietly, and went on, "I'll feel better, given everything going on, when we're safely under the bennaeth's roof and the protection of his hold, besides."

"Given what going on?" I asked, curious whether he knew something I didn't, but the question was promptly shushed by both the prince and Aerona. Facial expressions made it clear that I needed to stop talking.

The exterior walls weren't the only thing different about the northern elf town. As we continued through the gate the vision I got changed from wild west to medieval outpost. Granted, in all the wild west movies I'd ever seen, the buildings and doors and things were relatively square, while true to elf standards, Ganolog's buildings had the not-quite-regular shape to their features. Between the glow from the outer walls and the whimsical shape of the doorways, I almost felt transported to a magical realm.

Then I realized the silliness of that thought; I *had* been transported to a magical realm when I'd followed my father through the portal from Memphis the first time. The elves just refused to admit it. So there.

I'd gotten used to elf towns decorated in all the colors of the rainbow, but Ganolog was brown. Just—brown. The shades of logs and mud and roofing material were all a little different, granted. But it was all still very, very brown.

Brown, and foreboding, in fact, and so much of the latter that I could see Keion's point about getting to Padrig's quickly. There were a few elves out and about, but none of them seemed even slightly inclined to give us the same joyous greeting we'd always received in the villages around Cysegredig. Of course, when we visited the villages we were always tagging along with my father, who was extraordinarily popular. But Keion was a fairly popular—and, I must say, good-looking—prince, and yet he didn't receive more than a glance or two, and those were immediately severed.

After the gaily, noisy reception we'd received elsewhere, and the grand parade that had seen us off from Cysegredig, Ganolog's silence was spooky.

"How many live here?" I asked Keion, the sound of my voice surprisingly loud in the narrow, empty streets.

"A few thousand. As many as ten thousand in the deepest parts of winter, when people come in from their camps."

"Is it always this quiet?"

"Except at night when the werewolves come out."

Sure that I hadn't heard the elf word right the first time, I asked, "You said *werewolves*?"

He nodded. "Yes, I said that."

I shuddered. "Well, that's—scary."

"The part that is truly scary is how gullible you are, Princess. I've only been here once, so how would I know whether the quiet we are hearing is normal?"

"Gullible? I'm not gullible! A year ago I would've called someone that if they thought wyverns, fairy folk, unicorns, or moose actually existed. Well, not moose; I've actually seen pictures of those back on Earth. But now, I've seen each of them. I'm in a world where the fantasy of my old life is the reality of my new one, so whether you call it gullible or not, Prince, you *have* to expect me to believe what you're telling me about other fantasy creatures." I did my best to say the word Prince the same way I would've said other, far more insulting, terms if we'd been by ourselves.

"Hmmph," he grunted derisively. "What we have to expect is for you to get smarter, Princess."

"What we have to expect is for you to treat the crown princess with a bit more decorum and respect," Seph said, her voice extremely biting.

"A ranger is lecturing the first prince on decorum and respect?" Keion asked, raising his eyes skyward as though to appeal to whatever deity he believed in. "How ironic."

Sephaline's glare could probably have killed a lesser man, but the prince's haughty countenance deflected all of her energy.

Into the void Aerona hissed, "The bennaeth might, in his wisdom, be using the silence as a means of listening to and seeking to understand the crown princess's party so that he may evaluate her candidacy. Have any of the *younger* members of the party considered that?" Seph nodded, a smug look on her face, while Keion just shrugged sullenly and rode on.

I spent the next several minutes ignoring Keion as obviously as I could, bless his blackened little heart. As we traveled down the muddy road deeper into the capital town, it jogged to the right–to keep invading armies from having a clear shot in, Aerona explained in a whisper–and then it aimed us straight at a large open area behind which had to be Padrig's home.

The clearing presented another significant difference between Ganolog and the other elf towns I'd visited: there weren't any children. Anywhere else they'd've been out in droves, kicking balls and rolling hoops around. In front of Padrig's home, though, the central clearing consisted of about half an acre of muddy ground just that lay there, silently taking up space.

Looking around, I could see other paths radiating out away from the clearing. None of them flashed us with any more color than the one we'd come in on, though. All we could see in every direction was the mud and a few people slogging through it. It was brown, brown, and more brown.

As we approached, the twin oak doors–probably the only two doors in town that could actually be called rectangles–swung outward and a couple of familiar faces emerged from the first stone structure I'd seen since leaving Cysegredig.

"Welcome, Crown Princess and Prince of the Realm!" the large man bellowed. I'd met the mighty Bennaeth Padrig at the week-long party leading up to my coronation as crown princess, and he'd warmed up to me. He still seemed to hold the same regard as he hoisted a broad smile my way, and his welcoming gesture was as friendly as a bear-sized man can probably manage.

Beside the mighty bennaeth shrank Llew, the eleven year old son Padrig had tried pushing on me as a possible future romantic interest. As silly as it seemed to me, Llew actually had ardor in his eyes. *Oh, boy, here we go again*, I thought as I looked at the scrapling.

Next to the large man's son stood one of the most beautiful, and also one of the largest, women I'd ever seen. She lacked maybe an inch, if that, of Padrig's height, and she carried as much weight as the northern clan leader did, only distributed more in her chest and less around her waist. Arms and legs every bit as large and well-muscled as her husband's were visible thanks to her short sleeved, unassuming tunic. Her blond hair fell in braids past each shoulder and down nearly to her waist. Her wide smile was glowing, infectious, and seemed entirely genuine.

Dad's soldiers went to work, two of them taking their warhorses around toward the side of the longhouse. The other four leaped to assist us, one each grabbing the reins of our horses, and the fourth holding his hands out to help me down from Awel's back, as courtesy demanded of a soldier in the company of the crown princess. Or so, anyway, they'd told me. I hadn't allowed it in our camps along the road, and I sure as heck wasn't going to allow it in front of Padrig.

I was pleased to see that my denial of what they'd called 'simple courtesy' worked. A wicked smile turned the sides of Padrig's beard up toward his ears as I vaulted from Awel's back to land opposite the soldier who was still crouched there awaiting my foot. Hoping the soldier wasn't too offended by my rebuff, but not having the ability to show that I cared, I strode over to where Padrig stood. He and I clasped arms, each of us palm to elbow in the northern elves' gesture of deep respect.

"You have not forgotten our ways, little one," Padrig said, nodding approvingly. From anyone else *little one* would have been an insult, but from him it was a tender statement of relative fact. "It is good to see you again."

"I feel the same, Bennaeth," I said, trying to work just the right combination of formality and familiarity into my response. The queen's Lady had lectured me for hours on the way to approach this meeting, bless her heart. There'd been eight different possible reactions that our arrival could've triggered in the northern clan leader, and she'd required me to memorize each one, since the way I reacted to each would make the difference between being welcome in his home or being sent packing with war imminent, or just about anything else in between.

Have I mentioned that elf society is complicated?

Since I'd successfully broken the ice, so to speak, and there were people in the group who hadn't officially met, I stood silently waiting for the host to introduce his party. That part was backwards from what they expected back on Earth, but it was how the elves did it.

I didn't have to wait long. "Crown Princess," Padrig said directly to me, showing Keion surprisingly sparse respect, "You already know the light of my eyes, my heir, my son Llew. It now provides me the greatest of pleasure to introduce to the crown princess the light of my soul and my beloved wife of many wonderful years, Esyllt. Esyllt, this is Crown Princess Alyssa, daughter of Cadfael, King of all Kiirajanna, of whom I spoke to you so strongly about upon my return from Cysegredig."

In far southern regions of Kiirajanna, the queen's Lady had informed me, they had as many different titles for women as for men, and even more to the far west, but that wasn't so up north. Padrig was Bennaeth Padrig, while Esyllt was merely Esyllt. Still, I could always get away with a generic honorific. "It is a pleasure and an honor to meet you, Lady Esyllt," I intoned and gave the customary female-royal-to-female-royal peer two-finger gesture from my forehead. It was imprecise, and I knew it; generally one female elf outranks the other, and then the gesture tips itself toward the ranking member, but I'd been coached enough about the peerage of Ganolog to know that a show of equality would be rewarded.

It worked. She beamed and returned the salute.

That gave me the courage to go a little off-script on a hunch. "Your name is very nearly as beautiful as you are."

Esyllt blushed and smiled with pleasure as she thanked me for the compliment by executing the gesture of meeting someone who outranks you in royalty, her palm coming up vertical, shoulder-high, and then each finger, from index to pinky in order, coming up to the same vertical line. I was impressed by her precision in doing it; it's a lot more difficult than it sounds to get it just right with the elves' long fingers, and I wouldn't have thought she would get much practice up in the frigid north.

It was my turn.

"Bennaeth Padrig, it is my pleasure to introduce to you and to yours my companions. You already know Prince Keion, light of Queen Talaith's eyes and more than capable partner in battle. This is Ranger Sephaline, my cousin and excellent teacher in all matters of the natural wonders that surround us." Padrig's family nodded their greetings as Keion waved his palm, index finger up in the male version of the peer's salute, while Seph performed the dance non-nobles were expected to do when meeting nobles for the first time. When well done, it's an elegant gesture, but Seph was just a little ungraceful with it. She'd shown me the night before, and blamed the lack of grace on her having spent too much time out in the woods, but I countered that it was her own nobility coming out in rebellion. She was, after all, the first niece of my father, the king, and cousin to the future queen.

Padrig smiled openly at Seph's rough gesture. He was, according to all I'd heard, the kind of leader who would respect you more if you were worth something, as the king's niece in charge of training the future queen certainly was, than if you curtsied well.

I started to introduce Aerona, despite the fact that the queen's Lady had told me not to, but Padrig didn't give me a chance. He cut me off as I drew a breath and said, "and you must be Aerona, ever-present protector of the crown princess. The king has spoken highly of your battle prowess in the past, and I have even, I admit, tried unsuccessfully to trade for your services at times. It is good to see you all safely arrived. Princess, and prince, and ranger, and guardian, it is a pleasure to greet you and to welcome you to my hold. We are a humble settlement compared to the finery you are used to in Cysegredig, but I pray your stay by my hearth is comfortable and warm for as long as your journey allows."

The bennaeth and his family turned and went back inside, and we followed closely.

Well, that went well, I congratulated myself.

Padrig

The inside of the bennaeth's great hall was huge. I mean, I suppose the inside wasn't technically any bigger than the outside had been, unlike a certain blue police box I've seen. Still, the outside was set up against a large elf settlement, and so it hadn't looked all that big. Once we were inside, though, I could see just how massive the building was.

The two front doors had to be at least eight feet wide. They only took up, maybe, a tenth of the total front wall. To either side of the twin oak slabs–which could be barred, I saw, with three squared logs the size of railroad ties–the stone walls were decorated every few feet with either a stuffed animal's head or a sconce containing a thick candle.

The hall was lit by sconces hung on the walls and attached to the posts that stood along the middle of the room, as well as the four large chandeliers that dangled from the ceiling on ropes. Along each side wall were a series of large-paned windows that also let in the light from outside. Imperfections in the glass refracted the rays of sunlight to cast dancing rainbows, which played with the flickering glows and shadows created by the light of the candles. The shifting, shivering light gave the room a magical feel.

Stuffed animal parts of every variety I could imagine, and some I could not, provided the only wall decorations. Counting them and estimating the distance between led me to say that the great longhouse of the northern clan leader was a little over a hundred and fifty feet long.

I was so mesmerized by the immense feel and the dancing lights that I barely heard Prince Charming clear his throat meaningfully from behind me. I swiveled my attention to the front just in time to step around the huge pot-bellied wood stove that stood in the middle of the hall. Luckily it wasn't burning—too early in the season for that, I guess. If it had been, though, I'd've been burned, thanks to the lack of guard rails.

On Earth, they had guard rails around such things.

I guess they don't expect elves to be stupid enough to walk into hot stoves.

I checked to make sure I wasn't about to walk into any-thing else and then turned my gaze up into the top of the hall. It was impressive. The main roof trusses were supported by log posts, and they, in turn, held up the remainder of the roof through a complicated series of triangles constructed from what had apparently once been whole trees.

I sensed, rather than saw, a large person in front of me, and by putting on my brakes I barely missed walking directly into Padrig's enormous back side. A low growl that was his ver-sion of a chuckle rumbled from his chest. "Impressive construc-tion, is it not, Princess?" he asked.

"Very impressive," I agreed. "It must have taken a lot of strength to hoist the logs up that high," I said, hoping that complimenting his people and their construction would help my cause.

"We didn't do it by hand," Padrig said, turning a strange look my way. "We do have hoists and chains and levers, you know."

Oh, great, I thought. Now he thinks I'm stupid.

"I am pleased, however, that you thought so highly of my people as to believe we could do such a thing," Padrig rumbled. "Do you use much log construction where you came from on Earth?"

"None, Bennaeth," I said, shaking my head. I'd seen log cabins in books and on TV shows, but I couldn't think of a single one anywhere near where I'd grown up.

"Well, that is too bad. Log construction is not just warm in the winter, it is extremely strong too. As you see above you, the triangles create great structural strength and stability. That, and they also create a wonderful obstacle course for Llew, the Agile, to climb around on. Wouldn't you agree, Son?"

"Yes, Papa," agreed a much smaller voice from behind Padrig. Hearing it made me smile. Hey, I couldn't help it; the boy was cute.

Padrig took off again. I followed, wondering if I should have made more of a big deal out of his log triangles above our head. Probably not, I figured. One thing the queen's Lady had told me was that in the event of a situation that was outside of the scope of her briefings, I should just be natural and honest.

Just—not *too* honest, she had added quickly.

At the far end of the cavernous chamber was a concrete platform about half a foot high that held two thrones, each carved out of the same grey stone that formed the walls. They were decorated in rich purple velvet fabric like my father's throne.

I'd been briefed, both by the queen's Lady and by Keion, on how important the bear was to the northern clan, not only as a source of fur and food but also of inspiration. It didn't surprise me, then, that I saw a lot of bear representations on the platform. Each throne had bear claws carved into the end of the arms and a relief of a bear in the top panel. To either side, back against the wall, stood large, stuffed brown bears, each of their eyes glittering menacingly in the candle light. If I hadn't been pretty sure they were dead, I would have sworn they watched us walk up to the platform.

Behind the thrones and centered on the wall I saw another trophy. This bear had been pure white, and its head was easily half again bigger than the heads of the two brown bears standing below. It was just a head, but that was scary enough with its gaping mouth set into a permanent roar.

"That's the biggest bear head I've ever seen," I said. It was true, too, though technically it was the only bear head I'd ever seen. The rest of them had had bodies attached. I glanced backward toward the walls and confirmed my memory that the stuffed heads surrounding the dining area included foxes, moose, deer, and many other creatures, but not bears.

Padrig nodded and said, "Medraud. Took me three weeks of tracking across the barren ice fields in the northwest to find him, and even longer to come close enough to have a chance at ending his miserable reign of terror."

I recognized the name. I'd spent some time in the library of the abbey since we'd returned from the larger one, using the opportunity mostly to brood over what had happened in Alecsanddrha.

Yes, that was the library I'd burned down. The legendary Library of Alecsanddrha, a repository of information that was as important to the elves as the Library of Alexandria had been to the ancient world of humans. And I'd burned it down. Yay, me.

Granted, that was a different story. Still, I'd been haunted by the vision of the fire rushing from scroll to scroll, book to book, shelf to shelf, every night since.

Forcing myself out of my brooding vision, I asked, "Medraud? That's a fairly famous name both here and in the legends on Earth. I wonder if your bear was named after the legendary villain, or the villain after the bear?" Medraud is the name for one of the big bad guys in the ancient story that, on Kiirajanna, parallels Arthurian legend back on Earth. In fact, he was the guy who killed King Arthur, according to the tales on both sides of the ley-gates we used to travel between the worlds. The only thing was that it was considered a legend on Earth, but an actual piece of history to the elves.

"Probably neither," Padrig said.

"It is likely that both were named for someone else," the prince added. He'd been silent through the long building, so hearing his voice from behind surprised me.

"Oh?" I asked.

"There is an ancient story you should hear some day, but I am certain the bennaeth does not wish to waste time with stories," he said.

"The prince's certainty is well placed," Padrig said, and I wondered again about the icy formality in both of their manners. Keion hadn't told me of anything between him and the northern clan chieftain, but something was off. "I shall have one of my storytellers delight you with its telling some evening, but for now we should see your party settled in and comfortable. You are under my roof now, little one, and my honor will not stand to have you tired or dusty from the road, or in want of anything. Now," he said, turning and waving toward the throne area, "for meals my people bring tables up onto the platform, and here is where you and the prince and your cousin will dine." I noticed he left Aerona out, but she didn't seem to mind. "Should you hunger or thirst at any other time you have but to inform one of my people. Through that door," he said, gesturing toward a stout oak door in the corner of the room with a ferociously-posed brown bear painted on it, "are my personal quarters, should you ever need my presence. Through that door," he said as he turned and pointed at a much plainer oak door at the other end of the wall, "are our guest quarters as well as the house's guard post for your protection. Please, follow me."

"Protection from what?" I asked Seph quietly as we turned left and followed him toward plainer of the two doors. She shrugged, but Padrig heard me.

"Protection from every worry, little one. This portion of the continent, unlike the tamed central region you have become used to, conceals many dangers underneath the pretty white snow caps and beams of light in the sky. I will be pleased to brief you on some of those this evening, once you have freshened up from your long ride."

This being the second time he'd outright said we needed to freshen up, I wondered how much we'd come to stink on the long ride. The librarians at Alecsanddrha hadn't said anything about our cleanliness, but then again they'd been concerned about other things. Things like keeping us from ever leaving again, but like I said, that's another story.

The door in the corner of the great hall opened into a hallway that led further down the length of the building, and I noticed that the windows that had opened up that side of the building to the sun were gone, replaced by a continuous thick stone wall decorated with more of the candle sconces. Gone, also, were the heads of dead animals; in their place hung a tapestry showing a hunting scene with yet another ferocious brown bear.

The hall turned right after several yards, with a doorway at the bend and other doors spaced out down the new path.

"The guard post," Padrig explained and pointed to the first door, a two-piece contraption that opened down the first hall we'd entered. We walked past another few doors, and then he held one open and gestured Seph in. He didn't linger long enough for me to look at her room, though; instead, he walked to the last two doors at the end of the hall to deposit Keion, to one side, and me, to the other.

"Remember, if you need anything at all during your stay, please let my people know, and it will be our pleasure to ensure that your every need is met. Now, I will leave you to your relaxations from the long and arduous road," Padrig said from the hall. With a brief nod, he turned and retreated.

"I–" I started to say something to Keion from my own doorway only to see his back disappear and the door to his room slam shut. Fine; I guess he didn't want to talk to me.

"Can I get you anything, Your Highness?" the bubbly girl who'd been assigned as my personal maidservant asked. "Something from the cupboard, perhaps, or a drink? I have already begun heating water in the tub for a bath."

"Hmm," I said, still stinging a little from Keion's door being slammed in my face. "Let's start with the Your Highness part. I already have the helpers"–I refused to call them servants–"at Cysegredig not fawning on me so much. I know it's not the standard practice here, but it's how I was raised. So how about if you just call me by my name, Alyssa?"

She nodded. "I will be happy to call you by your name if it pleases you, Crown Princess Alyssa."

"Yeah, thank you very much. Can we get to just Alyssa?" I measured my tone carefully, trying not to let the frustration into it. It had been a long ride, and a rough introduction, but more than that, this name thing was the same issue I'd faced over and over at Cysegredig.

Would anyone ever be willing to just call me by my name?

She blinked in confusion. "You—you wish me to refer to you as though we were familiar? Is—is this a trick, Princess?" she asked, her eyes narrowing slightly.

Apparently, the answer was no. I let a sigh be birthed into the world before continuing.

"No, no trick here. I'm just a familiar kind of girl."

"Oh. Okay, thank you, Your Highness. I—I can't. I couldn't. It would get me beaten, or—or worse." The way she trembled and held her head down, looking intently and respectfully at my toes, made me believe she was being far more honest than I'd have believed otherwise. Beaten?

"Who would beat you?" *And what would be even worse*, I wanted to ask, but the first question scared the girl enough.

"They—I—if it would please Your Highness, I will need to see to the bath water," she said as she beat a hasty retreat.

While she was out I looked around at the rest of my new apartment. It was nice. The entry alcove, or *mud room* as Padrig had called it, led to a small but comfortable sitting room, off of which was the bath in which I could hear my—*servant*—bustling about. Past the sitting room was the bedroom, its simple furniture granting it a ton of old country style charm. The bed frame was made entirely of stripped-down logs, their white wood polished till it gleamed. The heap of blankets on the bed, an assortment of all possible fabrics and colors, made me think of just how far north we'd come as I wondered just how cold it might get. The bedroom also held a couple of wardrobes, a chest of drawers, and a dresser, all made from rough-hewn lumber and, like the logs of the bed, polished to a fine sheen.

A small wood stove in the corner put out both a little bit of heat and a snout-full of the most incredibly aromatic wood smoke. It instantly reminded me of being out in the woods camping back on Earth. On its flat surface bubbled a small bucket of water, and the warped glass inset into its door displayed the flames inside in a distorted way that would've pleased Picasso.

It looked like the servants had been busy preparing for our arrival.

"You should not be too shocked over the plight of the house elves, many of whom are slaves, up here in the north," Aerona's voice entered the room from behind me. I jumped, having forgotten for the moment that she was there, and then I snickered. *House elves* made me think of one named Dobby, which in turn made me wonder if the young elf lass could disapparate. Maybe if I gave her a sock she could be free? Would she be interested in helping Hermione SPEW?

"Did I say something funny, Princess?" she asked.

"No. At least, not intrinsically funny. I just–oh, never mind." I gave up explaining the funny topic to get back to the serious one. "Slaves? They practice slavery up here?"

"All that training you received on the clan to the north, and they didn't cover that with you?"

"No, it seems my trainers left that part out."

"Oh. Well, then, yes, they do, Princess, though it's become less of a practice these modern days." Aerona said the word modern like it was a bad thing, and I barely held back that chortle. She continued, "I could explain to you what I know of it, or you could ask someone who's much more familiar with the process, as long as you don't scare her off." Aerona indicated over her shoulder where I could see the maid crossing back toward the bedroom.

"Princess," the younger girl said, but she was interrupted by a knock on the door. I started toward it out of habit, but I stopped when I noticed Aerona subtly shaking her head. I stood quietly while the maid answered the door, accepted my saddle bags from somebody, and bustled with them into the bedroom. She placed them carefully into one of the wardrobes, and then led me into the bathroom gingerly.

She never met my eyes at all. I guess I'd really shaken her up with my strange and progressive commentary.

As I let her help me into the tub, I tried again. "Look, I'm not trying to get you into trouble. Your culture up here is different from what I'm used to, is all. I don't even know your name."

"Ellga," she said quietly. She still wouldn't meet my eyes, but at least a pleasant smile started shimmying its way onto her face.

"Ellga. That is a very pretty name. Are you from around here, Ellga?"

"No, Princess," she said, shaking her head as she leaned over to get the spoon and sponge to bathe me. I still wasn't used to being bathed. It had only happened once, on coronation day in the castle at Cysegredig. I didn't want to scare her off again, though, so I sat passively while she started scrubbing the dirt of the road off of my body. "I am from Thurso, far to the west."

"The Western clan?" I asked. There was a clan separate from Padrig's people who lived way over that direction. They were an exotic group who made their home in the desert.

"No, Princess, though I have often wondered what life in the ever-present dry warmth would be like. I am from the Digonol tribe. My village stands where the Bull River empties into the ocean."

"I see," but I didn't. I had no idea where the Bull River was. I wanted to foster the conversation, though, so I asked, "What's it like there?"

"It is nice," she said, her voice still guarded.

"Would you tell me of it? I have never been to that area of the continent, and would enjoy hearing you describe your home."

That did the trick. Ellga relaxed and started speaking in a quiet, sing-song voice that, while it was still the elf language, was accented in a way that made her sound foreign, exotic. As she scrubbed the layers of caked-on dirt from my hair and my back, she told me of tall, rustic mountains that were always capped in snow and of lush green expanses of forests whose trees grew up, way up into the clouds and had trunks so big around that three or four elves together couldn't encircle them. Large, red-meat fish filled the rivers almost every year, and many ended up in the nets of fishermen along the way. It was a perfect life, and in a perfect climate, too. The ocean air kept it cool and breezy in the summer, and never far below freezing in the winter.

Ellga told me of the mountains that sheltered Thurso and the other villages, keeping the ocean air from dissipating over the rest of the north. There was a road her father and other leaders, and tradesmen, too, used to pass from her idea of paradise to the much colder interior of the continent. She'd only made the trip a couple of times, but every spring a trader made the dash in his dog sled carrying all manner of things, from pelts of far north animals to frozen slabs of red meat to plants of the far north that loved the cold and came brilliantly alive beside the chilly ocean. She and her people would trade, in most of the years when the fish was plentiful, and the grizzled old trader would sit around their fire for the night telling tales and news from the rest of the land.

Her people, she said, were generous. The trader, in fact, had called them the most generous people on Kiirajanna, and he would know. He didn't even bother haggling for prices, since they would give him beaded works and baskets that, he claimed, none others could rival. That captured the Digonol, she agreed. They would never let a visitor go without shelter or food, and everything they received would be rewarded with a return gift more valuable. And they were happy, too, extraordinarily happy with their simple lives.

I could tell, from the way she'd spoken of the fish filling the river *almost* ever year, that something had happened. I asked, and she smiled wistfully and nodded, meeting my eyes again for the first time since I'd gotten too familiar.

"Every half-score or dozen years, Princess, the *eogiaid* fail to return in numbers as we expect them to. Generally my people can tell that the short year is coming and store some extra in the years before, but we did not see the shortage coming this last time. As a result we were faced with a choice: pay our normal tribute to the ben and the bennaeth and starve, or feed ourselves and suffer the consequences with the chieftains."

"And you decided to make sure everyone had food to eat." I got a grim picture of the politics of the clan.

"We did, Princess. The ben understood our plight and did not take any penalty, but the bennaeth had to act to preserve his position. He held back his raid at the cost of two slaves."

"And you were one of the slaves," I added, horror growing in my heart. The Digonol had just wanted to feed everyone, to merely keep all of their friends and family from starving. How callously—*callous!*—was all my brain would give me as it spun up the level of irritation. How callous could a leader be to take as a slave such a beautiful young girl when the tribe's only sin was ensuring that everybody had food to eat?

"I was," she said, nodding. "But I was lucky to be taken into the bennaeth's household where we have always been warm and dry and fed well."

"Wait. *Padrig* took you as a slave?"

"He is the bennaeth, Princess."

"I know that. I'm going to have to talk to him about this slave business," I said, and as soon as it was out of my mouth she tensed right up again.

"Please, do not attempt to speak on my behalf, Princess. My stay has been happy enough, and I have but one more year before I can be returned to my village. I so desperately want to see my home again."

"And if I open my big mouth, Padrig might keep you longer."

Her only reply was a meek nod.

"Well, I have to say this all sounds completely foreign to me, but I will agree not to discuss your plight with the bennaeth," I promised, choosing my words carefully. I still planned to ask him about the whole slavery thing.

She nodded and helped me out of the tub. She insisted on drying me off, an activity that was weirdly invasive of my private space. On a shelf nearby there was a fresh set of clothes that looked and felt more like flannel pajamas. I was pleased to see them, but concerned over the impression they'd make.

"Aren't these for after dinner?" I asked, and she shook her head.

"These pants and blouses serve as dinner wear here, Princess. Except during times of battle, of course, at which time everyone is expected to attend in their armor. Now is a time of peace, though, and Bennaeth Padrig's sense of honor rests on your being warm and comfortable by his hearth."

With Ellga's help, then, I made sure my hair was tidy and my flannel pajamas were all buttoned up, and then off I went to dinner.

AMDDIFFYNFA

a fortress, stronghold, citadel, or just a great big ole' rock. Elf language is awesome that way.

Argument

"Is your room to your liking?" Padrig asked me once we were seated at the dinner table.

He hadn't been kidding about the transformation of a ruling hall into a dining hall. It was impressive. The table that replaced the thrones was made out of a single long, wide plank that had been sliced from a massive tree. Just like the furniture in my guest room, all the knots, blemishes, and soft spots had been buffed and polished till the whole thing glowed in the candle light. The high-backed chairs we sat in were simple, austere even, but despite the lack of embellishment each one was beautifully formed with lines that seemed to flow together naturally. Each was just a little bit different from its peers, obviously handmade by a master craftsman. The other tables and chairs in the room, though not as high-backed or polished, were just as well made.

Padrig sat at the center of the table, Esyllt to his right. I sat to his left, and Keion was placed way over at the right hand of Esyllt. Seph, to her unspoken horror, had a seat all the way down the table to Keion's right. Padrig explained that northern clan protocol called for alternating boy-girl-boy-girl at the head table, but I figured he wanted to give Llew a chance to sit next to my left hand His son certainly didn't seem to mind that spot, not one bit.

The regular people, to use Padrig's term, sat at tables arranged in angled lines on the floor. Most of them seemed content to just sit there patiently, talking quietly and only occasionally glancing up toward us new arrivals. One, though, made his way directly up to our table. He stood out from the crowd immediately; most of the northern elves were big, burly, simple types, but the one who approached was short, wiry, and haughty-looking. Padrig introduced him as Grigor, his advisor. I wanted to ask him what he advised the bennaeth on, but I remembered the queen's Lady's suggestion to leave my sarcastic wit at the door. Instead, I just mouthed a "nice to meet you" kind of thing, and he quickly turned his hawk-nose away from us and strode over to sit at the head of one of the lower tables.

I was relieved to see that everybody was wearing the same style pajamas I was. Everybody, that is, but Grigor, who wore sparkly blue robes. It seemed weird to me that a bear of a chieftain like Padrig would maintain a short, slight, and eccentrically-dressed man as an advisor, but then again, it wasn't much weirder than the huge stuffed bears that overlooked the table as we ate, or the fairy-driven moose that had charged through our group on the way.

We were served Viking style, to nobody's surprise. Flat wooden plates and linen napkins were laid out in front of us, along with an assortment of wooden and horn and stone cups that were obviously all carved by hand. That was it, though—no silverware, and the only knives were sharp carving blades used to slice through the massive shanks of meat that Padrig's servants brought out to us.

It ended up being fun, eating with our hands. Hunks of bread helped, and the meat and roast vegetables were dry enough to handle. It was still messy, but nobody seemed to care. While we ate, we swapped small talk, much of it centered on stories about our ride up to the rim. Keion piped up from his puddle of glowering to pay Padrig's kitchen a sideways compliment, by way of complaining about how bad the food on the road had been compared to Ganalog's noble fare. His comment had its desired effect on Seph, whose expression clearly showed a desire to do bad things with the carving knife in front of her.

I glanced over and noticed that the prince's insult and Seph's resulting glare hadn't been lost on Grigor, whose dark eyes were watching the three of us closely. As soon as he noticed me watching him watch us, though, he nodded a small but respectful gesture my way and turned his gaze downward toward the food on his plate.

As they cleared the plates and platters away to bring out the little sweet bread things that were our dessert, I got the chance to ask a question that had been bothering me since we arrived in Ganolog. "Bennaeth Padrig, where are the children?" I asked, trying to make my question sound as light as possible instead of the probing that the queen's Lady had warned me against. I couldn't help it; the lack of kids playing outside in the clearing had just been too creepy after seeing other elf villages.

He shrugged. "The children are—around. Where should they be?"

"I—well, I'm not sure where they should be, but in every other village I've visited, they've been outside playing. Hoops, and balls, and sticks, and things. Elf children are some of the most active I've ever seen. When we came in through the city today, though, I was surprised at the lack of childish play."

"Oh! Yes, well, the lack of children playing outside at this time of year is not unexpected, little one. Every other village you've seen is in the lesser—or, rather, you say lower regions, yes? Down there where it is warm all day, the younglings have plenty of time to run around without a care in their heads. Up here in the north, though, when the days begin shrinking and the temperature dips at night, every hand is needed to prepare for the coming winter."

"Forgive my ignorance, but what do they prepare?"

"Everything! They prepare everything. One matter that surprises southerners who visit is how thoroughly we must prepare for the coming winter, because it will be upon us in a single moment, like this." Padrig laughed heartily, and then brought his frisbee-sized hands together to illustrate. "It is not unheard of to awaken and find that anything—tools, toys, anything—that you mistakenly left laying about outside has become hidden by deep snow overnight. Unfortunately such a thing will not be found till either it is stepped on by an unfortunate person, or it is revealed by the melt as the sun god once again vanquishes the dark."

It was the first I'd heard of a sun god, so I made a mental note to ask about it later.

"Here in the great white north," Llew intoned from beside me as though it were a lecture he'd memorized recently, "we have three seasons. Did you know that? Our three seasons consist of this winter, last winter, and next winter. What we mean by that is that we live in this winter, we learn the lessons of last winter, and everything we do when it's not technically winter is in preparation for next winter."

"Oh," I said delicately, not sure whether to come back conversationally or with a chuckle. A glance toward Padrig confirmed that it wasn't meant as a joke, though. "So how long is it, do you think, Llew, before I might get to see some snow fall?"

"Up here, we do not say the snow falls. We say the snow flies. It is more—descriptive," the boy said. "More honest. But to answer your question, Princess, I would say you might see that in another three, maybe four weeks. Would you agree, Papa?"

"That's about right," Padrig said before stuffing another sweet bread puff into his mouth.

"Again, please forgive my ignorance, but what are people doing to prepare for winter? It seems to me that putting away the things that are out in the yard should only take an afternoon."

Llew took up the lecture as he responded, "There is always work to be done repairing homes after the rains of the summer so that they may successfully face the cold and the weight of the snow on the roof during the winter. Most of our people's time, though, is spent preparing and putting up enough food to last the winter through."

"Food, like wild game?"

"Well, yes, of course. It's not like we have many *melysffrwythau* orchards to harvest up here."

Padrig chortled at his son's joke at my expense, but I managed to keep my game face on.

"That's a good thing, too. I don't know how they manage to harvest those without eating them all," I said, referring to the little fruits grown in the very southern reaches of the continent. They were smaller than a peach and yellow-orange all the way through with a single large pit. It looked like an apricot, but was firm like an apple. I'd never seen anything similar on Earth, so I had no idea what the English name might be, but I sure did love when we had some in stock at Cysegredig.

"Are you old enough to hunt?" I asked to continue the conversation, and only after it tumbled ungracefully out of my mouth did I realize how dumb it was to ask that question to an immature kid who had a crush on me. Oops.

Sure enough, it stung him, and he reacted as all young males would. Chest puffed out, voice pushed louder and artificially lower, he said, "Of course I hunt. I've taken a brace of rabbits by myself this year, and I was along on the trip last year when Father took a bear whose meat fed us for days."

"How do you eat bear?" I asked, and when he turned a disbelieving expression my way I spread my hands in supplication and continued, "I'm really sorry, Llew, but all of this is brand new to me. And interesting! I'm so fascinated by your way of life and the ways it differs from what I'm used to. I'm not mocking you, I promise. I was raised in the far southern region of my homeland, in a place known as Mississippi, where we didn't have any bears or moose. Our deer, in fact, were only about this tall," I finished by turning a little to the side and holding my hand out a few feet high.

"Princess," Padrig's voice rumbled, "you are in luck. We have a hunt going out tomorrow. Perhaps you would be willing to accompany us in order to learn more of our ways and see something larger than a *ginau*?" I grinned; the word he'd used meant a very young puppy.

"I would very much enjoy the opportunity, Bennaeth," I lied through my teeth. Of all the things I wanted to experience in the great white north, a hunting party was extremely low on the list, if not dead last. "Will we be hunting bear?"

"No, Princess. We do not hunt bear for food this late in the year."

"Why not? I thought all hunting seasons were in the fall."

"Springtime and early summer are when the bears have just come out of their winter rests, and those who have eaten at all have eaten berries and leaves, which makes their flesh taste sweet. This late in the year, though, the bear has had a steady diet of fish and carrion, and that makes the meat taste harsh."

"That makes sense, I guess. So what will you be hunting on this trip?"

"Elk, primarily. Our larger version of deer. Did you change your mind about going already?"

"No, why?" Padrig's sudden turn of question confused me.

"The way that your question was worded sounded as though you are now planning to stand to the side and cheer the hunters along our way out of Ganolog."

He was right; I'd used second person instead of first. Silly me. "Sorry. In my native tongue there's a pronoun, *y'all*, that can be used for just about anything, including first person plural. I slipped back to it since I'm tired after a long day of travel. If I may ask, though, why elk and not moose?"

"Ah, a good question," he said, and sounded surprised that it was. It should have upset me, but in truth I hadn't done the queen's Lady very proud over dinner. "Up here on the edge of the Rim the elk are the primary game animal that we see. Moose are found in numbers far to the west where the trees are smaller and the hills settle down into plains."

"That moose we saw must've been ridden quite some distance, then," I said.

Padrig sat up straighter. "Moose? You saw a moose? Where?" His booming voice caught the attention of some of the nearby elves, who stopped talking and peered at me with hunters' eyes gleaming in eagerness to take off after the moose that we'd sighted.

I explained what had happened on the trail nearby. Esyllt nearly choked on her drink when I described the tylwyth teg's expressions as they rode past us on the moose's antlers.

"Well, we will not hunt a moose out from under the little people," Padrig said when he was done chuckling. "They are good luck to us, and to anger them just before winter sets in would be a very dumb thing. We hunt elk tomorrow, and we will leave five bells prior to noon. Please be packed and mounted at that time."

The bennaeth's family rose from the table, wished us a good night, and retired directly to the part of the long house we hadn't been invited to tour. Everyone seated at the lower tables took that as their cue to rise and begin their own exodus, and the servants swooped in to start gathering dishes up. As I watched the men and women of the serving class, I couldn't help wondering how many of them were slaves like Ellga.

As he retired, I noticed Grigor casting a glare my direction, but as soon as he saw me looking his expression vanished. Quickly he turned and exited through the crowd, and as much as I wanted to follow him to find out what all the rudeness was about, I knew I needed to get settled in and not cause any more waves my first night.

We gathered back in the sitting area of my room at my request. For one thing, I wanted a chance to go over what had happened so far. For another, Prince Charming had charmingly sulked his way through supper, and I wanted to know what had flown up his butt.

"Nothing, Princess," Keion growled when I asked him what was wrong.

"Right. We can all tell that nothing is wrong. You've been as happy as a lark since we got here."

"Nice sarcasm face," he sneered and then continued, "I must advise the Princess that it was not within the scope of her father's orders for me to be or to act as happy as a lark. I am only here to keep his daughter safe, as some sort of super guard."

"Well, you could at least quit growling and snapping toward our host."

"I am doing no such thing."

"You have a strange definition of no such thing," I argued.

"You have a strange definition of growling and snapping," he countered.

Aerona sighed and rolled her eyes. It was the most expressive thing I'd seen her do all day.

"Look, at least maybe you could enlighten me on why there's such tension between you and the bennaeth."

"Why?" he asked, and the way he asked it reminded me of a little five-year-old. I was surprised he didn't stamp his foot at the same time.

"Because I worry that it may get in the way of the mission."

"I doubt that the bennaeth's ability to insult the first prince will have any bearing on your mission."

"The bennaeth insulted you? I can't imagine anyone insulting the mighty Prince Keion. What did he say?"

Keion glared at me for a moment, then apparently decided it was worth telling. "Some years ago, on his visit to celebrate my becoming an adult. He called me a *paunbach*."

Seph snickered once, earning her a bright glower before she could force her expression neutral again.

I hadn't heard the word before, so I looked around for an explanation. When none came, I asked, "Okay, I'll bite. What's a paunbach?"

"A paun is a type of bird, Princess," Aerona said from her corner, her face carefully straight. "It has glorious coloration, usually green and blue, and it can spread its tail feathers into a shimmery fan shape. Each feather has a green and blue sheen to it, and—"

"I've seen them!" I said, nodding. "He called you a little peacock! That's actually kind of funny, Keion."

Keion shrugged. "I did not find it so then, nor do I *now*," and he turned his glare briefly back toward Seph, silencing the little snickers that had returned. "I am content to be peaceful within his hold in support of your mission, Princess, but do not press the matter further."

"Ah. Silly me, I thought maybe you were here as my friend."

"I am not now, nor will I ever be, your friend," Keion said in a voice that slithered into my gut and ripped everything in there to shreds.

See, ever since he and I had a go at a sultry kiss, my guts had been tragically exposed to his verbal slicing. The very next day he'd pretended like it was a mistake. Granted, his hand was already promised, and that to a very young girl he'd never even met. Then there was the fact that tradition forbade me, the most likely future queen, to consider the most likely future king as a likely future mate. So there was plenty of reason for me to be messed up in the head over my feelings for him, but for him to verbally slice me open like that made my blood boil.

Seph caught my mood. It didn't take much, I'm sure. "If I may suggest something, Alyssa?" she asked in a carefully pleasant, conversational tone.

Keion hurled a glare her way and spat out, "You may not."

That really lit my fuse. "She may *so*. She *is* my cousin, after all," I argued.

"I believe the prince's moodiness will be easier to understand within the context of the upcoming sporting season that, I am certain, he is anxious to get back down to," Seph said, her eyebrows perched meaningfully above her eyes.

"Oh, don't bring cylchoedd into this," Keion snapped.

"Is it true?" I asked.

"Is what true, Princess? It is true, yes, that I promised your father that I would keep you safe on the journey up to the miserable, godforsaken northern realm for as long as it was required for you to gain Padrig's favor. It is also true that I plan to see that promise through, even should it somehow require that I miss the first days of practice for my team. It is also true that my missing too much of the early season would be disastrous for me, for my team, and for our game. Do you need to be let in on any further *truths*?"

"I take it this cylchoedd, whatever it is, is an important sport?" I asked, and got my answer from Seph as she shot me a shocked look followed by a vigorous nod. Keion just snorted.

I'd never heard of this cylchoedd. Fine; I really didn't care. I didn't care whether it was like football, or like baseball, or even like quiddich for that matter; sports to me were as useless as running circles around a stadium on an asphalt track. In any event, Keion had not only taken an insulting tone, but he'd even given me the peer-to-peer hand-flit gesture of respect, only twisted to the side to make it into a sarcastic insult, and that made me even angrier.

"The only further truth I need to know, then, is that we need to be done and back in time for you to play your precious little sport."

"Perhaps the future elf queen should show more interest in the sport of her people," he sneered back, this time looking away at the wall rather than at me. With the elves, that, also, serves as a display of deep disrespect.

"Perhaps the future elf queen should determine that for herself," I growled.

Without turning his face my way, the prince widened his sneer and shot back, "Perhaps she should, if the future elf queen is capable of making such determinations. Sadly, though, she has proven herself entirely incompetent since we arrived here, which has but further exacerbated my own desire to be done with this place."

"*Look at me!*" I yelled, tired of him as well as the obvious disrespect he was rubbing in my face.

He rose to his feet and fixed me directly with a glare. "*Better?*" he bellowed. When he spoke next his voice was quiet, but it rang through the room like a sword leaving its scabbard. "I am looking at you, *Princess*, but I do not see what I have been hoping to see, what this realm needs. Instead I see a scared, stupid, careless, and spoiled little girl who has no real hope of becoming an effective queen. And now I must retire to my own room. Good night, *Your Highness*."

"*Get out*, Keion," I replied, my own voice sharp enough to cut the stone of the walls around us. I wanted to say so much more: *get out, go home, I don't need you, go back to your stupid archery and your silly cylchoedd.* But I didn't dare say any of that, because he'd been right about one thing. I really was scared—scared of doing the wrong thing, scared of sending away the guy who'd been my ally when I'd needed one the most, scared of losing—

No, not losing him. He wasn't mine to lose. We'd already worked that out, after the dance and the ill-timed kiss. He was taken, fated to be the husband of a girl who was still too young to know better.

Besides, I was too angry to know what to say. I was so angry, in fact, that everything in the room turned a deep shade of red.

The door slammed shut, and moments later I heard another slam from across the hall. Then—silence. Through the stiff webs of silence I could hear—or maybe just sense—Draignerthol's buzz, as though the pendant wanted to see some action.

"Cousin, I–" Sephaline started to say, but I cut her off.

"You get out, too," I said, my voice a little harsher than I wanted. "No, I mean it, Seph. I'm madder than a hornet right now, and it's no time to talk. I have–some thinking to do."

Silently my cousin left, closing the door much more carefully than Keion had. When she and Booboo were both gone, I took a deep breath and turned to Aerona, the only person who was still standing in the room. "I don't suppose you have anything to add?" I asked, feeling a little peevish.

"Would it matter if I did, Princess?"

"Oh, probably not." Aerona, in the months I'd known her, had proven herself able to cut to the chase in a direct and honest way, and that had earned her not only my respect, but also my own direct sincerity in return.

"Well, then, might I merely, and gently, recommend that you call for Ellga and allow her to do her job in assisting you toward your bed for the evening?"

I nodded and, ignoring my misgivings over the whole slavery thing, let the girl help me get ready for bed. Aerona ignored her own resting area in the entrance, since she had rested over dinner. Now she was ready for duty. She took up her post, guarding my bedroom and glaring at the shadows, just exactly as she did back in Dad's palace.

GWERSYLL

a campsite, usually an established one with buildings instead of tents. Elves are funny that way.

Hunting Camp

The hunting expedition launched early the next day, just as Padrig had warned me it would. Luckily, considering the lack of sleep I'd had the night before, it wasn't quite as early as I'd feared. Ellga had explained the northern elves' concept of time to me while I was settling down for the night. The word for noon meant, literally, midday, which was the time that the sun was highest in the sky. That put the occurrence of noon during that time of year right about two in the afternoon, which in turn put five hours before noon at a nice, comfy nine o'clock in the morning instead of seven o'clock.

Prince Charming was up and ready to go and, surprisingly, he was actually pretty upbeat in spite of the blowout we'd had. Not to me, of course; he still turned a cold shoulder my direction. To everybody else, though, he acted as happy as a hog in fresh mud.

Seph and Booboo were up and prancing around, too; Seph explained that they'd been on plenty of hunts before, but never for such large–and excitingly dangerous–prey.

Aerona was, well, Aerona. She was every bit as expressive as a telephone pole, and just a tiny bit tougher. She held Awel's reins as I jumped onto my mare's saddle, and then she climbed up onto her own mount, announcing her readiness to be off with a stoic gaze forward.

Ellga, sweetheart that she was, packed me a food pouch that held sausage and cheese and even a few sort-of-apples—they were squishy like a plum and bright green inside, but they tasted like apples, anyway. She'd even filled the pouch with enough that I had some to share with Aerona and Seph. Keion didn't need any of mine; it turned out that he had his own slave-servant named Aleifr who'd provided him with a travel pack too. Not that he'd've taken any of mine, or even talked to me about it, or even looked at me, but—well, whatever.

We rode west for most of the day, passing from the rolling plains into foothills with a line of towering and majestic mountains gradually coming into sight to the north. I and the rest of the visiting group rode at the head of the column with Padrig and Llew, while several dozen northern elves, gussied up in their best hunting furs, rode along fanned out in formation behind and to either side with a knot of pack animals ambling along in the middle. Llew glommed onto me for the first while, his face smiling this little dopey-eyed expression that seemed to be constantly turned my way. Finally he happened to glance past me and caught the glare that Keion was sending his way, and then he excused himself to ride alongside his father for the rest of the trip.

Bless the poor kid's heart, and I mean that in the good way.

After saving me from my enraptured little prince of the north, though, Prince Charming went back to ignoring me. I think he actually said more words to Aerona than he did to me, and that was just to ask her if she intended to hunt using only her daggers. From her nod, it was apparent that she did. Honestly, I was willing to bet she'd have better luck with her daggers than I would with my bow. Heck, she could probably scare a beast to death with her glare, and between her and Keion's grumpy faces I figured we had all the death-stares we needed lined up for the hunt.

We arrived at the clearing that served as base camp after about six hours of riding. I was surprised that the sun was already sinking toward the horizon. At least it wasn't freezing cold yet; that had been my greatest worry. After spending most of my life in Mississippi, the thought of spending a night out in the cold northern air of the Rim of Kiirajanna frightened me.

Luckily, we didn't have to spend the night out in the cold air at all. The permanent camp was built of fairly solid little log cabins, each about twelve feet wide and fifteen or sixteen feet long, and each had just enough room for eight bunks and a wood stove with a small table at the back. The one closest to the middle turned out to be ours, and as we stepped into it Aerona insisted on taking the top bunk in the back with me right underneath her. Seph took the bottom bunk against the other wall, and looked disappointed when nobody moved to take the one above her. Llew claimed the top nearer the door when it was clear Keion wanted the bottom, and of course Padrig got the other pair of bunks all to himself.

I'd hoped for cabins, but I'd also expected them to be chillier versions of the ranger stations we'd been sleeping in along the road. When we arrived, though, we found that chilly was pretty much the opposite of what the cabin was. Padrig pointed to the roaring wood stove and explained that runners had come by to set up camp and light the stoves to warm the cabins well in advance of our arrival. I was impressed.

"You like, Princess?" Padrig asked as I walked over to the small black canister that was popping and roaring from inside its belly, amazed at the warmth it put out.

"I do," I said without turning away. Between the sound of the fire inside it and the occasional deep gong of its metal stretching in the warmth, the song of the wood stove fascinated me. I put my hands closer and marveled at how deeply, comfortingly warm it was. "I've not been in much wood heat before, and this is both comfortable and mesmerizing."

The snort from the front of the cabin let me know that I'd said something else that Keion thought was silly, but it was well past time that I cared what he thought as long as he didn't get in the way of my gaining Padrig's acceptance.

"My father's house has wood heat," Seph reminded me. It was true; he'd invited us in after our trip to the library, apparently for the purpose of hazing me about my use of magic, and I remember him fixing tea from a boiling pot of water on his wood stove. "So do the ranger cabins."

"That was different, though," I argued. "It felt different, anyway. It was warm outside, and so the heat wasn't cranked up as much. And we used the stoves primarily for cooking, not heat."

"The level of fire does make a difference, but so does the kind of wood you use," Llew lectured as he walked over to join me at the wood stove. "The lowlanders like to burn lots of pine and fir, which burns fast and hot for cooking but doesn't give off the sustained, comfortable heat that you're feeling now from the birch."

"Different types of wood burn differently?" I asked, and this time Keion's snort was unmistakable.

"Prince Keion, might I suggest that you would do well to avoid insulting your future queen on such a regular basis," Padrig's voice rumbled.

Keion shrugged and left the cabin, his face a red, angry jumble of lines.

"Youth," Padrig said, the word sliding through his teeth like a curse.

"Not all of us are so uncouth, Papa."

"That you would criticize Prince Keion openly is just as troubling, Son. You and he are both of the peerage, and there is a solid chance that he will one day be your king. You must learn when to hold your thoughts within the head that birthed them."

"Yes, Papa."

"I'm sorry," I spoke up a few minutes later to break the uneasy silence that had settled over the cabin. "I just—"

Padrig shook his head and interrupted me. "You have much to learn yet, Princess. For one thing, a queen never says the word sorry. Acknowledge a bad decision if you believe it to be in your best interest, but never apologize, not to anyone. For another, it would be best if you cast your doubts and uncertainties as far from you as possible. You are a very fortunate young woman, to have such capable companions along on a journey to see the wonders of Kiirajanna. You should be cherishing the excitement that these new experiences and discoveries bring. To go on a hunt with the people of the north, for example, is an experience your father has never enjoyed. What the prince forgets in his youth is that once you have experienced everything, there will be very little left in the world that is worth springing your buttocks out of bed for."

I nodded to Padrig. "Thank you. Some of that, my father has also told me. I have yet to perfect this becoming a queen business."

"Good. For both, that is, for once you perfect the becoming a queen business, as you describe it, then all that will be left is to be queen. Her Majesty rules with both grace and honor, but I have seen it in her eyes that sometimes she wishes she could return to her own journeys."

"I understand. Thank you."

"Good. Now, to answer your question, yes, different woods burn differently. Anyone who has grown up in the great north would know that, but someone from Cysegredig, and anyone from this Mississippi place that you describe, would have no reason to have obtained such knowledge. Soft wood like pine and fir lights quickly, burns fast, and is best for warming up the heat box inside a wood stove, or for quick cooking, as my son has already explained. Hardwoods–oak, maple, and so on– burn much slower, and it's those woods you'll want to lay in to the stove as we bank the fire for the night, for they'll give you a nice bed of coals to use in waking her up in the morning. Birch, which is what we're burning now, is a nice in-between wood for general heating. With it, you get a good warm fire, long-lasting logs, and a nice aroma, as well."

"So a northerner wants all three types of wood stocked in the wood pile," I said, feeling a lot smarter already.

Padrig shook his head, his beard swaying back and forth. "Not necessarily. Most of us concentrate on birch. We don't burn much soft wood except for starting the fire, and if you're running the fire box full-time then you don't need to start it but once."

"Why not stock it with oak, though? If the hardwoods burn longer than birch, and a longer fire life is a good thing, then why wouldn't you use them instead for all around heating?"

"Well, it is a good thing, yes, except for two problems. Up here on the Rim you don't find a lot of hardwood growing, for one, so it's hard to lay in the cords you need to heat through a cold winter if you're looking just for oak."

"Oh. That makes sense. What's the other problem?"

"Ah, thank you for paying attention," Padrig said with a grin. "The other problem is, simply put, hardwood is hard, Princess. Birch is easier to cut and to split, and it's more forgiving when you're splitting it with a little sap in it."

"That's a strange thing to hear a tough northerner say."

"Why would being tough make us want to do things the hard way? You would understand if you'd ever split wood for any length of time, I am certain. I've already told you how much effort we go to in order to be prepared for when the snow flies. Why make any part of that more difficult—and much more difficult, in the case of splitting hardwood?"

Figuring his question was rhetorical, I let silence slip back in to the moment, enjoying the crackle and pop and roar inside the stove. Quietly, the rumbling voice continued from right beside me as the great northern chieftain said, "Tomorrow night we'll have to burn some hickory, Princess. It does make for the finest aroma, and you'll appreciate that permeating your clothes as we travel back."

"That sounds good, Bennaeth. Do you worship the sun god up here?"

"The sun god?" Padrig paused to think, but if I'd thrown him for a loop with the change of topic he didn't show it. "Oh, you refer to the old idiom I used when you arrived."

"Right. I figured you all might worship some sort of sun god, perhaps versus a winter god, in a—I don't know, cycle of deities?"

"You all? Alyssa, your greatest mistake is in lumping all of us together. Our spiritual beliefs are a very personal thing up here. There are some elves who do believe in a rotating pantheon of deities, pulling and stretching the world around as the seasons turn. I do not, though."

"So what do you believe?"

"I believe that my beliefs are personal, Alyssa."

"Oh. I am sorry I asked, Bennaeth."

"What have I told you about saying that word, Alyssa?"

"Right," I said, shutting up for good. The snarky part of me wanted to tell him I was sorry for saying sorry, but there was no way I could see that being taken well, and I still needed to remember that his approval was the main reason I was there. Obviously the word sorry, at least up in the great white north, was stronger in meaning than the flippant sorry of the great American South.

Dinner that night was served outside, with all of us sitting on logs that were laid out around the bonfire. As soon as we rolled in they'd started the stew, and after a long day of riding, the meat and vegetables in the hot thickened broth tasted like heaven. Seph and I sat side by side, happily sopping up the liquid with hunks of bread and licking what was left off of our fingers. The chill in the air was only broken a little by the warmth from the fire, but the colder temperature was refreshing after the warmth inside the cabin, and so nobody seemed to mind.

From across the fire I could see Keion's eyes glaring at me as he worked on his own bowl of stew.

"Think he'll ever be nice to me?" I asked my cousin quietly.

"Eventually. He has a lot to get used to, though. You should go easier on him, I think."

"Easier on *him*? Shouldn't he go easier on me?" I asked, forgetting about the crush Seph had on the prince.

"You're both destined for great things," she said, shrugging as she looked up to meet my eyes. "Why not go easier on each other?"

I let the wavy, crackling flames of the fire lure my mind away, way off deep into somewhere unknown, as I pondered whether there would ever be an answer to her question.

Winning Padrig Over

"I haven't done all that well in winning your approval, have I, Bennaeth?" I asked and then turned my face toward him, trying to peer through the dark for any hints I could glean from his expression. The chieftain gave up nothing, though, his solemn gaze staying right where he'd had it, boring deep into the dying flames of the bonfire.

"Why do you think that, Alyssa?" he asked, his voice neutral.

I looked around at the now-deserted seats. The elves had tired themselves out after a short while, hastened in the process by Padrig's suggestion that the morning would come quickly. He'd even glared the prince and Seph back to the cabin, but I'd stayed. It was clear to me, somehow, that Padrig wanted to sit and chat with me by myself.

Finally I shrugged, knowing that it was a useless gesture in the dark. "I don't know. I just figured coming up here that I'd have trained enough and be able to lead more, to be more—queen-like, I guess. But I've only been here for one whole day, and you've already had to correct my speech and bearing a couple of times. I feel like I should've been better prepared."

A sardonic chuckle burst from the large man's chest, and then he said, "I do not believe you could possibly be prepared for what is to come, Alyssa. You are aware that you are to be the Dragon Queen, yes?"

"Yes, I am. At least, I know that's what's in store for me as long as I don't make myself too much a fool in front of you."

"I am not the one you should worry about that with."

"What do you mean, Padrig?"

"What do you think I mean, Princess? Can you use that brain in your pretty head for thinking, or is it just for swooning over the first prince?"

The comment stung, but he was right. I did need to think for myself, and at the same time, I needed to quit playing the little games with Keion. The boy was a heck of an ally in a fight, but the arguing we were doing was nothing but a distraction. Besides, it seemed to lower me in Padrig's eyes as well.

I took a stab at it. "I know that I need to impress the members of your clan as well as you, but I thought that the ultimate decision about whether to bless my coronation was yours to make. Was I incorrect?"

Padrig sighed, and that made me nervous. I had him pegged as a guy who didn't do that a lot. In the dim light of the bonfire's remains I saw him shake his head, and then he said, "That was not what I was referring to, but no, you were not incorrect. For the most part, anyway. It is–complicated. Far more complicated than you probably believe the northern tribes can be, I would say. Very complicated."

The only thing I could tell from his cryptic response was that I'd failed in my own answer, and that left me even more confused. Still, it was impress Padrig or be exiled back to Earth, and Momma and Dad needed me to succeed. Not having any idea whether I was making the situation worse, I plunged ahead with the question that was bugging me the most from his answer. "I'm not certain how complicated it is, but why do you say I wouldn't believe it?"

"Alyssa, since you arrived you have worn the superiority of the Cysegredig elves about you as a cloak. 'Why aren't the children outside playing?' you ask, and then 'Oh, what's to preparing for winter that would take more than a day or two?' Your disregard–disdain, even–for my people and for our way of life is what we would expect from a southerner, but I am sad to see it from you."

"Padrig, I–" I stopped for a moment to collect my thoughts. I was genuinely shocked; I hadn't intended any of that. I figured, though, that my response needed to be very well-worded. "I–look, Bennaeth, you know that I am not from here. I was raised for most of my life in one of the hottest places in–where I'm from. I don't even know what winter is, really. Back home– what used to be home–if it snows this much," I held my thumb and forefinger out in the flickering ember light, about an eighth of an inch apart, "they close down schools for a week and everybody raids the grocery stores for all the bread and bottled water on the shelves. And you probably have no idea what I'm talking about with grocery stores, do you? What I'm trying to say is that I don't look upon your people with disdain. My questions were naive, perhaps, but genuine. I have no idea what a winter is like. I'm ssss–" I barely reined in the *sorry* that I was about to voice, remembering our talk earlier, "it appears that I have miscommunicated, and I will try to do better in the future."

"You were about to use that word again, weren't you?"

"Yes. Old habits die hard, it seems."

"I like that you are honest enough to admit that. I also honor that you paid attention to my earlier talk. There is a high degree of promise in you, Alyssa. I just wonder whether you are ready for the stage you are in."

"Didn't you say earlier that you figured I would never be ready?"

Padrig chortled. "Ready for what is to come, Crown Princess. That is correct. I will accept your explanation, in any event."

I let the silence carry for a few moments, and then asked the next question that was bothering me. "So, as much as I hate to make my ignorance known, I am curious as to how complicated it is."

Padrig's head moved slightly up and down in a slow nod. "You are paying attention, Princess, and that is good. There is the way that a future queen would ask questions, and the way that a *merch* would ask, and I am glad to see you taking on the queen's approach."

I tried not to take insult; the word he'd used just means girl, but he'd slid into it as though it were meant to describe a young, silly girl. Still, it was Padrig, and I reminded myself that I needed his approval more than I needed to allow myself to be insulted by what he said.

He looked down at his meaty hands as he continued, almost to himself, "My people are nothing if not complicated. We keep secrets from each other for the sole purpose of doing so. Plus, the long winters are plenty deep enough to cause some introspection about prophecy and so on, and so we have far too many who would oppose you just because they think it will save us from our own predestined fate. Plus, we—and I'm not telling you anything your father doesn't already know, but I'd appreciate you not sharing it with the others—we're far from the unified front that the rest of Kiirajanna sees us as."

"You and the bens don't always see eye to eye, I take it?"

The question earned me a sardonic chuckle before he answered, "We rarely see each other in any manner, regardless. We are an independent people, Alyssa, and I do not tell the bens what to do in their territory very often."

"Will I meet the bens while I am here?"

"Most likely not. Remember when I said that most of us are busy preparing for winter? That includes the bens, and even more so sometimes. If I were you, I would not take it as an insult if the bens do not come to meet you."

"Like they didn't come in the summer to meet me at the coronation?"

"Yes, exactly like that," he said, but I could hear a concern whispering through what he wasn't saying. I let it go, though. Their approval wasn't my concern; his was.

"So, Bennaeth, what can I do to earn your blessing as the crown princess?" I asked. It took a lot more gumption to ask than I'd thought I had, but I still figured that showing gumption was the best way to approach Padrig.

"Hmm," he mused, and then he turned his face directly toward me, making me wonder if he could see better than I could in the dark. "What do you think will earn my blessing, little one?"

"They say you are impressed by strength, mighty Bennaeth, and so—" I started to explain, but he cut me off.

"*They* say? They say many things, Alyssa, wise things occasionally and some strange things, too, sometimes. It is humorous, I guess. I should not have expected you to be any different from your father. Cadfael is always asking, probing, studying, researching. Not that it is wrong; perhaps that is the best approach for a king, or for a queen. Perhaps, hmm? But I did not ask you what they say. I asked what you say. How do you see the best path into my approval, Princess?"

The question stopped me for a moment. What was he looking for? How could I answer his question in a way that would impress him? Then I thought about the only queen I knew, Keion's mother. How would she answer the question?:

"Well, as I was saying, mighty Bennaeth, they say you are impressed mostly by strength, but–" I slipped the last word in quickly before he could object again. It wasn't what I'd been about to say, truth be told, but he didn't need to know that. "Padrig, you're a softie. A smart, calculating, caring softie, who uses both his great strength and his intellect to protect and serve his family and his people. To you, the heart and the mind are just as important as the muscles and the willpower. That's why you appreciate my father's rule so much. That is also, I think, what you see in me."

I was rewarded by another gentle nod of the clan leader's head. "Nicely said, Princess. You are smarter than many of my people give you credit for. Do not be insulted, little one," he added, somehow sensing my irritation rising. "I said it was complicated, and that is part of it. There are many in my clan, and, I would venture to guess, in the others as well, who without even having met you have already judged that you are too young, too non-native, too stupid in the elf way. None of that is true, but were I or any of the other high chieftains to grant you our acceptance without evidence of a trial, it would give the people reason to rebel."

"The prophecy already says I'm destined to do that, Padrig," I quipped, and earned another sardonic chuckle for my effort.

"Well, yes, that is what I have heard, though I have never, myself, read the work. There is something about you bringing the people together while driving them apart, is there not? I suppose, then, that it doesn't really matter what we do."

"I disagree."

"Why so, Alyssa?"

I exhaled slowly, giving my brain time to put my recent thoughts into an order that would make sense. "For a few reasons, Padrig. First, while fulfilling the prophecy is a certainty, the method–the path–for doing so is not. Second, I think that sometimes we actually have to do something to bring the prophecy to fruition. Take my trip to the library, for example. I would never have burnt a library down on purpose. But when I faced a couple of dozen Cult members and the prospect of my friends and I all dying, I did what I had to do. It fulfilled the prophecy even though I hadn't intended it to. Then there's the bit about 'all the king's horses and all the king's men.' That wasn't anything I did, myself, at all. Seph reached out through her ranger bond and asked for Dad's help, and so it happened that on the day of the battle, and the fire, across the blight came thundering a legion of black-cloaked warriors led by my father. I think that we have to keep doing what we believe to be best, and somehow the prophecy already has that calculated into its outcomes."

"And if we do something that it hasn't calculated? What happens to the prophecy then?" he asked.

"I–I don't know. It may be that someone else will do what the prophecy calculated, and it will come to pass anyway. Or maybe the prophecy will just miss in that case. Regardless, I think that in this case you and I should proceed in a manner that will bring about the most support from the people."

"A good answer, Alyssa."

"So do I have your approval yet?"

"Hah! No."

We sat in silence for several minutes, listening to the light popping of the embers punctuated occasionally by the soft crash and fizzle of a branch losing its ability to support itself and topping into the coals. It was awfully peaceful; all the other elves seemed to have already gone to sleep.

Just as I started thinking about joining the others in slumber, Padrig spoke up again. "Alyssa, what is it that you like most about Kiirajanna?"

I'd actually prepared for this question, so I started in rapidly. "The people. The elves are a hard-working yet joyful lot, and I've enjoyed nearly every encounter I've had with the various groups here. I can't wait to begin serving them as their leader."

"Uh huh. Why did that speech sound so rehearsed?"

"It–well–I–guilty, I guess. This is so vital to me that I prepared the answer to one of the more important questions I might face."

"I see. Could I trouble you for your unrehearsed answer, then?"

"The answer is still the people. I've–"

"You've met five percent of its people. Less, probably. What, the inhabitants of the castle, a few of Ganolog's residents, and a couple of villages in the center of the continent? How can you say the people are what you like most when you've met so few?"

"Well, I've read a lot about them."

"Ah, so you like the books of Kiirajanna the best."

"No! That's not–heck, Padrig, I can barely read some of them, written in ancient variants of the language as they are. But I see where you're going with it, and truth be told, I'm not sure I can come up with a satisfactory answer. There's so much to like about what I've seen so far."

"Like what?"

"Like not having to mow the lawn." I'd had my best responses from him when I'd been a little tongue-in-cheek, so I tried it again.

"What is this cutting of the property?" he asked. The translation into elf hadn't been anywhere near exact.

"Towns where I come from are built with the houses in rows, all lined up."

"Like Ganolog."

"Yes, but a little bit farther apart."

"How do you fit them all within the walls?"

"Well, there aren't any walls."

"No walls? I did not realize that the Earth was such a peaceful place."

"It's far from peaceful, Padrig. Well, my town is peaceful enough, at least till the night of the football game against County." I chortled quietly, thinking of all the ruckus that had been raised last Homecoming, but I plunged back to the topic as quickly as I could. "But even in the less peaceful areas, our weapons have become so large, so dangerous, that there's nothing to be gained by building a wall. With a single bomb, you can kill thousands. Millions, even. What's the point of walls when you have bombs?"

"These *bombs* sound like magic," Padrig growled. I'd had to use the English word, since I was pretty sure Elf didn't have one that even came close.

"Pretty close to it, Padrig. But in part because of that, I think, the people on Earth build houses farther apart than in Ganolog, with swaths of land between each of them. The wealthier you are, the more land is in between your house and your neighbor's."

"Ah, and so instead of letting it grow wild, you go out and cut the brush down and the trees back. That is what you meant."

"Well, no, not exactly. Most of the time the trees and the brush are completely removed when the houses are built."

"So you have faster travel? Does that not become too mud-dy?"

"Well, it would become muddy if we didn't plant grass there. We don't use those areas to travel between houses, no."

"So if you do not use them to travel, what is the purpose? Do neighbors communicate that much on Earth?"

"No, usually we try not to communicate with our neigh-bors. I mean, we pretend to have Southern hospitality where I am from, and so the first time someone moves in people come say hi and bring pies and stuff—sometimes, anyway—but after that we don't really want to see or hear them."

"Then why do you make it easier to see and hear them?"

"I don't know, Bennaeth. That's just how it is."

"You come from a strange place, Alyssa. But tell me, then, if there are no trees or bushes, what is there to be cut in this ritual that you are glad does not exist here?"

"The grass that is planted."

"So you plant the grass to keep it from becoming muddy, and then you cut the grass down to keep it from becoming gras-sy."

"Yeah, that's about it." It made even less sense to me after I'd explained it than it had before.

"I see why you are glad the ritual does not exist here, then. You are a good, practical woman, Crown Princess."

"Thank you, Bennaeth. Do I have your approval now?"

"Hah! No."

"Had to try," I said.

"Is fine. But now we should probably get some sleep." He and I quietly made our way back to the leaders' cabin.

The Hunt

Stop glaring at me, I mentally screamed at Aerona. I knew she couldn't hear the thought, of course, but it was all I had. As much as I wanted to actually scream it at her, I'd been threatened with a punishment that had been unspecified yet very un-Princess-like if I spoke even a single word aloud once we got out to the things the hunters called blinds. Thus, I wasn't about to open my mouth. Besides, the little scratchy knitted scarf covering the bottom half of my face to keep my cheeks from freezing off would've just made it sound like *wofp wawwin wah wee.*

They'd jounced me out of bed way before the hour that any reasonable human—or elf, either, for that matter—might rise. Seph had helped me don the long, scratchy underwear that went below the other few layers of clothes. Then they'd handed me something that, in the dim light of the wood stove, looked, and tasted, an awful lot like cement. The first time my teeth hit a chewy part I almost spit it out for fear of finding a bug, but after a little bit of checking I figured it was just a dehydrated berry of some sort. Well, that, or a sweetened worm, but at oh-dark-thirty, when my whole being really wanted to be back in bed, it seemed easiest to just keep chewing.

Padrig held a short briefing in the gloomy predawn moonlight in the center of camp. Besides the admonition to not say a word and to move as silently as possible, he also let us know that scouts had seen moose droppings in addition to the regular elk droppings. The hunters around me started grunting and stamping their feet on the ground, leading me to wonder if that was how the northern elves showed their excitement in general, or just on a hunt.

Padrig also warned us that there was fresh bear scat to the north, which prompted another admonition from him to be very quiet as we moved through the woods. Because, I guess, surprising a bear by walking into it is somehow better than scaring it off by hooting and hollering.

Since I was the crown princess, I got the only two-person blind. Everybody else fanned out by themselves, but they couldn't risk my safety like that. Not with *dangers* about, Padrig whispered, and his sweeping James Bond stare out into the woods around us made me wonder just how much he knew about my earlier problems with the Cult. Besides, I couldn't help but wonder whether Padrig envisioned the poor Mississippi girl shooting herself by accident. He didn't say anything to that effect, but the look he'd given me as he'd explained that I would be sharing my early morning spot of hunting bliss with Aerona spoke loudly enough. I could've protested, arguing that I'd done fairly well for myself on the approach to the library, but there wasn't anything to gain by it. Aerona wouldn't have allowed me out of her sight, regardless, and I needed Padrig's approval.

The code for a successful kill, used to bring others in to help with something they called "field dressing," was to be the call of a beast known as a ptarmigan. Since I'd never even seen a ptarmigan, much less heard one's call, I found myself hoping that if anything did wander into my kill zone, Aerona could back me up with the call.

The walk was rough. It's one thing to move around a forest in the daytime, or a central-continent, manicured forest in the light of a full moon, but in the dark in a chaotic northern forest the moon's shadows do really weird things to the shape of the plants around you. Besides, there isn't any depth perception to be had in the gloom. As I stumbled along I found myself wishing I was back in the ranger-tended central forest–that, or the nice, warm, soft, comfortable, sleepy little bed in the cabin. Aerona growled and hissed at me a couple of times when I missed my footing, but I just kept bravely feeling my way forward, reminding myself how much I needed Padrig's nod.

Meanwhile, I still wondered what the heck a ptarmigan call sounded like.

The wool scarf gave me a hard time, too. It did keep my nose and cheeks warmer, but it also slowed my breathing through my nose, and then when I made the mistake of trying to suck air through my mouth I ended up with little fuzz balls on my tongue. That, and it was claustrophobic. Some princess I was turning out to be.

The worst part, though, was sitting still once we'd climbed up into the stand. I'd heard people talk about stands back home, but I'd never really seen one. Turns out, it's got nothing to do with standing. Instead, a hunting stand is a cold wooden platform up about a dozen feet high in a tree with branches draped around it for camouflage, built so that you sit there dangling your legs off of the side in the chilly pre-dawn wind while you lean back against a frigid slat of wood. Oh, and all the while, your bow-shooting hand goes numb because the thin leather gloves they give you aren't warm enough to be comfortable.

That was what kept earning me Aerona's glare; I rubbed my hands together several times to bring feeling back to my fingertips.

I didn't mind her glare much, though. I figured if the animals got frightened away by the sound of me keeping my fingers from freezing, then more power to them, bless their hearts. Besides, I didn't know how to call for help for field dressing, anyway, so as much as I wanted Padrig's approval, I secretly hoped to come back empty-handed.

We'd been sitting there freezing in the dark for what felt like hours when the sun finally decided to pay us a visit. I didn't even notice the brighter light at first; it just gradually crept up on me. Once I finally realized what was happening, it looked like somebody had flipped a switch and turned the darkness filled with darker shadows into a dim landscape featuring actual colors.

I've never felt so happy to see sunlight before. I didn't dare express my delight, though, for fear of more silent glares of doom from Aerona.

Suddenly, brush crackled off in the distance. In the still morning air I couldn't tell if the movement was right down the ridge from us or up near the mountains, several miles away. Still, I looked over at Aerona, my eyes bright and and my spirits up for the first time that morning.

My staid guard just shook her head my direction. Putting two fingers to her eyes and then pointing them out to the field, she gave me the universal hand gesture for *eyes front, dummy*.

A few minutes later I heard a low clucking sound from the same direction. It was nothing like any bird I'd ever heard, but it brought me hope. Was that what a ptarmigan sounded like? Again, I looked at Aerona for guidance. Time for us to move to help? Pretty please?

Please, let it be time to get out of this stand, I thought as strongly as I could, trying my best to project it all the way to Aerona. My heart sank, though. Once again she shook her head and gave me the two-finger gesture.

It wasn't much longer before I nearly fell out of the stand in surprise as something–something big, I thought–rattled the bushes down the hill to our right. Immediately my bow was up with an arrow nocked and ready to fly. Aerona's hand crept into my field of vision, moving up and then slowly down in a warning I needed but didn't really want: *calm, patience, wait.*

Padrig had warned us about shooting anything we couldn't see clearly. The last thing we wanted, he said, was an elf tracking an injured target being shot by another elf. They didn't have any of the cute little orange hats and vests that I'd seen back home, either, so I understood the concern.

Soon enough, the shape moved out from the bush so that I could see the target clearly. *Uh, uh*, I thought. I looked a question over to Aerona, and the quick shake of her head gave me her firm agreement with my assessment. Neither of us were of the opinion that I ought to shoot. Lucky us, we'd found the source of the bear scat.

That, or I guess, technically, it had found us.

I'd never imagined I'd see a bear that big, especially not in person without a cage between us. At a distance of about thirty feet, it looked bigger than my horse. The beast was huge.

A gust of wind blew past us down the hill, and the bear stopped and sniffed. Our scent must've been interesting, because it swung itself around and started lumbering directly toward our little blind.

It was all I could do to keep from screaming. The bear's head, a massive block of fur and bone that was well over two feet wide, angled up to catch more of our aroma as its powerful legs padded our way. Brown, coarse fur stood out at all angles and enhanced the beast's fierce look.

I was hoping that the bear's slow, methodical pace would carry it past our tree. "Please go past, please go past, please go past," my mouth formed wordlessly, my hand tightening, loosening, and then repeating the cycle many times about the grip of the bow. Then the bruin stopped below us and sniffed, and I once again barely held back a scream. Its nose easily found the spots on the trunk we'd used in our climb earlier.

Aerona and I both leaped up as one, each of us rising to stand on the narrow perches where our butts had been, putting our feet high enough, we hoped, that the bear couldn't reach us.

It wasn't far enough. The bear sniffed a few more times around the base of the tree and then rose on its hind legs. Its head continued along our scent up the bark, taunting us with its measured pace, bless its black heart. When it was standing fully against the tree, nose slowly sniffing upward toward our perch, I could see that its massive arms would be able to reach the wood we were standing on.

Terrified, I looked over at Aerona. The battle ax of an elf woman had her daggers out, one in each hand, and with the same sharp gesturing style she'd used before she told me *I will fight down there. You run.*

I shook my head. Terrified as I might be, there was no way was I leaving her alone with that bear, no way was I running back to the camp alone. I held up my bow and arrow.

She sneered. She shook her head even more vigorously, trying to out-do my head-shaking. *No.* She jabbed a forefinger at me, knife still held in that fist. *You.* With a swish of her arm back around to the rear, she made it clear what I was to do. *Back to camp!*

I honestly don't know whether I'd have taken her instructions. I'm sure my father would've wanted me to, but at that moment I was still just as terrified of running back through bear-infested woods by myself as I was of leaving my guardian to fight such a huge bruin nightmare.

Luckily, I didn't have to make that decision.

Off to our left, another brushy sound rattled through the dim morning. This time it was accompanied by the soft thud of something hitting the forest floor, followed by another low-pitched clucking sound. The noise caught the bear's attention, and with a stare off into the distance, and then a glare back toward us, it seemed to decide we just weren't worth the effort. It snorted and bounded off.

"Come quickly," Aerona whispered and leaped to the ground. I followed her down, and then she pushed me ahead of her a lot more roughly than she needed to as the two of us practically sprinted through the dawn air all the way back to camp.

It wasn't far, a half mile, at most. It had seemed much farther in the dark, but in daylight and at our pace it was a short run. Still, with each of us following Aerona's quiet exhortations to run faster, we both arrived back at camp breathless. The porters and scouts gathered quickly at the sight of the crown princess and her guard sprinting back into the middle of the hunting camp, and Aerona gave them quick instructions on what we'd seen and where we'd been. They all took off at a sprint.

"We—we have to go back," I gasped, still trying to catch my breath. Now, after listening to how she'd describe the situation, I was worried for the others. "Aerona, that could be Padrig, or Llew, in trouble with the bear."

"No, Princess," Aerona forbade, her voice making it clear she wouldn't hear otherwise. "The northern elves are much better prepared to fend off the creature than we are, for one thing."

"What's the other thing?" I challenged her as she pushed me forcefully toward our cabin, which I admit had a tantalizing curl of aromatic wood smoke rising from the chimney.

"The other thing? Are you mocking me? Princess, I am charged with your safety. *Yours.* Not Padrig's, not Llew's, not anybody else's. Your father assigned me the mission of guarding your life as though it were my own, and I intend to make good on that assignment. Once, you and he arranged for me to be fooled and left behind as you rode into danger, but that will *never* happen again. My entire purpose of being is in keeping you safe till you are crowned queen, *whether you like it or not.* Which, by the way, brings me to the other thing," she said, her voice growing even more heated and dangerous. She shut the door firmly to close us in the cabin by ourselves and then rounded on me. "Princess, when I tell you that you need to run, I mean that you need to *run.* Do *not* argue with me."

I flushed from the heat of her last sentence. "But Aerona, no offense, but that bear would have killed you with just your two daggers to fight it."

She wasn't done with the anger, it seemed. "*No,*" she said in a voice that made me flinch. "The bear would have stood a fighting chance against me, it is true, but do *not* underestimate my abilities, Princess. Not with twin daggers, and not ever. Nor should you ever again underestimate my level of experience in combat situations, upon which I draw my actions. Have I ever told you how I earned this scar?" she asked, pointing to the triple scar across the right side of her face.

"No, you haven't," I said, genuinely curious. My guard hadn't opened up to me about anything, really, and so the history of that scar was a good start.

"Well, I'm not going to, now, either. But you should know that I earned every scar on my body, and also that in every case my opponent, a danger of some sort to the crown of Kiirajanna, suffered more than just a scar. When I tell you to *run*, Princess, *run. Is that clear?*"

Meekly, I nodded. I was completely cowed. Aerona had never shown the slightest bit of emotion, but she was practically glowing with anger and indignation, and after months of stone-cold Aerona, red-hot Aerona was completely terrifying.

"Besides, Princess, that little arrow you had would've done nothing but make the bear angry," she growled as she turned to pile more wood into the stove. "Those creatures have several inches of thick fur and strong, knotted muscle to get through before your arrowhead could approach anything that was important to the bear. Never bring a bow and arrow to a bear fight, Princess."

"You don't—suppose...."

"Suppose what, Princess?"

"It seems silly, but I can't help but wonder—there's no way the Cult of the Wyrm could've been behind the bear attack, could there?"

Aerona held me in her glare for several long moments. I kept wanting to flinch away from it, not sure if I were about to be mocked or not, but I knew I had to get used to standing up to glares. Finally, she shrugged. "I cannot say for certain. I doubt it, as there is no conceivable way to have pulled that off in a planned sort of way, and if they had, it seems there would have been more direct means of attacking you. But it is good that you are thinking along those lines. Always search for connections, even when it is most likely that none exist."

"Always search for connections, never bring a bow and arrow to a bear fight, and run when you say run. Got it," I said, and got a glare in return for my snarkiness.

I managed to get the scratchy wool underwear and the other layers off with a little help from Aerona, thankfully replacing it with a few layers of nice comfy cotton, before a supercharged Prince Charming came banging through the door. Seeing me, he planted his feet and began ranting excitedly about the hunt. "Alyssa, that was incredible! There I was, waiting for something to present itself, when suddenly a magnificent stag stepped out into the clearing in front of me. He was beautiful, with sixteen tines on his antlers, and there he stood, back steaming in the morning coolness as I drew a bead and loosed the arrow. It dropped the stag immediately, a clean kill, of course!" He stopped ranting for long enough to flip his ebony hair up and around his face as he always did when bragging. "I signaled for the others to help, and then just as I was getting to the elk's body, you wouldn't believe what stepped out to challenge me!"

"A grizzly bear," I said. "One with a head this big," I held out my hands wide, "that stood at least twelve feet tall."

"Uh, yes," he stammered, wind completely gone from his storytelling sails. "How did you know?"

I sat heavily on my bunk. So it had been Keion who our flight had put at risk. I wasn't sure how I would have explained that to his sisters, much less to his mother, if it had gone badly.

"Your timely shot actually saved us, Keion. The bear caught our scent and came after us, first," I explained quietly. "We were about ready to leap out of the stand and do battle with it when your kill called it away. Aerona made sure that I made it back to camp safely while she sent the porters and scouts to help you with it. We didn't know it was you, though. We figured it was—"

"Thank you," Keion said, interrupting me as he moved over to Aerona. "I had no idea she was in danger, but I am glad I was able to pull it away from her."

"And Aerona," I said.

"Hmm?" he asked, his gaze darting back to me with a confused look.

"You pulled it away from both me and Aerona."

"Oh. Right, but.... I mean, right."

"But what?" I asked, and when I glanced over I saw that Aerona also looked curious.

"But I misspoke, Princess. I am glad you are both okay."

"Yeah." I stood silently for a moment, ready to punch him for ignoring my guard's safety, or to hug him for actually being concerned about me. I wasn't sure which one I wanted to do more. Finally I gave up and asked, "So what happened to the bear?"

"He went away."

"He just—went away?"

Well, he didn't just go away, no. He took my elk with him."

"You let the bear take your elk?" I asked, dumbfounded. Having seen the bear myself I knew what a smart choice that would have been, but to be honest, that was a smart choice that I couldn't imagine Keion making.

"Yes, I let the bear take my elk. Sometimes that is how the circle of life is maintained, Princess. Besides, the scouts told me that the bear I'd given my prey up to was none other than Halbiorn, the great grizzly. To have provided a feast for Halbiorn is a great honor among these people."

"I see." Unfortunately, what I'd actually seen was the exuberance of the hunt dying away to be replaced by the more familiar brooding desire to be anywhere but near me.

The door slammed open again, this time admitting a jocular Padrig, Llew, and Seph.

"Ho ho, Crown Princess, it is a hunt of historic proportions that you have been on!" Padrig boasted as the trio removed layers of clothing and converged around the wood stove. "Are you all right?" he asked, correctly guessing the measure of my emotions from my face. "I heard that you came face to face with the mighty Halbiorn himself."

"I'm good," I assured him, widening my face into the elf grin I'd been working on in the mirrors. The elves have a way of including their entire face in a true smile, and just one of those can light up an entire room. As expressive as it is, though, it's hard to fake, so I had worked on that ever since. Apparently I succeeded; he grinned back. "Luckily, it never got to actually be face to face. It was touchy there for a while, but with Aerona there to protect me and then Prince Keion's timely slaying of Halbiorn's breakfast, all ended well."

"Ah, yes," Padrig said, turning toward Prince Charming with an expression that was half grimace, half grin. He'd obviously missed the touch of sarcasm I'd slipped in. Keion hadn't, though; I could tell that from the glare he shot my way. Padrig continued, apparently unaware, "It is, among my clan, a portent of things to come to interact with one of the great brown bears and live to tell the tale. For both of you to do so, and with Halbiorn, himself, is none other than incredible. We must feast tonight, and from the reports I have received, we have much to feast on. Your cousin, our dear southern ranger friend, dropped a large elk by herself."

Seph's face glowed with pride as she nodded, but she was too busy struggling out of her warm hunting garb to say anything.

I helped, my stomach growing as I did. I'd been promised a sumptuous meat feast, and after getting up early, eating nothing but hardtack, and then going through a fear-fueled sprint, I was looking forward to eating whatever meat they put in front of me.

First, though, I investigated and learned that my guess had been correct. The low-pitched clucking I'd heard was the call of a ptarmigan. A ptarmigan's a bird, I learned when I got Seph alone and asked, and it clucks instead of chirps. She added that they'd chosen the ptarmigan because its clucking sound carried easily in the morning quiet, and also because the ptarmigan itself isn't known to make much noise in the morning, which meant that any ptarmigan calls would likely be elf imitations.

Padrig had sensed my mood going south with Keion's change of attitude, but he guessed the source wrong. Several hunting stands came back as empty as my own, the chieftain assured me, and so I had no reason to feel like a non-contributor. While the assurance was nice, I really didn't care at the moment. As good as it was to know I hadn't lost much standing in the efforts to gain his stamp of approval, it was impossible to get past caring about Keion's mood swings, and then being upset because I knew I shouldn't care about his mood swings.

I did, however, manage to clear my head a little by going around to look at the kills that the hunting party made. There were several elk, none as large as Keion's, as the prince reminded me, but one of the proudest of Padrig's takings was a huge bull moose. "That will feed many families," he crowed as he toured with Seph, Keion, and me following, all of us watching the ongoing butchering with varying levels of interest.

STIW

a stew. I didn't have to work real hard to learn this word.

The Feast

I went back to the little cabin to rest while they finished the job of butchering the carcasses. It was good to rest, but it was also nice to be by myself. Nobody else seemed to share my aversion to watching animal flesh being hacked into large pieces, so they all stayed outside to watch and even participate. That gave me plenty of blissful quiet.

Even Aerona left me alone. That was rare.

I didn't even notice the cabin getting darker inside, the windows catching less and less sunlight, until the door creaked open. I glanced up from my mattress to see the darkened silhouette of a scrawny young man draped in a cloak of fur.

"Hiya, Llew," I called out.

"Princess, are you all right?" he asked as he entered the room. I nodded and raised my head up onto an elbow. The young prince of the northern tribe came over to perch on the bunk across from mine and continued, "You haven't been out enjoying the festivities. I was worried after your encounter with Halbiorn...."

"No need, I'm fine. I'm the most well-protected princess ever, I think. I was tired, though, and I've spent so much time around so many people that I came looking for, and found, a chance for a little bit of quiet time. How have the festivities been?"

"Wonderful! We got to play peremichku. I won."

I was feeling pretty good after my rest, so I took the bait. "What is peremichku?"

"Oh, right. You seem so like one of us, with your natural beauty and grace, that I keep forgetting you weren't raised here. It's a game. We build a small bonfire—a cooking fire, really—and while it's building coals for the actual cooking, we jump over it. That's after stripping down to our shorts and sticking ribbons down into our belts. Each of us starts with two, and we all try to yank each others' ribbons out when they're over the fire. Whoever ends up being the only one with ribbons wins. You should play. I mean, girls don't play very often, but you're the princess."

"It does sound like fun," I agreed carefully, nodding to hide the lie. It actually sounded pretty pointless. "I just don't think anyone would want to see me strip down to my shorts and then jump around."

The young northern prince's face screwed itself up into a weird expression; I could tell he couldn't figure out how to reply safely. I managed to hold back my chortle, but only barely. Finally, after watching about fifteen different things to say make the journey across his befuddled, testosterone-riddled expression only to be rejected by his better, more regal verbal filters, I took pity on him.

"Besides, it smells like they're already cooking on the fire that you used," I said with a grin. He returned the grin with one of his own that was thankful, and humorously so.

It really did smell good out there. I had noticed the woody smell of camp smoke mixed with a heady soup aroma when he'd opened the door, and my stomach reminded me about it again.

"Oh, they are!" he came alive once again, leaving the confusing, awkward moment in the dust. "That's what I was sent in for, to let you know that the food is ready."

"I thought you came in because you were worried about me after my encounter with the big bear," I teased.

"I was! A little, anyway. But I knew that you are such a strong and tough princess, and so you'd be fine. It was Pa who told me to come invite you outside to dinner."

"Oh, well, if your pa said, then I'd better get moving!" I jumped off of the bed with a smile. Indulgently, I held my hand out for his, and it brought a smile to my face when his warm palm connected with mine.

"Princess!" Padrig's roar cut across from the fire as we exited the cabin. "You are just in time. Come, join us for the tastiest of treats!"

I walked over to where he stood beside the fire and looked in. Next to a huge vat of boiling soup, I saw several large bones laid on the hot rocks.

"What are the bones for?" I asked, a little scared of sounding ignorant, but curious enough to ask anyway.

"Mm, the best part!" Padrig bellowed and lifted something that, with its row of round teeth, could only be a jawbone.

I eyed him skeptically, not sure how a jawbone could be the best part of anything. "Do we beat each other over the shoulders with the bones while jumping over the fire as we try to eat the soup?" I asked, and the Keion-shaped shadow across the fire snorted. I stuck my tongue out and was rewarded by a grunt of derision. He went back to glaring, his eyes shifting from me to Llew to the grasped hands that the boy and I still shared.

Padrig, on the other hand, bellowed a laugh. "No, I will show you," he said, rapping the bone against a rock and listening to the sound. He nodded in satisfaction. "It is done," he said. He held the jaw across a nearby stump and brought a hatchet down sharply into the widest part, splitting it neatly down its length. He set the hatchet down and, with a heave of his massive hands, broke the bone apart into two pieces.

"Here. Eat," he ordered, grinning as he presented a piece of the marrow to me. In the light of the fire it was dark, and it felt rubbery, but I obediently slipped it into my mouth and chewed.

"You like?" he asked, smiling around his own mouthful as he passed the jawbone around to the rest of the royal party near the fire.

"Mm hmm," I said, truthfully this time. "It's a little chewy, but the flavor is really good. Strong, but not in a bad way. It reminds me of a well-smoked jerky. I'm surprised by how chewy it is, though. I always thought marrow would be soft."

"The moose's jaw bone is tough, so the marrow is chewy. Most of the marrow is more pliable," Llew offered.

I nodded, finished chewing, and accepted another piece from the other jawbone.

"So is this the only thing I'm going to eat that I haven't had before, or are you going to give me some whale fat?" I asked, mostly joking.

Padrig actually snorted then. "We are not the Digonol. Whale fat and seal oil are only for those who cannot manage otherwise. They are not nearly as good as moose head stew. Right, everyone?"

From the sounds of agreement and the longing looks at the huge soup pot, I gathered I was just about to get a taste of moose head stew. *Yum,* I thought–who wouldn't want a big bowl of moose head?

"At the risk of sounding even more ignorant than I've already proven myself, what all goes into moose head stew?"

"Moose head," Padrig said, and I heard another Keion snicker from across the fire.

I rewarded Charming with a glare of my own and then continued, "Oh. Of course, but what parts of the moose head, specifically?"

"Well, all of it," Padrig said. "Nearly all, anyway. Not the skull, nor the eyes," he added, correctly interpreting my expression. "Also, we save the brain for turning the hides into useful leather, but the rest of the flesh is really quite tasty."

"We trimmed the nose hairs out, Princess," Llew added. I'm not sure if he was trying to be helpful or not, but the expression on my face must have gotten really bad. Even Seph, who was normally deadpan and completely on my side, spewed out whatever she was drinking through both her mouth and her nose.

"Thanks," I said, both to Llew for his comment and to Padrig for handing me the first bowl. I couldn't help looking down into the depths of it for nostrils, but all I saw were chunks of stuff that looked like regular meat and potatoes.

It wasn't bad. In fact, it was actually pretty good. The meat had a stronger flavor than beef, and the broth had that and plenty of salt and pepper. There were root vegetables, too, though I wasn't sure what they were. I wasn't about to ask, either. I'd already made myself out to be ignorant enough.

Padrig handed me a skewer with chunks of deep red meat on it and then motioned that it was to be handed around. I took a bite, held my taste buds in check, and forced the hunk of medium-rare, squishy liver down my throat. I hadn't liked the rich, bloody taste of liver the first time I'd tried it, and now I found that moose liver cooked on an open fire isn't any better than cow liver with sautéed onions. Padrig took the skewer, snagged a hunk off of it with his teeth, and passed the stick on to Seph as he explained that eating the liver of the just-killed animal was good luck as well as a way of transferring good health to the hunter. It was good health as long as it wasn't overcooked, he added. I just nodded, glad that a single bite was all I'd be required to enjoy.

As everyone else lined up for a bowl of the delicious stew, someone handed me a hunk of the bread we'd brought. It was crusty and heavy, but nowhere near as hard as the rations Seph and the other rangers traveled with. I dipped it into the stew as they showed me, and then the flavors came alive. I hadn't realized how hungry I was until I scraped the last drops out of the bowl with the bread and looked over at the pot, hoping there was enough for seconds.

Padrig chuckled. "More, Princess? It has been a long, long day, and the last time we ate was early this morning, so you must be starving as much as we all are."

I gratefully accepted a second ladle-full along with another plug of bread.

Llew came over to sit beside me as I finished the second serving off. "So, do they do a feast like this in Missi—Massa—Messachippi, is it? That place you're from originally?"

"It's Mississippi, though technically I was originally from Wales, I guess. No, they don't do anything like this in the South, at least not with large game. Close by where I lived, there's an annual slugburger festival, which is sort of similar, I guess." I tried to work out a translation into elven for *slugburger*, but I couldn't figure it out so I used the English word. It brought a curious look from Llew.

"Slugburger? What is that?"

I felt like messing with somebody after everything I'd been through, and poor Llew happened to be close by, so he was it. I explained to him what a burger was first. Then I told him that a slug is the English word for a snail without a shell, and then I got to totally enjoy seeing someone besides me blanch from a gross mental image.

"You eat—snails, in these—these burger creations?" Llew asked, revolted.

"No, no, that's just what most people think, and it's why the slugburger festival is such a big deal." I laughed as I added, "But you have to admit, eating snail sandwiches is about as gross as eating moose nostril hair."

"I suppose that I deserved that."

"Well, it's a common joke down home, actually. The truth is, slug also used to be a slang term for a five cent coin, and to make a burger cheaply enough so they could sell it for a slug, or only five cents, they added grain to the meat."

"Can you still get these burgers for a slug?"

"It's actually called a nickel, now, but no, you can't. Even as cheaply-made as they are, they cost almost a dollar these days."

"And a dollar is a larger coin than a nickel, I take it?" Llew asked. I noticed that most conversation had died down as the northern elves listened in.

"When it's a coin, yes. More often a dollar is a piece of paper."

"You buy things with pieces of paper?" Llew's forehead held furrows from his confusion.

"Well, yes. It's special paper," I added, realizing as I did that it still wouldn't make any sense to the elves, who did all their trade through barter and had no common currency.

"Is a nickel available as a piece of paper, too?"

"No, it's only a coin."

"But a dollar can be either?" he asked.

"Correct. It's the only unit of currency that can, I think."

"Ah. So how many different coins do you have there in Mississippi?"

"Several. There's a penny, which is pretty much useless but they still make them. Then there's a nickel, and there's the dime that's worth two nickels–"

"So it's twice as big, right?" he asked.

"Um, no, it's actually smaller."

"How can it be worth twice as much, then?"

"It's–well...." I looked off into the night sky searching for a reason to give. I'd never considered the question, really, and "it just is" didn't seem like a good enough answer from the future queen. Finally, I shrugged and, taking the easy way out, said, "It's worth twice as much because the government says it is."

"Your money is worth what it is because your king says so?"

"Well, we don't have a king where I'm from. We have a set of people who have won elections, and they get together to tell us what the money is worth, among other things."

"Elections? Voting?" Padrig joined in. "Sounds inefficient. How do your people ever get anything done?"

"Well, they don't. Not really, anyway. We're taught from a young age that having kings and queens is a very bad way to govern society, and yet democracy doesn't seem to be the answer either. I'm awfully glad to be here. One of the things I like most about Kiirajanna is the simplified form of leadership and government that you–that *we*–have here." Padrig nodded approvingly at my insertion of the topic from the previous night, and I felt relieved after the long line of silly questions I'd posed.

"This money thing is such a strange concept to me," Llew said, shaking his head solemnly. "What else might you buy with a dollar?"

"Not much. A, um...." I thought about it for a while, but couldn't think of anything else that cost less than a dollar back home. I started to realize how long I'd really been away.

"So they are poorly valued, then?" he asked when I shook my head in defeat.

"Right."

"And people make a festival out of the fact that these burgers consist of coarse, poorly-valued food?"

"Um, right, I guess." I knew where he was going, and wasn't sure that I liked it.

"This Mississippi sounds like a strange place, Alyssa."

"Honey, you ain't just whistlin' Dixie," I quipped in English, and then, a little too late, wondered how appropriate that response had been.

The conversation was interrupted by a couple of beats of a deep bass drum. A higher pitched drum added a few raps, and then there was some chatting over in the drumming circle that I couldn't quite hear from where we sat. As I watched, others joined in and the group expanded to include nearly a dozen different drums of various sizes and timbres. Soon the beats combined into a complicated, driving rhythm.

I looked around the fire, expecting the dancing that I would've seen down around Cysegredig. There was none; instead, elves were sprawled out contentedly around its warmth and light. Some clapped in time to the drums, while others hummed softly, but most just bobbed their heads. The night darkened even further, and a chill descended on the camp. A couple of elves brought wood from a pile and heaped it onto the bonfire, which responded by crashing and crackling in time to the drummers as it sent blazing embers into the sky. Wood smoke filled the clearing, there being very little wind to spread it around.

Through the smoke, dark eyes jabbed at me from across the fire. I could feel Keion's desire; even after he'd renounced our kiss I'd known it was still there, and in the depth of the night's darkness he wasn't bothering to hide it. Meanwhile Llew sat beside me, his feet tapping excitedly to the rhythm, his head turning toward me occasionally to cast a longing stare my way. Soon the boy reached out and took my hand in his.

Before long the love triangle got to be too uncomfortable. I yawned and stretched my arms out over my head, holding onto the move for as long as possible in the hopes that both Keion and Llew would get bored and go away. Finally, bringing it down, I wished Llew as well as Seph, who'd taken up a seat on my other side, a good night.

Aerona met me at the door of the cabin. She held it open for me to enter, and then shut it tightly behind us. She reached onto a shelf, took a candle from it to the wood stove, lit it, and then brought the tiny light source over to me.

"It would seem you have more fans than you are certain what to do with, Alyssa," she said, her eyes meeting mine. For a rare moment I thought I saw a smile crease the skin beside them.

"That's a nice way to put it," I answered.

"One whom you would have, who cannot be yours, and one whom you would not have, who would do anything to be yours."

"Yep, that's just about it."

"It is a—one might call the situation entertaining, if one were not in it."

"Great. You're laughing at me, too, now. Bless your heart."

A good-natured chuckle answered me. "I am not laughing at you, Princess. I would not enjoy being in your position, to be certain. But it is a tale for the bardds, you must agree."

I nodded. I'd heard a tale of the bardds much earlier, and I had to admit that this one would probably make it eventually into their registry as well. I said, "I must, I guess. Why are boys like that, Aerona?"

She shrugged, and for the second time in a short period I actually saw a smile play across the old battle-scarred warrior-maiden's face. "If I knew the answer to that, well, then I'd be the wisest woman in the land, Princess. I suppose they have to practice being impossible when they're young in order to be so impeccably perfect at it after they've grown up."

"They get even better at it?" I asked, faking the sourest expression I could make. Deliberately, I let a loud sigh of exasperation escape my lips.

"Much better. I suppose you weren't raised around many men, were you?" I shook my head, and she chuckled softly. "Well, as I said, it is one for the bardds, Princess."

"I suppose it is. We'll have to see how well it ends, though," I said as I slipped under the sheets and let a yawn loose.

"We will, indeed. Good night," she said as she sat down in her chair and snuffed out the candle.

LLETCHWITH

sorta clumsy. Not physically clumsy, as that would describe no elves ever; this is more of a social thing, like when a boy asks a girl out for the first time.

To Crush A Heart

The ride back was uneventful, and blessedly silent as well. The ben's men—I'd taken to calling them that though his title was technically bennaeth—rose early and lashed the massive piles of meat onto a couple of large sleds, tied the skins on another, and stacked the bones into a wagon. Each of these was hitched to a team of horses, and then, after a breakfast that consisted mainly of elk meat and some cheese we all mounted up and headed back toward Ganalog. We seemed to move faster on the way back than on the way there; by mid-day, we were back within the log bastion of the northern elf capital city.

Everybody, and I mean *every*body, celebrated our success as we pulled into town. Esyllt herself met us at the gates and led a procession of dancers down the main road into the central courtyard. Our arrival was expected, as they'd sent runners back the night before with the good news, which explained why the town looked like an entirely different place than the one I'd entered just two days previously. Before, it had been literally, entirely, brown. For our return, the muddy ground and the roofs were the same, but the walls were decorated in a rainbow of colors. Windows were festooned with masses of ribbons. Every door had a sheet of colored fabric tossed over it. The whole thing created the atmosphere of a carnival.

Meanwhile, the village drummers were out in force, making the drumming circle of the night before seem like a minor rehearsal. I'd heard drumming circles in the villages near Cysegredig, and those were fun, but the drums of Ganolog ranged from tiny hand-carried units to massive, cart-drawn six and eight foot tall bass drums, and they seemed to fill every street in the town. The thunderous beats shook the ground beneath our horses' hooves and actually caused little pebbles to jump on the sides of the road.

The powerful beat gave the dancers something to go on, and they responded just as powerfully. There ended up being several hundred of them, all pressed together and undulating in the road with just a small strip down the middle left open for Esyllt to move from where she'd greeted us at the gate to the head of the dancing column. It wasn't just women, either; apparently everyone in the small city turned into either a drummer or a dancer for celebrations, and gender seemed to make no difference which. All the dancers were decked out in leather clothes that were brightly dyed, beaded, or both. They followed the drum rhythm on the way in, hips swaying and arms flailing overhead to the loud, complex beat.

It was colorful. Colorful, and loud. I, as the future elf queen, needed to learn to appreciate it, I could hear Sternyface telling me through Padrig's face from miles away. That was fine; at first I busied myself smiling and waving whenever someone smiled up at me, figuring that if nothing else it was more fun than sitting in a hunting stand. Before long, though, the infectious mood drew me right in, forcing me to break out into the sincerest bout of grins and chuckles I'd had in a long time.

In the main town plaza the procession widened, and we could see that Esyllt and a few of the ladies of the court stood in the doorway of the great hall swaying side to side to the steady beat. Our procession came to a halt as we reached the center, at which point Esyllt, still swaying side to side, advanced toward us. Padrig dropped off his horse impressively lightly for such a large man, handed the reins to somebody, and started swaying with his wife. Finally the pair swayed into the hall, and the main drums cut a dramatic end. Everyone cheered.

Eager hands helped the rest of us down from our horses. I looked back at the sleds with the meat and skins on them, but Seph told me, "Leave it, Cousin. It is time to celebrate!"

Celebrate, we did, as large glasses of something sweet and highly alcoholic were put into our hands as soon as we walked in. I tried to object, remembering my father's suggestion that partaking in strange alcohol may be too much for an inexperienced palate, but nobody wanted to listen. They wouldn't let my glass get less than full. It felt strange, drinking that much for a celebration, but everyone including Llew, young as he might be, seemed to be reveling in it. I watched out of the corner of my eye as he downed his first glass and eagerly snatched a refill.

A smaller drumming circle quickly set up off to the side of the hall, and as they started to play a group of women started dancing in front of the dais. The royal party had already been led to the main table, and there I sat sipping the drink that had been shoved into my hand. I was keenly aware of both Keion's and Llew's eyes on me, each pair growing hungrier with each sip. We all drank and watched as the girls performed in unison an intricately rhythmic yet highly athletic dance, one that reminded me vaguely of the hula but with more kicks and leaps. We all applauded when they finished. A hand came out of nowhere and refilled my drink once again, and I didn't argue. I noticed quite a few slaves, or servants, or whatever, wandering around the hall making sure drinks were full as the drumming circle and the dancers launched into another round.

The dancing was hypnotic enough without the level of alcohol in the beverage being served. The two, though, worked together to completely befuddle my senses.

I blame all of that on what happened next.

Suddenly I felt a masculine hand grasp mine. I looked over and found myself staring through an alcoholic haze into Llew's love-twisted face. As soon as we made eye contact, he raised my hand to his chest. Out of the corner of my eye I saw Keion start up, and then stop, fury evident in his face. Still, mostly to keep myself from doing anything stupid in my drunkenness, I concentrated on staring into Llew's eyes.

"Will you—will you be mine, Crown Princess?" Llew asked.

His apparent and suddenly soul-baring sincerity, combined with the amount of alcohol I'd drunk, was my undoing. Rather than brushing him off delicately, I laughed. As my laughter pealed, his face crushed in on itself.

I tried to react but only made it worse.

"Llew, look, you're a great kid, but you're only a kid. I'm too old for you. You need to find some young–" I said, but I stopped as I watched him bolting from the table.

A hush set over the nearby crowd momentarily, but Esyllt motioned for everyone to start up again. They did, obediently and a little bit woodenly. The boy's mother seemed to put effort into not meeting my eyes as she set off after her son. Keion, meanwhile, moved over to the now-vacant chair, murmured, "Smooth work there, Princess," and then returned to his own chair, leaving me to gape.

As soon as Keion moved away, Seph jumped over to the chair Llew had vacated, winked at me, and whispered, "Don't worry about it." I couldn't help but notice she was slurring her words, more than a little.

"Thanks, Cousin, but I think I broke the bennaeth's son," I said quietly, looking down at the glass I held and wondering if snakes would be coming out of it next.

"He'll get over it, Alyssa" she promised quietly, and then she motioned for me to continue enjoying watching the dancers. I did, or at least I enjoyed it for as long as I could remember before the alcohol took over my brain.

I awoke the next morning with Booboo jumping around on my head. Okay, honestly, it just felt like Booboo was jumping up there. In reality, I figure it was what most people call a hangover. I'd had no idea what they had served me at the celebration the night before, nor any idea how often they refilled my glass. It was several times, which probably amounted to a level of drunkenness that I'd never experienced before. All I knew was that I woke up the next morning with my head hurting like it had never hurt before, and my tongue feeling like it needed to be shaved.

The water basin clinked, a sound that amplified itself several times as it clanged between my ears.

"Stop!" I growled, glaring at the one inhabitant of the room I could glare at—mainly because she was the only inhabitant of the room. Ellga shrank back from my voice, and if my face had hurt less I'd have felt guilty about the tone I'd taken with her.

"What are you doing?" I asked.

"Setting Your Highness's washing bin up and the clothing out to be worn, my lady," she said, flushing demurely. I was impressed in spite of my hangover; she was a fisherwoman from the north who'd learned to flush demurely.

"Who asked for that at this early hour?" I demanded.

"May it please my lady, you did," she said.

Oh. Crap.

"Was I drunk when I asked that last night?" I asked, not sure what I hoped the answer would be.

"My lady seemed to have imbibed a little," she replied, her voice defensive.

Oh. Crap.

"Okay, thank you," I said. "I don't suppose you could get me a rather large drink of water, could you? And a Tylenol?" The few times I'd seen my mother inebriated, she'd asked for a Tylenol the next day, so I figured it was the thing to do.

I was wrong. "Your Highness, I do not know what a Tylenol is. I would be happy to get you some water, though."

"Sure. Just–make it soft." I winced as she left. I had no idea what I'd meant by soft, but I hoped she would figure it out. If she didn't, I supposed I had the rank to yell at her, even though it didn't seem right to do so.

"Here I come, honorably bearing some soft water for the crown princess," Keion shouted from the door several minutes later as he sauntered loudly into my room. Seph and Aerona followed him, tentative expressions on their faces.

"Thanks, asshole," I knew was the wrong thing to say, but I said it anyway. He grinned. "This spot on my forehead still requires a little bit more trouncing on to reach full pain levels, if you wish." I pointed to a random spot.

"I would love to help you out with that if we didn't face a serious challenge to our diplomatic presence, Princess," Keion said, continuing just as loudly.

"I bet you would. So what is this challenge you speak of?" I asked, raising my head off of the pillow. The movement prompted yet another wave of pain, which in turn caused my stomach to threaten to lose its meager contents. I grabbed the water that Keion really did have, thankfully, sipping it as quickly as my queasy stomach would allow.

"Llew is gone," he said, and his words brought me up short on every account.

"Gone? What do you mean, gone?" I handed him the water glass back so I could try to get out of bed.

"I think the word's meaning is pretty obvious, don't you, Crown Princess? The bennaeth's son left the party last night shortly after you smashed his ego along with every last one of his romantic dreams. He told his mother that he was going for a walk. His footprints lead out through the gate and into the wilderness. He has not yet returned. Do you need for me to spell it out any further?"

"Not particularly." My brain flipped wildly over, trying to come up with other possible reasons the poor kid could've gone missing. Unfortunately everything I came up with included me as the primary culprit.

"Wow. So much for 'he'll get over it,' right?" I asked, looking around Keion to catch Seph.

Seph shrugged and said, "Some men's egos are more fragile than others, it would seem." Her comment earned her an unsure glance from Keion as the prince weighed her words to see if there was an insult to him hidden within them. She noticed, and grinned at me to draw the moment out, and then said, "No, Prince Keion, I was not referring to you. No one would suggest that your ego is–fragile."

"Your cousin has learned to be almost as good at verbal barbs as you are," Keion muttered to me.

"I'm sure she didn't mean to hurt your feelings, Keion," I said, finding the strength to turn my body so that my legs could dangle off the bed, which in turn gave my head leverage to move. "Hey, how come the room is spinning like that?"

"It's called a hangover, Princess," Aerona said. "You should remember it from the last time, that night out dancing near

Cysegredig, if I recall. Would you like me to show you a warrior's cure for your malady?"

"I remember, but this one makes that one seem like a minor thing. I don't recall wondering whether my head was actually going to explode. As for the other, I'm not sure. What's a warrior's cure?" I asked, knowing my voice sounded weak but not really caring.

"It needs to be experienced rather than described, but it is very invigorating," she said, and from Keion's evil chortle I could tell I didn't want to experience it.

"No, no, I'll be fine. I just need some more of that soft water you have there, Keion. And then I need to go talk to Padrig."

"Not entirely certain he wants to talk to you, Princess," Keion said as he brought over the glass of water.

"Fine, but I need to talk to him anyway," I muttered before I tried to drown myself in the glass. It was the best, most refreshing water I'd ever tasted.

"Careful, don't gulp," Seph said, and within moments she was by my side, pulling the water away from my protesting lips. I didn't have the strength to fight her, though, so I gave in and let her have the glass right as my stomach started complaining.

"Well, at least get some food into your stomach before you head over to take your verbal beating," Keion said.

"We don't know that she's going to get a verbal beating," Seph argued.

Keion shrugged. "We don't know that she's not, and you have to admit that with the thought of it she's turned an awfully attractive shade of green."

His joy at my pain gave me back some of my vigor. "Get out, you. And you, too," I said to Seph. "Let me dress, and I'll meet you at the breakfast table."

"As you wish, Princess," Keion said with a bow and a smirk that made me want to punch him. He and Seph both managed to get out of the room before I could drum up the strength, though.

MALU CACHU

literally, to smash feces; it's used to suggest that somebody's saying something nonsensical.

To Search, Or Not To Search

"Bennaeth," I started in, trying to keep my voice strong. I had so much I wanted to say, so huge of an apology to make, but I also knew that he would neither accept nor respect it if I came from a timid, apologetic stance. I knew I was on awfully shaky ground, my fate teetering between future elf queen and exile to Earth, but that was less important to me than Llew and what I'd done. "Highness—"

"I thought we already established that you would call me Padrig, Alyssa. I don't appreciate all that simpering 'Your Highness' *skit* they do down south." Despite his civil words and tone, I could tell he was seething. For one thing, *skit* is a harsh cuss word in the north; it's a strongly derogatory way of referencing a pile of poop. More obvious, though, was that he refused to raise his eyes from the map on the table to acknowledge me.

"Padrig, yes. My colleagues informed me that Llew is missing," I said, trying to imagine, and then match, the coolness and in-control tone you'd hear from James Bond.

Padrig shrugged dismissively, but he still didn't raise his gaze. "He is a boy. We do not keep them leashed up here in the north. He goes missing from time to time. Why does it concern you?"

"I feel partly responsible, so I would like to help find him."

Finally Padrig did look up at me. He couldn't hide the depth of concern in his face. It was only a moment, though, because suddenly his face lit up in a delighted grin, lips curling all the way up into his cheeks and eyes shining. A thunderous laugh erupted from his chest, and he kept at it for several long, awkward moments, till he finally stopped himself by slapping the table with the palm of his hand.

"You look like *skit*, Alyssa."

I nodded gingerly and smiled as far as I could make it go up my face; near the temples it felt like tylwyth teg were driving nails into my skull and so nothing I could do would bring the smile up to there. I wasn't sure how best to address the fact that I'd gotten way too drunk at his party the night before, but the direct approach seemed best. "I haven't had the courage to spend a lot of time gazing into the mirror this morning, but I suspect I feel even worse than I look. I don't know what the servants were pouring into my mug last night, Padrig, but it would probably be illegal back where I came from."

He gazed at me curiously. "What kind of fool would make a law prohibiting inebriating beverages? No offense intended, of course, Alyssa."

"None taken," I said, holding my hands up to match the words. "There are—fools—back in my original homeland who believe that outlawing all alcoholic beverages is best, while others believe that just outlawing certain types of them is best, and still others who think that keeping adults under a certain age from consuming them is best. It's a mess, Bennaeth. I wasn't talking about that, though. I was referring to how wonderful it tastes in relation to the wallop that it packs. It's not fair. It feels so good going down, and then *vrrm-boom*!" I waved my hands over my head crazily to indicate what I meant by the sound.

"Ah. I'm glad you like it. I will send a cask or two back with you when you return next week."

"Thank you, Padrig. But–wait–did you say next week?" My heart sank, and I had to work to keep tears from my eyes as the image of me walking back up to Momma's front door, exiled forever, sprang to mind. I think I did a good job keeping panic out of my voice. At least, I hope I did.

"But Padrig, I need more time yet to get to know your culture, to–"

"You have done fine, Alyssa," he interrupted me, a tell that the queen's Lady had warned was rare with him. Rare, and dangerous. "I shall send you back to your home with my recommendation for your coronation."

I think I actually did stagger backward, the impact of his words hitting me squarely in the chest. His recommendation! I'd done it! But....

His recommendation was what I'd come for, but it just didn't feel like a victory.

"Well, that is very good news to me, but I would still like to offer the assistance of my party in finding Llew."

Steel entered his tone as he looked me directly in the eyes. "He doesn't *need* to be found, little one. You must have misheard me when I spoke on it earlier. My son can handle himself in nearly every conceivable wilderness situation, which is, I suspect, more than we can say for the current realm's crown princess. If he needs tracking down, then I shall send my own trackers out–trackers who, I must point out, were also born and raised in these lands, just as my son was. I have every confidence that their skills are more than sufficient for the task. So thank you, but no thank you."

I could tell by his tone we were done, so I just turned and left. There were plenty of protocols for such a departure, but I knew that he would respect me more if I just ignored them.

"Well, that was smooth," Keion said over my shoulder as I walked out of the bennaeth's area to go around and back into our rooms. I kept my pace steady and my lips closed till I entered the my own room again, and then I rounded on him.

"And how would you have handled it, oh mighty prince?" I asked, and both Seph and Aerona, hearing my tone, stood up at the ready.

"Calm down, okay? I mean, seriously, are you that hung over? I offered you a compliment."

"It didn't sound like a compliment," I argued.

"Well, it was. You really didn't think you handled the bennaeth smoothly?"

"No, I did not. At least, I'm pretty certain that on a different day I could've handled it more smoothly. In any event, I'm not certain what smooth means to you, but to me it doesn't involve getting tossed out of the bennaeth's home and shut down on an offer to help find his son."

Keion held my eyes with his own for a short while, thoughts darting across his face like fairy folk. He seemed to be weighing what to say, and changing his mind four or five times a second. Finally he sighed and said, "Okay, look, Alyssa. You and I have had some challenges in our ability to see eye to eye, but I recognize both your progress and your prowess. You did handle the bennaeth as well as anyone would have possibly expected you to, and probably better than most would have. He is giving you his recommendation, which was our primary mission in coming, and I have to agree with his assessment that his son really doesn't need your help, and so the good news is that we'll be able to head back soon."

"Head back soon with his recommendation. So, I suppose, you'll be back in time for your precious cylchoedd, right? Is that all you want out of this?"

"Well, sure," he said, cocking his head to the side with another of his annoyingly cute smiles. "What more should I want out of this?"

"The bennaeth's son may not specifically need my help, but I'm the one who caused him to run off. I know you want to get back, but I want to see at least some sort of tiny resolution here, some glimmer of Llew's fate."

Keion's eyes traveled down toward my waist, where my fists were busy rapidly clenching and unclenching. "You really are messed up over this, aren't you?" he asked, his expression softening.

"Yes! Yes, I am. Why is it impossible to go make sure Llew is okay?" I looked past him to Seph and Aerona for support, but they had their poker faces slapped on tight.

"By the same token, Alyssa, why is it impossible to believe Padrig when he says Llew is fine?"

"Because he doesn't really know, and he's probably dismissing the depth of the boy's hurt after what I said to him, and of course the ruler is going to assume his son is doing fine. It's not like he's going to go outside of his circle to ask for help. At the same time, he probably has no idea of how dangerous the Cult can be."

"Right," all three said at the same time, and then they looked at each other. Keion shrugged and gave what was apparently the group consensus, "No matter how dangerous the Cult can be, or perhaps more appropriately, especially because of how dangerous the Cult can be, why would he want help with his son from outside of his circle, when doing so would signal weakness in both father and son?"

"Well, he might not want it, but what would it hurt for us to give it?"

"What would it hurt? Alyssa, you're talking about potentially starting a war," Keion said, his face completely serious.

"A–a war? Why? Because I helped Padrig's son?"

"Because you stuck your nose into Padrig's business. His next step would be to complain about it to your father, who–" he said, but I cut off the lecture.

"But why would he complain to my father? Doesn't he like him?"

Keion breathed an exasperated sigh. "Alyssa, why is it that every time I forget how little of your life you have spent with us, you make what seems to be a concerted effort to remind me? You are here as your father's daughter, guarded by his best men under his banner, and so your actions naturally reflect upon him. Yes, every indicator is that Padrig has both a healthy respect for and a solid appreciation of your father's warrior history, his ruling style, and his personality. No matter how much he may like your father, though, it wouldn't stand up to a slight like this."

"But why a war?" I asked.

"I was getting to that when you interrupted me. A lot would depend on how your father chooses to react. Now, since you're the crown princess, you could be considered the representative of my mother, and so the smartest thing for your father to do would be to let the queen respond–so sorry, youthful vigor, we'll discipline her, and so on. But if the king responds, he has to protect his daughter; otherwise, he's being weak. A strong response from the king could very likely lead to an escalation of accusations which would, in turn, lead to a clash of warriors."

"Oh," I said, still wanting to protest.

"You two," Seph admonished. She'd been silent for most of the day, but I noticed that for the first time in a while, Booboo was growling at the two of us. My cousin shushed the wolverine and continued, "You're both getting worked up over nothing. Padrig isn't sending us home till next week, by which time I bet Llew will have made it back by himself. The bennaeth is right; the boy really can take care of himself out there. If he's back before we return, then Alyssa can make her peace with him and we can head home happily. If not, then perhaps Padrig's attitude toward outside help will have changed."

Seph was turning out to be a wonderful voice of reason, I thought as I nodded. It didn't take long for my head to make me regret the gesture, though, as pain stabbed from one temple to the other and kept bouncing back and forth.

Keion shrugged, still unwilling to show much respect to my low-born cousin. "Sure, if it pleases you ladies, then I suppose we can put off the conclusion of this argument for a few days." He stalked out of the room, closing the door a little harder than it needed.

"I suppose we can put off the conclusion of this argument for a few days," I mocked after he was gone, mimicking his voice and then throwing a hair-flick in at the end just for fun. Aerona raised her eyebrows in disapproval, but Seph giggled.

"I wonder what Grigor has to do with all of this," I muttered.

"He's Padrig's advisor. Why would he have anything to do with the disappearance of the bennaeth's son?" Seph asked.

"It's just a feeling I get when I'm around him. It's like being around a viper who's ready to strike, you know? I just have this feeling that under his fancy sparkly robes he's wearing the pin of the Wyrm as well."

"That's a pretty severe accusation to make."

"Remember how we didn't think to accuse the librarians until it was too late?" I asked.

Aerona flinched. She was still feeling put out by us leaving her behind, I could tell. Seph just shrugged, though. "You're right, but that doesn't mean we should start assuming every strange person is a member of the Cult, Cousin. Out of curiosity, what did you two talk about last night?"

The question brought me up short, and so I quickly scanned the events in my memory. Nope, Grigor wasn't there.

"What do you mean?"

"After Llew left, and then the show ended, Grigor invited you to dance. You accepted, though it was pretty obvious you weren't fit to do much of that. You don't remember a bit of this, do you?"

I shook my head and looked at Aerona, who nodded her agreement. "It is common, Princess," she said, "for periods of memory to vanish when alcohol is involved. That is why you should be more careful with your intake at public events in the future."

"Gotcha, thanks for the wisdom," I said, only half sarcastically, and turned back to Seph. "So, I danced with Grigor." I had no idea what to do with that information.

She nodded vigorously. "And talked, for quite some time. You two seemed to be having quite the discussion for a couple of dances."

"I sure do wish I could remember what we talked about. So, then what?" I asked, scared of what she was going to say.

"By then it was pretty obvious that you were done for the night, and so Grigor carried you to bed."

"Grigor? Grigor—carried? He carried me here, to my bed?"

"All was suitably handled, Princess," Aerona said. "I was on duty."

"I–I'm sure. But he–we–I–dance–talked–ugh. Now I really do have some things to think about, don't I?"

A banging at the door suddenly had Aerona tense, alert for any threat. Seph moved toward the door, but Ellga beat her to it. She opened the door a tiny bit carefully, peering beyond it, and then opened it wider so I could see.

I gasped. The elf in the hallway held Little Treebeard! I could tell it was my little elm familiar because all of its branches were stretched out toward me. Meanwhile the elf looked nervous, holding the pot as far from his body as it would go.

"LT! Put–put the pot over here," I stammered, shocked, as I motioned toward a side table. Ellga was quicker than I was once again, and she cleared off space for the pot before the royal courier got to where I'd pointed. "Thank you," I finished as the guy handed me an envelope and left as quickly as he'd come.

I opened the envelope to find a short note written in the script I'd only seen on official documents so far: my father's handwriting. *Uh oh*, I thought, but after scanning it to make sure it was shareable, I read the note aloud to Seph, Aerona, and Ellga.

My dearest daughter, I pray your visit is progressing well. Padrig is an old and dear friend of mine, as you already know, so please make sure to ask him for anything you may be absent of, and do so in my name. In the meanwhile, please accept custody of your little tree, with what you may take as my blessings. As much as I respect his kind, this little guy has been, as your mother would say, raising a ruckus since you departed. One of my men went in to water it, and the tree quite nearly strangled him. Do not fear; my man is quite skilled in various forms of hand-to-hand combat, a skill that he says translated into hand-to-branch combat quite well, and as a result he managed to retreat safely. That said, the tree creates another problem by beating against the walls of the room at night. I do not know what is causing this, and neither does S.F. When you left for the library, there was none of this. I am confident that the tree will grow out of such displays, but in the meantime, for the love of all that is beautiful in this life and beyond, please keep Little Tree-beard with you.

I looked up when I ended the letter to hear a strange sound. It was Seph unsuccessfully trying to hold back a chortle. When I glared, she actually lost control and broke out in loud guffaws.

Aerona just shook her head, holding her hand up to her mouth to hide her grin.

L.T. picked up on the mood—or maybe the little trouble-maker really was just overjoyed at being returned to my pres-ence—and the elm sapling started to shake. The back and forth motion of the limbs made Aerona and Seph laugh even harder. I looked on proudly, feeling a little bit responsible for the little tree's bushiness, since I'd been the one to sing it back to health in the first place. Before long we were all laughing hard.

"Who is this S.F., Cousin?" Seph finally asked when she could breathe again.

"Oh, that," I said, my laughter stopping suddenly as I wondered how much to let my cousin and Aerona in on. It wasn't a huge deal, I thought—surely nothing that would surprise anyone who'd ever spent time in the castle—and so I continued, "I probably shouldn't tell you, but S.F is short for Sternyface. High Priestess Naissa earned the title early on, and Dad thought it was—well, he thought it was cute." Seph redoubled her laughter, this time adding strange little snorts of glee. Obviously I'd been right about the understanding of anybody who'd ever spent time in the castle.

"Crown Princess, I must ask you a question, one which I beg of you to answer honestly," Aerona said once Seph's joyous laughter had died down again. I nodded, still too tickled to object to her use of my full title, and she went on, "Do you have any entertaining nicknames for me?"

"You? Of course not," I said, and she nodded, satisfied and apparently relieved. Her expression went back to startled, though, when I added, "I was way too scared of you at first to make one up."

"And now, Highness?" she asked, a rare grin cracking its way through her guarded facial lines. She actually crossed her arms in a show of trumped-up peevishness.

"Still no nickname," I said, shaking my head. "Sorry. I'm not terrified of you any more, at least not in a bad way, but 'Aerona the Supremely Competent' just seems lame as a nickname."

"Ah. I see," she said, and then she allowed herself to finish forming the grin before falling back into her normal habit of glaring at the shadows of the room.

PROFFWYDOLIAETH

*prophecy. With a term as difficult to say as that,
it's a good thing it's rare.*

Prophecy in the Weirdest Place

"I'm bored," I said to nobody in particular.

"If they played cylchoedd up here you could go to a game," Seph said. Tired as I was of hearing of Keion's little sport, I glared at her. She just snickered evilly.

We'd already spent one entire day sitting around not doing much. Granted, it had given me the opportunity to present Essylt with her house gift. The queen, knowing that I wasn't quite a hundred percent on elf customs, had recommended I bring something to give the lady of the house in return for her hospitality. I'd flailed around for ideas till the queen's Lady stepped in with a suggestion. She happened to know, just as she seemed to know everything else worth knowing, that Essylt loved green, and that northern elves were famous for their love of any fabric that wasn't fur or the hide of an animal. In the store room they had a swath of forest green lace held together by delicate jade and silver hoops. It had come from some trade with the elves of the southlands, she explained. The Lady Essylt would love it, she said, and she was right. Essylt had not only oohed and ahhed over the gift personally, but she'd even brought in the entire household staff to do the same.

That made for a supremely exciting half hour, I'll tell you what.

"Ellga, is there *anything* going on in Ganolog today?" I asked.

"The market is open, Your Highness," Ellga replied. That got my attention. An elf market! I imagined vendors in their little stalls, hawking their wares, just like at a Renaissance festival back home. I couldn't wait to see the real thing.

"Let's go!" I said, eagerly jumping up off of the chair.

"Wait, we need–" Seph started to object.

"Need what? We're dressed, and I already have Padrig's permission to poke around the town. C'mon, it'll be just like old times!"

"Cousin, we never had any 'old times.'" Seph shook her head in confusion, but she still rose to her feet.

"It's just a saying."

"You Missiliffians have some strange sayings, bless your– what is it again, your hearts?"

I sighed. "Hearts is correct, yes, but I don't think it means what you think it means. Let's go get Keion." I stepped out into the hall, ignoring my cousin's repeated mangling of the name of the state I'd once lived in.

"I am sorry, Your Highness, but the prince has stepped out to practice his martial skills with the bennaeth's guards," the servant informed us. Oh, well, his loss, I figured, and neither Aerona nor Seph seemed to disagree. Not that either of them seemed particularly overjoyed at the idea, but I was going to drag them along with me regardless, and they both knew it. At least the dragging was easier without Prince Charming and his weighty sidekick, his blessed ego.

"I wonder what they use to–make transactions," I mused as we walked along the side of the muddy street that Ellga had directed us down. It took me a second to even form the question, since the elves didn't have a word for *pay*.

"The people simply trade what they have for what they need," Aerona said. "It is a standard way of conducting transactions."

"So it's just like the central region. Are there many markets around?"

"I believe that there is probably one in each major town," Aerona cited the obvious. Conversation had never really been her strong suit.

"How many major towns have you been to?"

"A few."

"Did you go to the markets there?"

"When my presence was needed."

I gave up and lapsed back into silence, thinking about the differences between the two elf places I'd seen so far. Ganolog was a typical town, with a concentration of houses and streets and, as we were on our way to see, a market. Cysegredig, on the other hand, didn't have a market, but that made sense. The castle and cathedral built into the hill, and their inhabitants, made up what was called Cysegredig, and the remainder of the population was spread widely around in much smaller villages.

As we approached it, our steps lightened. For one thing, we could actually hear the murmur of conversation. I hadn't realized till I heard the noise how gloomy the silence of the empty, muddy streets seemed. That there were people ahead, and based on the sound of their voices, they were actually in pleasant moods, actually brightened my own mood.

That changed as we stepped out into the open courtyard, though. As soon as one elf saw us–well, me–he stopped talking and gestured to the ones standing beside him, who gestured to those around them, and so on. My presence was rapidly signaled through the square, and all talking ceased.

"Awkward...," I whispered in English.

"Yup," Seph agreed from beside me.

I couldn't just stand there, though. I felt all the weight of the queen's kids' training, all of my father's advice, and all of Padrig's words about the complexities of my acceptance, propelling me forward to make an entrance regardless of how I felt about it, and so I plunged ahead into the silence, dragging Seph and Aerona forward solely with my own willpower. Donning the smile I'd practiced, I started down the row of booths, greeting each trader as respectfully and cheerfully as possible.

I stopped at the fourth merchant. The woman, hands misshapen and spotted with age, had some of the prettiest, reddest apples I've ever seen. I complimented her on them, and she made a show of selecting the most perfectly rounded and colored fruit in her stock and then handing it out to me.

"I—thank you, but I have nothing to give you in return," I objected.

She shook her head, her lips and eyes joining in a surprisingly sorrowful smile. "You have honored me with your presence and your kind speech, Draignerfrehines. If I could beg anything, it would be to remember this moment when your time of prophecy comes, and to—" her voice faltered briefly, but she raised her eyes to fix mine and, in doing so, found her courage once again. "Please, please, in the terrible times ahead, go easy on my family and hold, Draignerfrehines."

Draignerfrehines, I repeated in my mind. The word, even unspoken, brought a chill to my chest. So that was it, I realized. I was already the instrument of horrible prophecy to these people. It wasn't mistrust of an outsider or of a royal, as I'd assumed at first, that caused their reticence.

No, it was fear.

The realization made me want to turn and run, but I didn't dare. Instead I held back the tear that threatened my face, nodded as regally as I could manage, and continued down the aisle of booths. Wearing the smile had suddenly become much harder, but I think I managed it as I greeted each person, and once we were done I kept walking straight ahead down the road without looking back. I heard conversation slowly, cautiously, return to the merchant area once we were gone.

A few dozen paces led me to a corner to turn, and I gratefully took the opportunity. Around the bend and safely out of sight, I let myself sag against a wall, holding the apple in front of me as though it represented something deadly.

"Princess, we should get back," Aerona said, her voice flat.

"Did–did you hear what she called me?" I said, and then I let a single sob course through my body. Once it managed to escape, I steeled my courage once again and focused my attention directly ahead and slightly downward.

"Yes, Cousin, we did. She called you the Dragon Queen. Is it not what you are?" Seph stepped in front of me, reached out, and pulled my chin up to meet her eyes.

"Yes, but–I've never–it's not–I haven't had it put right in my hands like that, Seph. I mean, wow. All of those people, every one of them, think I'm going to ravage them."

"Yes. You are, aren't you? At least, according to the prophecy. Isn't that right?"

"No! No, not at all. It's not right. I'm going to turn the elf practices and traditions upside down, certainly, and I think I'm going to start with the prohibition against the good kind of magic, followed closely by the whole fear of prophecy *skit*, but no, I'm not going to ravage them," I argued, though it was tough to get the argument tone right while still whispering.

"I think perhaps you are not as sensitive as you would like to believe to what might be considered a ravaging by your future subjects, my queen," Seph observed drily.

I sighed and breathed slowly to calm myself down. Finally, I responded, "Okay, Cousin, we can bicker all day long about the meaning of certain words. That doesn't change the fact that the woman back there seemed to believe I will do actual harm to her family. Certainly you know me well enough to know that I would never do that intentionally."

"Not intentionally, no. Alyssa, I don't know any more than you do what lies before us. I know that the prophecy makes many claims, and that those claims have made their way to the populace in a way that may or may not properly represent their original form. It's–"

"Well, then, we should go back and tell the people what that proper form is, right?" I said, marshaling my courage. It was, I knew, what a queen would do: face the fears of the people and calm them with words of truth and kindness.

"You two might wish to quiet down and watch what is happening," Aerona said. She pointed back toward where the market was, and as she did I noticed that the area back around the corner had quieted down once again.

I glanced around back the way we'd come, and I hissed. Grigor was there! He was walking like a hero through the crowd, smiling and chatting softly. Every so often either he or a merchant would point down the road toward where we had disappeared, and Grigor would laugh and make a comment. I couldn't hear what he was saying, but I could only imagine how he was poisoning the minds of the people against me.

I looked back toward my team, small as it was. I was seething. "We need to–"

"To what? Charge in and confront the bennaeth's advisor in public? That will go badly, Princess," Aerona said.

As much as I wanted to get angry at her, I knew that she was right. We didn't have any standing to confront anybody, at least not yet, and certainly not Grigor himself. Once I was queen, I promised myself, we'd be able to clear all of this up. Till then, they'd just have to continue thinking I was evil.

I growled, and then jerked my head down the street in the direction we'd been traveling. "Let's go, then. We might as well get back to the keep."

The street we were on intersected another radial street, and I was ecstatic to turn that corner and head through the muddy path toward Padrig's home. I started thinking about how good it would be to get back and wash the mud off of my feet.

A little ways down we saw an elderly lady sitting in the mud on the same side of the street we were walking down. We stopped, and Seph and Aerona actually started gesturing between themselves, asking each other whether we should cross the street and avoid her.

I'd had enough, though. I was the good guy in the story, and I'd be darned if I wasn't going to show it.

I strode directly between their hands and continued down the street toward the old woman. As I approached, she cocked an ear my direction and then turned sightless eyes my way. She held up her hands, asking for something.

Apparently even the elves have their beggar class. It shocked me at first, considering how carefree, hardworking, and equal everyone around Cysegredig had been. Then again, Ganolog was in so many ways nothing at all like Cysegredig, and so I had no business being surprised that they had slaves and beggars.

"How are you doing?" I asked when I got close.

"Oh high one, please, my lady, please help an old woman. I am so hungry," she said, her voice thin and reedy. She stretched her hands out toward me.

I'd felt less attached to the apple the merchant had given me with every step since, and so it seemed natural for me to give it to her. I heard Aerona say "No" as I reached out to hand it to the woman, but I didn't care about Aerona's worry. The beggar was, after all, blind; what was she going to do?

My hands made contact with hers as her fingers started curling around the small round fruit, but the apple suddenly dropped through loose fingers to the ground as the old woman gasped and spasmed. Film-covered eyes suddenly cleared and found something to look at way out in the heavens, and a completely different voice came from her mouth as she began reciting.

"Massive maw of fire and bone,
Armor-clad teeth, so sharply honed,
Serpent body, ancient mind,
Seeking power, elves will bind,
Nesting tall, of glass and steel,
Culture crushed by heavy heel,
Hunger fuels the dreadful war,
The elves must find the ancient core."

She came out of her vision as rapidly as she'd gone into it, grasping for and finding the apple. She brushed it off on her shirt and took a gleeful bite of it. Wordlessly, Aerona and Seph led me away from the noisy sound of chewing.

"What in the heck did that mean?" I dared to ask my two fellow travelers once we were safely ensconced in my room of Padrig's hold.

"I–" Seph said, but Aerona cut her off, looking meaningfully at Ellga. My young servant took in the wild expressions on mine and Seph's faces, and then extrapolated that into the meaning in Aerona's glare, and she vanished with a muttered apology to the air for being in it.

"It would seem that you have been blessed with your own private prophecy, Princess," Aerona observed drily.

"Oh, that's just joyful. I was just, this morning, hoping to come across someone who could grant me my own private prophecy," I said.

"Your sarcasm face is impossible to miss this time, Cousin."

"Oh, good. I'd hate to have you think I really wanted to find out about gloom and maw of fire and bone and crushing heels," I said, my voice rising in pitch to almost a hysterical level.

"Calm down, Alyssa," Aerona ordered. "We are in a safe place now, and I will also remind Your Highness that we do not yet know the meaning of the prophecy."

"That was pretty hard to miss, I think. If the gods of prophecy are trying to be subtle here, I think they suck at it," I said, still totally in the mood to spaz out a little bit over what I'd heard. "Nesting, serpent, ancient mind, sharp teeth–any question, really, about what kind of foe she was talking about?"

"Well, you are the Dragon Queen, Cousin."

"I know! I know that I am called the Dragon Queen! No, I will not be quiet, Aerona. I think I deserve this little breakdown that I feel like having, don't you? People hate me, others campaign against me, some even try to kill me, and now I am told I'll bring a dragon to bear on anybody who's left on my side."

"Sounds like somebody had a far more entertaining morning than I did," Keion's voice called from the door. I glared, but didn't do anything else. I knew that right then would be a really bad time to scream at the walking ego.

Seph interpreted my glare correctly and shooed Keion out of the room, closing the door after herself. I could hear her in the hall telling the prince that I'd had a rough day and needed some time to digest. He didn't protest, at least not that I could hear, and I vowed to myself that I would give my cousin a big hug next time I felt like hugging anybody.

"Ellga!" Aerona shouted, and the willowy servant girl appeared almost immediately. "The princess needs a bath to wash the mud from her feet, and also a mug of that good strong ale that your people serve."

Ellga nodded and got to work, and I forced myself to relax and allow her to do her job.

The Celebration

On top of everything else, at a time when I didn't feel like celebrating anything, they threw me a party.

I shouldn't complain; it was a cool party. I'm not sure how much of it was Padrig's planning, as opposed to the word I got that the partiers had wanted to come meet me before I headed back to what they were calling the lesser part of the continent. But I'd been hoping for a chance to experience the four tribes of the northern clans for myself, and somehow that chance magically appeared right outside of Ganolog's gates. Who was I to complain?

Ellga woke me the day before we were to leave for Cysegredig. L.T. sensed the girl's excitement and quivered her own little boughs. "Wake up, wake up, Princess! The people of the north have come to welcome you." I glared at the maid and the tree equally, the maid got a glare of irritation and the tree one of suspicion. Somehow the little limbs seemed much closer to me when I woke up than they'd been when I'd put the tree's pot in the corner of the room before going to bed. At first I wondered if I remembered it right, but after wading carefully through my memories, I wondered how the tree had managed to convince somebody else to move her in my sleep.

"Why did you move the tree?" I asked Ellga.

"I didn't move the tree, Highness."

"No, it's okay if you did, really. I'm just curious why."

"Crown Princess, I'm being completely honest with you. I have not moved that tree, not ever. It—she—is too much of a close companion to you for me to interfere."

I was both charmed and insulted by the close companion comment, and I wasn't sure which was greater, so I just let it go. "If you didn't, then who did?"

"I do not know."

"Aerona! Who was in here last night?"

My guard stepped out of the corner she'd been stationed in and shook her head. "No one was in here last night, Alyssa. Are you sure you're not just remembering the placement of the tree's pot incorrectly?"

"Yes, I'm sure." I sighed, wondering if I'd ever resolve it. "Please keep a closer eye on it tonight."

"I will," was all she said as she stepped back into the corner.

I joined Seph and Keion, Aerona at our tail, and walked eagerly through the hall. Padrig and Esyllt caught up from the other side, the bennaeth stage-whispering to me a grumpy comment that expressed his concern over how much of the recent hunt's meat would go to feed the assembled crowd.

I'd already earned his blessing; he'd announced it at dinner, so I felt a little more relaxed than I had earlier. "It's a party for me!" I returned in my most gleeful, childlike voice. I tried putting on the full-face grin I'd practiced. Padrig looked at me, harrumphed, and then started to laugh deeply, from his belly, as he joined us in our hurry.

"They have all come to meet the prophesied one, High-nesses," Grigor explained when we got there, his arms held wide to indicate the collection of tents to our front. He stood square in the entrance, facing me with his ever-present dour expression and hawk-sharp gaze. His presence, especially before I managed to arrive, made me wonder whether I really wanted to be there after all.

Padrig nodded happily; apparently he was oblivious to my distrust for his advisor. "Yes, they have come to meet you, but more importantly, my people have come to introduce you to their culture, Alyssa. You are a strong young Princess, to be honored so." Elves have a lot of words for strong, as I'd learned on the road with Keion discussing these very tribes, but he used the one that meant strong in leadership, in a dictatorial sense. It was the word that would've been used for someone like Hitler. That wasn't me, not at all, I thought as I scanned his face for hints of sarcasm. Seeing none, I glanced over to Grigor's face to see no change in his expression either. Keion and Seph, likewise, didn't see anything wrong with the term, so I set it aside to consider later while I followed the bennaeth past his advisor and into the circle of tents to its center.

The games were a lot of fun. Each tribe sent its own trans-lator over to sit beside me and explain as we went through their feats of strength. The events of the tribe of guardians and the central tribe were the least interesting, since I'd seen, or at least heard of, ax tossing for accuracy and log throwing for dis-tance before. Their warriors were the ones who participated, and they did so with gusto.

The high kick was fun to watch as the elves from the sea-board demonstrated their favorite sport. They suspended the ball on a string, and their contestants had to leap to kick it. Each round they tied the string a few inches shorter, making the kicker reach higher each time. Some of the elves who managed to kick it fell on their back sides on their way down, earning both a disqualification and a loud round of laughter at their expense.

First they did a round kicking with one foot, and then they held another round kicking with both feet at the same time.

The winner of that round, declared so because he'd missed fewer times than anybody else, asked me if I wanted to try it. I certainly didn't, but neither he, nor Padrig, nor my cousin and Prince Charming, were willing to take no for an answer. The expression on the bennaeth's face sealed the deal; I could tell that this princess was expected to go along with whatever they asked me to do, and I'd gosh-darn better enjoy it, too!

For my first try, I concentrated on kicking the ball but completely forgot about the landing part, so I fell on my back side just like others had done. Everybody laughed, even Padrig. Embarrassed, I let my guide, a tall elf named Garon, help me up.

"Princess, that was a nice first try," he said softly.

"Then why is everybody laughing at me?"

Garon chuckled and shrugged. "It is our way, Highness. We are taught from a young age to find joy and merriment in anything we can, since the opportunities to find those are so rare in our everyday lives." He gave me the most sincerely happy smile I think I've ever seen, even among the elves who generally smile with their whole face. That distilled all the em-barrassment right out of me.

"I see. So how do I kick the ball without falling on my rear end?"

"The secret is in the hips. That, and the order of motion. You tried to kick the ball and then land on your non-kicking foot, which would have gotten you disqualified even if you had somehow managed to stay upright. Keep your eye on the ball, but concentrate on rotating your leg up, and then down, as you match the direction that your body is going."

"Okay, I think I've got it," I lied. I proved that I didn't have it a couple more times, to the assembly's raucous laughter, but the fourth try was perfect. I stuck the landing on my right foot, watching the ball jiggle around on the string. Applause greeted my success, and Garon explained that being successful in the first ten, twenty, or even fifty kicks was rare. I sat down feeling pretty happy with myself.

The people of the ice had the most interesting competition. They tied strings to bags of flour, and then they made a loop in the other ends. The loop went around a warrior's ear, and then it was used to lift the sack by a few inches. Once the sack was supported only by the guys' ears, they made loops around the circle till their—well, till their ears gave out. It looked very painful. That was the point, according to that tribe's interpreter. Frostbite attacks the ears first, making them hurt, and the ear-carry competition mimicked enduring the pain of frostbite.

The winner gave me a chance at this one, too. I'd already learned something from the previous game, so I gave it a try. I made it once around the circle—far short of the winner's thirty-seven loops—before I gave in to the pain. Still, my effort earned me a fair amount of applause, and looking around I thought I saw a decent measure of sincere appreciation in their faces.

The athletic games gave way to the eating, and I enjoyed most of that. I was handed bear, and elk, and moose on a stick. It was all pretty tasty. The strip of dried salmon was chewy, but it tasted better than any of the canned salmon I'd tried. Then the fishermen also gave me a small sardine-looking fish, and unfortunately it actually tasted like a sardine, so I didn't eat much of that.

The blubber was the most surprising food of the day.

They didn't call it blubber, but that's what my interpreter explained that it was. The mammals–whales, seals, and sea lions–that swam off the shore were taken by the fishermen, and while their flesh was prized, the fat was even more precious to them. It was a source of energy over the winter, she said, and as she told me the story she glared toward the interpreter from the ice fields. Apparently both groups fight over the substance, they both explained later.

I tried a little piece. Trust me, it's not worth fighting over. The texture of the fat is like oily Jell-O. It tastes a little fishy, but then when you dip it in the oil they provided for that purpose, it becomes even more fishy.

"Thank you so much for letting me sample this part of your life," I told the blubber-bearer. She grinned a huge, thankful expression at me and then wandered away.

"Did you actually enjoy that skit?" Padrig breathed into my ear.

I shook my head in a minute gesture, careful to maintain a neutral expression.

"Good. Thought I was the only one," the bennaeth whispered. "The Digonol and the Pobl'yrhew absolutely love it!" he said with more volume.

"Your people–our people, now–have interesting and wondrous traditions, mighty bennaeth," I said, trying to make my voice carry to all nearby ears.

"We are proud of your willingness to join in the festivities with us, Princess. We would enjoy hosting you for the actual games next summer. Not only is it an entire week of sporting and feasting, but it is also a time to listen to the greatest story-tellers in the realm spin the history of our people out before you as only their melodic, silvery tongues can." Padrig turned a sincere smile to me, making it obvious he'd actually meant what he'd said in his too-pronounced voice.

"I'd love to," I said, dropping the stage-speak. It was the truth; other than the floppy fish blubber, everything I'd experienced was incredible.

"Excellent. Well, as much as I'd love to sit out here in the crisp air and enjoy the festivities into the evening, I'm afraid Ganolog still needs some preparation done for the coming winter. I will leave you in excellent company, Princess."

"Oh, but Bennaeth," I said, panicking. As much fun as I'd had, I wanted to spend a little more time with him. Besides, I had a question to ask. "I am tired, and have a long journey to begin tomorrow. I would walk back with you, if you don't mind."

"Not at all," Padrig said and started off. Luckily Seph, Keion, and Aerona all read my intentions correctly, and all three hung back a bit before following.

"So why did you call me a strong princess?" I asked once we were out of earshot. His use of the term we'd have used back home for Hitler had bothered me all day.

"You are, little one. Or, at least, you are going to be." He spared me a single glance that seemed full of kindness and even regret before putting eyes to his front again.

"What do you mean?"

"Isn't it obvious? No, I suppose that it may not be to one so young and still, and I mean this without disrespect, a bit naive. Alyssa, you are a nice young lady, and I do not doubt that you mean at this point to be a happy, equitable ruler, but...."

"But what, Padrig?"

"But I do not know how to say this without risk of offending you, though that is not my intention at all. You already know some of what the prophecy says you must do. To accomplish all that is in your future, you must be—or become—one of the strongest rulers the realm has ever seen. You have already demonstrated a little of that strength, being willing to burn a library to the ground to save the lives of your friends. You were willing to battle one of our most storied, and feared, bear brethren so that your guard would not have to face him alone. You are definitely, completely, your father's daughter, Alyssa, and I have no doubt that you have it within yourself to live up to the strength that the prophecy promises."

"But that's horrible," I said, shaking my head. All I had ever heard of strength like that was that it killed masses of people. I'd burned a library to the ground because of it, and Padrig was right. I was prophesied to do even worse, more terrible things to the people of Kiirajanna.

"No. No, it's not," Padrig argued, and to make his point he spun and stopped me, forcing the two of us to face each other in the middle of the clearing. "Alyssa, Crown Princess, *Cadfael-merch*," he rambled. The joining of my father's name with the elf word for daughter made his point clear. "The people of Kiirajanna need strong leadership more than you realize. We have grown lazy and unconcerned about the shadow that, in turn, grows stronger every day. We need you, Princess. We need you to be every bit as strong as you were born to be."

Point made, the bennaeth turned and marched silently beside me back into Ganolog.

Waiting For Llew

I spent the rest of the day in a weird kind of terrified apprehension, stuck inside for fear of meeting more prophecy in the flesh while hoping to see Llew walk back in through the front door, yet at the same time dreading the conversation I'd need to have with him if he did. Meanwhile, I was also petrified of the decision I and the rest of the party would have to make if he didn't come back.

He didn't come back.

"Why does Grigor hate me?" I asked Padrig late in the afternoon. I'd finally gotten him alone, and I really wanted to get some closure to at least one thing before we had to leave.

"Hate you? I do not understand," he said.

"He's always glaring at me. No, before you object, I'm used to elves glaring at me in Cysegredig. This is different, Bennaeth. Most elves glare at me to intimidate me, or to make it seem as though I'm going to be in trouble. His glares radiate anger, and sometimes even worse."

"Anger, and worse? Well, that should not be happening to my guest. I shall discipline my advisor."

"No! Please, no, Bennaeth. I was only curious about my interpretation. I am not looking for—I do not see a reason why your adviser should be disciplined. I should not have brought such a minor matter up in your presence."

"You are a strange case, Princess Alyssa," he said. "I would not presume to advise the crown princess in matters of politics, of course, but I might suggest to the northern snows in the air above that, perhaps, there is a level of desirable decorum at which you do not complain to a clan leader about his chief advisor, unless you have something specific to complain about."

"Your suggestion will be taken to heart, mighty Bennaeth. I was only inquiring. I will be more careful in how I phrase my comments in the future." Bless his heart, I wanted to add, but I left it off. Too many elves had started figuring out what I meant when I said that, especially since I said it in informal tone: *bendithia i'ch calon*.

Padrig only nodded in dismissal.

The next day, it was obvious that Padrig expected us to leave. He called a council in the grand hall with everyone, including glaring Grigor, and in his typically short-spoken fashion the bennaeth proclaimed me the rightful heir to Queen Talaith. Everybody, including Grigor, cheered and applauded, and then they all gave me a strange gesture that was halfway in between the hand-swish they'd give a friend they respected and the temple-touch you would present to the queen herself. It would've brought an emotional moment on if I hadn't already been feeling emotional in the other direction. Dang it, I wanted to know where Llew was!

Meanwhile, during the short period of time that we were in the meeting, the bennaeth's minions packed up our stuff for us so that we had nothing left to do but to leave.

If that's not an obvious "*Get out*," I don't know what is.

On our way out of the royal building we were given a massive farewell reception. They even formed a line, Padrig and Esyllt at the end, to shake our hands. It felt like way too much pomp and circumstance. In fact, it started to seem overdone on purpose.

As I shook his hand, I leaned in to Padrig's ear and whispered, "Are you certain we can't help look for Llew?"

Padrig gave me a stern glare and nodded. "Yes, I am certain. Thank you, Princess, but you have done plenty for my son," he said, his voice a little bit louder than mine had been.

"Well, that was direct," Seph observed as we stood outside in the chilly mid-day air, the double doors of the mighty keep having been abruptly closed behind us. Winter was descending quickly, I could tell by the way the breeze cut through my clothes more than it had the day before. I shivered my agreement.

"And loud," Keion agreed. He sprang into his saddle effortlessly, whirling his sable hair about his face in a way that still irritated me nearly as much as it made my knees weak.

"And final," Aerona stated. She wheeled her horse toward the gate and motioned firmly for me to take my place in the little procession. The half dozen of Dad's guards took their stations in a wheel around us while Seph and Keion led us out.

Passing through the gates of Ganolog left a bittersweet taste. Despite gaining Padrig's approval in my bid to be the next Queen Talaith, I felt like I'd lost status rather than gained it. The elves tearing down the fairground from the day prior accentuated the feeling by ignoring us as we clopped our horses around the ring of tents and then back onto the trail to the south.

In the tree line, it was even more obvious that the seasons were changing quickly. As we left for the hunting trip we'd seen a little bit of green, but as we looked around just over a week later it seemed like even the scraggly evergreen spruces had given up the battle against the coming onslaught, their spindles turning dark and drooping downward to point toward the earth.

Once we'd passed deep enough into the bleakly foliated tree line to be out of sight, I nudged Awel to catch up with Sephaline. To my pleasure, the mare proved once again that she could move as quickly as the wind she was named for. Seph looked at me in surprise when I reached out and stopped her from spurring her own mount out to begin her traveling search pattern.

"No, wait," I said, and was immediately answered by groans from all three of them.

"What are you thinking, Alyssa?" Seph asked at the same time that Keion said, "No, no waiting, Princess." I looked around to see that everyone, including the members of my father's guard detail, was glaring at me.

"I just want to look," I argued.

Keion shook his head. "Bad idea, Princess," he said, and I was both frustrated and infuriated to see Seph actually nod her agreement.

"Look, y'all, I won't be able to sleep until I know what happened to Llew. I know he doesn't want my help, nor does his father, but we have the perfect party to saerch, and the bennaeth can't really stop us from following a little bit longer path toward home."

"Actually, he can, Cousin," Seph said. "He has his rangers patrolling all through the land looking for Llew, and he is within his rights to demand that we return via the most direct path, especially so that we do not generate suspicion of changing the signs of the boy's passage."

Keion's scowl deepened as he added, "And even if he really could not, why can you not accept that the boy is a child of the north, and, further, that he's doing just fine, and if not, then Padrig's rangers are more than capable of dealing with it?"

"If they were, then why hasn't he been found yet?" I asked and rounded on Keion.

He shrugged and held his arms out wide. "Big forest," he said, and then he held up two fingers close together. "Little boy. Trust me, Princess, if I'd wanted to vanish when I was his age, I could have done so easily. Besides, we need to get down off of the Rim before the arrival of winter prevents cylchoedd season."

That did it; I was tired of hearing about his precious sporting event. "I don't care," I growled, "about your stupid sporting season, Prince. I care about a little boy whose health, even though you would prefer to presume the best, is still, as yet, in question. I am not saying we need to bring the boy back in; I am only saying that we—I—need to find where he is. I am confident in my cousin's ability to out-track any of Padrig's rangers. I am confident in your ability to out-fight anything we come up against. Am I being clear?"

"Crystal clear, Princess, *but*–" Keion started, but he was cut off.

The sudden support from an unexpected backer surprised me so much I whipped my head around as she spoke. "But nothing, Prince Keion," Aerona said, her voice taking on a patina of steel. "The daughter of the king, the crown princess herself, has spoken. Surely you do not need the king's most humble guard-servant to describe basic court precedent to one as elevated in position as you?"

Keion turned his glare toward her, his eyes opening wide in his fury. "No," he said, his voice quiet but deadly, "I do not need–"

He was interrupted again. "Keion, she's right," Seph said simply. I almost snickered at the prince's injured expression;

not only had my cousin, the non-royal royal, put him in his place, but she'd also done it entirely and noticeably without the customary honorific.

I didn't snicker, though. Instead, I recognized that it was time to take charge. "Of course she's right," I snapped. "Now, you," I stopped and pointed at my father's honor guard, who'd long since passed the point of being needed. "You go on back to Cysegredig. Let my father know that I'm going off on a side trip that won't take more than a day or two," I said and then stopped to glare at Keion, silencing his protest, before continuing, "and please make plenty of noise and tracks on your way, in order to disguise the fact that Prince Keion, Sephaline, Aerona, and I are not traveling with you."

"We cannot do that, Your Highness."

I rounded on the guy who'd just spoken. He was big, and he wore the single chevron of leadership over the stag-and-raven crest of the current royals on his black cloak. I tried staring him down, but failed. His coal-black eyes just returned my glare with his own unemotional gaze.

"Why not?" I finally asked.

"His Majesty, your father, charged us with your safe transport to and from Ganolog, Your Highness. It is our duty to see you safely home. To leave you on your own while we head back, no matter how sound the plan, and no matter that it was by your order, would invoke your father's wrath."

"See? We need to head back as a group," Keion said, his voice actually pleading for once..

"Shut it, you," I said in English. I saw his eyes widen at my tone, but otherwise he did as I ordered. *Good*, I thought. "So, what if we didn't head back as a group, then, but rather sent only a few back?" I asked. "The few would be a diversion set up to ensure our overall trip was safely made, while the others could keep us safe directly. You'd all be doing my father's bidding."

"Who would be the few that you are thinking of, Highness?" the guard leader asked. Aerona's eyebrows raised in curiosity, too, and Seph tilted her head to the side.

"A few of your team, I'm thinking. Say, four. You and one other can come with us to ensure our safe return, while four others head on back to perform the diversion we were talking about. You can take the prince with you, to make sure he makes it back for his little athletic practice."

"Over my dead body," Keion growled. "I was sent to protect you through this journey, and protect you I shall, *Princess*."

"Good to see you've changed your mind about the trip, Prince Keion" I said, and grinned when my comment brought the expected, silent glare. "Okay, so does the plan meet with everybody's prior orders?" I asked. I looked around; nobody said anything. I actually got the feeling that I was in charge, for once.

The arrangements were made quickly. The toughest part was convincing Little Treebeard to not protest being sent away from me. It's weird, I have to admit, to stand in the woods arguing with a potted sapling, especially in a sing-song voice. She didn't want to go, though; she'd only just been reunited with me. I actually sensed a strange combination of loneliness and protectiveness from the little elm sapling.

I sang a few lines from *Blue Suede Shoes*, in English, and pushed through them mental images and sentiments showing the thankfulness that I had that L.T. felt the way she did. Then I tried to express, in my thoughts, the need that my party continue on for a while with her returning in the midst of all of the baggage to the castle so that the ruse would work. It was an awfully complex message to get across while singing an old Elvis song, but I finally managed. I felt her capitulate, and then I felt sick as I watched her carried away. It was weird, missing a tree, but I actually was starting to be attached to my little sapling friend.

The rest of us set off to skirt around the settlement, just inside the cover of the tree line, headed west, the direction we'd heard Llew had gone.

Seph's horse disappeared into the trees ahead, my ranger cousin going to find hints of the boy's trail. The rest of us were stuck on slow so that we wouldn't overtake her. Keion took the opportunity to say, in a surprisingly humble tone, "Okay, so my command of your tongue must not be as thorough as I once thought. I understood *blue* and *shoes*, but why would you address a sapling with the command *go, cat, go?*"

I looked over at Aerona while wondering how much to explain to the prince. She had been the one stationed in my room through my initial exercises learning to sing to the tree. It was her sardonic comments, in fact, that had clued me in on how the meaningfulness of the song to the singer was so much more important than the words that were sung. The first time I'd really connected with L.T. had been while singing an old Elvis song that Momma taught me, and that was after hours of singing lovely little ditties about love and peace and trees to no effect.

Aerona was no help; she just smiled back at me. I finally settled on the simple, straightforward answer. I turned to Prince Charming and said, "It's an old song Momma and I used to swing around to. The emotional connection in the song helps me connect with L.T. better."

He nodded, apparently getting it. "You were very close to your mother, weren't you?"

"Yeah, I was. Very, very close. Dad was here running the kingdom, and that just left the two of us together, fending for ourselves."

"Did she ever tell you? About who he was, and who you were?"

"No. She told me just before I came here that she'd started to explain several times, but it hadn't ever come out right. I mean, how do you tell your daughter that her father is a a race that you've always known as a myth?"

"So what did you think happened to him? You did wonder, didn't you?"

"Sure, I wondered. I wondered a lot, in fact. But when I finally managed to bring the subject up, I could tell that I'd upset Momma by asking about it, and because seeing her like that hurt, I told myself I wouldn't do it again. Instead, I just went on living in a great big fantasy world, inventing stories about where, and who, my father must be."

"Oh? What kind of stories?"

I paused, wondering how much I should open up to Keion. He'd been a total jerk so far on the trip, but now that the decision to dally was made he was back to being a nice guy. Well, as nice as any conceited jerk of a prince could be, anyway.

Finally I shrugged as I realized that it didn't really matter. The worst that could happen was he'd go back to being a jerk. "All kinds of stories," I said. "In some, he was a pirate, even though there really aren't any pirates left on Earth. Except in Africa, I guess, but—well, never mind. Sometimes he was a CIA man, a secret government spy working on something so important he couldn't manage to get any word back to us. Just, anything a little girl could imagine, really. Anything but an elf king, I should say. That would've been too far-fetched."

Keion snorted. "I bet it would have been."

"What about you? I never hear anybody talk about the queen's husband, your father. Where's he?"

"He's—not around, and I'd prefer not to talk about it."

"Oh," I said, feeling the temperature of the conversation drop abruptly. "Um, sorry? I think that's the best thing to say?" I asked, tentatively, hoping to revive the feeling of warmth and caring I'd felt from him.

"It's fine. Thank you for your concern," Keion said, ending the conversation.

Luckily, especially considering how cheerfully the prince and I *weren't* getting along, Seph proved her worth quickly. We only spent only an hour or so riding along, deep enough in the tree line that the bennaeth's rangers couldn't detect us, before she came riding back to the party.

"I found it!" she said, her eyes bright with excitement.

"Llew's trail?" I asked.

"Yes, Llew's trail. What else would I have been looking for? I found it, leading off that direction." She pointed to the west. "You'll need to stay slow, so that you don't overtake me too much, but I'm pretty sure I can follow it."

"*Pretty* sure?" Keion asked, derision coloring his voice. "That a ranger is pretty sure she can follow a boy's trail is underwhelmingly helpful to my faith in our eventual success."

Seph glowered but visibly ignored Keion as she replied to me, "My apologies, Cousin. I was excited over finding his path. I am certain that, no matter how skilled the young man of the northern tribe is at moving through the woods of his homeland, I can follow his trail."

"Was he running away, or was he walking out as though on an adventure?" I asked.

"Oh, right, we forgot the important questions! And does his gait indicate he was carrying his pack on his left shoulder or his right? Was it a blue pack, or a green one? Was he, you know, hobbling along with a crushed heart, or moving along on a sudden desire to hunt and kill something?" Keion asked. I looked at Seph first to see if she reacted, and when she leveled her glare directly at him, so did I.

"He was walking, I think," Seph answered me without removing her glare from Charming. "That doesn't mean much in the overall sense, though. Even creatures who are fleeing from predators will get tired and walk part of the time. Llew is a smart young man, so he was probably choosing his path carefully."

"Well, then, you should follow his trail, and we will in turn follow you," I said decisively.

"I shall do that," she said, just as decisively.

Keion groaned and asked, "Can we *just* get on with it? I feel it getting colder as we speak."

HUD

magic. I'd've figured the realm of "hud" would have a fancier word for it, but no.

Through the Portal

We followed Seph along Llew's trail for what seemed like hours. It was impressive, really. I couldn't see anything to be followed, but she seemed to know right where she was going. Of course, the prince acted less impressed than I was, but then again, that's just Keion being Keion. Meanwhile Aerona and the guards continued traipsing along beside us with an air of acceptance and trust. I felt the same, and so I tried to adopt their solid, trusting demeanor if for no other reason than the hopes of annoying the prince with it.

We caught up to Seph directly, the ranger on her hands and knees near the middle of a clearing. She was busy, focused, starting intently at something I couldn't see on the ground. Soon she crawled a few inches and stared just as intently at a different, still completely unremarkable, spot. We all sat in our saddles and watched her scuttle about like that for a while.

It was an unusual place, the clearing to our front. In the center stood a small ring of vertical stones that, in the brisk afternoon air, emitted the quiet but persistent hum of energy that I now recognized. It looked, and sounded, and felt just like the portal I had come through to get from Earth to Kiirajanna in the first place, back when Dad led me from Memphis to a ring of menhirs just outside of the castle grounds at Cysegredig.

Having been through one once, I knew a portal when I saw a portal, and this was definitely a portal.

Finally Seph rose to her feet and ambled over to the party, looking at the ground and shaking her head absently as she walked. A couple of times she even seemed to mutter to herself.

"Lost the trail, ranger?" Keion asked. I glared over my shoulder at him. He ignored me, as he usually did. Meanwhile, she ignored him, as she usually did.

I heard an audible sigh from Aerona.

"The trail ends here, Alyssa," Sephaline said, shaking her head.

"What–" I started, then stopped when I realized I was about to ask something that Keion would make fun of me for. Launching on another approach instead, I asked, "How could the trail end here? Did he go back? Or do you think that Llew stepped through the portal?"

"Either he stepped through the portal, or he learned to levitate and flew away," Seph said, her proclamation earning a snort from Keion.

"So where does this portal go, do you think?"

"There's no way of knowing, Alyssa," she answered, finally looking up to meet my questioning look with her own confusion. "These things just connect to the other side, usually somewhere on Earth. We've mapped most of them out, but the northern rangers won't let us do that up here."

"Usually? They don't always go back to Earth?"

"No, not always. In fact, there's a portal far to the south that transports anyone who steps through it to another portal on the other side of a fairly small hill. Kids use it to play games. And no, nobody really knows why they connect to where they do."

"But you're pretty certain that Llew went through it."

"There's no way of knowing that, Cousin," Seph said over Keion's exasperated sigh. "There's no traceable residue left when someone goes through a portal, unlike when they pass next to a bush or through a swath of grass. But the alternative requires him to have walked away leaving no tracks for a ranger to find, which would in practice require levitation, and so I have to say that the most likely option is right through the center of the stones. And Booboo, please stop growling at the *nice* prince." The way she said nice suggested anything but a literal interpretation of the word, but Keion just grinned, his teeth showing and his eyes glinting.

Booboo turned his glare toward his mistress, briefly, before extinguishing the growl and pacing over to her side. Absently she reached down and scratched the mean-looking creature behind his ears. The wolverine turned its coal-black eyes on the prince, growl-lessly this time, and received a similar black-eyed glare in return.

The rivalry between the prince of the realm and the wolverine nearly made me laugh out loud despite the seriousness of the mission.

"So, let's quit wasting time," I urged and pushed Awel closer, remembering my father's advice to be strong, take charge, and show that I could be a ruler. Unfortunately, my horse stopped cold, refusing to move into the clearing and thereby destroying all hope of looking strong and in charge. Instead, the mare shook her head and snorted one of those long, loud horse noises that Keion somehow echoed perfectly a moment later.

"What?" I demanded.

"Highness, the horses can't go through the portal," Aerona reminded me gently.

Right. Once again I'd forgotten one of my lessons. When the prince and his two sisters had caustically set out to teach me the history of Kiirajanna, they'd explained that the open portals were used initially to bring armies of humans and beasts of war across from Earth to serve as fodder in the tremendously violent wars of the first age. After centuries of decimation they'd closed the portals off, but only at great cost. Eventually, of course, that great cost was forgotten, and so the elves re-opened the portals. To prevent warfare on Kiirajanna from ever returning to that fury, though, they restricted the use of the portals to magical beings, a category that included elves and the occasional unicorn but neither humans nor horses.

"Oh. Right. Thank you for the reminder, Aerona. We'll probably be through and back quickly," I said, trying to salvage as much regal pose as I could. I turned to the guard leader and ordered, "One of you needs to remain here to look after our horses, please."

The leader turned a sardonic expression to the other member of the king's guard, who shrugged and dismounted to gather leads. The selection was pretty much automatic, then.

As the guardsman gathered the horses together, the rest of us made preparations for travel on foot. Luckily our side packs became backpacks easily, and we all took on part of the load of food and equipment and then prepared to set off.

My pack was heavy, but not as bad as some of the camping packs I'd worn growing up. I shouldered it, earning a quickly-hidden look of approval from Charming.

He stepped through the portal first and disappeared, followed immediately by Seph and Booboo, the non-magical wolverine apparently able to pass through thanks to his bond to the ranger. I stopped for a few seconds to give them a chance to establish a safe perimeter on the other side, and then I stepped through, moving forward quickly to make room for Aerona, who I knew would be following me almost immediately. She pushed through rapidly and moved to the side to make room for the guard leader, who brought up the rear.

It felt like we'd walked into a blast chiller. My teeth instantly started chattering, and I closed my eyes and raised my hands to protect them against a solid force of wind that whipped thousands of little sandpapery things against my face.

"*Move*, Princess," Aerona's growl startled me as she pushed me forward, and not very gently. The shove from behind forced me to open my eyes, and for a second I forgot all about the cold and the withering blast of tiny ice shards as I was suddenly blinded by the sun's brilliance reflected off of the whiteness of everything. I slammed my eyes protectively shut again and tried another gentle step forward.

"It's going to be hard to find the boy with your eyes closed, Alyssa," Keion's voice drifted across the wind gusts.

Left hand held up protectively in front of my eyes, I forced them to open once again. Everything–the snow on the trail, the snow above and below, even the snow that was blowing in the wind–was white, and the sun's closeness to the horizon turned that white into a ferocious, sparkly light show. The hand helped, though, both in shielding against the sandblasting and in lowering the brightness level to a more indirect glare. As my eyes slowly adjusted, I looked around.

"Where are we?" I asked, knowing that I wouldn't be able to figure it out by myself. "Iceland? Greenland? Alaska? Canada?" I was guessing, naming northern places at random. "Norway, maybe? Anybody know?"

Seph's voice carried to me from a little way off, "None of us have any idea where those places are, Alyssa, and even if we did, there's no road signs. There doesn't seem to be anything dangerous about, but finding Llew's trail is going to be impossible with this driving snow blowing our own tracks to nothing." She walked up to the party from a little way off where she and Booboo had been scouting.

"Unless he suddenly has become a *mwfflon*, I can't imagine him taking but one path away from here," Keion said, pointing down the only open trail. I wasn't sure what a mwfflon was, but it had to be some sort of mountain goat. The portal stones we'd stepped into were perched on a flat spot way up a steep cliff, high enough that in the blinding snow I couldn't see either the bottom or the top. The spot we stood on was wide, nearly thirty feet across, but the trail leading away on the mountainside narrowed to five or six feet of blowing snow.

It looked dangerous. No, perilous is a better word. Between the whipping wind, the blinding light, and the slick piles of ice crystals, I could easily see an accident in our future.

"Do you think we can make it down?" I asked Seph. She didn't respond immediately. I managed to catch her cold-induced shiver out of the corner of my eye.

Keion exploded. "Have you somehow in the recent past completely lost control of your senses, Princess? Are you stark raving mad? If Llew passed that way, it will be some time before he can return, and that's *if* his corpse isn't lying at the bottom of the cliff somewhere. The conditions are horrible for travel, one, and we have no idea how far we are away from anywhere else, two, and we're not even close to being equipped to stay out in this cold, three. We don't even know where we are. And that, dear Princess, is four."

Despite my own terror regarding the trail to our front, I warmed up a little at the chance to argue with Prince Charming. "How nice to learn that you can successfully count, Prince. But there is still a teenage boy out there somewhere and I am certain that it is my responsibility to help him get home. You do understand responsibility, do you not? Or are you just too scared to attempt a walk in the snow?"

That did it. Charming's face turned dark purple and then pivoted to point directly down the trail away from the portal. He stalked off into the snow.

"Um, Princess?" Aerona muttered behind me. "It is certainly not my desire to cross your word, but the prince was correct in his assertion that we are not equipped for this weather."

I barely heard her, at first, through the glory I felt at taking him down for once, but I shook my head when what she'd said registered. "We'll be fine. We're better equipped than the boy probably was. Let's go a short distance down the trail, at least, to see if we can find Llew's path. Hopefully he'll have marked it somehow. If we don't find it shortly, then we can turn around."

"Okay," Seph said, her voice shaking a little from the cold. "I'll do it, Alyssa, but I also must agree with the rest who aren't sure that this is such a good idea."

"Et tu, Seph?" I asked, drawing on what I imagined was my most Caesar-like voice.

"What, Cousin?"

"Never mind. It's a line from a movie, I think, or a book, anyway. I can't remember which right now because my brain is shivering. Can we just get to moving? Walking will warm us up."

We started down the path as a group, the rest of us catching up to Keion soon enough. He was moving slowly and carefully. "I wasn't sure you were brave enough to follow," he taunted, but I couldn't formulate a good reply at the moment because of my own need to concentrate on not losing footing in the blowing snow.

Instead, I fell back on the old standard: "Bite me."

As we inched forward, the trail descended, and that lightened my worry a little. I actually started believing that we might get out of the walk alive, in fact. We turned a curve that sheltered us from the wind, and the stinging spray hitting my eyes died down. The sun was still blindingly bright, but by shielding my eyes with a hand I was able to see just fine. Without the wind whipping up a snow cloud, I was able to tell that we were going through a mountain pass. I could even see the expansive white valley before us. All we had to do was get to the base of the mountain we were on and we'd probably find something or someone who could tell us something useful.

It wasn't that bad, I allowed myself to believe. It was cold, but not bad.

Keion coughed, a loud bark that made us all jump. It carried in the cold, echoing off the mountain opposite the one we were on, and then rebounding from behind us, getting louder with each bounce.

Suddenly the whole mountain above us seemed to groan, a low, rumbling sound that increased in volume.

"That's not good," Seph said.

"Um, no, it's not," Keion agreed.

"Everyone to me," Aerona ordered, pulling me physically up against the side of the mountain and then pushing me down into a crouch. As she added bodies to the group it felt like she was trying to squish me into the granite.

"Hey, that hurts," I tried to say when an elbow was thrust into my ribs, but the groaning noise above was too loud to speak over. Then came the solid rain; in addition to the low tones of rocks against granite, I also heard shrill whistles and distinct plops of things hitting the trail near us. The little plops turned to thuds as the screaming, groaning noise grew louder. I looked up through the crush of bodies and saw a massive wall of white hurtling down toward us.

Someone screamed. I think it was me, but I wasn't sure at the time. There were probably others joining in the screaming as well, but it was awfully hard to pick out the minor details through the roar of a full-blown avalanche.

Suddenly the vivid image of Momma handing me her pendant cut through the panic that welled in my mind. Draignerthol! Its power, forbidden though it may have been, had saved us once. I'd caught heck for that, and even agreed not to ever do magic again, but that moment, sitting underneath a raging avalanche, seemed like a perfectly good time to forget that I'd made that agreement.

I managed to wriggle my arm up through the crush so that I could lay a hand over my chest, my cold skin enjoying the warmth of the dragon-shaped silver pendant. Blue light suffused through my blouse, spreading out around and over us as we pressed ourselves against the wall in a great big group hug. I pressed my own energy through the relic, grasping toward the nearly bottomless well of magical force that I could sense right there on the other side. Energy like electricity coursed through me as the power of the magic filled my body. I snatched it up, rejoicing in its limitless power, and pressed it out and away from the party, envisioning a solid bubble of titanium shielding us from the coming onslaught.

Then, it hit.

The roar was deafening by the time the leading edge of the snow pack reached our level. It pushed everything that stood before it downward, straight down toward the ground so many hundreds of feet below. I managed, somehow, to hold tight to Draignerthol as the whole mass of people was plucked from the side of the mountain and washed away like a pebble in a river. We fell together, tumbling end over end, as the scream of the avalanche died away slightly to be replaced by the whistling of the wind as we sailed out, away from the rock face and down toward the valley floor below.

We hit the floor hard. The jounce of my body and my head against something solid made me lose both physical contact with Draignerthol and magical contact with the energy I commanded. The silvery-blue sheen of the protective bubble snapped and burst outward, and then the blinding whiteness of our surroundings went black.

A Long and Winding Road

"Princess, come back to us," a voice called, slowly slicing its way through the fog that swaddled me. It started as faraway song, intoned from the other side of a dark grey mist. "Alyssa, I need you to wake up," the voice said again, closer, sharper, and somehow more—more urgent? I wasn't given much chance to consider that, though, as a slap to my cheek sealed the deal.

I was awake.

My eyes opened to blue skies, white surroundings, and Aerona's worry-creased face.

I moaned. Of all the sights to wake up to.... Still, the urgency in her voice, aided by the slap, managed to cut through the fogginess in my skull, and I quickly remembered the avalanche, the terrifying fall, and the crushing impact with the ground. I also remembered that I should be on my feet, moving, finding Llew, but I needed to go through a short checklist first. One hand up in front of my face; fingers wiggling—good. Other hand up; fingers wiggling—good. Feet move, even better. I rolled over onto my side and then forced my aching body to rise to its knees, and then precariously to its feet, holding its balance through some strange, mysterious force.

"Wow, that was some fall," I observed. Hey, it was the smartest thing I could come up with at the time.

"Are you okay, Cousin?" Seph's voice sounded from right behind me. Then I realized that it had to be her arms that grasped me about the ribcage, steadying me on my feet.

"Yeah, I guess. How's everybody else?" I shook out of her arms to stand on my own, feeling stronger already.

A snort and a chuffle from beside me said that Booboo had survived the fall. Seph said, "Aerona is fine, and so am I. The prince is as grumpy as usual but fine nonetheless. And now it looks like you're going to be fine, too. All limbs attached, all spirits high!"

Keion grunted.

I ignored him. "What about the guard?"

"The guard? He, um...." Seph looked away, her eyes traveling the length of the ravine.

"He what?"

"Well, he–" Seph tried to continue, but stammered, and then brought her gaze back around so I could see the sadness in her eyes.

"The guard didn't make it, Alyssa," Aerona's voice cut in, its steel softened by velvet undertones.

"What? He didn't make what?" I peered at her, not wanting to understand what she'd said, and shocked that she could say anything with that much feeling.

"He–Gerallt was his name–the guard, your guard, did his duty to the end. Unfortunately that meant being outside of our group, and so he was not included in your little–sphere–as we were knocked off of the cliff face by the power of the avalanche. Your–display of power, perverse as it might have been, saved us, but it could not save him."

It hit me in the gut, and hard. Not the bit about perverse; that reaction to my spell was expected. I was past the point of caring, really. I'd saved us all with it. Nearly all, anyway. I'd saved all, except the one.

Gerallt. I hadn't even asked his name before he'd given his life for me. That hit me in the gut again.

I looked over to where Keion was engaged in pulling a twisted and broken black-cloaked body to the side of the valley. I felt like crying, but knew I couldn't for way too many reasons.

"Aren't we going to bury him?" I asked.

"In what? Ice? Alyssa, there isn't any unfrozen ground within days of here. We need to move on before we all join him," Seph said, grabbing my hand and gripping it hard in a physical show of support.

"We can't just leave him here."

"We have to, Cousin. To try to carry his body would likely bring us to death, sacrificing the very thing he died to save."

"I know, but I just—" I started, but she interrupted me.

"I know." She engulfed me in a hug, and it was all I could do to keep from breaking down. The thought of Keion being there to witness it was the deciding factor that helped me hold it together.

The prince gave me a dark, questioning look as he tramped past in the snow, shouldering his backpack as he moved. "Princess," he said, "you, personally and quite by yourself, ended the lives of dozens of Cult of the Wyrm members when you burned the library down, and that didn't seem to faze you. Now you're shaken up over one death?"

"Yes. Yes, I am," I said, holding myself back from using the derogatory word I really wanted to send his way. "They died trying to kill me. This man—Gerallt was his name—gave his life to protect me. I've never had anyone do that."

"Well, if you intend to be the queen of the realm, you should attempt to get used to the idea," Aerona said gently. "It has been peaceful for most of my lifetime–what?"

I stifled the giggles that had erupted in spite of my morose mood and said, "With your scars, and your skills, you seem like the last person to be able to say something like 'it has been peaceful for most of my lifetime,' Aerona."

"My scars, and my skills, have been well earned, Princess, but not in any large conflicts such as those that once scoured the land, and will once again very soon. The prophecy says that when the Dragon Queen returns to Kiirajanna, death will follow close behind as entire armies assemble for war. It also says that dragons–actual, living dragons–will return with her. It is further said, as you know, that you are she, so it is not a stretch at all to suggest that the time has come to remember wistfully the ages of peace."

"Bah. Fairy tales, nothing more," Keion interjected, earning him a look of surprise. While he hadn't been present for the prophecy in Ganolog, he had been at the library when parts of the prophecy had played out as true, so he should've known better. "What we really need to be remembering wistfully is the warmth of a shelter and a fire, and our worry should be that the sun is well on its way down toward the horizon while we stand still in a frozen land of ice and snow with no way back to the portal we came through. We need to get to shelter, and sooner rather than later. Let's go, folks."

We started trudging along after him, our feet kicking through the shin-deep snow as we blazed a trail. At one point Seph told us that we were walking along the top of a frozen stream, a fact that seemed to impress no one but me. Hey, I'd only ever heard of walking on ice; I never figured I'd be doing it.

"We still don't know where we are, much less where we're going," I lamented when the rest of the party insisted on stopping briefly to eat some cold sausage and cheese.

"Princess, if I may offer you an educational word or two," Keion said from across the shivering circle, following his sarcastic words with a sullen glare, "when you are ostensibly in charge of any troop movement, as you will be if and when you are crowned queen, you should never give voice to the idea that you do not know where you are going. To do so is to invite dissension and despair. Far better to keep your mouth closed and leave your followers wondering if you are sane, than to open it and let them know for certain."

"Thank you for the educational word or two, Prince," I grated across to him. "But I doubt there are any here who were not already aware that we are rather low on geographical information, and I'm sure y'all know just how sane I really am."

"Yes, well, your high degree of insanity notwithstanding, it is still often the words of the leader that hold the power to inspire the party to stick it out and trudge farther along. Your words were simply not very inspiring."

I sighed. "Okay, I give. I'll admit, Prince Keion, you have a point."

Seph spoke up. "I have a point, as well, actually. Two points, perhaps. Three, if you count the point that I am definitely not looking to be a leader here. Anyway, I believe that I do know where we are, and second, I'm pretty certain that I know where we're going."

"How?" Keion and I asked in unison.

"Simple deduction, really, at least for the 'where we are' part. When we first came through the portal, Alyssa named some far-north places on Earth, places I'd only ever heard about. Places, I must add, that my guidance skills would be completely useless in. But one thing everyone knows about all of Earth, not just its far north, is that it completely lacks magical energy flowing about it. Alyssa, you have told me before that when your mother gave you Draignerthol it was a beautiful pendant that was completely inert and devoid of power, correct?"

"Correct," I said, sitting up straighter. I could see where she was going, and it was promising.

"So, since this is a realm where magic exists, then we can't be on Earth, and the only other option is that we're still on Kiirajanna. We rangers have legends of an ancient portal to the far north, way above the mountains, up in the great ice fields. It was a trapper's paradise way back when, because it let them drag their furs from the town just at the base of these mountains a short distance up an old riverbed and poof! Less than a day's travel later, they could be near the center of the realm. Common sense says that such a portal might still be used—it must be, in fact, given the quality of the path that we just fell off of." Seph paused to grimace upward, and then continued, "As to where we're going, my training says this frozen river path is heading southward, and combining that with legend, I believe that it will likely will take us to Abergarhewi, a well-known northern tribes trading village and probably the northernmost collection of elves on all of Kiirajanna."

"So will this Abergarhewi have warmer clothes for us?" I asked, starting to shiver as the adrenalin from the rapid walk dissipated.

Keion muttered, "Well, it is, after all, a trading village. For furs, by the way. I'm sure they'll have something warm that you can wrap your body in." I stuck my tongue out at him, and he shrugged. "You'd probably look good in a *drychiolaeth* pelt, actually."

Aerona even rolled her eyes at that.

"I may not have the widest vocabulary, Prince, but I do know what a *drychiolaeth* is, and I don't see myself wearing a pelt of one anytime soon." I retorted, and then shouldered my backpack, ready to trudge off along the frozen river.

A ghost's pelt, indeed. Bless his blackened little mealworm-infested heart.

After a while the walk turned into a numb shamble for all of us except Aerona, who seemed to be able to put her physical body's sensations out of her mind and just operate it like a machine. I tried to ask her about it, but after uttering something that sounded like "muh, muh" a few times, I gave up and stayed as silent as everyone else. Even Booboo looked like the cold was getting the best of him, in spite of his fur coat. I thought briefly of using Draignerthol to warm me. At the mere thought of it I felt giddy, in fact. But no, I realized, I couldn't. While I was perfectly fine with using magic when needed, everybody else was still not, and I knew I'd feel guilty and lose everyone else's respect as well if I used my supposedly evil powers to warm myself while they were freezing.

Besides, if they could keep going with their teeth chattering, so could I.

The sun dropped like a lead weight behind a mountain past our right shoulders. You could actually watch the change as the shadows lengthened into darkness. We went from frigid daylight to freezing shadows to the darkness of a closed blast freezer in what seemed like just a few steps. The only part that was even slightly comforting was that down in the valley we were sheltered from the biting wind we'd felt above on the path.

"Are we going to walk all night?" I mumbled out loud. I wasn't sure anybody could hear me or translate my mouth's frozen murplings, but it turned out someone could.

"We can't stop moving or we'll freeze. Besides, Abergarhewi can't be too much farther." Aerona said, looking over at me with concern in her voice and her face.

She was right. On both counts, that is. Soon after she spoke her wisdom, we came around a bend in the river to see the moon glimmering low on the horizon, illuminating a small village. I'd like to say that we all took off running for the warmth, but the truth is that we just shambled faster, like zombies toward brains.

Yes, that is an ugly example, but it's how it felt.

We reached the village quietly. It was weird, walking through ankle-deep fluffy snow that turned our footsteps into rhythmic whispers into an elf village with no other sounds at all. This place was quieter, even, than Ganolog had been upon our first entry. It seemed like the dark was covering our ears as well as our eyes. There was no grand communal fire, of course, no party on the green. Granted, there wasn't a green to party on. All I could see was silvery-grey of resting snow shimmering in the soundproof moonlight.

Keion and Aerona both headed toward the closest house that had light streaming from a window. The prince banged on the door, and I was relieved that it opened quickly. Inside I saw a beautiful woman, but what struck me the hardest, had me almost fainting in pleasure, was the warmth that gushed out through the now-open doorway to bathe my frozen face.

"You look like walking icicles!" the girl cried. "Come in, come in right away. Please, come sit by the fire and we'll make some tea. Where in the five hells have you come from dressed like that?"

Strong hands—Keion's, Aerona's, I neither knew nor cared whose—propelled me inside and to a chair near the wood stove. I sat there like a lump for a while, mesmerized by the little flickers of flame that danced through the glass front. The wood smoke aroma I'd come to enjoy took on a whole new level of pleasure as I let it suffuse throughout my body, warming as it went. The pin-pricks of pain as my nerves unfroze were annoying, but my brain was still so numb I didn't really give the pain much notice. I saw Booboo shake himself out vigorously in the edge of my vision, an action I found strangely humorous, and then the beast harrumphed and wound itself into a tight, warm ball of fur under Seph's chair. Aerona and Keion joined us silently, nobody having the energy to answer the woman's question. She didn't object to our silence, though, so we just sat and wrapped ourselves up in it as we allowed our bodies to thaw.

More hands–the girl's, I guess–shoved a cup of warmth into mine, and I sat there for several seconds just blowing the steam that rose from the liquid into lazy circlets. It was fun, but I could think of better things to do with a warm cup of tea. I sipped, and instantly my tongue objected to being scalded as a large piece of it went numb. It occurred to me then that the girl's ignored voice had been warning that it was hot, but her words hadn't brought a lot of meaning until the pain jolted my mind back to life.

Motion returned slowly to us all. Keion leaned forward and started clapping his hands together in the warmth. Seph slowly rocked back and forth. Aerona–well, Aerona just sat there and glared at the darkness like she usually did.

Me? I smiled, at first. We'd lived through it, after all. All of us but Gerallt, that is, and my heart knotted up again as I reminded myself of his sacrifice for my safety. My smile vanished.

"So, now that color returns to your faces, our curiosity bubbles again. Where are you from, to be dressed like that in the winter?"

I glanced around, curious who the 'our' included. The girl seemed to be the only inhabitant other than us, and my glance didn't take in anything to contradict that.

"The south," Keion said. He countered with, "So where are we now?"

"The north," the girl answered, quirking her eyebrow in a roguish expression. Seph and I both snickered, and she grinned.

"We're from Cysegredig," I said, ignoring the dark glare I received from Keion at my admission. "Long story, that, and I don't mind telling the interesting parts if we have time later. For now, though, are we in Abergarhewi?"

"Well, sure. Where else could you be, Alystyw?"

I grimaced. Alystyw is an elf paradise far to the south, a place to enjoy tropical weather along a long, beautiful, white stretch of beach. To be honest, I'd been looking forward to visiting that town ever since they'd told me about it. After all, there's got to be something good about being the queen.

"There were other guesses, but they were all pretty far off, too. We weren't certain after going through the portal."

"Through the portal in this weather! And in those clothes! You're lucky you survived!"

"Well, yes, we are, but we didn't know that at the time. We were hoping to find a young boy who's been missing for a little while. Have you seen one of those?"

"Nope. Stray little boys are eaten up here."

I chortled once, hoping she was joking.

"Sorry, the sense of humor doesn't come off well when the recipients are nearly frozen to death. But no, no strangers through here in a couple of weeks."

"His name's Llew, if that helps."

"Llew? Padrig's son? He's no stranger, lass. But no, he hasn't been seen. So what are a group of folks from Cysegredig doing chasing after the bennaeth's son?"

"Well, um–" I floundered, not sure how much of the story I could tell without her being either offended or laughing us out into the cold again. "Padrig said he'd gone away for a bit; we were just testing out our ranger friend's abilities to track him on our way home." Seph started to glare at me, but thought better of it and just nodded weakly. Too late, I remembered her words about the northern clans requiring southern rangers to obtain permission before entering their lands.

Luckily, our savior didn't seem to mind. "Oh. Well, in that case, good luck tracking anything out there, between the fresh snowfall and the wind blowing everything around," the girl shrugged, and Seph again nodded weakly. "But no, we haven't seen Llew pass through here, and we're fairly certain that he'd've stopped by if he were through."

"Are you sure? He might've–"

"Yes, it is certain. His family and ours are old friends, and besides, you've already seen how bad it is out there. No one in their right mind would pass up an opportunity to get warm before heading on farther south."

"Oh. So, um, I suppose that we should just head back to the portal in the morning?" I asked, trying to judge the reaction of the others in the group. Unfortunately, everybody else just seemed too beaten down to gloat over having been correct. It was just as well, because I still didn't want to give in on having been wrong.

"Just–just head back to the portal?" the girl asked, incredulous. "The way you came, you mean? Did you happen to see the avalanche that rumbled down the mountain behind you this afternoon?"

"Yeah. We did," I said, still not wanting to share too much. What would this elf do if she found out that Keion had caused the avalanche? Worse, what would she do if she learned that I'd cast a magical spell?

"Well, there's more up there waiting to come down. And what fell just adds to what's already stacked up on a very treacherous trail. The path to the portal won't be safe for a week or more. You're better off warming your feet here for a while."

"I'd prefer not," Keion growled.

"Well, if you're really in a hurry, you can take the land route to the south."

I glanced over at my companions, who were still playing it completely cool. "Land route? How long does that take?"

"On foot? A couple of weeks. You'd be stupid to try that, but you're in luck. Your timing is superb. Cai, our local merchant, starts his fall run to Ganolog tomorrow, and he's always looking for friendly tagalongs to help guard against the beasts of the north. You could be there in just four or five days if you hitch a ride with him."

"Well, we should go talk to Cai, then. Which way–" I said, starting to rise from the chair, but the girl put out a hand to stop me.

"No offense, traveler, but you look like the walking dead. There will be plenty of time tomorrow to worry about tomorrow's business. You three ladies can have our bed. We'll put out blankets for you, sir, to sleep on."

"Fine, and I do so very much appreciate your help. Before we take your bed, though–we don't even know your name," I objected.

"Blodwyn the Grey, at your service, fair traveler. And yours?" she said. Out of the corner of my eye I noticed Keion hide a twitch with some effort. Apparently the name meant something to him, more than he was willing to let on.

"I'm–" I started, but Keion interrupted me with an over-acted glare.

"You're forgetting your place, girl," he chided me, and then he smiled at Blodwyn. "I'm sorry. Down south, we men always make the introductions. I am Eonil, first armsman to His Majesty, and these are my companions." He gave us each a made-up name that I realized, too late, that I shouldhave tried to remember. "We were sent to Ganolog to establish a trade agreement for this winter, but after we finished we heard Llew had gone missing and wanted to gain the honor of finding him."

"First armsman to His Majesty? Traveling with trade ambassadors. That sounds important."

"Not at all. A common rank, I assure you," Keion covered.

"So, do you know his daughter?"

"A little. She spends most of her time with the nobles, not us common folk," Keion lied. I managed to keep a completely blank face, I think. Seph and Aerona buried their faces in their tea, and after seeing that, I decided to take the same course.

"Is she as arrogant as they say?"

"More, I'd say. She's always flouncing about, and she has a tongue that is sharper than the tip of an arrow." Keion said, nodding simply to her. I held back the exasperated gasp.

"Ah. Be careful whom you speak to so frankly up here, especially around Ganolog. The old man and his whelp still have some friends."

Everybody nodded mutely, and I found myself nodding along as well despite my desire to challenge this Blodwyn the Grey. *Whelp?*

"Ah," she said finally, as if acknowledging the silence that had surrounded us. "Well, Eonil, we're glad to be in your presence and that of your companions. Now, let us see to some blankets."

Before long we were all laying down pretending to be asleep. I couldn't sleep. My mind kept racing over why Keion had taken the sudden turn down the path of deception when he'd learned the girl's name. I could tell Seph wasn't asleep, either; she kept gently fidgeting beside me. Besides, I'd noticed that Booboo always curled up once Seph was safely asleep, but the wolverine still lay by the fire glaring around the room. Meanwhile, Aerona's breath slowed down, but not by enough for me to believe that she'd actually fallen asleep.

Who was this Blodwyn the Grey, and why did she dislike the king's whelp? She'd never met me, officially. More important, why did Keion react so strongly when he heard her name? I pondered those questions for as long as I could keep going as we all lay there in silence. It wasn't very long, though, till I fell into exhausted slumber and dreamed about dark-cloaked men following me off of perilous cliffs and falling to their own deaths, heartily accompanied to their doom by my screams.

A Day For Dogs

I slowly came to, the aroma of bacon filling my nose with happiness.

Mmm, bacon....

There's nothing quite like waking up to the smell of bacon and Momma's coffee. I laid there for several minutes, sniffing the air with my eyes closed, memories filling in my vision.

Eventually I *had* to open my eyelids, though. As much as I didn't want to leave the warmth and comfort of the bed, the need to go to the bathroom snagged my attention and then grew to a dull, throbbing pain.

Seph's elbow to my midsection didn't help.

"Thanks, Cousin."

"What? Oh, sorry. I wasn't quite awake yet."

"Me neither. Dibs on the bathroom, wherever it might be."

"Outside, around to the right. Make sure you wear something warm, though. It's a frigid one this morning!" a voice chirped from over near where I could hear the spattering of bacon grease. A glance confirmed that Blodwyn was making a huge pan of the thin slices of heaven.

After the weirdness of the evening before, which in turn had fueled weird dreams about being eaten alive by large, grey potted plants named Blodwyn, I wasn't sure whether to trust the bacon or not. That, or the coffee. Or anything else, for that matter. One thing I had to trust, though, was her instruction on how to get to the outhouse.

I didn't really have much choice in that matter.

Now, if you've never used an outhouse in freezing weather, you'll have to take my word for it: it's a horrible experience to be avoided at all costs. I mean, it's better than the other alternatives, but it's really strange, frightening, and literally chilling to bare certain parts of your body to that kind of cold, especially once the outside air gusts up between your bare legs. I was glad to see that Blodwyn's outhouse had a seat cut out of some sort of soft spongy material, so it wasn't as miserable as the bare wood itself would've been, but still–just, take my word for it, and don't.

I giggled to myself as I left the outhouse and saw the line to get in. Seph was the next up for the frozen butt award, followed closely by a grumpy-looking Keion, with a glaring Aerona right behind. Apparently both the need and the morning grumpiness were universal.

Of course, since I'd gotten to the outhouse first, I got back inside first. I went over to the bustling cook, who was still smiling widely. "Can I help?"

"Sure!" she said, more cheerful than anyone had a right to be that early in the morning. "Would you mind setting the table?"

I began to wonder about my strange, dangerous dreams, and also about Keion's reaction. Blodwyn seemed to be as perfect a hostess as they come–nice, chipper, sweet, and so on.

Once I'd finished setting the table, Blodwyn asked, "Is Alis doing okay this morning? She slept restlessly last night."

I panicked for a second, with no idea who she was asking about. Then I remembered Keion's made-up names, and though I couldn't remember exactly, it seemed like Alis was one of them. Which one didn't really matter, as I made up a neutral answer: "She's fine, I think. We haven't talked much yet."

"Ah," she chirped back. "And so would you like some coffee?"

"No," Keion answered for me, coming to stand behind my shoulder. "Thank you, kind Blodwyn, but we really should be heading out to find Cai and arrange for our passage back to Ganolog."

"We can send word asking Master Cai to hold off his departure for a moment or two, though."

"No, thank you. I've met my share of merchants, and if he did delay his departure for us, I'm sure any of his fellows would take that out on us."

"That's too bad, but you are probably right. Some bacon, at least?"

"Thank you," Keion said as he politely lifted a few slices from the tray and held them out away from his body as he put his pack on. Seph came in from looking after Booboo at that moment and, ranger that she is, immediately picked up on Keion's body language. She handed me my pack and grabbed her own.

"No, thanks," Seph turned down the offered meat. "My stomach is a little turned around from the freezing last night. Thank you for giving us a warm place to sleep, though."

"And these fine cloaks," I added. Blodwyn had insisted on pulling out a few of her old cloaks and giving them to us, and no matter what danger she did or didn't pose to us, the weather would be a greater danger without them.

"Yes, we do appreciate your hospitality," Keion said, and I murmured something similar as we walked out the door.

We were halfway down the row of homes before anyone dared to speak. Only when the coast was obviously clear did Keion hiss under his breath, "Princess, next time I go to the trouble of making up names for us on the fly, could you at least try to remember them?"

"What do you mean?"

"You were Bron, Sephaline was Elen, and I was Megan," Aerona's somber voice sounded over my shoulder. "There wasn't any Alis."

"Oh. She was testing me, wasn't she?"

"Hmm. Ya think?" Keion said, giving me a glum look.

"Hey, that's *my* sarcasm face. You can't use it."

"I can, and I did. And, I should add, even better than you do."

"What's done is done," Seph said wearily. "I really did sleep poorly last night, so perhaps you two royals could try to avoid irritating my headache even more than it already is."

"Sorry, Seph," I apologized, and then turned back to Keion. In a whisper, I asked, "So who is she, to scare you like that?"

"Glad you asked, Princess. After the battle of the library, your father's men were able to question a few of the surviving Cult of the Wyrm members. While they didn't get much that was very useful, the name Blodwyn the Grey was brought up by more than one person as a senior leader up in the north."

"So once again I managed to walk right in to the net of someone who wants to kill me."

"Technically, no. The Cult doesn't want you dead, remember?" Keion asked, giving me a half-smile.

"Right. That was what the librarians were telling me, right before they tried to kill me."

"Well, okay, *they* did, but they couldn't get over the part of the prophecy that said you were going to burn their library down. I can see a librarian getting a little bit extreme in his methods over that, myself. It's too bad the only full copy of the prophecy burned with the library, or else we could see what other exciting predictions it has in store for you."

"I know," I lied. While the battle was raging, I'd slipped the prophecy scroll and a book on magic into a bag which was now safely hidden in my room back at the castle. That was a secret that even Seph didn't know, though.

"What else did the Cult members say, Keion?" Seph asked.

"That they weren't trying to kill the princess."

"Who were they trying to kill, then?"

Keion caught Seph's light sarcasm and chortled quietly, his apparent happiness making me wonder how he could pick the worst mornings to be in the best moods. Then he replied, "They weren't trying to kill anybody. What they want is to protect and control the princess."

"Protect?" I asked.

"From unsavory influences."

"Oh. I'm sure they're not the only ones," I muttered.

He shrugged. "Probably not. But they're the most active at it. At first they just wanted you to go home. Now that you're so well established along the path to succession, their goal is to guide you into not fulfilling the prophecy. Apparently they're really worked up about the idea that you'll bring magic back to the realm."

"Magic never left," I interjected.

"I know that, but they fear its possible return to mainstream use. As do most of us, I should add," he said.

"Yes, I am painfully aware of that. In the questioning, did anybody find out what this wyrm thing is?"

"A wyrm is a dragon," he said, looking at me like I'd asked a stupid question.

"Thanks. Now tell me something I didn't already know."

"That is as much as I know, actually, oh mighty Dragon Queen."

Right. Dragon Queen. I didn't feel like much of a Dragon Queen, dragon-shaped birth mark or no. Didn't feel like much of a queen at all, honestly, after what was obviously a foolish expedition into the northlands got a loyal guard killed, and nearly took my friends and me with him. But my father had been pretty firm that the only way he'd be able to "retire" from his own rulership and cross back to Earth to live with his beloved, my momma, was for me to go through with the succession thing. Seph and Aerona already knew about the birth mark, though, and Prince Charming didn't need to know, so I just grunted and kept trudging down the street.

Cai wasn't hard to find. When I heard Blodwyn talk about dog sledding, I'd imagined a few, or maybe as many as half a dozen, cute white furballs with tongues out, all jumping around playfully. Having seen it in the movie *Balto*, I was really looking forward to meeting a dog sled team up close and personal.

Reality wasn't at all like that, though. We loped around a corner to see one of the noisiest, most chaotic scenes I've ever been in. Far from cute little white fluffy puppies, there were dozens of sled dogs, each of them big, rangy, and snarling. The ones who had noticed our approach were snarling–at us. The rest were yipping and howling and snarling at each other, and generally raising a ruckus. They were all on chains, too, each staked into a circle that wasn't quite big enough to reach any of the other dogs.

"Ah, visitors!" a stooped elf called from near the front of the long leather line that stretched down the road. He stopped whatever it was that he was doing and ambled over toward us. "Comet! Genen! Tino! Shut up! Back! Back, you!" he yelled as he jumped aggressively toward the dogs that were snarling. He pointed his finger at each, and each in turn lowered its head and backed away.

"Sorry, sorry. I've trained 'em to warn away thieves on the trail, and it's just impossible to teach 'em to behave different here in the yard. They listen to me, though, even if only by barely, and so you're not in any real danger. Oh, no, not my team! They're all excited, see, since they all know we'll be hittin' the trail soon." He thrust a gnarled hand out toward Keion. "Old Trader Cai, at your service. You lookin' for somethin' to buy, I'm the guy."

"Eonil," Keion replied, taking Cai's hand in an awkward-looking Earth-style shake. "My companions Elen, Megan, and *Bron*." He said my alias noticeably louder than the rest, and then Prince Charming leaned in toward the old trader and whispered, just loud enough that I could hear, "she's a little bit slow, you know, but she's good with a bow and arrow nonetheless."

"Oh, yes," Cai said, nodding and glancing at me through the side of his eyes. "We got our share of those up here, son," he whispered back.

I told myself to remember to punch Prince Charming as soon as we were in a private setting, bless his blackened little heart.

"We're a little out of our normal place up here," Keion continued, and Cai cut him off with a nod.

"I'c'n see that, you southerners up here without a stitch of good clothin' on, just wearin' Blodwyn's old cloaks. Talkin' like southerners, too. You're lookin' for a ride down south, aren't you?"

"We are. We're all pretty good with our weapons, and wouldn't mind helping load and unload as well."

Cai made a production out of sizing each of us up and down, looking at our packs and our bows, and then at our hands. He snerked a little when he looked at mine, which admittedly weren't nearly as calloused as the others, but instead of a comment he just shook his head and went on. At the same time I got a close look at him, though. Despite the rough speech, I saw a pair of wise old eyes peering out from under a furry cap with funny-looking floppy ear covers. His face had more lines on it than a road map. He was working in the cold with neither cloak nor coat on, and so I was able to see a wiry body that had still some strength left in it despite the hunch of his shoulders.

"You've seen a few runs, haven't you, cutie?" he asked when he got to Aerona.

The guard responded by flicking a dagger out of a hidden belt sheath and using its very sharp tip to scrape a fleck of dirt from under a fingernail.

"Well, you do look like you'c'n carry your weight, and the weihr could use a good run. But wait—how'm I to know you're not gonna kill me once we get out on the trail?" he asked Keion, who had become the leader of our party in Cai's eyes.

"The same way we know you're not going to kill us once we get to sleep. I'm pretty good at reading people, and I think we can trust you. You seem to be a pretty good trader, and so I bet you're better at reading people than you're letting on, aren't you?"

The flattery worked well. Cai knuckled his chest in a more familiar northern greeting, smiled, and said, "Well, welcome aboard. You kids finish loadin' them boxes ont'the sled over there while I go get the weihr ready."

"What's a weihr?" I asked once our voices were safely hidden behind the din of excited dog barking.

Keion sent a questioning look Seph's way. She shrugged. He replied as he hefted a box onto the platform of the sled, "A legend, or at least I would have said so before today. Stories tell of the great and powerful northern clans swooping off the shelf on the backs of mighty wolf-mounts they called weihr, or warg, depending on who was speaking. They were as big as a horse, or even bigger, again depending on who was doing the telling. Some said that a few weihr, working together, could take down a wyvern, though that's really difficult to believe. But they haven't been seen in the south in thousands of years, and stories say they are all gone."

"Hmmph," Cai grunted from behind. "Southern stories are as weak's the southern bardds who tell'em. Why, your bardds don't even make their stories rhyme."

I ignored the insult, as did the rest of the group. It was impossible to do anything, in fact, but stare agape at the magnificent beasts behind Cai. The three weihr—they really were very large dogs with thick, rough, grey fur—stood as tall as the horses we'd left behind at the ley-gate. Each looked at us fiercely through eyes that spoke of a scary level of intelligence.

I looked around and asked, "Where are the saddles?"

Cai looked at me incredulously, snickered, and whispered to Keion, "You're right." He turned to me and said, "Bron, we don't use saddles up here. You'cun'n put one on a weihr if you tried, and I'd strongly recommend agin' that. Their backs are perfectly good without saddles, anyway. Now, all of you are probably used to ridin' horses, so lemme tell you that the gaits of a weihr are very different from those of a horse. There's no uncomfortable trot, for one thing; these babies lope along perfectly smooth't any speed. They think, too, unlike any horses you've'er seen. They'll follow their pack leader—me—to the end of the earth, but don't you bother trying to tell this guy here to jump o'er a log or go a certain way around a bush. Won't listen; he just goes the way he think'is best. Got it?"

Seph asked what the weihr's names were, and her question received a similar response: "Weihr don't get names. They don'- come when called. They're *not* horses," Cai said after a snicker.

We lined up, one beside each beast, as Cai tightened a series of ropes over his cargo and double-checked the knots.

"What's in the boxes?" Keion asked.

"Stuff. Boy, don'e'er ask a merchant what's in his boxes. Might make him a little suspicious of your motives, if y'get me."

"I get you."

"Good. Now help me get the dogs in line."

In *Balto,* I remembered seeing teams of six or eight dogs, and somehow I'd thought that was reality. I was shocked, then, to watch Keion and Cai wrestle seventeen of the chained beasts onto the large sled's long harness, forming eight pairs of two with Cai's favorite by itself out in front.

"Been m'lead dog for nearly four decades," Cai said to Keion as the ancient man guided the very excited dog with pure white fur over to the front of the line. "She'c'n make the trip all the way to Ganolog and back without a single word from me."

"Four decades? Dogs don't live that long," I whispered to Seph.

"When bonded with a ranger, they do," she whispered back, a shocked expression on her face. "It shouldn't, I suppose, surprise me to learn that Cai started out as a ranger. It would make trail-riding both easier and more enjoyable, after all."

"But why would you become a merchant when you could be a ranger?" I asked.

"He probably sleeps in the nicest inns in every town across Kiirajanna, Alyssa. Have you seen where we rangers normally sleep?"

"I have, but I thought you preferred sleeping that way."

"We say we do."

"Moun'up!" Cai yelled, and we did obediently. Keion held my weihr steady as I climbed up onto its back, making me want to hit him just a little bit less in spite of the comment about me being slow. Then he leaped onto the front of the sled and nodded to Cai.

"Ayeeyee!" the old merchant's voice trilled, and his team leaped to action in response. As one unit, seventeen dogs started barking and pulling, and the huge sled full of boxes shot forward like a rocket with Cai standing up at its rear whooping like a teenager. Keion nearly rolled off, a sight that made me giggle for the briefest of moments, but then, without urging, the weihr lunged after their pack leader. The jolt caused a few startled whoops from us, too. Before we knew it the town, and its Cult chief Blodwyn the Grey, were far behind us.

CYTHRUDDO

to irritate. I'm glad I learned that word before I met Charming.

A Contentious Ride

The din at the start of the ride was soon left behind and forgotten. Once the dogs started running, concentration and physical effort took over and they quietened down. Soon the only sound we heard was the whooshing of the wind, the rapid poofs of the padded rise and fall of the weihrs' feet, and the steady shhhhh sound from the sled's runners gliding across the snow.

The path we followed down out of the foothills proved both bumpy and winding. The river bed we followed was the same one we'd walked to Abergarhewi on. We crossed it every so often as the open area shifted from one bank to the other. It seemed pretty well frozen, and the weihrs' thick, padded feet had plenty of traction, so after the first nervous crossing I stopped worrying and started to enjoy the ride.

Cai hadn't lied. The weihrs' gate was much smoother than that of a horse. They managed to lope along with their riders held perfectly steady while still moving fast enough to keep up with the sled. I thought of all the archery practice I'd enjoyed from the back of Awel and realized what a significant advantage a team of archers on the back of weirh would have.

I couldn't help wondering what it would take to get a herd, or whatever you call a group, of weihr for Cysegredig once I was queen.

At one point I yelled across to ask Seph how Booboo was doing, since her familiar was staying back behind us to avoid exciting the dogs too much. She stuck her tongue out at me. "You shouldn't ask if a wolverine can keep up with dogs," she replied.

"I'll remember that next time I'm talking to a wolverine!" I called back. I should've known the answer without asking, of course; Booboo had kept up with three galloping horses as we'd plunged forward through a host of dire wolves and ravens to make it through the blight that surrounded the library. Of course he could keep up with a dog sled team, though to be honest the dogs were managing what seemed like an unbelievably rapid pace.

We stopped every couple of hours to rest. The dogs didn't seem to need it or want it, but Cai insisted on keeping a very disciplined schedule. When it was time for him to pull the team to a stop, he'd first wave his right hand to let us know he was halting while trilling out something that sounded like "oleo" over and over. He then thrust a long, sharp brake hook slowly into the snow, and that would bring the team to a halt and anchor them there while he jumped out and, by himself at first and with Keion later, skipped rapidly down the line of dogs, checking their feet and their breathing on the way. On the way back he dropped a little food in front of each one, and with it, a little hunk of what looked like uncooked bacon.

I asked, and the old merchant explained, "Moose fat."

"Why fat in addition to the regular dried meat?" I asked, curious.

He nodded and explained, "Well, now, that's an awfully good question for a southerner t'ask. It's a whole lot smarter'n, 'where's the saddles,' anyway. The dried meat is their main diet, while the fat gets metabolized quicker'n so it gives them a much faster burst of energy and warmth. When you're runnin' trail like we are, the fat's a requirement."

Cai slowed his routine down the first time to show Keion how to check the dogs and the lead line. He was obviously an old pro, making it up and down the line quickly and efficiently, with every movement having a purpose. He also seemed to enjoy the chance to teach Charming, who in turn actually beamed with pleasure at the lessons. I marveled at the change from arrogant young prince to eager dog handler, and a glance told me Seph was wondering the same.

As we raced both southward and downhill the snow got a little bit lighter, though it still covered everything in a thin blanket of white. It was spectacularly beautiful; each of the pines looked just like they'd been flocked for Christmas. I was glad for the independence of the weihr I was riding, since it let me ignore guiding the beast in favor of swiveling my gaze from left to right to take in all of the beauty.

The silence of the ride let my mixed emotions have full, raging control over my mind. On one hand, riding a weihr through a winter wonderland was a treat I'd probably never be able to experience again. I wondered if Momma would even believe me when I told her about the majesty and beauty of it. On the other, Llew was still missing, Padrig was bound to be furious at us, and worse than anything else, Gerallt was still dead, his corpse laying abandoned somewhere along a frozen river bed. Was that what being a queen was going to mean? Was I to let people serve me right to death, just to abandon them in the name of my own safety?

The sun was half down past the horizon as we pulled up to a little ranger shack. I was glad to see it, as the action of stopping finally silenced all the voices berating myself in my own head. Nothing fancy, it had thicker walls than the other shacks Seph, Keion, and I had stopped at, but it was still the same basic overnight shelter for roving professionals. Inside by the door, a stack of firewood and tinder awaited.

Cai got right to lighting the wood stove. "Let's don'burn too much, since we'll have to replace it'n the mornin' before we'c'n leave. One thing you folks from down south don't ever realize is the importance of fire up here," he growled at us while he lit the tinder. "Down off the Rim it's uncommon practice, but up here everybody always leaves enough firewood inside for'th'next person. Once the snow flies it gets darker quicker, and it's really hard to find enough to burn through the night then. If you don't have enough wood to keep the stove going all night, well, too bad fer'ya. A person can go a night up here without food or water, but a night without fire and you won't see the mornin' sun, not ever."

"Earlier you said that we talk like southerners," Keion observed. "What does that mean?"

"You talk different, that's what it means. Don't feel bad; I do too. I get that way from travels elsewhere."

"How so? Blodwyn sounded weird, kind of strange, but I never figured out what it was."

"That's it, exactly. 'I never figured it out.' I, I, I. Pobl'yr-hew don't use a singular first person. There's no room for any I up here. To survive, we need all'f'us."

"I'd noticed that, but I wasn't sure if it was just how Blodwyn spoke. So tell me, Trader Cai, do you always stop at this cabin on your way south, or are there other cabins about?" Seph asked while she put together a ranger stew from the stuff in her backpack.

"Almos' never stop here," Cai said. "We usually push on through the night so that we can make town around noon. Gettin' there in the evening makes another day wasted. Besides, the trail gets pretty by moonlight."

"We don't have to stop on our account," Keion said. "We're perfectly capable of riding on."

"It's not you, though I can't say I've got much confidence that the thin one o'er there can sit a saddle all night," he said, pointing at me. I opened my mouth to protest but he kept going, "It's the season I worry about. The river's frozen o'er, but the ice isn't thick yet. Can't tell how solid it is in'the dark, and I don't wan'the dogs—us neither—crashin' through into the icy water. The wet added t'the cold will get you just like that," he snapped his fingers to illustrate, "and in the freezin' darkness with a fresh snow blanket all'round, who knows who'd be able t'build a fire quick enough to save your life?"

"I read a story once about a guy who tried to build a fire in the snowy wilderness," I said, and Cai snorted.

"I've lived more stories than you could possibly've read, girl. Just you stay with me, and old Cai'll keep you safe till you get home to your parents."

I glowered, and Keion chose that moment to duck toward the door.

"Gotta go? This shed's got a nice outhouse. I'll show you where't is," Cai said and walked out with him, leaving us three girls alone.

"Outhouse?" I asked Seph. "The other ranger sheds haven't had outhouses."

Seph shrugged. "I'm sure that it's an awful lot easier to dig a single large hole while the ground isn't frozen." She stroked Booboo's head, and the wolverine actually snorted in pleasure. I smiled; Cai had been the one to suggest she bring the wolverine inside for the night to get it out of the cold; his own dogs, he explained, were used to it.

A couple of minutes later the old trader walked back through the door and sat down next to the fire, looking directly at me. "Why did you feel the need t'lie to poor old Cai, Crown Princess?"

Aerona moved incredibly fast, but he had his hands up in the air by the time she reached him with twin daggers. "Hey, hey, I'm not threatening anybody. Can you put the stickers away, please?" He moved his body back gently, putting a much safer-looking inch or two distance between her daggers' points and his Adam's apple. "I'm just—well, hurt that you'd lie to me about who you were."

"How'd you know?" Seph asked, her eyebrows arched in suspicion.

"He told me," Cai said, pointing at the door that he and Keion had left through. "I was just showing him where the out-house was, and he came right out with it. Felt guilty for having to lie to me, he said. He's a good, honest man, the prince is. Honesty is a good thing to have in a ruler, don't you think?"

Footsteps crunched the snow outside, and Cai shushed us. "Shh, don't tell him I told you, please. I wanted you to know that I knew, though, and to tell you what an honor it is to have you all with me."

Keion entered the cabin to find us all quietly sipping from cups of hot tea that Seph had brewed. He took a cup for himself and sat down, his expression guilty and brooding, his eyes darting from Cai to me and back. The setting remained completely silent until after we'd each eaten a bowl of Seph's stew, at which point Seph excused herself to visit the privy. I, and then Aerona, jumped up to join her.

"Can you believe that son of a gun? That lying sack of bliss-fully boiled peanuts with less sense than a hound dog's got fleas. He just up and told that trader who we were," I swore quietly as we trudged through the snow.

"Actually, Princess, I'm not quite ready to believe that the prince is guilty," Aerona murmured.

"What are you talking about?" I demanded.

"Look, Alyssa," Seph intervened, "while you and Keion haven't always seen eye to eye, he's always been on your side. And I do mean always, literally. It was he who recognized Blodwyn's name, and he came up with the fake names in the first place. While I, also, want to know how the trader figured out who we really are, I'd prefer to at least hear Keion's side of the story before we accuse him of betraying us."

"Oh. Right." She *was* right. I felt like an idiot for jumping to the conclusion I had, but I still couldn't bring myself to fully trust Keion.

"Plus, did you notice the change in Cai's speech? He went from a rough, weird drawl to sounding like he'd just come from the castle. We need to keep a close watch tonight," Seph said.

"I will–" Aerona started, but Seph cut her off.

"No, you will not. You didn't sleep well last night, and two nights in a row with a lack of sleep makes an incredibly bad guard. We'll split the watch, thank you. Alyssa, you can feign inability to sleep for an hour or two, and so you'll take first shift. Wake me up and I'll take second watch. Since Aerona is intent upon suffering, I'll wake her up for the third watch. Aerona, you wake up Keion. Okay?"

I looked at my cousin for a minute, impressed again at how much she'd grown since the days she'd stood solidly behind me after uttering her battle cry, *meep*. "That's okay by me," I said.

Aerona looked like she wanted to grumble a little more, but instead she just pointed to the door of the privy. "Your turn first, Princess."

****

"Good morning," I said to Keion as he held my weihr's shaggy fur so I could jump onto the beast's back more easily. I put as much happiness as I could into my greeting, but a night in a drafty cabin and a guard shift that I wasn't used to pulling, followed by a quick, cold breakfast of more hard bread and cheese, made me about as chipper as a giraffe with a sore throat.

He smiled, sort of, his grin reaching almost all the way up to his eyes as he said, "Good morning. I hope you slept some of your grumpiness out."

"What grumpiness would that be?" I challenged, keeping up with the sweet voice.

"What grumpiness? You glared at me all night. Kind of a–" and he demonstrated with the most twisted version of a glare I could imagine.

"I did not. Did I?" I asked. I hadn't meant to glare at Keion, despite the fact that I still worried he'd ratted us out to the merchant, who as far as we knew could easily be best buds with Blodwyn. The prince nodded, and to clear the air I opened my mouth to tell him just exactly why I might have been glaring.

"Dawn's not far off, but the town still is," Cai's voice chimed as he walked up to us, cutting through the conversation Keion and I still had brewing. "You kids going to be ready to go today?"

I nodded, and Keion broke away to stand ready near the sled. Cai was right about one thing, I figured. There would be plenty of time to chat once we got there, but the morning was already brightening, and the sun would be up soon, and so we needed to get on our way.

The morning's ride went by quickly and quietly. Cai and Keion managed to have a quiet, lengthy conversation on the back of the sled, but the rest of us plodded along silently. I wasn't able to hear anything being discussed by the guys, and I wasn't sure I wanted to, anyway. The scenery was breathtakingly beautiful, though. Once the sun was fully up we saw the land flattening out ahead of us. We were still on a gradual downward slope just like the one we'd covered the day before, but by the time the sun was nearing its peak we turned away from the river and settled in to a steady run across flat, open field. At about that same time, the snow quit its job as ground cover, only appearing in small clumps.

Suddenly we seemed to turn the calendar back from winter to fall.

We broke briefly for lunch, Keion and Cai sitting quietly to one side of a hastily-built fire and us girls to the other. To call it awkward would be an understatement. It was so quiet that we could hear each other chewing on the sausage and cheese bites we'd pulled from our packs. The three of us on my side of the fire spent most of our time avoiding eye contact with the men. Cai ate quietly, flashing a big, happy smile at anyone he caught looking his way, while Keion glared his normal shadowed expression. The prince seemed to be trying to use his stare to bore a hole right through my being.

"Time t'be off!" Cai finally ended our nonverbal feud with a cheerful call. I couldn't help gaping briefly before I managed to school my face again; it was like the old trader had absolutely no idea what was going on among the rest of us.

Keion obviously had an idea, though. He sprang to his feet, sent an audible grunt of displeasure our direction, and then stamped off toward the sled, leaving us to mount the weihr by ourselves. Seph returned the favor with a quiet grunt in his direction while Aerona helped me onto the massive beast's back and then leaped into her own spot.

The sun was setting off to the right by the time Gidreffydd finally came into view. "It's a good thing we got here when we did," Cai called to us all, raising his voice to a surprisingly powerful level for a slight old man. "They shut the gates after dark, and if you're not in by then, you're not in at all till mornin'. Trust me, it's much more comfortable within than out. There's an inn here that I always frequent, and given the time of year, I'm sure Delyth'll have a couple of empty rooms for us to bed down for'th'night. I can do my trades first thing tomorrow morning and be off for Ganolog tomorrow afternoon. How's that for a plan?"

"Great," I called through the still, frigid evening air. I didn't try very hard to raise my own voice, but it carried well enough. Sound seemed to travel farther, faster, and crisper in the cold, and so I heard Seph's and Aerona's agreement clearly also.

Truth be told, after Blodwyn's pallet and a ranger shack of the far north, I was looking forward to a comfortable bed.

I was going to have a good night. I only wished I could tell what Cai was up to.

Delyth's Inn

As we neared the gates of Gidreffydd, I noticed the silver dragon pendant on my chest warming up. That was a sensation that I'd come to regard as a bad sign. At the library, when the pendant had healed me, the magical flow through it caused it to get warm. Later, when I'd used it to heal Seph and Keion, it had similarly heated up. As we fell from the cliff, and I blossomed the protective force field out around us, Draignerthol had actually gotten uncomfortably hot. I wasn't trying to work any magic, though, and the northern air in my face made the rest of me shiver in spite of the cloak I was wrapped in, so the warmth against my chest puzzled me.

I finally managed to figure it out as we closed on the settlement. The vertical logs of the town's walls glowed a faint blue light that grew more distinct the nearer we got. It was similar to the hazy blue I'd seen around the logs of Ganolog's fortification, suggesting the same "earth magic," so to speak. Still, here, it was just a little different–warmer, stronger. It felt more energetic–almost virile–and if such a thing could be, it actually felt hostile.

I thought back to my study of the tome on magic that I'd brought from the library. In it, the author described what, in the olden days, had been a simple, new initiate trick: divination of magical flow. I followed the author's description of the process, letting my mind relax and gazing at the wall through half-open eyes. It was difficult to do just right while riding on the back of a horse-sized wolf, but the smoothness of the lope at least made it possible. Finally, a feeling washed over me— strong, active, protection, almost in a preemptive strike sort of way—and I knew I had my answer.

Somebody had lain down a spell of super-protection on the walls of Gidreffydd. Even considering the town's status as a trade hub, that was strange.

"Good evening, Bran. So good to see you again," our merchant host called out into the deepening shadows as we pulled up to the closed gate. I was confused; I didn't see anybody there.

"Master Cai? I'd heard you were expected to arrive soon," a large man said as he stepped out of a guard shack while slipping a dark, gleaming kettle hat on. "Good to meet you again. Let me just do my regular checks, and we'll let you in where it's nice and warm and dry." He creaked and clanked as he lumbered; in the twilight I couldn't see much detail, but I caught a glint of metal from inside of his dark cloak.

"Does the Mistress Delyth have any rooms for rent this evening?" Cai asked, his voice quieter and much more casual than the one he'd used upon our approach.

"She should, she should. Not much custom this way, though—oh, my—uh—um, Master Cai, is your—are you, good sir, are you Prince Keion?"

"I see I am known even up here," Keion's voice sang out through the now-useless hood of the cloak that apparently failed to obscure his features enough.

Arrogant jerk, I thought. He'd gotten onto me for forgetting the names he'd gone to so much trouble to make up, and yet at the first chance to be fawned over, he sang his presence out.

"And the ladies behind you—they're not your sisters, are they, Your Highness?"

"Are you kidding? My sisters would never ride on a weihr. They're too well-bred." I bristled at the underhanded insult to my father as well as to me, but my fear about the danger we were in kept my mouth shut. I'd make him pay for it eventually, somehow. Meanwhile, I glanced over at Cai to read his face in the torchlight, but if the merchant chose to be insulted by Keion's comment he didn't show it.

"Of course, Prince Keion. It was too much of a grand coincidence to ask for, I suppose, hoping for seven royals in town instead of five."

"Five?" I asked, pressing my mount forward. Keion tossed a warning look back my way that made my blood boil, but I obeyed and backed off to let him continue all on his own.

"What my companion is trying to say is that it is unusual to run into peers, especially out here in this ruggedly remote area. If I may ask, who else is in town?" Keion asked.

"Of course you may ask, Your Highness. The four mighty bens of the northern realms are in town, and they are currently holding council at Master Synod's place. It will be my pleasure to let them know that you here to meet with them, my prince, and to arrange for them to pay their respects to you at Mistress Delyth's inn as well."

"No, no. I am profoundly pleased at the level of honor you show my household, my good man, but there is no need for that, I assure you. I am passing through on my way to Ganolog with Master Cai and his guards. It is merely a wonderful coincidence."

"But–" both the guard and our merchant argued, and Keion cut them both off.

"No, I must insist not. Master Merchant Cai, do you have any idea how much time we would lose in the honorable and ceremonial greetings due between peers? Perhaps, if it fits your plans to remain an extra couple of days in the hospitality of Mistress Delyth's inn, then we may enjoy such a court, but it was my understanding that your desire was to continue your trade mission as quickly as possible."

Cai nodded, and then the guard nodded once in agreement.

"Please, my good man, not a word, as I would not wish to offer perceived insult to the mighty bens with the lack of an official greeting. We simply do not have time to avail ourselves of the pleasures of a formal reception," Keion finished and then faded back away from the guard.

With that, we were ushered through the town gates just before they closed for a final time of the night. Cai drove his team up the main–and only–street of town. As we followed I looked around to see pretty much the same thing I'd seen in Ganolog–brown mud covering brown walls with brown trim. The northerners just liked brown, I supposed as Cai stopped us in front of a larger than usual building. I looked at it curiously, wondering about its lack of sign or any indication that it could be an inn. The elves weren't big on signs anywhere we'd been, but it seemed weird to be expected to know that this building was Mistress Delyth's Inn without any exterior statement or advertisement.

Cai led us in through a pair of stout wooden doors while a couple of thickly-cloaked handlers closed in on the dogs and led them around the side of the building. Inside was a large room that could easily have been a movie setting for a Middle Ages common room back on Earth. Its rough plank floor held up several tables, all hand-made and none the same size. The chairs looked hand-made also, with backs that were a jumble of branches and seats hewn from round ends of logs.

As the doors closed behind us, I couldn't help but notice the smell. I'm not sure if the rank combination of old beer and mold was a Middle Ages common room thing, or just a far north elf tavern thing, but the stink got to me quickly. It was all I could do to keep from pulling my cloak up over my nose and mouth.

Across the room from the doors stood a simple bar made from another rough-hewn plank, its surface stained from years of alcohol and–well, other stuff that I didn't want to think about. Unlike the bars I'd seen in the movies, this one didn't have any of the fancy maraschino cherries and lemon wedges and stuff. It was just a hunk of wood with a few steins turned upside down on it. Behind it, a slender elf stood watching us.

He didn't really have much of a choice, I guess. We were the only people in the room, a fact that both comforted and bothered me. Cai didn't seem to care, though, as he walked between the empty tables directly up to the bar and nodded grandly in greeting. "Good day, Master Dai," he said. "We're just in from a long ride down the slope. Does Mistress Delyth have anywhere a tired party can rest for the evening?"

The elf fixed Cai with a stern glare that didn't seem very authentic, but then after a couple of heartbeats he caved, frown turning into a broad smile. "I'm fairly sure you can take your pick of the rooms upstairs, you old codger, but if I don't give you the chance to ask her yourself I'll be in the weihr-house all night. Delyth! Come here, darling! You'll never guess what the wind just blew in through our door!"

Delyth stepped into the room.

Okay, now, look, I'm a little embarrassed to admit that I was expecting a plump, aproned, middle-age lady wearing copious amounts of flour in her hair and on her cheeks. You can't find a fantasy book with an inn where the innkeeper's wife isn't pleasantly plump, and aproned, and covered in cooking mess, after all. Old stereotypes die hard, is all I'm saying. I was, however, disappointed; she wasn't what I expected. The woman who walked in was even leaner than her husband. She didn't seem to have an ounce of fat on her, in fact. At least part of the stereotype played out, though; both members of the pair were, in fact, obviously middle-aged. Still, both looked like they could easily run a marathon tomorrow morning if they wanted.

"Why, you scoundrel!" she cried as she ran up and gave Cai a tight hug, an unusually personal gesture in elf society. Then again, I had no idea what practices served the far-northerners, so it could have been perfectly normal. The queen's Lady had briefed me on social expectations within Ganolog, but we were as far away from that capital fortification, both distance-wise and customs-wise, as I could imagine getting. Besides, I couldn't picture the queen herself ever coming anywhere near little Gidreffydd.

Some day they'd probably be saying that about me, I realized.

"You've avoided darkening our door for much too long, stranger," she chided the merchant.

He shrugged. "Business before pleasure, Delyth. You know that."

"Business, I understand, but you're a traveling merchant, Cai. You've never stayed away for this long. What kind of business keeps you running like you have been?"

"Oh," Cai paused, looking away at the wall before answering, "stuff. Just making runs for people, you know. Folks want me to go south to pick things up for them, and if the pay is right, this old merchant does. It's been a very busy summer, you know, what with—um, things going on. But I'm back now."

"Well, I certainly am glad to see you back here. I missed you, Cai. Do you and your team need a drink?"

"No, thank you. The kids with me might, but I need to be getting to bed. Long ride today, and a very long day in store for tomorrow."

"That's fine, dear. You two boys can take the first room down the hall, and the girls the second. I just put fresh linens in, and there's plenty of spare pillows and blankets in the wardrobe in each room."

Dai added, "And please, once you're settled, somebody come back down for a drink or two. You'll be my only customers tonight."

"We wouldn't want to disappoint the good man, would we?" I asked Keion as we hauled our backpacks up the flight of stairs. I really wanted a chance to corner Prince Charming without Cai around to hear it, and it sounded like a great opportunity to do just that.

"Oh, I probably would," he said in a droll voice. "I'm pretty tired, too."

"I'm sure the trip has been just exhausting for you. It's a good thing, though. I'm pretty certain you couldn't keep up with us girls in drinking."

"I'm pretty certain you just got yourself a challenge, little lady," he replied, and I tried hard to hide a grin. When all else failed, I knew I could always appeal to that part of him.

The room upstairs continued with the old stereotypical Middle Age guest room theme, even down to the three straw pallets on wooden box frames that we were supposed to call beds. Bare walls and a complete lack of closet space other than the tiny wardrobe stuffed full of old bedding finished off a perfectly dreary picture. It did smell better than the bar, but not by much.

"Anything I should check this for?" I asked, pointing toward one of the beds.

"Like what?" Seph asked, hefting her bag onto the end of another bed to claim it as hers.

"Like, I don't know. Bugs, maybe? Fleas? Ticks? Mites? Tarantulas of princess-killing?"

"You'll be fine," Aerona said. "An inn like this should be treated for bugs regularly. Now, are you going back down to the common room to challenge that impetuous boy to a drinking game or not? Because if you are, I want to be there to watch."

"Yes, I am, and I'm going right now. I have a word or two in mind for that boy. You coming, um–?" I asked Seph, realizing as I did that I'd forgotten her cover name completely. Granted, I'd probably already blown it, but at least I could try.

Seph could tell that I was searching for her name from my expression and the prompting gesture I gave her, but she just shook her head. We'd already talked on the ride about how we had to fear being overheard no matter where we were. It was important, then, for us to stay in character–even though that character had been shot in the head by Prince Charming's coming out at the gate. Still, we were determined to be good. She couldn't help with her name, so she just nodded and said, "Yes, of course I am."

"Well, then, let's go."

A Night of Drinking

Keion was already in the common room when we arrived. He raised his head, flicking his sable mane up over his eyes, and then gestured us over to his table. He'd chosen it well, back in the corner that was farthest away from both the bartender station and the outside entrance.

As we walked, I growled. I hated when he flicked his hair like that. Hated it, and hated my knees for their reaction to it.

Prince Charming raised his glass to us as we sat, and then signaled over to Dai for a drink for each of us. The bartender complied quickly, pouring foamless beer from a spigot in a large cask behind the bar into three mugs and then bringing them over to the table. I sniffed it, trying to appear to have a discerning palate, but really what I was hoping to do was cover up the smell of the room. It worked, mostly.

"On the house," Dai said. "Your master pays us enough when he's through that I couldn't justify charging his team for a few drinks. Enjoy, and just wave when you need a refill." He went back to where he'd been standing behind the bar and busied himself wiping steins down.

"How does Cai pay him?" I asked, switching to English to make sure we weren't being eavesdropped on. Not that there weren't a lot of people on Kiirajanna who could speak English, but I doubted we'd find them in a remote northern trading village. "I thought there wasn't any money in the realm."

Keion shot me a disgusted look and started to say something mean, but Seph cut him off with a glare of her own and then answered me. "He does stuff for them, probably. Deliveries to and from Ganolog, that kind of thing. The beer in your cup was probably delivered for free. That, or the cup itself, or both. Or he may bring Dai and Delyth treasures from his trips elsewhere that they use for their own private enjoyment—chocolates, fruits, and so on. You know, stuff that's hard to get up here."

"It's tough to get used to such a different system," I admitted. "Everything where I'm from has a price, and after you pay the price it's yours. That makes things so much more—well, regular, I guess."

Keion snorted, earning him another glare from Seph. I joined her this time, and so the handsome prince turned his face toward the wall and took a long drink from his beer.

Seph asked, "But how can it really be that regular? How does everything have the same price everywhere? Who sets the price?"

"No, no," I argued, wondering if my little bit of knowledge of how economics worked on Earth was up to the task of explaining it to an elf. "I suppose it's not—you know, I'm not sure, but I know that gas and food have different prices depending on where you go to buy them. Like, sometimes a gallon of gasoline," I paused, realizing that the English word wouldn't translate back to their experience in elvish, so I wasn't sure if Seph and the others would understand at all. I gestured at about how big a gallon jug would be, and when they nodded, I trudged on, "Well, it might be three dollars at one station, and three dollars and twenty cents at another station."

"Who determines the difference in prices, then?" Aerona asked, leaning forward. Her interest surprised me.

"Well, nobody, really. Each station owner sets his station's prices according to some logic that, to be honest, nobody's ever explained to me."

"But the trade is conducted immediately, and both parties are happy," Aerona said.

"Well, no. I mean, I guess the fuel station owner is happy, but the fuel purchaser rarely is."

"Why not?"

"Because it always seems to be too expensive. But you buy it anyway, because you have to have it."

"But the trade is conducted immediately?" Seph asked.

"Right. See, that's the benefit that using a currency gives us We don't have to wait for a trip to Ganolog to receive fair reward."

"So what you're saying is that you don't need personal honor in your system," Keion stated.

I felt myself getting frustrated. "Well, it's no longer my system, thank you, but yes, personal honor is required. Otherwise you get a poor credit score—um, trade score, I guess, is another word I could use for it."

"Trade score? Who keeps this trade score?" Seph asked.

"I don't know," I said. "Somebody. It's kept in a computer somewhere."

"But if transactions are conducted immediately, what might this trade score be based upon? Wealth? Bargaining power?" Aerona asked.

"No, it's—not all transactions are conducted immediately. When you try to purchase something that you don't have enough currency on hand for, they're consulted on whether or not you should be allowed to buy it."

Keion brought his focus back around to the table and said, "You know, in Alyssa's defense, my mother is from there, and she has also attempted to explain the system to me. I still can't help but believe that such a system sounds–stilted. Infantile, in fact. It's difficult for the sole purpose of being difficult, as though it were designed by a–how do you say it–*gwallgofddyn*."

Him saying it that way automatically got my dander up. "It's not infantile, nor was it designed by a lunatic. It's the way the system has evolved over time, thank you. And it works just fine."

"And yet you have to pay for everything in these–dollars, right? Okay, dollars, let's say for a drink in a tavern, regardless of how many dollars you had on you, right? And from what you're saying, and my mother has explained to me, in one tavern the beer in your hand might cost one dollar, and in another it might cost two? And if the tavern set the price as two dollars, but you only had one on you, then this–agency–would be consulted as to whether or not you should be allowed to have a beer?" Keion asked.

"Um, yeah, that's pretty much it, I think," I said. I had no idea what a beer cost in a bar, much less two different bars. Besides, I knew it was an oversimplification on the credit card thing, but there wasn't any way for me to explain it better. It wasn't like I'd ever owned a lot of credit cards, myself.

"That's not working fine. That's just lunaticky" he stated.

I shrugged. "Loony is the word you're looking for. And–okay. Fine. I'm not going to argue; that the system here is so much better is part of why I'm so happy to be here."

"Ah, yes. But would you still be happy to be here if you were not going to become our queen?"

"What?" Seph asked, jerking her eyes up from her beer. She seemed to have been enjoying it, but his statement really got to her.

"Why do you ask that?" I asked, more curious than offended.

His expression still completely unreadable, Keion shrugged and said, "Oh, nothing major. It's just that our well-traveled merchant has spent most of the day telling me that there are people all around Kiirajanna who are, more or less silently, hoping for tradition to change to bring the crown to Seren's head. Further, he tells me that scholars to the south have found a way, a passage in a tome that specifies circumstances to allow such a thing. He doesn't know what those circumstances are, however."

I stiffened. So that was why Keion had sat apart from us all day. Seren was Keion's older sister, the "first princess of Kiirajanna." She had been nice enough to me, at least to my face, and far more so than her younger sister Meriel ever had, but there still wasn't a lot of love lost there. Keion and Meriel, both, had outright told me that Seren would make a better queen than I could ever hope to, and to be perfectly honest, I had believed them.

I still sometimes did, in fact, even though the queen herself had said otherwise.

"That could get ugly," Seph murmured, and Aerona nodded. I could see why she'd say that. Were someone to push Seren onto the throne instead of me, I was pretty certain the current king and queen, and their corresponding armies, would try to stand against it. I had no idea where the leaders of the four clans would fall, but I could only guess that the people they governed would pull for Seren. That would pit an awful lot of elves against another awful lot of elves.

"It will be war," I mused, horrified at the mental images the thought brought to mind. My education so far included a great deal of the history of Kiirajanna, with the bloody warfare parts emphasized. They'd wanted to make sure I understood how bad military conflict could be when the warriors involved can put an arrow through a nickel a hundred or more yards away, and that didn't even include the dangers involved in using magic to fight. Patches of forest had been so devastated in the last major warfare cycle that one I'd recently been through still wouldn't support the growth of any living thing.

"It will be no such thing," Keion snarled, shaking his head. "You don't actually believe Cai's story, do you?"

"Well, yes, I do, now that you're so kind to ask me. I don't see a reason to disbelieve it, for one thing, and you've been glaring at me all day like you can't wait to see my head on a stick, which hasn't helped."

"Ah, yes, that glare. It is a glare I have perfected, would you not agree?" He gave me the same glare, and then spun it up into a pleasant smile. "It is useful for the prince of the realm to have such a glare at his disposal, you see."

"I see. I definitely see," I said with as much irony in my voice as I could muster. "I'll give you credit for that much. You have definitely perfected the fine art of the prince of the realm's death-dealing glare. Congratulations, asshole."

"Thank you." He swished his hair around his head once again.

"Don't. Just don't. I'm *not* in the mood, after a day of putting up with your glares, to be bothered over that hair-swishing thing you do. But please, do tell me why you don't believe his story."

"Isn't it obvious?"

"No," I said, and I was glad to see both Seph and Aerona shaking their heads in echo of my statement.

"He went back into the cabin last night while I was occupied and told you that I had outed you for being–important," he said, looking past us to make sure the barkeep was still safely out of earshot on the opposite side of the room. "Didn't he?"

"Yes. How'd you know?"

"I heard him steal away and enter the building while I was on the privy. I don't think he realizes how good of a tracker I am." He looked proudly at Seph, his expression kind of challenging, but she just shrugged it off. He shrugged, too, and then continued, "That was right after he informed *me* that he knew who we are because he had recognized my face, and what an honor it was to be traveling with the prince of the realm. And so when I walked into the cabin and saw your guardedly angry expressions pointed my way, I was able to put the pieces together."

"So how did he know who we are?" I asked.

"Well, it is actually possible that he might have recognized my face. It's been said by many that I am so handsome that my visage is recognized throughout the realm."

"Uh, yeah, Mister Handsome, that *must* be it, bless your handsome little heart," I said. "But given that, how did he know who I was?"

"Well, it's entirely possible that our connection as royalty from–the castle–brought him to a lucky guess, but it's just as likely that somehow, despite our haste yesterday morning, Blodwyn got word to Cai as to the identity of the prize she had sent his way. After all, she didn't fight very hard to keep us in her lair."

"So he could be–" I started, and then let the words trail off.

"Of course he could be a member of the Cult of the Wyrm. The barkeep could, too. For that matter, the whole town might be one big, happy Cult-ville. Which leaves us in–" Keion said, letting his own words trail off just as I had, a mocking expression on his face.

I sighed and sent another glare his way. "*Must* you be so difficult?"

He chortled and replied, "No, but it certainly is enjoyable."

"Well, ain't *you* smarter than a hog with a wrist watch?" I grinned at him, enjoying the little punch of my own. I missed speaking in English sometimes, though I bet truly English people like his mother probably get angry at what Southerners call English. Still, all my good stuff was in English, and when translated to elf it just didn't have the same *oomf.*

All three elves at the table cocked their heads to the side and blinked. Seph braved saying it: "I don't understand what you just said."

"Oh, never mind," I dismissed it. It wasn't worth driving home a Southernism when there were other fish that needed frying. "Anybody else notice how his accent keeps changing? He sounded rough and petty when we took off, but by the time we got here it was fairly polished."

"What you describe as rough and petty is actually distinctive in some folks from the very south, actually," Keion said. "It struck me as him trying to sound rough and unpolished by using an accent that is considered rogue-like elsewhere."

"So he's really quite the actor. Hey, on an unrelated note, why is the wall around this town magically protected?"

"What?" Keion asked, still blinking. "Why—how do you know it's magically protected?"

"I can sense magic, remember? Ever since I touched it, I can feel its presence. It looks like a blue aura to me. The walls are surrounded in it, and it struck me as odd. I could tell that it's some kind of protection spell. Ganolog was, too, but here it's stronger, more viable, and that seems kinda backwards."

"Is it possible for such a spell to remain in force since the magical age?" Seph asked.

I shrugged. "None of us has any idea, do we, since we haven't been allowed to study magic." I poked at them on purpose. It wasn't precisely true; in my studies of the tome I'd rescued, I'd read that dissipation of magical spells depends on the skill of the spell caster. Still, I allowed myself to enjoy sending the barb.

What I knew was that it had been well over a thousand years since the beginning of the current, magic-is-forbidden age in Kiirajanna, and for a protection spell to remain in place over the log wall for that long, it would have to have been cast by a very skilled and powerful mage. I couldn't imagine a sorceror of that skill level even knowing about a town this small, much less casting a spell powerful enough to protect it, so that logical conclusion was unlikely. Granted, the scroll had hinted of spells meant to lengthen the lifespan of other spells, but it seemed to me that I should have been able to detect those, also, if they were there. So no, the protection spell over the walls of Gidreffydd had to be recently applied.

"Huh," Keion grunted. He'd apparently watched the expressions float across my face, and he didn't seem convinced by my assertion that none of us knew or had studied magic. "So let's assume that the spell on the walls couldn't have remained from the Third Age. Who might have cast them?"

"The Cult," both Seph and I said at once. The Cult of the Wyrm had proved, after all, that they weren't averse to casting magic spells. They claimed to fight primarily against a return to the use of magic for the general population, which was why they didn't want to see the prophecies regarding the Dragon Queen come true, but it seemed like that was just because they wanted to be the only ones who could wield magical power.

"Right. Any idea what they're protecting against?"

I shook my head. "My spidey-sense doesn't get that specific."

"Spidey-sense?" Seph looked at me questioningly. "Is that another reference from the movers back where you come from?"

"Movies, not movers. And no, it's from—wait. Yes, I suppose it is from the movies," I said, not wanting to spend any more time on useless references. It was true, anyway. They had made movies about Spiderman, but I'd never cared enough to watch them. I hadn't really read the comics, either, but that wasn't the point.

Keion took a gulp of the vile-tasting yellow stuff and said, "So, to recap briefly, if I may, the town we are in is protected by magic whose origin we cannot identify, and we have been brought here by someone who is likely a member of the organization that wants to work against, if not outright kill, our friend here, and this is after we happened to spend the night in the home of one of the core regional leaders of that organization. Whose brilliant idea was it to come here? Oh, right—" Keion swiveled his glare around the group and finally let it land squarely on me.

"Look, I brought us here because it was the right thing to do," I argued. "We still don't know where Llew is."

"Everyone along the way has suggested that Llew is fine," he countered.

"Blodwyn was the last who said that Llew would be fine. And we know how far we can trust the word of a Cult member, right?"

"Yes, but I recall Padrig saying something along the same lines. Are you suggesting that Padrig is a Cult member, too?"

"No, of course not. I wasn't saying that Padrig's word couldn't be trusted, only Blodwyn's."

"And yet the fact remains that you didn't trust Padrig's word," the prince closed his argument with a satisfied smirk.

"I did–well, okay, I didn't–but it wasn't his word. It was Llew's safety, and I–oh, never mind." I was tired of the argument, tired of being reminded that I'd started this journey, tired of knowing that an elf had died because of my decision. Rising, I pushed away from the table. Aerona got up to accompany me, but I waved her back.

"I'm going for a walk. Alone, please. I need to clear my head, and I will be back shortly. While I'm gone, somebody else please drink that stuff for me," I said in a voice that allowed no argument.

I stormed out into the darkness, forgetting in my anger that we'd just been talking about how the town we were in likely served as a Cult stronghold.

CWRWTENAU

literally, watery ale. Used by the elves to indicate anything not worth experiencing.

Secrets in the Darkness

The door of the inn clattered shut behind me, blanking out the light of the candles inside and casting me into utter darkness. I stood and blinked for a few minutes till my eyes adjusted, and then looked down the street. The thin sliver of the moon brightened the setting just enough to see shadows of the buildings, barely visible against the dirt of the main road.

I felt myself shudder. In the nighttime forest the darkness hadn't felt like anything more than the absence of light. In fact, the glow of the full moon had seemed playful, joyful, in amongst the trees. Deeply ensconced in the streets of the northern trading village, though, the darkness brooded with a much more more sinister feeling. The hairs on the back of my neck prickled as much from that oppression as from the night chill.

More oppressive than the darkness, though, was the silence, a deep and smothering quiet that lay about the town. At night the elf villages near Cysegredig nearly always had a party going with drummers, dancers, and singers all gathered about a mid-village bonfire. Ganolog didn't have that outside, but they'd at least had some indoor gatherings during the nighttime hours. Gidreffydd, though, was completely shuttered, dark, and silent.

My terrified subconscious took over briefly, and I imagined a scary clown stepping into the road to ask me something silly about having Prince Albert in a can. I looked cautiously to the side, wondering if there were any storm drains to be carried down. The warmth of the pendant against my chest allowed me to shake the fear off, though, and I put the scenes from the old movie out of my mind. The northern air might feel sinister, but I was the Dragon Queen, after all. I was the one armed with Draignerthol. I was it, I told myself, and I knew it.

Confidence renewed, I started down the main avenue on what I figured would be a short, mind-clearing walk, and then I nearly jumped out of my own skin. A shadow suddenly lurched toward me from across the street! As I panicked, my hand flew up to cup Draignerthol in the hopes of getting something defensive going before the shadow could charge. I seized the power, but held off casting for a moment as reason took hold.

I realized that whatever it was, it wasn't attacking me. Instead, it just lumbered slowly across the street. Finally, I was able to relax as the shape resolved itself into a wolverine.

"Oh, it's just you," I breathed after a moment, letting the sweet warmth of the magical energy dissipate. It was pretty silly, of course, to talk to an animal. I knew that, and I could bet that Booboo knew it, too, but as heavily as the blanket of silence hung in the street around us, I found both the wolverine's presence and my own voice oddly comforting.

"Come on," I said, and then walked over to the wolverine. Kneeling down, I scratched Booboo's head. It felt weird. I'd only done it a couple of times, and no matter how many times I'd seen Seph do it, I'd never gotten used to the idea. Cuddly scratches behind the ears are what you give little Pomeranians, not wolverines. Booboo was too much of a thigh-high killing machine for me to even consider petting under normal circumstances.

It wasn't normal circumstances that we were facing, though.

Whatever, Booboo seemed to like it. The beast pushed his head up into my hand as a way of telling me to scratch harder, and so I did.

"Seph sent you to watch after me, didn't she?" I whispered. "Good cousin. Although—" I stopped and looked sideways at the wolverine before going on, "how'd you get in? Seph wouldn't let you get anywhere near the dogs of the team for fear of the reaction, so I thought you were sticking behind us quite a ways. They shut the gate behind us, and the walls are magically protected. Where'd you come in at?"

Booboo just stood there and gave me a look. I'm not sure if the look was meant to say *gosh, that's a stupid question*, or *I really don't understand a word you're saying*. Either way, it was kind of cute in the darkness.

"Well, if I'm gonna do this walk thing, I should probably get going, shouldn't I?" I asked, and as the words tumbled out I wondered why I was still asking for Booboo's advice. There wasn't any change in the wolverine's facial expression, though, so I gave up on it and rose from my crouch to start down the road. Booboo slipped back into the shadows, but through my contact with Draignerthol I could sense that he stayed close, shadowing me, probably relaying my location back to Seph in case I got into trouble.

In case is kind of a silly way to put it. One thing I've always been good at is getting into trouble.

I walked back to the gate we'd come in through, which took all of two minutes. Two and a half, maybe. I turned around and walked back down the road, past the inn, to the other gate on the opposite side of town. That took less than ten minutes. It's just not a very big town, and closed gates aren't conducive to long nighttime strolls.

Bored, I decided to go ahead and walk all of the roads in town. From my initial survey, I figured it wouldn't take me that much longer. I'd just walked the main strip, and there were a half-dozen or so side jaunts. I set off back down the main road, and the first side street I came to was wide, nearly as much as what I'd started calling Main Street. It was perfect, so I turned the corner, moving quietly past the darkened houses. A few hundred yards down, though, the road ended abruptly at huge wooden double doors. These doors entered a building unlike its neighbors in that all its lights still blazed. I decided to walk the length of the road, turn around just in front of the closed doors, and then head back to Main Street to continue the walk.

"Now is not the time!" a voice bellowed from within the building as I reached the door and turned. The sudden shift from silence to a man yelling surprised me so much that I jumped and barely held back a gasp. I froze and looked around; there was an open window off to the building's side from which light and disagreeing voices both streamed. Slowly, curiously, I crept over to where I was hidden by shadow but could still see in.

The leading voice shouted, "Yes! Yes, it is! The bennaeth–" and stopped. I stood like a statue, having heard Padrig's title and wanting to hear more. Suddenly a shadow darkened the window. It was a silhouette that featured black, wild hair and a thick, braided beard backlit by the gleam from inside. Luckily I was well hidden, and his eyes were too used to indoor light, and so whoever it was didn't see me as he slammed the window shut.

I huddled even farther down into what I hoped was the deepest shadow available, wracking my brain to remember a listening spell from the magic scroll. Finally I gave up, reached to my chest, and grabbed Draignerthol to take an intuitive stab at it. The silver of the pendant felt cold at first, but it warmed up quickly as I gently probed my mind's energy into it. As usual, it was a nice, beckoning, welcoming warmth. It felt almost like the pendant wanted me to fold myself into it and use the power it presented. I allowed a couple of moments to pass as I luxuriated in the sensation, and then, gingerly feeling my way through the magic, pushed the energy out toward the building I'd heard the voices from, extending my senses into and then through the log wall.

"It will be over soon enough," a gruff voice said once the spell had infiltrated into the room.

"What?" a challenge rang. It was the same voice that I'd heard bellowing about it not being the time. At the same time the voice sounded both energetic and old. "Why do you say that?"

"Our forces will soon be—" the second voice, the one that had stopped to close the window, started, only to be interrupted.

"Soon be where?" the challenger growled, quieter and even more dangerous.

"Where do you think? Ganolog, of course."

"Ganolog? You actually intend to take down the bennaeth?" I could tell from the challenger's incredulous tone that he wasn't a fan of the idea, and that, at least, brought me some hope in spite of what I'd been hearing.

"No, I intend to play dice with Padrig. Yes, of course I intend for us to take him down, and then, further, to unite with our brethren in the east, the west, and the south, and remove the king and his whelp. As a matter of fact, we already have several hundred warriors camping right in front of the town's gates, pretending to be a silly northern games demonstration for the king's whelp and her accompanying pawns. And so, my fellow bens, what do you think of that?"

This time the challenger's answer started with a barked laugh as he said, "I think you are an idiot. Did you really start an attack without consulting us? Really? How stupid do you have to be to do such a thing?"

"Iolyn consulted us, Merfyn. You weren't there," a third voice spoke up, his accent a lilting melody that sounded gentle despite the deadly tone of his words.

"Of course I was not there. This was one of your little meetings for which I received the invitation just a little bit too late, was it not?"

"We cannot help the vagaries of the message transportation system, especially when the meeting has to be kept quiet," another voice commented.

"Bah. You have started a war for us all without consulting me. What will happen to your little plan when I pull my forces back home?"

"That will be difficult to do, as they are already on the march toward Ganolog."

"On the march? Well, that is a new low for all of you. And if *our* forces are on their way to battle, should we not be heading out to lead them?"

"That is why–hey," the gruff voice said, this time getting quiet. "I sense–"

I could tell from his sudden change of volume and tone what he sensed, and so I yanked the spell back as quickly as possible and slipped farther away into the darkness. Within seconds I was rewarded for reacting quickly, as four large men tumbled out of the front doors looking around. They stood there for a moment blinking the same way I'd had to when I'd walked outside, and that moment gave me a chance to meld into the darkness of another building and then slow down my breathing.

The four men split up, two coming around the inn my direction and the other two going the other way. I got a look at the two on my side as they passed slowly, swiveling their heads to peer in each direction. One was tall and thin, with long age-creased caverns in his face and neck, and he wore a floppy brimmed hat from which scraggly hair streamed. In his hand he carried a staff with a long, bladed hook on one end. His search partner carried a wicked-looking double-bladed axe in one meaty hand, and he looked like he was wearing a bear's paw with its claws extended over his other fist. Unlike the guy with the staff, he had a beard, though his face was shaved from his ears to the edges of his mouth. From there, though, deep-black hair cascaded down past a massive chest and tucked into his pants.

I'd thought Padrig was large, but he had nothing on the bens that I saw. The largest elf that passed in front of me could've been a match for Halbiorn, himself, in size.

I held my breath as they passed by, willing them with every ounce of my mental power to miss me in their search. Somehow, thanks to the darkness, they did. The foursome met up behind the inn, and after passing some quiet, though obviously agitated, words among themselves they walked around the other side of the inn to go back inside.

I let myself breathe again once the door shut completely. One breath filled my aching lungs, and then I let myself exhale, and then I pulled in a second breath that felt even better than the first.

That was when a hand slipped from behind and covered my mouth, shutting off my ability to draw a third breath, while another hand grasped me around the chest, the heavy force of both yanking me back even further into the shadows.

A Fast Way Home

"You have an interesting idea for what 'nighttime walk to clear my mind' means, Cousin," Seph mouthed, her voiceless hiss barely reaching my ear. When I relaxed and nodded silently, she released her hold on me. The pair of us slithered through the narrow darkness between the buildings to get even farther away from the now-quiet inn.

"You've been following me?" I whispered.

"Only after Booboo signaled you were in trouble. Funny thing how a wolverine can tell better than a princess when she's getting somewhere she shouldn't be."

"That's not fair. I—"

"Not fair? I had to leave a perfectly good drink back there. Luckily I still have a throat in one piece to drink it with, and even luckier, you do, too. Now shut up and come back to Master Dai's with us so we can talk."

"Us?"

Seph had already started back around the building, but at my question she tilted her head meaningfully in the direction of another moving shadow. It looked like we were being shadowed–literally–by a linebacker with breasts, and so I realized that it had to be Aerona.

"Great. Where's Prince Charming, then?"

"Back at the inn. If we'd all left, it would've looked even stranger than it did. And at some point, Cousin, you might wish to consider cooperating more with him."

"He should consider cooperating more with me," I said, sticking my tongue out. It was no use; the gesture couldn't be seen in the darkness, nor did Seph try to look for it anyway. It was childish, I knew. It wasn't befitting a crown princess, either. Still, I really had been in a lot of danger back there, and so I couldn't help if it felt good to joke a little.

The rest of the walk was silent. We weren't too far away, but then again, nothing was too far away in the itty-bitty town. In moments Aerona held the door open for Seph and I as all three of us walked in and joined Keion at the table.

"An invigorating walk?" Keion asked, switching back to the elf tongue.

"Yes. It's quite pretty out tonight, with the sliver of the moon illuminating the town, but only barely. I'm so glad you could step out and join me," I said, aiming the last at Seph and Aerona.

"Gidreffydd is a good, safe town for walking at night," Dai said, bringing over another round of beer. "Few partake in that pleasure, though. I hope you get to see townsmen out and about in the daylight tomorrow. The people here are quite friendly, and especially so to visitors from the south who bear both news and stories."

"I would enjoy it, myself, but I'm sure Cai will be the first person out of town heading toward Ganolog. He's said he wants to get business taken care of quickly so that he can get to Ganolog and back soon," Keion said.

Dai shook his head. "Cai won't be the first. Tomorrow the courier leaves before sun-up. He drives a fast energy-powered carriage, and it is said that if he leaves while the moon is still high he can make it to Ganolog on the same day. With Cai's team running full-out, it still takes him three solid days to get there."

"Oh, the courier!" Keion said. "Right! Where does he leave from? I have a message I need to get to Grigor, Bennaeth Padrig's–"

"I know Grigor," Dai interrupted, nodding with a neutral expression. "If you'd prefer sleeping in a bit, it would be my pleasure to make sure the message makes its way to the courier in order to leave for Ganolog on time."

I held back a sigh by quaffing a slug of ale, which was getting less vile with every quaff. I was so tired of the duplicity within every meeting. Dai knew Grigor, and since Grigor was probably one of them, that meant Dai was too. Then again, Dai knew Cai, and we were pretty certain that the merchant was a member of the Cult, so the fact that Dai also knew Grigor shouldn't have surprised me. It was all one big, stinking game I had to play.

"No, no, I rise early enough anyway. I always enjoy a brief walk in the cold morning air, you know. Thanks, but I'll take it there; I just need to know where there is."

Dai nodded again, accepting Keion's reasoning. "Eastern gate, but you had better be up early. He shows up, loads his carriage, has the early morning guard open the gate for him, and poof! Out he's gone into the morning, racing the sun."

Keion nodded and downed his beer in a single gulp. He motioned for us to do the same. "Drink up, ladies. We have an early morning ahead of us, helping Master Cai prepare to leave."

Even Seph, who had been nursing her beer with the look of an okra-hater eating a bowl of gumbo, followed Keion's lead as we all guzzled our beer. It was harder than it sounded, because what the elves call beer is dark and flat. Dai's ale is also heavy, and very intoxicating. One beer, then, is just fine as a meal by itself, and guzzling my second managed to make my head swim and my stomach bloat while my taste buds continued to try to protest through the fog of intoxication.

We followed Keion up the stairs, and at the top he gestured toward our door. We all went in to the girls' room and closed ourselves tightly in, Aerona taking care to lay a towel along the bottom of the door to keep our voices inside.

"Okay, so what happened?" Keion asked in whispered English, looking at me over crossed arms. "You left, and then suddenly Sephaline and Aerona darted out after."

I related to him the conversation I'd eavesdropped on, and was rewarded by his eyebrows lifting clear up onto his forehead.

"You're quite certain you heard the names Iolyn and Merfyn?" he asked when I was done.

"Yes."

"That's troublesome."

"Ya think?"

"Alyssa, I could do without your sarcasm now. Iolyn is–" he started to lecture me, but I'd been paying attention on the way up to Ganolog the first time.

"I know, I know. He's the mysterious leader of the Pobl'yr-hew. Merfyn is the leader of the Digonol. Which one of those looks like a bear with a goatee, by the way?"

"Did he have a scar here?" Keion whispered, using his finger to draw a line from his right cheekbone to his jaw.

"I couldn't tell. It was dark."

"Right. Well, Rhodri and Madog are both known for their size, but Rhodri is usually the one with the goatee. At least, he was the one with the goatee, last I heard. Madog is known for keeping a close-cropped beard that just graces his cheeks and chin with a hint of blackness, which, it is said, matches his soul. Regardless, the one you saw was probably Rhodri."

"Who cares who is which?" Seph asked in a furious whisper. "They're going to attack Padrig."

"So it would appear," Keion said.

"We have to do something," I whispered, drawing the last word out into a hiss.

"Princess, aren't you the one who insisted on doing something when Llew went missing?" Keion asked.

"Okay, *fine*," I said, forcing as much vehemence into a whisper as I could. "So going after Llew was a bad idea. But it got us here, and it uncovered a clear and present danger to Padrig. The northern elves are moving against their bennaeth! We have to make sure he knows."

"Well, I'm sure that'll be no problem. But wait, our first problem is going to be getting him to listen, after running off after his kid even though he ordered us not to, and then returning without the kid. 'Oh, but Padrig, we bear this news,'" Keion said.

"He'll–" I started, and then let my voice die off. This far on the trip, I'd proved myself worthless as nipples on a boar hog at predicting what Padrig would say, believe, or do.

"Yes, he'll ignore you. Right," Keion said, nodding his agreement at what I hadn't said.

I sighed. Keion *was* right, no matter how much I wished he wasn't.

"So, we just–what? Sit here and hope he wins the coming battle?" I asked.

"No," Seph said, and in a rare show of solidarity, Keion nodded at her. "We have to present the information about his subordinate bens to him, and as quickly as possible."

"I am not certain how to make the bennaeth believe the story," Keion said, "but I agree that we must present it to him, regardless, in order for him to make his own decision."

"So we need to travel to Ganolog with the courier?" I asked in confirmation.

"I am not sure what the trader will do with his weihr if we leave him behind to travel to Ganolog without us," Seph complained.

"I am not sure I care," I argued.

"We don't all need to travel with the courier," Keion said. "Maybe you could go with him, and the rest of us could, well, just–"

"Just what, tell him I felt like calling in sick? He's got to know that the courier runs tomorrow. He'll tell his Cult friends, including probably the bens, the moment he realizes that any of us has gone ahead. Anybody who's left behind, then, will be in danger, if not immediately, then on the next few days' ride with him to Ganolog. No, we all need to go with the courier," I argued.

"If we can. We don't know what his capacity is," Aerona said.

Keion saw the distressed look on my face and explained, "The courier is actually in the employ of the king and queen, not the bennaeth, and he makes deliveries all across Kiirajanna. His position requires that his sled have a fairly large capacity in general, but we can't know how loaded down he already is. If we're lucky, this being one of his earlier stops on the cycle, he'll be fairly empty."

"Okay, right. Let's hope, then, that his remaining capacity is four. But, I suppose I have to ask, if only one of us can go, who should that really be?" I asked, already sure I knew the answer.

"You," Keion and Seph said at once. Keion's expression told me I should have known better than to ask.

"But the bennaeth already doesn't listen to me," I objected.

"He doesn't listen to what you have to say in the audiences you gain with him," Keion said, "but at least you gain audiences with him. If anyone else goes, they might as well start throwing paper wads over the wall with messages for the bennaeth to read."

"Fine. Let's just hope we can all go. That said, if we're going to get an early morning start, we should probably get some rest now."

"You can rest?" Seph asked me. When I shrugged, not certain what the truest answer to that should be, she shook her head. "All right, well, somebody needs to make sure all are safe, and then make sure we're up and moving in time."

"You doubt my position, ranger?" Aerona asked from the corner, glaring over the point of the dagger that had suddenly appeared in her hand.

"No, not at all. I was just pointing out how well you do what you do, Aerona," she answered with a smile.

"That is good. Prince, if you wish to sleep in here, you should probably get your bag now. To sneak in during the early morning hours would be too suspicious. I will make sure everyone is up in time, trust me."

"We trust you," Seph said with a wide grin, while Keion nodded and stepped through the door.

The door opened a couple of minutes later, and Keion stepped back through with his backpack on his shoulder and a grin on his face.

"You look—pleased with yourself," Aerona observed, still keeping her voice pitched very low.

"It is just humorous. The merchant awoke when I entered, but I told him I was likely to get lucky tonight, and he nodded and went back to sleep," Keion whispered back in English.

"Lucky?" Seph asked, a confused look on her face. Aerona looked confused also; I guess they don't teach English idioms in whatever class she'd taken.

"Which of us were you suggesting that you might have sexual intercourse with, Prince?" I asked, choosing my words carefully to make the meaning clear to everyone. That did it; both of the other girls' faces flushed.

"None of you, but get real, Princess. It was the best line I could use to have him not question me," the prince argued, and I had to grudgingly agree.

We settled in, with Keion, Seph, and me sleeping in the three beds while Aerona calmed down into her elf-trance that resembles sleep and is nearly as restful. It's not sleep, though; I've seen her snap right out of the trance on cue.

In what felt like a only few minutes later, a hand shook me awake. "Princess, it is time to go," Aerona's voice hissed.

The four of us sneaked out of the room into the darkness of the hall, Keion leading the way and Aerona bringing up the rear. Keeping enough space in front of me was tough; I could sense but not see Keion's frame as he moved slowly and deliberately.

Somehow we managed to make it down to the bottom of the stairs and out of the building without making any noise. I remember playing Dungeons and Dragons a couple of times, and in that game elves could always see in the dark. I'll tell you, it's not like that. I could sense, through Draignerthol, the life forces around me, but I still couldn't *see* anything, and by the tentative touches and gentle brushes I could tell that Seph and Aerona were in the same boat, only they walked without my magical pendant's assistance.

The four of us crept quietly through the dim shadows toward the eastern gate. I hoped all the while that nobody would discover us, that the courier would be at least sympathetic to our plight, and that he would have four seats open going to Ganolog.

To avoid frightening him, we stopped being stealthy as we entered the light from the courier's lantern. Apparently, it worked. The elf, a grizzled old veteran, ignored us and kept at his task of loading his sled as we walked toward him from the side.

"Courier," Keion said, and as I heard his voice, I realized that nobody in our group really knew the elf's name. That might have been something to have already found out, I thought, especially since we intended to beg for travel assistance.

"What do you want?" came the challenging reply, the elf's head swiveling to face us.

"A ride to Ganolog," Keion said.

"This isn't a bus," the courier said and returned to loading his carriage. At least, the elven wording he used kind of translated to bus.

"I can tell," Keion said. "But we're not looking for a bus. It's just a few of us seeking transport, and we'll help provide for it."

"How do you plan to help provide for it?"

"Well, we can help with security," Keion offered.

"Don't need help with security," the elf replied. "Nobody ever attacks the royal courier."

"Okay, then how about this offer. I am Prince Keion, son of Queen Talaith. I seek the fastest possible transport to Ganolog for myself and my traveling companions. Does that clarify the situation?" Keion asked, striding forward and lowering the hood of his cape so that his flowing sable mane was visible.

"M–my prince," the courier exclaimed, dropping to one knee as was customary. "Your words clarify the situation substantially. I would be pleased to convey you and your party to Ganolog, or even further to Cysegredig if desired. Forgive me for my earlier–"

"Of course, of course," Keion interrupted. "You had no idea who we were. Time is essential, though, so please make us aware of anything we can do to hasten our departure."

The courier stopped to look closely at me. "Yes, yes, I guessed that you must be the Crown Princess Alyssa of whom I have heard so much, and I must proclaim that your beauty surpasses even those tales that I have heard of it, Your Highness. This will be a highly honored journey." I smiled broadly in spite of Keion's audible snort. The courier turned back to loading his carriage and continued, "I rarely have even one passenger, and now I have you four plus one other. It might be a little bit crowded, but I pray you will not find that disagreeable, as the trip to Ganolog should pass very quickly."

"One other? Who is this other?" Keion asked, his voice tense again.

"Oh, none other than the bennaeth's only son, Highness. I was honored to be able to provide him rapid transport back to Ganolog, but now I am even more greatly honored by all of your august presences."

"The bennaeth's–" Keion started speaking but finished whatever he intended to say as a growl. A familiar, grinning face popped up over the back of the carriage, illuminated by the courier's lantern.

"Hi, guys," Llew's cheerful voice piped over Keion's growl.

"Llew!" I gasped. My heart did gymnastics–flippity-flops of happiness that he was alive and kicking, and somersaults of agitation that he'd been invisible for so long and now showed up here, of all places. "Thank goodness you're okay. We've been searching for you."

"Let's not wake up the town before we depart, Your Highness–rather, Highnesses," the courier chided us gently as he finished piling the last of the small boxes onto the back of the carriage. "I can tell that there's some talking to be done, but I am sure you can all settle whatever needs settling once I get underway."

We all climbed silently up into the carriage to sit beside and across from the boy we'd been searching for. Booboo climbed aboard, too, once Seph successfully argued that this was one of the few cases where there was no way the wolverine could keep up. All aboard, the carriage lurched into motion, driven by magical forces powered by energies as old and powerful as time itself.

I joined the rest of the party in glaring at Llew in silence. I couldn't decide whether to hug him or to wring his foolish neck, though I was certain that I shouldn't do either.

The carriage's runners slid silently and magically over pockets of air onto the main street and then stopped as the early-morning guard opened the gate for us. He and the courier exchanged wordless salutes, and then we shot off into the darkness, gaining speed very quickly.

As we headed off to the east, the sunrise caught up to us, brightening everyone's faces. Llew stared at us, and we glared back at him, each of us daring the other to speak first.

Meanwhile, I wanted to laugh out loud in exultation for so very many reasons.

TUAGHAUL

literally, toward the sun; eastward, in general use. The actual word for east is dwyrain, but everybody uses the compound tuaghaul even when the sun is in the west.

The Journey East

"Why did you come looking for me?" Llew finally broke the silence, his voice sounding hurt. "I was fine. I've been fine in my father's lands and holdings for many years. I don't understand why you continue to consider me such a young, helpless baby boy."

All four faces turned my direction, their expectant looks pressing my mood downward, and I sighed. The decision was rightfully mine to defend, after all. I took another deep breath and then launched into an attempt. "Llew, look, we both know that you're not young and helpless. Well, okay, you're a little young for where I'm from, but I am sure that you've been more than capable of handling yourself for years in your own realm. I was just...."

I let my voice trail off, not sure how best to put how silly I'd been into words, especially words that his father might agree that a queen should say.

"You feared that your rejection of my adoration would cause me to go off and do something stupid," he accused.

"Well, yes," I said, nodding and shrugging sheepishly. He really did have it in a nutshell, as dumb as it sounded when he put it that way. "I mean, I get that you're competent and capable, and that's easy to talk about now that we're both safely here, but I really didn't know you that well, and I had no idea what you were going to be thinking or doing, or—"

Llew interrupted me, which was just fine since I was floundering, "Thank you, Crown Princess Alyssa, for caring so deeply about my welfare. I had no idea that anyone would be afraid for my well-being, so I did not think to let you know, and for that I apologize. I knew that my mother and father certainly wouldn't worry, for they know me very well. It was insensitive of me, though, to go off and leave you to worry."

Insensitive, I thought. The kid was managing to out-class me.

He continued, "That said, I have been on an important mission since I departed."

"Oh? How so?" Keion asked. He leaned forward intently. It was strange, seeing the boy not only gallantly apologize for my needing to make an apology, but then also utter something that pulled Prince Charming's interest as solidly as it had.

"Um—" Llew looked meaningfully toward the courier. "Alyssa, I was led to believe that you have rediscovered the art of magic. I've also heard stories that tell that ancient magicians could create a spell that could keep sounds inside from being overheard outside of their perimeters. Are those two statements correct?"

"I—um—well—I—" I stammered, out of sorts from the sudden role reversal. I was used to being looked down on and threatened with exile for using magic, not having spells requested. "I—*guess* that I might have read something about that kind of spell before. Are you suggesting that I create a perimeter of that sort?"

I admit that I was being a little coy. One of the spells I'd read about would do exactly what Llew was asking for, and I was pretty sure that I could reproduce it. Still, that I could actually be asked to work magic was weirding me out, making me feel important in a way that the already-routine "Crown Princess" stuff didn't.

"Yes, I am," Llew said, lowering his voice. "Though I trust our friendly royal courier well enough, I am still loathe to chance him overhearing certain state secrets which need to remain state secrets."

I found myself wanting to reach out and pinch him on the cheek, cute as it was that he was using such formal talk while still looking so much like a young boy, but then I realized that that sentiment was exactly what he had run away from in the first place.

"But it's magic," I objected.

"Which is forbidden by tradition and so on. Yes, I know about magic. I've never quite understood why we sit so firmly upon our traditions, honestly. At this point, the only thing that might make a difference in what is coming is your ability–and willingness–to cast spells of power against the bad guys, and so I am hoping that what I have heard is not exaggerated."

I looked back and forth from Keion and Seph, both of whom appeared horrified by Llew's words, to Padrig's son, whose eyes seemed to be daring me to claim my own power. Finally I nodded, giving in to the reality that was my birthright. "I can cast that spell," I said, and as I spoke the words I reached out mentally through Draignerthol to grab hold of the ancient energy. Once I found it, I pulled it through into current reality and made it blossom, surrounding the company in the carriage in what would be to everyone else an invisible blanket that deadened every sound coming from within.

I glanced toward my companions from Cysegredig to gauge their reaction. Seph looked like she'd just eaten a live bee and was trying to keep it down—eyes bugged out but mouth firmly clamped closed. *Good cousin*, I thought. Keion raised one eyebrow in a minute, but very meaningful, gesture. I figured that Sternyface would quickly hear of my transgression from him, assuming we made it back to be heard. Aerona, meanwhile, ignored the magic and just kept glaring around at the shadows that were passing by at a rapid pace.

Llew looked around, studiously ignored their reactions, and then nodded. "Good," he said, a smile forming on his face.

"You can see the flows of energy?" I asked.

"Sure," he said, smiling. "My family line was once regarded among the most capable of magic-users. In fact, I am a direct descendant of Rhiannon, the White Queen of the North. Why are you looking at me that way?"

"It has been suggested to me that my mother was also a direct descendant of Rhiannon, Llew. More than suggested, in fact; the picture I saw of Queen Rhiannon could easily have been one of Momma. Plus, she gave me—um, my love for so many things that are elf," I stumbled. I'd been about to tell him about Draignerthol, but nobody knew about the pendant Momma had given me but Seph and Keion. Well, and Aerona. Well, and Dad, and Sternyface, too, I guess. Anyway, the point is that there were already too many elves who knew about my possession of the powerful magic relic.

"If what you are saying is correct, then we must be cousins," I finished.

"Cousins? You speak of your mother on the Earth side?" he asked.

"Right." I wondered what he was getting after. It wasn't like I had more than one mother, after all, and everyone knew she was from Earth.

"Then at best we are only distant cousins in lineage. It is an interesting suggestion, though. But aren't you curious about the state secret I mentioned?"

"Of course I am. It's just that you surprised me so much with the mention of Rhiannon that I haven't gotten there yet."

"Oh. Well, enough about Rhiannon. Here it is. My father is about to be attacked," Llew said, his voice lowering to a conspiratorial whisper.

"We know," Keion's voice droned.

"You–you know? How do you know this? You're not part of the attackers, are you?" Llew's grin morphed into a glare as he inched away from us. It was hard to go very far, sitting next to Seph as he was. Still, it was cute watching him try to fold his gangly torso into the spot behind her shoulder blade.

"No, no, relax, Llew. We're not part of the attackers," I said, holding up my hands in a calming pose, sparing a quick glare Keion's direction. "We just overheard the wrong thing at the wrong time, or maybe it was the right thing to overhear at the right time." I related to Llew what I'd heard the night before.

"Oh," Llew said after hearing my story. He relaxed, and then he nodded. "So that aligns with my observations of movement through the forests, then."

"Oh? How much movement?" Keion asked, wrapping what looked like a concerned tactician's expression onto his face. That was cute, too.

"I saw thousands of armed men, camouflaged by a massive ranger presence. I just assumed that it was *my* father who was the target, not mine and yours both."

"Well, they have to get through yours to get to mine, so let's make sure that first part doesn't happen."

"A massive ranger presence?" Seph asked, her ears perked up.

"Massive," Llew nodded. "At least two hundred rangers, probably more, flanking the force and covering its tracks. Warriors scouting the way, too, though not quite as many out in front."

"There aren't two hundred rangers in the north," Seph argued.

"Correct. There are closer to a couple of thousand," Llew said, his voice dismissive. He looked out over the landscape as if he could see them all.

"A couple of–what?" Seph exclaimed, sounding completely flabbergasted by the idea. "No, no, no, no, no, Llew. We keep track of every ranger in the realm, and the northern reaches have produced disturbingly few rangers for centuries. The only way you could have a couple of thousand rangers is if none of them had died in the past millennium."

"Well, we do live quite a long time, but–ah, forgive me, I need to be silent now. I've already revealed too much of our internal business to outsiders," the boy said, turning his face away from us.

"Outsiders who are as intent on saving your father's neck as you are, Llew. Maybe–and I'm just suggesting this–your father's future height might benefit from you sharing what you know," Keion said, his voice liltingly convincing.

Llew sighed. "Okay, right. We have our own order of rangers," he muttered to the floorboards of the carriage. "It is an order that the southern rangers–the *lower* rangers," he added, his tone of derision grating even for me, "don't know about. I am one. I pledged solidarity and silence, and had every intention of keeping my pledge until that order, or a large part of it, anyway, decided to attack my household."

"So–that's–I'm–wow–you mean," Seph said, her voice coming out breathlessly as her eyes met Keion's in a furtive look, "the northern rangers have been operating separately from the rest of us for–for how long now?"

"I don't know. At least ten years. Twenty? Maybe a hundred?" a defeated Llew replied.

"More than that," Keion said. "Do the math. For the population estimate to be that far off, you have to have been getting bad data for centuries."

"Centuries. Right. I have to get word to the order next time we stop," Seph said, still breathless, her face white.

"Well, the bad news is that we're probably not going to stop anywhere you can get word to the order prior to the coming battle," Keion said. When Sephaline glared at him, he shrugged and gestured in front of the carriage, pointing out that there wasn't a team of animals needing rest pulling us. "The good–I don't know if you'll call it good, really, so I'll just say other–the other news is that there's nothing the order, or the king, or the Cult, or anyone else can do at this point to stop us from getting to Ganalog in time to warn Padrig of the coming storm."

"Other is a better descriptor for that last bit than good, to be sure," Seph said, and Llew, a terrified expression on his face, nodded.

"Don't worry, Llew. We'll protect your father," I said.

Keion snickered.

"What?" I shot a dark glare along with the question his way.

"'We'll protect your father'? Really, Princess? Against an incoming horde that includes numbers of warriors and rangers we haven't ever been able to accurately measure? And let's not forget that the Cult of the Wyrm, with its magic users, is apparently quite strong up here. Do you plan on stopping them all? Shielding them all? It's going to be incredibly violent, and you have no idea how it will turn out." Out of the corner of my eye I saw Llew flinch when Keion mentioned the Cult, and so I decided to interject a little confidence if I could.

"If you will just think back to the action in the library, you'll recall that I do have some abilities to draw upon, Prince Keion," I retorted with a glare, trying my queenly best to make my voice sound level and dangerous.

The prince's return chuckle infuriated me, though. "Yes, I do recall the action in the library," he sneered. "I was there, after all, if you will recall that much. While it was quite impressive to watch you blow a fire around the dry books with a tornado, I'm not certain that a wind storm would have the same effect on a large group of attacking warriors and rangers. It might blow their smells away from us, come to think of it, and that's something, I suppose."

"All this time I thought you were afraid of magical spells, and now you're just mocking them like a child."

"Like a child? A child? You're the one suggesting that the four of us–five, if you count the beast over there–can make a difference against thousands of armed men."

"My father has a large number of armed men who will come to his side," Llew offered in my defense.

"Yes, he does," Keion answered, his tone softening for the boy. "He has a mighty force, full of well-trained and motivated fighters, but whether or not they can hold against the thousands who are coming is a question I'm not prepared to answer. It's the suggestion that the four of us will make a difference that I find ridiculous," he finished his sentence while turning toward me and returning to his harsh voice.

"And so what would you do, run away? All this time I've thought Prince Keion to be a strong fighter, a brave man, and you're going to flee like a little boy, arguing the whole time that we can't do anything about it so why even try?"

I could tell I'd hit a nerve; Keion's eyes flashed and his lips drew back in a snarl. "No," he growled, "you little fool. I–"

"*Would* you two please stuff it?" Aerona barked. We both looked at her, Keion's face showing as much shock as I felt at her intervention. Still, she glared defiantly from her perch across the carriage. She nodded and continued, "That is good; you two spring chickens can feel free to report me to your father or your mother, or both, for breach of protocol when we return to Cysegredig safely, *if* we return safely. In the meantime, though, your spat is doing nothing to help us move toward a solution. All it is accomplishing is making me wish I had a good set of earplugs."

"She's right," Keion said. I looked at him, surprised to hear reason from the arrogant boy's mouth. He shrugged. "You know that she speaks the truth of it, Alyssa. Look, sniping back and forth with you has actually become a rather enjoyable pastime, but we would accomplish a lot more toward surviving the coming threat by being pleasant with each other and discussing the situation as a group, I think."

"I agree," Llew said, nodding.

"Oh, shut up." I intended the line to be a joke, but as soon as the words were out of my mouth his face melted into the same expression that I'd seen the other night. Lowering my eyes in what I hoped would come across as conciliation, I smiled, made my voice as pleasant as I could, and said, "I mean–what I mean is–well, Llew, I'm just not sure what I mean. I've been on edge for this entire trip, and for that I apologize. To everyone. Even to you, Keion. I guess I enjoy getting into it with you as much as you do me, though you did hurt my feelings with the comment about being ridiculous."

"You need to find less hurt-able feelings, then, Crown Princess. That was mild compared to what my mother has been through."

"I'm aware of that, Keion. I've never had a problem with getting my feelings hurt before. Somehow it always seems to sting a little bit deeper than it should when it comes from you."

"Well—" Keion started and then paused, finally shrugging to show his apparent inability to come up with a good response.

"That's—interesting," Llew said, looking from my face to the prince's and back. I felt myself blush, and the boy's gaze grew sharper. "Prince Keion, you're—"

"Oh, shut up," Keion mimicked me, taking his own turn at putting the kid in his place. He followed it with a wistful smile, though, and that seemed to cut the tension. "Look, we really do need to figure out what we're doing here, and I don't know how long Alyssa can hold her magical sound shield in place. And speaking of magical energies, Alyssa, please know that I neither fear them nor mock them. They are, as I am sure you are aware, firmly and explicitly forbidden by a tradition older than all of us combined several times over. You pulled the wind down to save us at the library, and for that I am and will always be truly grateful. You also used your power to save our lives in the fall from the cliff. Your spell is useful now. But all of this still makes me extremely nervous, as one who grew up in this realm and was taught the destructive nature of the forces you wield, and even more so as those of us near you seem to grow more accustomed to it. Your magical prowess is significant, but we must—" he paused for a moment, looking off toward the horizon as he searched for his next words. Finally he came back, "I would simply prefer that we not ever be treated to a display of your power at spell casting again, honestly. That said, I trust that the way ahead of us will ever become more dangerous rather than less, and so instead of completely forbidding it, we should—and I know how silly this is going to sound—reserve it for those moments that are truly life and death."

"You're right, that does sound silly, Keion," I argued. "How am I supposed to know those moments that are truly life and death? If I'd taken the time to think about it when we fell off the cliff, we'd all be dead now."

"I know that, Alyssa. But I also know that we cannot allow ourselves to be eased into the trap of using your magic whenever we desire it." Keion looked as serious as I'd ever seen him.

"Not planning on it."

"Good. To do so is to revisit a very dark place in our mutual past."

"I'm aware of that."

"Good."

I got tired of the serious discussion between Keion and me and decided to change the topic. "Hey, speaking of falling off the cliff, Llew, how did you manage to evade the tracking skills of one of the best rangers in the land," I paused for a moment to gesture toward Seph, who glowed a little at my comment, and then continued, "in order to get from the portal circle to Gidreffydd without us tracking you there?"

"As much as I appreciate the compliment, Cousin, we have far more important issues to talk through," Seph contradicted me. I glared at her in my best royal look, but she just shrugged and said, "Okay, so please report me along with Aerona when we return, but first let's make sure that we return. And just out of curiosity, how long *can* you keep that silence shield going?"

I shrugged. Touching Draignerthol through my shirt, I pushed my senses out toward the sphere that surrounded us and found that it was still solid. "A long time. Forever, I think. The power to keep it in place is maintained mainly by Draig-nerth—er, my, um—" I stammered, suddenly suspecting that I'd given more away to Llew than I'd wanted to. The sudden light in his eyes made it clear that I was right.

"You—have found—you have Draignerthol?" he asked, his voice coming out in breathlessly excited spurts. Then he shook his head, suddenly serious. "Sorry, that was a silly question. Of course you have. You're the Dragon Queen! Besides, I've noticed you touching your chest where a pendant would be, usually unconsciously, like you're just checking to see if something precious is still there. I just haven't been comfortable enough to ask. May I—may I see the relic, Crown Princess?"

"I don't—" I started to object, but Keion and Seph both shook their heads. "I mean, I'm pretty protective of this, since my momma gave it to me, but yes, I guess it won't hurt to let you look at it." I pulled the ancient pendant out from underneath my shirt, and the blue gem in the eye socket glowed brightly.

Llew gasped.

"It's—" I started to say something dismissive as I slipped the pendant away safely beneath my shirt again. I suddenly felt naked in front of the boy.

He shook his head and interrupted me. "It's *beautiful*, Alyssa. Far more beautiful than the stories say, in fact. And it's powerful, too; I could sense the power erupting from the pendant as you took it out from behind your blouse. You're right to keep it hidden, but I must thank you so much for letting me lay eyes upon it. When you become queen, I will gladly follow you to the ends of the realm and back."

I'd imagined myself hearing those words, usually at night in my little pre-sleep fantasies of a blissful future. I'd always thought they would mean the world for me to hear—someone would follow me! Somehow, though, no matter how many times I'd dreamed of it, the fact that the first time I heard them was from an eleven-year-old boy sucked a little of the joyful punch from the event.

"So Prince Keion, I can see your point in that you don't think the four of us could have any bearing on the outcome of the battle," Aerona cut in. "So what are your thoughts on a winning strategy?"

I shot her a thankful look. She nodded, her chin moving the smallest fraction of an inch but just enough for me to tell. I'd always figured her to be a fighting and defensive machine—a linebacker with breasts and blades—but I was coming to see that there was more to her than that.

"I'm not sure I agree with our having *no* bearing, but I don't think there's much chance that we could have *much* bearing on the outcome of the battle," he responded, his eyes once again thoughtfully off in the distance. "Alyssa and Sephaline and, I suppose I must add the wolverine, have already displayed their prowess in battle both in getting to and safely out of the library, and I've heard all sorts of wickedly good tales about *your* exploits in the king's guard. I think the five of us would be fairly epic in any evenly-matched fight. But is it really enough to counter thousands? I'm hopeful, but not certain. More important, if we bravely and epically die here without getting word to the king about the upcoming challenge, is that better than us living long enough to warn the king? And, I have to add, if we allow Alyssa to fall into the Cult's hands no matter how bravely we fight up here, have we not just lost the most important battle of all?"

Sephaline and Aerona both nodded and then shifted their gaze to me in a way that suggested it was my role to counter the prince's speech.

"I think that with the benefit the courier's speed is granting us, we might have time to warn the king and still participate in the fight here. I think, one way or another, we should find a way to do that, as Llew and Padrig are unquestionably our allies and thus deserve our support. It is not for certain, of course. I have to admit that I don't know enough to predict whether we'll even survive the fight, much less win it."

"Who ever really does?" Llew asked, his voice wistful. The question, softly spoken though it was, brought us all up short. I looked over to meet Aerona's eyes, and for once my guardian met my gaze with something other than her flat, supremely confident stare. I could tell the question made her think, and when I looked at the other two from Cysegredig, I could see the same pondering.

"Who indeed?" Keion asked, nodding. He snorted derisively and then continued, "I wonder if the lack of warfare hasn't made us all soft. No, don't go getting insulted, Llew. Your people haven't fought any major encounters in as long as there's been relative peace in Cysegredig. But it doesn't matter, does it? We're elves. We roll into battle proudly, supporting those who deserve it. And you know what? Here I've been ar- guing with the crown princess, the only one of us not brought up immersed in our customs and history, and all this time she's been holding to the most elf-like attitude. That is—strange, to me." He leveled a gaze my way, and I could tell that, at least for the moment, he was proud of me. I don't want to admit what that did to my heart.

"I haven't been taking an elf-like attitude on purpose, though," I protested. "I just don't want to leave Padrig and Llew and—and god forbid, Esyllt—to face the oncoming horde without helping them somehow."

"That is an elf-like stance, Cousin. It's exactly the way we have been taught from childhood to think," Seph added, nod- ding. "Don't get me wrong. Prince Keion's desire to cut back toward Cysegredig and your father's army is sound tactically, and, I suppose, it is prudent." Keion nodded appreciatively to- ward my cousin. I held back a snort as I watched in her face the same heart-fluttering that I'd just experienced.

"I have to say, though, that I'm uncertain as to which path we should take," she finished.

"Let me suggest a middle ground, then," I said, and I wasn't sure whether to bridle in irritation or smile in pleasure when Keion nodded approvingly. "Let's get back to Ganolog and discuss this with Padrig, and then we can decide which path we're taking, after we hear the bennaeth's recommendation."

"Good, but there's one question. What makes you think he'll give us a recommendation? We already ignored his first one," Keion asked.

"Right, we did. Which reminds me, young man," I said, turning my stare back toward Llew. "How *did* you managed to evade all the trackers, including the magnificent one who is sitting right there, and then show up ahead of us when nobody on the trip had seen you?"

My intent had been to cow the boy and make him feel just the slightest bit remorseful for being gone so long, but it didn't work. Padrig's son just sat up straighter, his eyes widened in excitement, and he began to tell us his story.

FFOI

to flee. The elves put a whole heap of nastiness into sounding the double f, even more than it deserves, bless its little heart. It's a really bad word to them.

A Long Run

"So, everyone probably thinks I ran away because of a broken heart, right?" Llew asked. We agreed, and a cloudy expression washed over his face as he said, "Well, I sort of did, to be truthful. I mean, I left feeling pretty sorry for myself, never having been turned down in quite that manner before—no, Alyssa, it was not your fault, but rather my own for making the proposal in as abrupt and clumsy—and, I admit, rather inebriated—a manner as I did, and though I do hope that you and I—"

"Llew, the story, please," Keion interrupted. He motioned impatiently.

"Why? It's not like we don't have all day," Llew retorted. "I mean, we're stuck with each other, literally, all day long." His smirk was actually taunting the prince.

Somehow I managed to hold back a blush as I watched Keion's face darken and tense up and then, in a slow, measured, disciplined way, relax. The First Prince of the Realm, Light of Her Majesty Queen Talaith's eyes, and so on, was actually as jealous of Padrig's son's affections as Llew was of

Keion's. After a moment spent getting his emotions back in check, though, the jealous prince gestured gracefully for the boy to continue.

I suspect that Llew was smarter than Keion believed possible, and thus he observed the bulk of what I caught, but he managed to hide it, mostly, behind a glum little nod. He continued, "So anyway, after I'd thought about it for a little while, I realized that you were absolutely right about our age and background differences, Alyssa. But I also knew that people had seen me leave upset, and I realized that would be a great cover for checking out a report I'd overheard Papa receive of unusual movements around the region—reports of large numbers of warriors gathering for no apparent purpose, specifically. He'd been worried about who to send to check it out, because he doesn't really trust his rangers, and for obvious reason. So I set off to track it down for him."

Realization hit me square between the eyes, and pretty hard, too. "That was why he told us not to go after you!" I closed my eyes and shook my head; I'd seriously, embarrassingly, underestimated both Padrig and his son. They both had perfectly logical, tactical reasons for what they'd done, but I'd assumed it was just pigheadedness and boy drama. Along the way, a terrifically dedicated guard captain—named Gerallt, I reminded myself—had died for me—for my stupidity in misjudging the bennaeth and his son, actually. I'd already realized that I had no idea how to ask for Padrig's forgiveness for taking off after Llew, but that was turning out to be the least forgiveness I needed asking for.

Llew nodded. "He knew I'd overheard the briefing, and I'm one of the very few in the keep that he trusts. I'm sure he guessed why I left, and then assumed that the rangers he sent wouldn't have any desire to really track me. But he also wouldn't have wanted you southern folks running into any northern tribesmen armed for war, as they probably would not have been gentle to the king's daughter or to the queen's son. Papa can handle an attack on Ganolog by his own people–it wouldn't be the first time–but the embarrassment and sorrow of having anything happen to one of you in his realm would very likely break him.

"That's why we went on the hunting trip so much earlier this year than we usually do. While it's true that the cold is setting in earlier than normal, Papa's main desire was making sure that Ganolog's larders were well-stocked against an attack that he sensed was coming. Plus, I think he really enjoyed having you all out there with him. He thinks highly of you, Keion, and you as well, Alyssa. You're both strong, smart, and competent."

"Thank you," I said, appreciating the compliment despite the fairly low opinion I held at that moment of my own smartness. Plus, I'd learned that the elf language has several words for strong–one is *gryf*, which means strong in the brawny, weight-lifter sense. It was the kind of description you might apply toward one of the northern elf leaders. Another was the one Padrig had used at the fair, a label I still doubted I deserved, meant for someone who is strong enough mentally to do what is required as a ruler. The third, *gadarn*, is the one Llew had used, and it's more about being strong like steel or granite is strong–everlasting, unbending. It was a word any elf would be proud to have applied to him or her. I felt truly honored.

"You're welcome," he said, shrugging it off as though it were an obvious thing. He blithely continued, "So I took off on a scouting mission, and I very quickly located a few camps within an easy half day's march of Ganolog. They were pitiful in size compared to the garrison Papa keeps, though, and so at first I wasn't worried. But then I thought about it, and the possibilities worried me more than if there had been huge camps. The bens know how many soldiers Papa keeps in garrison, after all. Why would they send a force that was insufficient? What if part of the force they were counting on was already in Ganolog? More suspiciously, if I could find the camps, young as I am, why hadn't the rangers from Ganolog? Were they complicit? It wouldn't be the first time that part or even all of a bennaeth's garrison turned against him. So, all these problems plaguing me, I covered my tracks and headed toward the ley-gate to the north, the one you must have found, to pop through and see if I could see any other armies massing."

"Why the north?" Keion asked, leaning forward. I'd noticed him leaning closer and closer as Llew's story spun out, his tactician mind completely engaged.

"It's where Papa's at his weakest. His family is from Ganolog, and Mama's is from the great cliffs, so he has close ties in those tribes. The ice shelf to the north, though, is a growing sea of discontent, mainly with Cysegredig and the Dragon Queen—sorry, Alyssa—but also with Papa's leadership. I've been through there several times checking it out for Papa, but this time it seemed more urgent to get a lay of the land from the top."

"You have ranger training, don't you?" Seph asked, her voice curious. I nodded, seeing where she was going. She'd explained to me once that the only elf who could out-track a ranger was another ranger. She had to be right; she'd been pretty quick to find Llew's trail leading to the ley-gate, but she hadn't detected any of his other running around. Obviously, though, she needed confirmation of his ranger training to satisfy her own self-confidence.

"I already told you I'm a peer, Ranger Sephaline."

"Yes, you have, but there's a difference between coming out of the *hunhymgais* a ranger and actually having gone through the extended training, which, as you know, is traditionally sanctioned only through Master Owain," she said. The hunhymgais was the vision quest that all elves have to go through to become adults, and my next stop on the path to coronation once I'd visited all the chieftains, so any mention of it interested me.

"Of course, that is how it works down in the lesser reaches," Llew said. "I am not sure about your sanctioning, but we have our own set of rangers, remember? I have been fully trained in the entirety of our skill set from an early age."

"But we—but most rangers—" Seph sputtered, and I could see her wrestle with how to frame her argument. She paused, then forged ahead. "Llew, we don't choose to be rangers. Rangers are chosen by the hunhymgais itself. Our familiars find us, bond with us, and make us who we are."

"I am bonded to a familiar, though," Llew said with a shrug as though to explain the disconnect away with that simple fact. "One who found me during my hunhymgais just as you describe. I fail to see how my earlier choice would disqualify me."

"You have a familiar?" Keion asked. "I've never seen evidence of a beast near you, and, being an actual warrior rather than a ranger, I'm trained to notice these things. I can't even miss noticing *our* ranger's smelly little fur-beast, no matter how much I want to."

"My smelly little fur-beast, as you describe him, Prince, has saved your neck before," Seph retorted, and then her face scrunched up in concentration as she peered back toward Llew. "He's a *bear*, isn't he?"

Llew nodded, pride filling his face. "Indeed. *Slwtubytffest* has to stay away from people, as his countenance is so fierce that he even scares the soldiers away."

"Wait, what did you say his name is?" I'd heard it the first time, but I couldn't believe I'd heard it right.

"Slwtubytffest," Llew repeated, puffing his teenage chest out with pride. "Does that please you, Crown Princess? I named him after a great and noble character in a famous work of literature from your native Earth, one that we use frequently up here to improve our own English language abilities."

I shook my head, trying to remember the famous work of literature he could have found with a character named—well, *that*. Slutty butt fest, he'd said. Twice, even. Finally I had to admit, "Sorry, Llew, but I don't remember ever reading anything that had a character named—that, and I would probably remember it if I had." I glanced at my fellow passengers to see if they knew enough English slang to find the same humor in the name, but they just looked puzzled.

"Oh. That is surprising; I was led to believe that it is truly a widely-read masterpiece. Perhaps just not where you are from? Do people there read? Oh, that is a silly question; of course the wealthy do, but you were raised as a commoner, were you not? Regardless, it is truly a well-written work, so that is unfortunate. It will be my pleasure to lend it to you so that you may read it, once this matter blows over. It is called the Galactic Guide for the Passenger."

Something about the way he said Galactic Guide started me thinking, and then it hit me that I'd actually read that "famous work of literature" several times. "Wait. You're talking about Hitchhiker's Guide to the Galaxy, right? It is well-read where I'm from, but it's hardly literature."

Llew looked confused again. "How can it not be literature? We have a copy of it here."

I shrugged, realizing that I'd made a nonexistent point. The elf word for literature is the same as the elf word for book, which is in turn the same as the elf word for scroll; they don't differentiate between formats. "Never mind. The way you said it made me think of Chaucer and the rest of the really old, hard to read stuff that they forced us to write essays on. Hitchhiker's Guide was fun to read."

"It is, Alyssa, but–were you raised wealthy, then, to be taught to read by your tutors?" Llew asked. The poor kid had no idea how much he didn't know, but I didn't have the desire to explain.

"Llew, everybody where I'm from is taught to read. Except the Alabamans; I'm not sure what they're–no, scratch that, I'm just poking a little fun at our regional rivals for the extreme end of the educational spectrum as we both were. It's–just never mind. But, back to topic–you're kidding, right? The character is Slartibartfast," I said, laying heavily into the *ah* sounds to distinguish what I was saying from what he'd named his bear.

"Oh, I see," he said, nodding. "Where did you say you were from? Misikipippi?"

"Mississippi," I corrected with a sigh, figuring that I knew what was coming, and wondering what it was about rangers that made it impossible for them to pronounce my former state's name right.

"Mississippi," the bennaeth's son repeated, sounding it carefully. "I like the way that name feels on the tongue, I really do. It is a beautiful name, one that speaks boldly of deep winter snows and magnificent game animals. Alyssa, I understand your confusion, as they have taught us well how different dialects on Earth say words differently. I will assure you, my noble Mippissippi native friend and peer, that my highly qualified English language teacher would agree that I am pronouncing the name correctly as Sluttybuttfest."

I looked from Llew to Keion to Seph and then to Aerona, and then ran my eyes around the circuit once again. I know I shouldn't have expected anyone else to see the same humor I found in the situation, but I would've hoped for at least a faint glimmer of a smile out of somebody.

Nope, nothing.

"Well, bless your heart, Llew, I'm sure you're as right as rain." I was getting better at tossing my good ole' Southern euphemisms out in proper elvish, but it didn't help the situation. I watched confusion take hold on everybody's faces, and that just made the whole situation funnier.

Seph rescued me from the imminent bout of laughter by bringing us back to task in her own direct way. She glared at the kid and growled, "Well, dialect differences aside, that's all well and good, Llew, for you to have a familiar, but for you to have trained as a ranger from an early age is—"

"Nontraditional," Llew said, nodding.

"Precisely," Keion injected. "It would seem that the northern elves find tradition something to be spat upon. Is that true, Llew?"

"Spat upon? Of course not. My people do not spit upon tradition, but we also do not consider it to be sacrosanct. Life is to be lived in the present."

"I see. The northern tribes didn't fight much in the wars leading up to the beginning of our current age, did they?" Keion asked, his gaze leveled at Llew.

"No, of course not. The outsiders' battles mean little to us."

"*Guys*," Seph said, her voice sharp to cut off the battle that was brewing. "We can worry over tradition later. Continue, Llew, please. What happened after you went to the ley-gate?"

Keion grinned, and before Llew could open his mouth, he said, "You have come a long way from the unsteady ranger who leaped behind her cousin with a battle cry of *eep*."

Seph flushed, and I stepped in. "Thank you, Prince Charming. Now, let's please continue with the story at the ley-gate." It was Keion's turn to flush; it was the first time I'd used my nickname for him to his face. Granted, Keion was right, and Seph and I had already had the same conversation so she knew it. Seph *had* used a battle cry of eep, and she'd been jumpy and unsure of herself when I'd met her. Since the battle for the library, though, and especially after she'd saved us from a wyvern attack with her own special kind of ranger magic, she'd stepped up into her role. I was proud of my cousin, as I'd told her myself.

So was she, as I could tell from her grin.

So was Keion, apparently, and that realization brought me an unexpected bit of jealousy. That, in turn, left me wondering why I would be jealous of my own cousin. More specifically, why would I be jealous of her over a guy that neither of us could ever have?

"Well—that was interesting," Llew uttered quietly, his gaze passing around the circle of expressions. He sat back and crossed his arms as he continued to peer at the rest of us. Several long moments passed as eyes flitted from target to target: Llew's, from Keion to me to Seph; Seph's, from Keion to me; Keion's, from Seph to Llew; and mine, from Keion to Seph. The magnificent First Prince was, it seemed, just noticing for the first time that he had feelings other than contempt for my cousin, and she was noticing it in reverse as well. I was noticing that he hadn't noticed it yet. Llew, meanwhile, was noticing everything, taking it all in with the apparent wisdom of a soothsayer.

Through it all, Aerona managed to keep glaring at the trees in the distance to make sure they didn't come to life and attack us. I don't know how she maintained her total aloofness.

The moment finally passed. Llew let it drop and continued, "So, at the ley-gate, I stepped through and jogged up to an overlook from which I could see most of the northern plateau. When I didn't see anything noteworthy there, I realized the troop concentrations that must exist had to have already made it to the grassy plains. So I ran back to the ley-gate, passed back through, and realized that the courier would, fortunately for me, be passing by the very next afternoon."

"Up? We didn't see an up," Keion argued.

"It's well hidden, back behind the stones, and you'd have to have seen it in the summer to know it was there."

"Doesn't he have a name?" I asked, tired of always referring to him as just the courier. It made him seem like the same kind of mysterious character that the Doctor was on an old Earth TV show.

"Maybe. Probably, but no one knows it," Llew answered.

"What do you mean, no one knows it? Nobody has ever walked up, shaken his hand, and said, 'Hi, I'm Jim, what's your name?' Really?" I asked.

"Really, Alyssa," Keion answered. "The position of courier is hereditary, and no one has ever asked his name. He is The Courier," Keion made the capitalization of the name obvious in his pronunciation, "in the same way my mother is Queen Talaith, no matter what her birth name may have been, and in the same way that you will also one day be Queen Talaith."

"Oh. Well, then," I said, not really sure what else to add.

"So, I caught a ride with the courier," Llew added for me, circling back around to before my faux pas, "and he brought me to Gidreffydd from where I was able to move around and quietly observe the movements of troops and—well, and other folks—from both inside and outside the town for a few days as he went about his business elsewhere. It finally came time for him to pass back through on the way to Ganolog, and I had asked to leave with him. That was when you showed up, and, well, you know the rest."

"We do know the rest," Keion said, "but you glossed over the movements of troops and—other folks, you said—and I'm curious what, where, and how many they are."

"They're just troops, mostly. You know, I'm sure, how northern battle formations can be a little bit–well, random. Each company is raised from a region, and so I saw groups that ranged in size generally from one hundred to a few hundred. There were a couple of smaller groups, numbering twenty or thirty."

"Total?"

"Two thousand. Troops. I saw three squads of rangers, too, and you know what that means."

Seph nodded intently. "For every squad you see there are five or six more."

"Others?" Keion asked, his eyebrows steepling.

Llew sighed, looking a little bit worried. "Advisors is probably the best word. One per company, wearing a black cloak. You've seen them before?" Llew asked when he caught us exchanging meaningful glances.

"Did they wear a silver clasp in the shape of a dragon?" Keion asked.

Llew nodded. "That, and they were unarmed, which was–weird. Beyond weird, up in this area. Nobody leaves town without a bit of steel strapped to his hip."

"A lack of steel does not make these men incapable of defending themselves, or of attacking others, if my suspicions are correct," Keion observed.

"Magic?" Llew asked. When Keion and I both nodded, the boy shook his head. "If they cast a spell within sight of the companies they are with, odds are that the northern warriors will turn on them. Few up here are as accepting as I am of the practice of spellcasting. Who are they?"

Keion and Seph both looked at me, letting me take the lead in explaining what we knew. "They are, or at least they represent, the Cult of the Wyrm, which is the reason for the shape of the clasps. They're the group who attacked me when I first arrived, and they're also who poisoned and later tried to kill the three of us at the Library of Alecsanddrha. They're apparently convinced that I'm the prophesied Dragon Queen who they need to either kill or control."

"Where does the wyrm come in, though? Dragons have been extinct for thousands of years."

"We don't know," I lied. At least, it was sort of a lie. I didn't actually know the answer, despite the suspicions I held, but I wasn't about to share those with the boy.

"And why would killing you even cross their minds? Wouldn't it prove that you're not the prophesied one?"

"Again, we don't know, at least not for certain. I do know that I ticked them off so much that they didn't seem to care whether they proved the prophecy false back at the library."

"Oh. Well, that's a problem, then, I'd say, both because they may be ticked off at you, and because we don't know whether they are or not. Do you know how far their influence spreads?"

"Far. One of the survivors of the library battle was questioned by my father's men, and apparently Blodwyn the Grey's name was mentioned as a key leader."

"Blodwyn? Blodwyn, really? That's too bad. I like her."

"So she said. You might want to be on your guard if you see her again, though. She saw through our little change of names pretty quickly, and now that the Cult is playing its hand up in the north, the reception you receive on your next visit may not be as pleasant as what you're used to."

"Noted. Father will probably give her to me as a slave."

"Oh, good, just what you need. Another slave," I said, trying unsuccessfully to keep the sarcasm out of my voice. The taking of slaves wasn't right, and I was going to deal with that practice once I was queen, even though I wasn't sure how. I still had a long row to hoe before that had to be dealt with, though, so I let my mind wander as my eyes took in the rapidly-passing landscape. Nobody questioned my comment, though, so I figured either Llew hadn't caught my sarcasm, or he agreed with me, at least a little.

"So, if you have so many more rangers up here than we realized, why aren't the forests kept more pristine?" I asked idly as the trees flew by.

"Why should the forest be kept pristine?" Llew asked. "It's beautiful the way it is."

I just shrugged. I get the whole different strokes thing, but there was such a huge difference.

Letting the silence bubble dissipate, I relaxed and started paying attention to the passing scenery. As I looked out across the acres of woodland, I imagined thousands of tramping feet moving between the trees, disturbing the few clumps of grass that resisted doggedly in the path of the deep winter. I wondered what the tylwyth teg would think of the martial passing of entire battalions of troops. At the same time, I also wondered what Padrig was going to say when we told him the news.

Mostly, though, I wondered if any of us would make it back to Cysegredig alive.

In the hopes of getting rid of that dreary thought, I let myself nod off to the rhythm of movement of the magic-powered sled. It was a smooth ride, all things considered; the runners seemed to glide on cushions of air a couple of inches over the ground. Still, there was an underlying pulse to the motion forward, as though the currents that powered us were more of a cyclical ebb and flow than a steady pressure.

My last thought before surrendering to sleep was to wonder how the sled propulsion system worked.

The peacefulness that put me to sleep didn't last long, though. I was jolted awake by the sled grinding to a halt.

ADREF

literally, towards home, but used to describe any pleasant trip

To Get There First

At first the fog of drowsiness was difficult to shake off, but when the brown bear that stood directly in our path growled menacingly, it sent shocks through my body, bumping me awake instantly.

Through my fog I watched several things happen at the same time. Aerona's daggers sprang out of her belt sheaths, and my guardian assumed a defensive pose in front of me. It was effective; I had to move sideways to continue watching the bear. Meanwhile, both Seph and Keion had arrows pointed toward the beast nearly as quickly as Aerona had her daggers out.

Llew and the courier, meanwhile, had both taken up screaming.

The initial peak of adrenalin subsided quickly so that my ears quit ringing, and I realized that the two screamers were yelling very different things. The courier, far from any fearful reaction I would've expected, was hurling elven obscenities at the beast that was blocking our path. I recognized about every third term, and the words I knew were so shockingly profane that I wondered how bad the other ones were. His hands were busy gesturing in motions that are entirely unfit for public description.

Llew, meanwhile, was yelling at everybody at the same time. What I heard was, "Sluttybuttfest! Lower your bows! That's my Sluttybuttfest! Don't threaten my Sluttybuttfest! Lower your arrows! Don't shoot Sluttybuttfest!"

"*What* are you laughing about, Princess?" Keion asked.

His tone and glare killed all the humor I'd seen in the situation. Sitting up, I sucked a deep breath in and then answered, trying to project my voice over the screamers. "Nothing is funny, Prince. It does appear that the beast blocking our path is Llew's familiar, and I am sure that–Sluttybuttfest–is standing there for a purpose. I would suggest that we lower our arrows."

For once, everybody listened to me. Keion and Seph relaxed and let their bows slip back to neutral, while Aerona made her daggers disappear back into their belt sheaths with a flourish. Looking around the side of her face, I thought I caught a hint of a grin. The courier finally stopped screaming at the bear, though I could tell by his expression he was still very annoyed, bennaeth's son's familiar or not.

Llew leaped from the carriage and ran over to his beastly companion. The two younglings put their heads together, literally, and conferred through that strange bond that exists between ranger and familiar.

I took advantage of the quiet to whisper at Seph. "I thought Llew's familiar was a *medium*-sized bear."

"I think that is a medium-sized bear, at least up here, Cousin," she replied, gesturing at the beast that matched Llew's height while still on all four paws. "You saw Halbiorn, the bear that took Keion's kill, right? Now that was a large bear."

Shrugging, I said, "I only saw Halbiorn from the top, so I guess I missed the proportionality. Aerona, you were going to fight that thing for me, weren't you?"

"Crown Princess, I would fight a dragon to ensure my king's daughter's safety. That is my duty, and my honor," the older woman muttered, still not taking her eyes off of the bear.

Keion snorted softly and rolled his eyes at Aerona's noble words. She ignored him, but I was about to get on him for it when Llew made a little gasping noise and dropped to his hands and knees.

"Llew, what's wrong?" I leaped out of the carriage, intending to go to him. Suddenly his familiar switched back to raging bear mode and roared protectively at me over his ranger. The bear had some lungs, enough to stop me in my tracks.

"It's okay, it's okay," Llew reassured his familiar, and then he stood and walked over to us. "I'm fine, Alyssa. The news isn't good, though."

"What news, Llew?" Keion asked, suddenly using that deep, stern masculine *I'm-in-charge-so-bow-to-me* voice that men love to use. It didn't bother me, princess or no; the prince really was the best to be in charge considering the battle training he'd had, and the unavoidable fact was that battle seemed to be what was awaiting our arrival in Ganolog.

"Slutty has been scouting for us in the Sprucegrass Hills region just ahead of us, where we knew the troops were concentrated. He's noticed a lot of strange movement back away from Ganolog, retreating toward the path we're following now. When I listened to the earth just now, I heard many–hundreds, maybe–moving toward us to intercept. We can't use this path to get there."

"Wait," Seph and I both said at the same time. I turned to her and nodded, yielding the first question.

"When you say that you listened to the earth, you mean you could tell where the troops were and where they were going?"

"Sort of," he said after a pause. In the moment between her question and his answer I read three expressions cross his face: pride that he knew something she didn't, followed by stubbornness, I assume at not wanting to give any of the northern rangers' secrets away, and finally acquiescence. "I have heard that the southern rangers can't do this, at least not as well. I'll show you how it's done later, Sephaline. In the meantime, yes, I could tell general locations as well as direction of travel."

"Wow, that's—something. Something impressive," she said.

I shook my head, still confused. "How could they know we're traveling this way, though? I can see how the Cult in Gidreffydd would have an idea, but we left there at a rapid pace, far too fast for any of their runners. We should have been safe to make it all the way to Ganolog."

"They have both rangers and sorcerers on their side," Seph explained. "Remember how I passed word from the library to your father's troops that we seemed to be in trouble? Rangers can pass messages to other rangers, and I would suspect the same ability from sorcerers to sorcerers, through the energies that pass through the realm."

"...which, of course, are not actually magic," I poked, unwilling to give up on a sore point. When nobody took the bait, I asked, "So speaking of that, Llew, why don't you pass word the same way to your father that we could use some help? Or that we're about to be attacked? Either one might be good for him to know."

"Three reasons, Alyssa. First, even if he tried, he couldn't get here before the other troops do; they have too much of a head start on him. Second, if he could somehow win that race, it would remove his tactical advantage, because Papa's guard is used to battling, or drilling, anyway, in his hometown rather than out here in the open foothills. Third, and most important, is that I don't have anyone I trust to pass the message to. Papa is not a ranger, so I can't send it directly to him, and we have to assume that any ranger-trained members of his guard are in league with the Cult."

"Okay, that makes sense. So what do we do?" I asked.

"I have an idea," the courier said, his voice bordering on insolently sarcastic despite the fact that he was speaking to members of three royal families. "Why don't we all get back into the carriage and let it run? It has its share of defenses, I am pleased to assure you."

I took advantage of the brief, slightly embarrassed silence as we piled back in to ask, "So are you going to turn us a bit to jaunt around the Cult forces? This thing runs pretty fast, so going a little out of the way shouldn't hurt us getting there, should it?"

"If I could, Princess, I would, but that's not how it works. Hey, Llew, if an army is coming through to crush us, you might want to load your bear up in the carriage, too!" the courier called, and then he returned to my question. "I–the carriage, that is–has to follow the energy lines, which create set paths on the surface."

"You didn't know that–ow!" Keion asked, starting his question off with a touch of scorn but getting a warm bear claw across his shin as Slartibartfast clambored in. "Courier, surely this carriage can't support the weight of that beast in addition to all the rest of us!"

"All due respect to you and to your mother, Prince, but do not insult the capacity of my carriage again." The courier nodded forward, and the source of his pride lurched into motion.

"I did not know that aspect of the courier's carriage movement, no. Apparently my teachers failed me on that matter," I said, aiming a glare toward one of my chief teachers. When the prince looked wounded, I assumed I'd won the point and called out over the wind, "So, if I may ask, kind courier, if you do not control the path, what do you control on the journey?"

"Everything," the courier called over his shoulder. "I control the speed at which the carriage runs, and I select the the line upon which the carriage travels. The only limit to my control is that I cannot create paths where they do not already exist. Well, that, and I cannot force the carriage to run over an obstacle in its path, which was a lucky break for the young prince's bear."

"Ah, that makes sense," I said, and while looking at Keion I added, "but since my training so far has been inadequate, I must ask where paths already exist."

Keion flushed and mouthed, *you go too far*, but while the prince expressed his wordless anger the courier answered, "The paths exist between nearly every current major settlement on Kiirajanna as well as the numerous ley-line portals, Princess."

Hearing his words reminded me of the potential trouble I'd left my father's guardsman in, and so I asked, "Hey, speaking of that, is there any chance we could stop briefly by the portal that's about half a day's ride at normal pace from Ganolog? The one you met Llew at? I left one of Dad's guards there, and I really don't want to be responsible for two guardsmen's deaths."

The courier nodded easily, but Keion snorted and said, "Alyssa, you were not responsible for either death, even if the one at the portal has somehow met his end. The first was killed by an avalanche, and the second, if at all, has been killed by enemy forces. You should not accept responsibility for that which is not yours to accept."

I considered his words for a minute, and finally I nodded. "Okay, fine, but let's try to get to the portal in time so that I only have to worry about how I'm not going to accept one death, okay?"

After a while, Llew called out a warning from his lookout spot, "Attackers to the left!" A small band of fur-clad warriors tried to charge through the trees. It was obvious that they were much too late, though. None of them came anywhere close to being in range to attack the carriage.

"Left again!" he called out a few minutes later, and this time there were a few mounted archers among the troops. The folks on foot weren't even close, again, but the ones on horseback were able to get off a few shots–powerful shots that made me duck till I saw them bounce off of a force field that surrounded the carriage in a blue, hazy light.

"I told you the carriage has its share of defenses!" the courier sang back to us as we shot out of bow range of the group.

Magic, I whispered to Keion, who just shrugged and grunted as he continued scanning the horizon.

For once, they couldn't blame me for it.

We whisked along right past five more groups, three to the left and two to the right, with only two of them able to manage anything offensive at all. One launched another volley of arrows that bounced off of the force field just as the first one had, but the second group had a black-cloaked Cultist with them. While his archers shot at us, I watched him reach out toward the ley-line that powered the carriage with a tendril of blue magical force of his own.

"He's trying to bend the ley-line toward him!" I announced as soon as I figured it out.

The courier snorted. "I wish him luck."

Llew nodded in agreement. "The ancients themselves reportedly tried to mold and bend the ley-lines to meet their needs, and even at one point tried to draw them together for a super-powerful transportation nexus, but it never worked for them, either."

"You're pretty smart on history," I said, and Llew beamed under my praise. Keion snorted softly.

The courier's words proved true. I watched as the Cultist gesticulated wildly to no avail. I finally waved a sarcastic farewell to him as the carriage sailed past the point he'd been trying to bend. I breathed a huge sigh; it seemed we were done and home free!

My thought seemed to draw the next comment from Llew as he called out, "One more group, but this one is directly ahead of us." The courier swore, and the carriage rumbled slowly to a stop. His hand flew in the air; it looked like he was consulting some sort of mental map.

"Why did you stop?" I asked.

"Well, there's no point riding full-bore into their ambush. All they have to do is wait till they're in bow range and then have somebody step onto the ley-line," the courier said.

"So, your defenses are a little thin in some places, eh? It appears that we get to do battle directly. How many are there?" Keion asked, and I was actually kind of surprised he didn't thump his chest.

"Only eight or ten, but others are coming up fast behind us."

The carriage driver swore and started the carriage moving slowly forward again.

"Will the folks back there have been able to communicate with the folks up there yet?" I asked Llew.

"Probably not. The ranger link requires being stationary. Why?"

"I have an idea. No, no, hear me out," I argued with Prince Charming against his snort, and he waved me on graciously, or at least mockingly so. I didn't care at the moment. "So since they really don't have any way of knowing who's in the carriage, let's use surprise to our advantage. Llew, send Sl–your bear familiar–off to the left, and Seph, send Booboo to the right. We'll all hunker down in the carriage till it comes to a stop in front of them, with the shield up around us. Call the animals to attack from each side, and let us know when they engage so that the courier can drop the shield and we can all pop up and shoot into the confusion. With their attention diverted, we can down–"

"That's a brilliant idea, Princess," the courier interrupted me, "but to make it work we have to act now. The enemy is close enough for me to sense them, too, which means they're just around the next bend."

Llew and Seph both nodded and looked toward their animal familiars, and suddenly the carriage got lighter as both furry beasts bounded out and into the wood line. We hunkered down behind the boxes, and the carriage rumbling along for a couple of the longest minutes I've ever faced.

"That really is a brilliant idea if it works, Alyssa," Keion admitted. "Where'd you learn tactics?"

"It's just–um, wisdom," I said, stumbling a little on the elf language. They didn't have a term for common sense. It was a lie, anyway; I'd found some time to go through the library in Cysegredig, and there'd been a few military tactics books in there. Somehow it seemed important for a future queen to have at least read a book or two on the subject. I didn't feel like admitting that to him, though, so I gripped the half-dozen arrows I held in my shooting hand tighter and beamed a half-hearted, nervous smile in his direction.

"Hmmph," Keion grunted, looking sideways at me. I realized I'd used the word for the wisdom that comes with age, which was the opposite of what I'd intended to say, but I didn't have time to correct it as the carriage rumbled to a stop. Challenges punctuated the air to our front. I glanced to the side to see Seph looking directly toward Llew, and both rangers nodding slightly.

Their eyes widened simultaneously, and then both said, "Now!"

All five of us—Aerona actually had archer skills that she just preferred not to use—sprang up to draw beads over the boxes to our front. There were eight targets, archers by the look, and six of them were more or less effectively drawing beads on the two animals as the familiars crashed into their line from both sides at the same time. Wordlessly we in the carriage launched arrow after arrow, the first volley causing just enough confusion among the enemy to prevent them from loosing arrows at the familiars. Instead, they tried to turn their arrows toward us, but the time it took them to refocus was more than enough for each of us to send two more arrows after the first.

Within less than a second or two, eight dead elves lay in front of the carriage. All of us leaped out to drag the bodies out of the way so that we could continue our mad rush toward Ganolog. With the help of the bear, the path was cleared quickly. We jumped aboard as the carriage floated by.

"Is it too much to ask for the rest of the journey to town to be safe?" I asked as we gained speed again.

"Probably, but I don't believe that any more troops stand in our way," Llew said.

"Ah, good."

"And if they do, Crown Princess, Slutty—"

"Yeah, about that, Llew? Could I ask you a great big favor?" I asked, interrupting his slaughter of the language.

"Certainly. It is but yours to ask."

"Great. Look, I know what you believe that you've read, but I, having grown up speaking the language, am just a little bit more qualified to teach you to pronounce things, okay? The character you named your bear after is actually called Slartibartfast," I said, drawing the soft *a* sound out once again.

"Does it matter that much, Alyssa?" he asked in accented, but solid, English.

"Yeah," I said in English, nodding. "Yes, it does. Slartibartfast means something completely different from slutty butt fest." I switched back to elvish and told them what the words he'd been saying meant.

"Oh. Well, in that case," Llew said, and then he broke into a laughing fit that was closely followed by similar fits from the rest of the party.

After a while, the boy recovered enough to say, "So, Slartibartfast it is. And by the way, and I meant to say this earlier, good job with the tactics back there, Alyssa."

"Yes, it was a spectacular display of tactical skill," Keion huffed. I turned quickly, wondering if I'd catch his chest poking out as much as it sounded, but he just sat there eyeing Llew appraisingly.

LLYFFANT

a toad. Have you ever noticed that men standing around a table talking shop, or military strategy, or just about anything else, sound an awful lot like toads?

Strategy Conference

"I don't like it," Padrig growled. I sighed in exasperation, Keion gave me an *I told you so* glare, and Llew shook his head. Aerona? She kept glaring at the shadowy corners, even though we had made it to the safety of Padrig's inner fortress.

"How can you not like it?" I asked.

"This is the way I can not like it," he said, smashing one fist into the other open palm and grinding it around in a crushing motion. "It is *garthion*. I simply do not believe that your idea is the best way to keep your party safe."

"What is *garthion*?" I took a moment to ask Seph sideways. My language classes hadn't included that word.

"You really don't want to know," Seph said, drawing her cheeks up into an *eww* expression.

"Something I should not have said in front of a lady and a peer, much less my future queen, and for the slip of the tongue I must apologize, Crown Princess," Padrig said.

"She needs to know our language, at least, Papa," Llew defended my question. "It is—it is when a large number of people's excrement is gathered together."

"Oh. Crap, then," I said in English. Keion snickered in spite of the seriousness of the situation, and then he nodded.

"Yes, Princess. Crap," he said, also in English.

"You shouldn't be so worried over my safety simply because I'm a lady," I turned back to Padrig and argued.

"I am not so much worried over your safety as a lady. Ladies up here fight alongside their men when the time comes, and the key reason you gained my blessing as bennaeth is that I am certain you will be strong enough to do the same." I looked at him sideways; again his choice of words for strong sounded like he was making me out to be a female version of Hitler. He didn't stop, though. "No, what concerns me is the safety of the daughter of my liege lord, the King of Kiirajanna," Padrig said.

"Well, I very much appreciate your concern, but I don't see any way to get me safely through the enemy's lines to Cysegredig at this point," I argued.

"True. I did not say that the plan you suggest was not the only one left available. I said only that it is garthion. If you'd gone home when I told you to, young Princess, we would not be in this predicament."

I nodded. It was the first time during the discussion that he'd brought up any sort of *I told you so*. He deserved it once, I guess. It was true that Llew had the situation more under control than I'd believed, though I was still pretty sure he wouldn't have as much intel as he did if I'd gone home earlier.

Still, it was late, and Padrig had a right to be grumpy. The five of us had dismounted the courier's carriage inside the tree line before it arrived in Ganolog, and then we'd followed a special path known only to Llew in order to sneak into town, and then into his father's chambers, under the cover of darkness. Padrig answered the rap on his antechamber door in his nightclothes, shock and then glee registering on his face. The great bennaeth ushered us in quickly, and then he gave his son a chest-crushing bear hug. He stepped behind a partition for less time than it took most people to undress, and in seconds emerged fully clothed. Now we all stood in a side chamber with Padrig and a map of the area while Llew and I told him all we'd seen, Keion professionally filling in some of the strategic dots of our story.

When the attacking troops, including those assembled right outside Ganolog under the ruse of a fair, were all fully indicated on the map, it became obvious that there was no way for us to go home. Then Llew's description of the forces arrayed around Ganolog deepened the lines on his father's face. Worse, when I described the faces and the voices I'd encountered in the darkness in Gidreffydd, his shoulders sank and his head fell forward. The news obviously crushed him.

"Yes, those are my four bens, if your descriptions are any-thing close to accurate," he announced, his fingers gripping the table hard enough to dent the wood.

"I'm sorry, Padrig," I said, trying to lighten the impact of our story, but he shrugged it off with a stoic expression.

"Go on," the bennaeth said.

We told him the rest of what we knew, and then he told us what he preferred that we do as a result. The plan, then, was that the five of us—six, since in any fight I'd be stupid not to count Booboo among the team members—would remain in the hall, the last bastion of defense, and fight for our lives along-side Padrig and his personal guard if it came to that. Seph and I would stay back as archers, while Aerona and Keion would fight in the melee with the bennaeth and his son, as well as the son's bear, whose appearance was sure to be a surprise.

Padrig insisted three times that I stay back behind the lines as an archer, taking up a position from which I could flee if I needed to. I wasn't certain whether to take his concern over my well-being, and the implied lack of faith in my abilities, as a good thing or bad, but I let it ride in favor of firming up the plan. Besides, it got me stationed where I felt most needed, which was in a position to oversee the whole battlefield in case the Cult members began casting spells.

"They're not really going to try using magic in battle, are they?" Padrig asked.

"They have before," I said. "Not offensive spells per se, but they've teleported, and on our way here they tried to stop us by shifting the ley-lines. Who knows what they're planning to use against us this time?"

"At least we have our own answer to that tactic," Llew said, turning a glowing face my direction, but his father shook his head grimly.

"The only good answer to that is no, Son. I have heard what Alyssa did in the library, as have many others, and she must not do it again. Not unless her own life is in mortal danger. Do you hear me? Do *you* hear me?" he asked me directly the second time. "Crown Princess, I fear a realm-wide revolt if word gets out that you are flouting one of our most precious traditions. I will not order you to avoid defending yourself using whatever tactics are at your disposal if you must, but you must not use magical powers in any other circumstance. Please promise me that."

"Bennaeth, I promise to only use my magical powers if I can see no other option available to lead to the best chances at preserving and defending my own life," I said, choosing my words carefully.

Padrig glared at me for several long moments. It was obvious that he distrusted my choice of wording, but after a long wait he apparently decided to accept the promise I'd given as the best he was going to get. With a harrumph, he went back to studying the map.

"Now, we do have a problem before us. My forces, fierce though they may be, are outnumbered by those we believe are coming, and I must admit that Llew is correct that we cannot even trust all of those who stand with us tonight. How do we face a larger force and get its leaders in here without most of their army as well? You have studied tactics, young prince, so I ask, as a simple liege of your mother, known most well for my simple bear-hunting ability—I ask for your advice for the coming battle."

"Oh? I haven't heard that story," I interjected, trying to lighten the mood a little.

Padrig answered, "They were telling it the other night, and in verse. You probably don't remember because you had passed too much liquid fortification down your throat and become forgetful by that point. Medraud was a great white bear far to the north. He was big, this big," he said, holding his hand up as high as his arm could reach, "and mighty. Smart, too; he was one of the few bears we've seen who would actually hunt us, and seemingly just for sport. It was a magnificent hunt, but now is not the time to retell the story. Returning with his head is what propelled me into the bennaeth's chair. Well, that, and my natural leadership ability, and my winning smile. Having a gorgeous wife didn't hurt, either."

"Cannae!" Keion exclaimed, stabbing his finger at the point on the map that showed the opening to the main hall we were in.

"What? Who had sung?" Padrig asked, looking confused.

"No, no, not *canai*. Cannae. The Battle of Cannae," Keion said, looking around the group with a sudden commanding energy. I was confused, too; it sounded like he'd said the same word, the third person past-tense of the elf verb meaning *to sing*. He went on, "It's Earth military history. I actually went back for a short while to improve my English and took some military classes to supplement what I'd learned here. There was a battle many years ago on Earth that was fought between the Romans and—well, never mind all of the detail. The short version is that the smaller force used a surprise tactic and wiped the larger force out."

"That sounds promising, assuming my bens have not also studied this tactic. Tell me of it."

"It was simple, really," Keion said, getting excited as he laid out several troop markers on the edge of the map to show two forces facing each other in lines. "So, as battle was joined, the larger army naturally assumed it would win and charged ahead. As they charged, the middle of the other army appeared to assume, again naturally, that it would lose, and they fell back, giving ground."

"They—retreated?" Padrig asked, his eyebrows furrowed in confusion. "Come, Prince. A warrior would never do that."

"Hopefully your warriors will do as they are told, ben-naeth."

"Well, yes, as long as the order is not a pile of dung."

"It is not. At least, this was not. You see, it was part of a master plan. The bigger army saw the retreat and charged even more ferociously ahead, assuming that they would quickly and decisively win the battle."

"Of course. I would, too." Padrig still looked very confused, shaking his bearded head from side to side.

"But then you would be charging into a trap, Bennaeth. You see, as the center of the smaller force retreated, the ends surged forward, attacking the sides of the larger army instead of the front." Keion excitedly demonstrated the maneuver, starting with his arms stretched out to the side and then backing away from us while bringing his arms closer together. "They were able to cut through the sides easily and then rip through the vanguard from the rear, killing all of the enemy forces." Keion demonstrated again using the units on the map.

Padrig shook his head as he watched Keion move the pieces to demonstrate the tactic. "I confess, I do not understand. Why did the soldiers in the larger army not just turn to face a new direction? If you come at my side you will certainly cut me down, but I can change that with one step. See?" Padrig displayed his ferocious glare as he pivoted to his left in one ponderous motion.

"That was the point of the trap. They couldn't. They were trained to move forward in perfect lines so that their shields interlocked and formed a protective wall. To turn to the side would mean completely redoing their entire formation."

"These humans—they were called Romans, you said?"

"They were."

"There must not be any Romans any more."

"That is correct," Keion said, his voice a little guarded.

"Good. The Romans were stupid."

"Well, your point is valid, Bennaeth, but regardless, I think that this tactic will succeed here."

"Why? Because you think Iolyn's men will be stupid as well? You want the center of my guard, my strongest men, to retreat in the hope that those we face won't think to turn to the side?"

"No, no, that's exactly opposite of what I'm hoping. I'm certain, in fact, that they will think to turn to the side," Keion said, his eyes gleaming with excitement. "Iolyn's troops aren't as stupid as the Romans were, after all. But you see, in *this* battle, turning them to the side is a good thing. The forces at Cannae were trying to destroy each other, but yours aren't. Iolyn doesn't want to kill the elves of Ganolog any more than you want to kill the elves of the other tribes. Their goal is to get to you, while your objective is to prevent that. Is all of that not correct, Bennaeth?"

"It is. Go on, Prince."

"Who will be leading the charge, right down the very middle of the lines?"

"The bens, of course."

"Right. And who do we want to get inside first, and alone, if that is possible?"

"The bens." For the first time, Padrig's voice softened, and he peered at the table for several long moments of contemplation. "I see what you are saying. This—yes, this might work. By sliding back to let the bens through to us while making their troops turn to the side, we accomplish what we need. That just might work, my good prince. Thank you, and thanks to your now-deceased Romans."

"There is one problem with this plan, Papa," Llew said.

"What is that one problem?" Padrig asked, looking up from the table and cocking an eyebrow in curiosity.

"Whom do you trust enough to tell of the ruse?"

"Grigor, of course. He will help me select the others."

A shudder ran up my spine. "No, not him. Please, Padrig, not him."

"Why not my advisor, Alyssa?" Padrig's voice reminded me a little of the time when I'd complained about Grigor earlier, but I could tell from the fact that he was asking the question that it was an act for the rest of the group.

"He's been giving me the creeps since we got here. It's the way he looks at me, like he would rather see my head on a platter than on my shoulders."

"Bah, that is just how he looks at everyone. Even when he is speaking longingly of the hunt, his face always looks like he wants to rip my head off."

"No, Papa, this time I agree with her," Llew said, coming to my defense in a move that obviously surprised his father. "Grigor has seemed a bit–odd–recently. Remember how you were saying to me the other night that you really weren't certain whom to trust? Let's make a wild, and probably completely invalid, assumption that he may not be entirely loyal, and bypass him just this once."

Padrig looked from me to his son, and then back again. He mopped his forehead with one massive hand, and then growled, "Grigor has been by my side for nearly my entire adult life, and now you urge me not to trust him?" He looked back and forth once more, and when our expressions didn't change he nodded. "Okay, fine. Is better to err on the side of caution, no? So, my son, grown up as you are, I will ask you who you would recommend to give the orders to."

The boy named a couple of lieutenants, and Padrig nodded. "Fine. It shall be so."

"So we have two more days before the leaders get here, if I recall correctly?" I asked.

"Maybe a little more, since they're moving with troops. Maybe a little less, though. We should prepare tomorrow," Keion said.

"Do you think they will know that those of us who are from Cysegredig are here?" I asked.

"Of course they will," Keion said. "Let's stop assuming ignorance on anyone's part. No matter how I tried to cover up our identities, we were still recognized by nearly everyone along the way. I'm sure the bens knew by first light that we were in Gidreffydd. That's why they sent so many of their forces away from their normal march to catch us. I wouldn't be surprised if the good innkeeper was questioned thoroughly. I also suggested to the good courier that his next trip take him directly south, and that he not return to Ganolog for some time. I gave him a letter for your father to precipitate that course of action."

"I saw. Thank you. It's good that Dad knows what is going on."

"Indeed. And now, may I suggest we get some sleep in order to be ready for whatever tomorrow may bring?" Keion asked.

"Tomorrow will bring nothing. The bens cannot be here for two more days, and their forces will not attack without them," Padrig stated.

"Those outside the walls, I agree, will do nothing. But we do not know what those inside the walls will do when they see us back."

"Hmm," Padrig said, scratching his chin and turning the exhalation into a deep growl. "You are right, Keion. We should be on our guard tomorrow. Regardless, now is a fine time to seek the comfort of sleep."

Battle Preparations

The next morning started completely wrong when Ellga shrieked as she entered the room. She shrieked louder, though only for a brief moment, when Aerona caught her shoulder from behind and clapped a set of calloused fingers over the maid's mouth. I sat up and motioned for my guardian to set the poor girl free.

"You—you came back, Princess," she stammered once Aerona released her. "But I thought that you had left us, permanently. It is good to see you again, but if I had known then it would have been my pleasure and honor to have some hot water drawn for you."

"It's fine," I assured her. "After the long, rough journey we've had, the luxury of a hot bath would have been wonderful, but I didn't expect it."

"Well, it is good to see that you are back, Highness. I just came in to clean the room, but please allow me attend to that service for you immediately."

Ellga scurried away and then quickly returned with hot water for my wash basin, and though I still felt guilty being served like that—and by a slave—it really did feel good to wash up after the stress of the trip. I dressed quickly, and was glad to see Seph and Booboo come in just as I finished.

We held our tongues regarding the oncoming battle, as the last thing we'd all agreed on was to not tell anybody who didn't specifically need to be told. We didn't want to give agents of the Cult, if there were any inside the keep, a reason to strike early. I felt bad not warning the slave who'd been assigned to serve me. Who knew if she would be safe? Unfortunately, we'd all agreed, and that was that, and so there was nothing I could think of to do about it.

"Prince Charming should be here already," I joked to Seph as we waited near the door. It was true; he'd said he would plan to join us first thing in the morning, and he'd always been quick to get going before. I decided to give him a little nudge to get ready quicker, and so despite the risk of seeing something I shouldn't, I crossed the hall, opened his door by a couple of inches, and stuck my head in to ask him to hurry it up.

Instead of tossing out a light-hearted joke, though, I managed to make the third shriek of the morning.

Keion, still only dressed in what apparently served as his underpants, sat rigidly in the chair in front of his mirror. In the reflection I could see his eyes flick around toward the sight of my face poking inside the door. His hair was still wet, his face expressionless. A blue haze of magic lay draped over Keion's muscular form. I marveled for a moment as I realized that I could actually read the weaves of energy that had been used to immobilize him.

On the other side was Aleifr, the servant who'd been assigned to this chamber. He stood rigid, trembling a little, holding Keion's black-pommeled sword pointed directly at the prince's chest.

Sweat ran down Aleifr's face as he glanced up at me and my still-shrieking mouth. Our gazes met, his full of doubt, fear, and self-loathing. Suddenly his confused, terrified expression reformed into a mask of determination, and as I stood paralyzed for an attenuated moment I watched his left hand reach up to steady his shaking right fist on the sword's long, leather-wrapped grip. The business end of the sword stopped quivering and slowly began its calm, murderous journey toward the prince's bare breast

The servant's hesitation cost him the chance to act, though. A rough shove pushed me out of the doorway just as the hilt of one of Aerona's throwing daggers buried itself in the boy's chest. It was followed immediately by an arrow, two more daggers, and then a second arrow as Aerona and Seph both entered behind me. The boy let the sword fall to the floor, clutched at his breast as if he could somehow keep the blood in, and dropped to his knees.

"Thank you," he breathed once, and then he fell dead. Instantly the blue energy surrounding Keion winked out. Prince Charming sprang out of the chair, and very nearly also out of the folded white cloth that was all that protected his modesty.

"That was very fortunate timing for you to open the door, Princess," Aerona observed, stalking over to retrieve her daggers.

"I don't believe he would have raised the courage to strike if your entry hadn't made it necessary," Keion said, crossing his arms over a very muscular, entirely hairless chest.

"Yeah, I could tell you were working him down from that ledge real effectively. You're welcome, by the way," I said drily, trying but failing to keep my eyes locked on his. Six clearly defined muscles delineated a perfect abdomen, and the prince's thigh muscles were—well, also perfect. With a supreme effort, I summoned my most business-like voice to ask, "You want to tell us what happened, Keion?"

Padrig barreled down the hall and into the room, the bennaeth followed by a couple of burly guards. "Someone said—oh," he said, entering the room around me. His eyes traveled from Aleifr's inert form to Keion's near-nakedness to Aerona, who was matter-of-factly cleaning her dagger off on one of the towels on the valise. After a long, low growl he said, "Well, this is—unexpected. Unprecedented."

"I can imagine, Bennaeth. The northern clan is best known for your hospitality, and the promise of safety near your hearth, not for attacks on guests in their chambers. We do need to talk about this," Keion said, gesturing at the body on the floor.

"Yes, Prince, but we should hold the discussion in private. Leave us," Padrig said, shooing his guards out and closing the door after.

"Actually, Padrig, would you mind if I got dressed first?"

Padrig shook his head, his jaws clenching, unclenching, and then clenching again in rapid repetition. He pointed to the wardrobe. "There should be a robe to satisfy your modesty, Prince. This is too urgent a matter to hold off for clothing. Please, let me know what happened this morning so that I can act quickly if a plot is afoot."

Keion's hot, nearly naked physique rippled its way over to the wardrobe, from which he extracted a tan robe. I actually heard Seph exhale a quiet sigh of disappointment as the hard muscles disappeared from sight. A curious glance proved that Aerona's eyes were, as usual, examining the darkness in the corners for potential threats. I marveled at her level of discipline, something neither Seph nor I could equal.

"I awoke to a shriek from the direction of Alyssa's room, actually, but my sitting up startled Aleifr, who said that he had just entered my room and wasn't expecting me to be here. He poured me a pitcher of hot water for washing, which was a luxury I couldn't wait to enjoy. But as soon as I sat down in front of the bowl, I felt tingly and cold. It was strange, Padrig. I couldn't move anything but my eyes. I watched as he went to my bedside, sat shaking for a while, and finally retrieved my sword, bringing it over and holding the tip up toward my chest. He actually apologized then for having orders to kill me if I returned, if you can believe that. He put it on my chest, but his hand started shaking so much that he lowered it again. He tried raising it up to the small of my neck, and the same thing happened. The third time he raised the sword, Alyssa came in and screamed, and just as I sensed some strength come to the boy's grip on the sword, Aerona took him out."

"Guardsmistress, you have my thanks," Padrig said, nodding to her. She nodded in return and then went back to glaring at the darkness. "Huh. So Aleifr was a plant. Huh. Did he ever tell you where he was from?"

"No, Bennaeth, he did not."

"Huh." Padrig looked back toward me, bushy eyebrows lifting. "Alyssa, has Ellga told you where she is from?"

"Yes, she has. She's described her home, the tiny, peaceful fishing village far to the west that your people raided because they couldn't pay their taxes." I wondered where Padrig was going.

"Huh." Padrig nodded and shrugged. "Yes, that is largely correct. Ellga's village, which is indeed tiny compared to Ganolog in spite of its being the capital of that region, fell behind in their duties, and so we requested a bondsmaiden in a—well, a fairly peaceful, mostly—I'll call it a visit—in order to satisfy the debt. You know, government must happen. We got her, and she has been such a good, hard-working helper that I will be happy to return her with a clean slate to her village by this time next year. Aleifr, on the other hand, was a good-faith trade with Iolyn. It is a standard practice up here, putting people in each others' keeps in order to communicate trust and good intentions. Unfortunately, it did not occur to me until this morning that if the master is suspect, so must be the pawn. I, too, am quite glad for your timely intervention, Crown Princess, and for yours as well, Lady Aerona."

"Just Aerona, Bennaeth," the guardswoman corrected politely, though I could see where the very tips and edges of her lips started to crack upward into a rare smile.

"Not just Aerona. You prevented a realm-wide tragedy, Lady Aerona, and so within my clan and hold you shall henceforth bear the honorific, and hopefully proudly," Padrig said.

She actually allowed herself a pleasant smile at that. "I will treasure the title for the remainder of my days, Bennaeth," she said convincingly.

"However long that may be," Padrig added, turning back to us with a dour expression. "We—Sephaline, are you okay?"

"I'm fine, Bennaeth," Seph said, but her expression argued that she wasn't.

I stepped in for my cousin. "I suspect she's wondering why the prince thanked Aerona for saving his life, but neglected to mention the source of the two arrows that are sticking out of Aleifr's chest."

"I'm fine, Alyssa," Seph argued again.

"I did not think to add her, since I hadn't noticed the arrows, but I do appreciate your help, your assistance in saving my life, very much, Ranger Sephaline."

"I'm fine, Keion," Seph said and followed it up with a sigh.

"You already are a member of the peerage, so there is nothing I can grant you but my thanks, yet—"

"I'm fine, Padrig."

"Then why were you glaring, Sephaline?" I asked, curious.

"I don't know, Alyssa." She started sounding exasperated. "Sometimes my resting face is a glare, I've been told. It might have been the dropping down from the adrenalin high of the attack. It might be concern over the coming battle. I don't know, but I am fine, thank you, everyone, for your concern."

Padrig looked at her for a few long moments and then nodded. "You are fine, then. That is good. We have a lot of preparation to be done, and the death of this young man is likely to herald a more proximate beginning than we thought earlier. Let us be about our preparations."

"What exactly do we have remaining to prepare?" I asked, confused. We had our plan, and we had all of our weapons ready.

"Simply to gather and prepare yourselves for the fight. I will have more arrows brought to you with your meals. I must go now, to meet with my key leaders. When the time comes, I look forward to fighting by your sides."

Padrig rose and left, the door slamming decisively behind him.

"Well, that was interesting," I said.

"Yes, yes, it was. Now, if you ladies don't mind, would you please leave my room so that I might get dressed?" Keion asked.

We minded, or at least some of us did, but we all said we didn't and left his room as requested.

ANHYBLYG

stubborn, unyielding. The elves are generally positive about things that are strong and unyielding, but this is the other word for it.

An Escape Plan

The next day dawned as unseen and bleak in my room as the last one had, but at least it started quieter. This time Ellga, knowing that we were present, took care of me with not only a warm bath but also a foot soak. I swear, if I could ignore the whole slave thing, I could get spoiled that way. Still, there was no sunlight inside, and we couldn't go out because we'd been asked to avoid public eyes in spite of the fact that the Cult obviously knew we were there. We hadn't even left our rooms for the entire day after the attack on Keion. It wasn't safe, we were told, and so Keion, Seph, and I sat around and played dice all day.

So—bleak. Sunless. Boring, even.

I hadn't missed TV and texting and the Internet the whole time I'd been in Kiirajanna, but that was because there was always something to do. Either I had archery practice, or a lesson to be learned, or sometimes I just had research I wanted to do in the abbey's library. Every single day had brought something new, which just made the day stuck in our rooms seem that much harsher. For the first time I missed cable TV, and I missed the Internet.

I also desperately missed Momma. I missed her smile, and I missed her breakfasts. I missed her cheerfully wishing me a good night and sweet dreams.

So, yeah—bleak. Bleh.

Knowing that there was a battle coming our way soon just added to the overall dreary effect. How soon was the only question. It wasn't that I feared death this time. I didn't. I vividly remembered what I'd done at the library, how through Draignerthol I'd called down wind and fire and turned a badly-outnumbered situation entirely around and actually into our favor. That was before I'd studied the use of magic. I was pretty sure that this time I could do it again, and in even greater magnitude and to more deadly result, after going through the textbook. I even figured that, wearing Draignerthol, I could conquer the world with the magic I now wielded, and I was fully prepared to carry that power into the battle like a suit of armor.

No, I wasn't scared of death—at least, not *my* death. What I was scared of was the decision that was likely coming. At some point in the battle, maybe even at several points, I'd hold in my hand the decision of whether to call upon the power of Draignerthol or—well, to not call upon that power. I didn't want to; I'd been made well aware of the penalty facing me if I became known as the one who flaunted magic. On the other hand, there was no way I could watch any of my party, or Padrig's, either, fall without doing all I could to prevent it. Even, I knew, if that meant forfeiting my own claim to the throne.

At the same time, I still felt like a teenage girl from Mississippi who shouldn't be called on to make that level of decision, to be honest. Who was I to pull in the massive power of nature and use it to snuff the life of anyone, even a foe? But then again, I knew I couldn't talk about that uncertainty, not with my party, nor with Padrig's.

The bennaeth stopped by to lead us to his chamber after we'd been served a private lunch by his most trusted kitchen staff. They were his only kitchen staff, actually; apparently the mighty bennaeth was awfully picky about who he let work in his kitchen, and slaves and visitors from other clans weren't invited. That level of security made a lot of sense to me, once I found out. I made a mental note to ensure it was that way for my own kitchens during my reign. Not that there would be slaves anywhere from anywhere, of course, but the main concept still remained valid.

Padrig led us through a secret door from the guest side to his chambers to make sure that we weren't seen. As he opened it he also made sure to tell us to use that path in the event we needed to escape. Keion and I both bristled at the suggestion that we'd flee.

"No, you listen," the bennaeth said, pointing a finger at each of us in turn. "I am not scared of death; it comes to us all eventually, and I am an old man already. If it happens that I fall, though, my passing will be in vain if the prince and crown princess, my liege lord and lady's son and daughter, perish with me. It will not happen, and that is my final word on the matter. Llew, I order you to see to their departure in that event if they delay even one small sliver of a second."

"Yes, Papa," the boy said, glaring at us to show his own resolve.

"Lady Aerona, you will also make certain that the prince and princess make their retreat if I fall?"

"I will," Aerona agreed, earning her a glare from me that she ignored.

"Okay, so—" Keion started, but Padrig cut him off.

"Promise me."

"Promise you what, Bennaeth?" Keion answered with a completely innocent expression.

"Promise me that if I fall, you two, at least, will flee through the path I have shown you," Padrig said with a forceful glower. He crossed his arms in a stance that elves rarely use, though I recognized it. It was one of Momma's stances, the one that always meant I wasn't getting my way no matter what. He had us; once Keion gave his word, we all knew that he wouldn't go back on it even under penalty of death.

"I promise that if I see you fall, I will flee with the crown princess through the path you have shown us," Keion said after a brief staring match. Every word sounded like it pained him.

"Not good enough, Prince. Promise me that even if you do not see me fall, but rather hear it, or sense it, or come to know of it through magical or mystical means, you will flee with the crown princess through this path."

Keion's face narrowed; he'd tried to give himself a loophole but Padrig wasn't having any of it. He nodded once, grudgingly. "So promised, Bennaeth."

"Good," was all Padrig said as he turned and led the way through the secret passage into his area of the keep.

The secret route was a good idea. There was a closet in the back of Padrig's chamber with a sturdy wooden door that locked from the inside. Behind one cloth panel was hidden a wooden door that opened into a narrow hall that connected to the fake wall in a closet in Keion's room. That hall was home to a well-hidden trap door that led down to a tunnel. The tunnel, Padrig explained, opened up onto a landing on the cliff that was obscured from view from above, from which, in turn, a path led gradually up and away.

Only bennaeths were aware of this escape route, he assured us, and I believed him.

Back in his chambers, we met the bennaeth's personal escort of guards. Not that I hadn't seen them before, but in elf custom, V.I.P.s and guards never, ever, get involved with each other any further than pleasant smiles and an occasional nod. Aerona had become a very personal part of my entourage, true, but that was because she'd been thrust on me—we'd been thrust on each other—at a very stressful moment. It was also the case that she was so incredibly good at her job, and such an interesting person to boot, that I'd kind of started looking at her as more of an older sister than just a guard.

"Prince Keion, Crown Princess Alyssa, these are the members of my royal guard. The short one is Bors. He may look diminutive, but Bors can swing a mace like nobody else." The "diminutive" guard who nodded was a head and shoulders taller than Keion, and could easily have been in the N.B.A. back at home. He smiled and waggled his fingers at us, patting his mace with his other hand. I waved back, respectfully.

"Over there is Ithel, my archer who is equally generous at helping his targets lose blood with his daggers. Ithel, wave at our guests, please." A lithe elf waved from the wall opposite us. It wasn't an unpleasant wave, not really. It was more of an acknowledgment of understanding that we should not even consider threatening the elf's bennaeth. Nobody laughed as we waved back, despite Padrig's pun, which made use of the fact that Ithel means generous lord in the elf tongue.

Two more elves whose names I can't remember were introduced to us, and then came their leader, sort of. Technically, she *was* the leader, but only technically. Padrig had appointed her the leader of his personal guard, and he introduced her that way, but I could tell from everyone's body language that the appointment was in name only.

Sarah grinned as she was introduced, and then she clomped over to us, produced a muscle in one bicep and said,

"Feel this." Keion indulgently poked it and agreed that it was strong. Sarah then insisted on showing off for us, doing pu-shups and, at the same time, a neat dagger trick where she spun twin blades around her fingers and up over her head, suddenly springing up to her feet while bringing the blades back down to waist level with a flourish. Her lips curled up in a feral grin as she curtsied.

"Nice," Keion said, though his voice lacked conviction. I glanced at Aerona's face, hoping to gauge some truth about the quality of Sarah's display from our own dagger expert, but she just stared at the corner of the room.

"Nice," I parroted Keion, and Sarah responded with a glowing smile. The rest of the guards somehow looked even more disgusted, though the actual expressions on their faces didn't change in the slightest.

"Okay, get back to your posts, all of you," Padrig ordered, and all but the leader departed immediately. Sarah looked back over her shoulder once to make sure we were still impressed by her prowess, and then she followed her fellow guardsmen out the door.

Padrig waited till the door was completely shut to explain. "I knew her parents," he said, shaking his head. "She was always a special one."

"Huh," I grunted, and was amazed to hear the same sound from Keion, Seph, and Aerona, all at the same time. Apparently *special* could be given the same connotation in elvish that it has in English.

"A knife *savant*," Aerona said, surprising me with the word. It wasn't an elf word, and I don't believe it's actually English, either, but still it seemed appropriate.

Padrig nodded. "A warrior *savant*, actually," he said, shrugging with a sad look on her face. "She cannot tie her own boots most of the time, and as you saw, she has no concept of social graces, but she can use any weapon she has ever touched like she was born with it in her hands. She has the superhuman strength of a colossus, too. She's simply amazing, unmatched in battle."

"I bet she is," Keion said in a tone that didn't mirror his words, and then he shook his head in dismissal. "So, Padrig, is there anything further needing done to prepare for tomorrow's battle?"

"My scouts tell me it will be tonight's battle, actually," Padrig said, eyes tracking from Keion to Llew and then to the rest of us.

"Dang," I said in English. The elf language just didn't have some of the tools that we needed—tools like savant, and like dang.

"Why dang?" Padrig asked.

"Well, I—" I started, and faltered. Why dang? It was a good question. I didn't know. I really wasn't sure if it would be better to wait until the next day or to just get it over with, and so I shrugged.

"Do you need further preparation for tonight's battle?" Keion asked.

"No. Really, no, I don't," I said, shaking away everyone's questioning looks. "It's just that—I have this weird feeling. I've already seen so many people die. What if tonight is the last time I see one, or all, of you?"

"Alyssa, you are still so very young," Padrig said, his voice soft and tender. His bear paw of a hand reached up and gently stroked my cheek once. "I do not mean that as an insult—very much the opposite, actually. It is exhilarating to be around someone young, and especially so with you, because despite the rapid rate of change you have been experiencing in your new life here, you still have a view of that life that embraces constancy, permanence, and a degree of invulnerability. No, no, let me finish. It is entirely possible, should the bens somehow change their minds and turn around and thus the coming battle never happen, that one of us might perish peacefully in our sleep tonight, thus making this the last day you see that person regardless. Yesterday, in fact, could just as easily have been the last day you saw one of us. Thus, I ask you to consider, what is it now, what is it about this battle, that makes that potential any more poignant? Certainly, the battle increases the odds of one or more of our deaths, but we are all good, strong fighters, and we have a good, strong plan. The thought of potential death is merely a head game that you are playing both with and against yourself."

"Also remember," Keion jumped in before I had a chance to counter. I was relieved that he kept his voice soft and non-sarcastic as he continued, "that an elf should honor a good, hard-fought death in battle. That honor is a significant part of who we are as a people. The elf queen must always personify that."

"You sound like a Samurai, Keion," I objected.

"I am not certain what that is, but it must be a good thing."

"Didn't you study the history of war on Earth? You told us about this Cannae thing. How could you not know what a Samurai is?"

"I did, and I did, and yet I do not. Perhaps you could explain?"

"Samurai are Japanese—um, warriors," I started, suddenly realizing my own knowledge of them was limited to having watched a few movies. "They pledge to serve as fighters for a lord, but if they're disgraced, they become—oh, I can't remember the word." I'd seen it in a movie a couple of times, but that wasn't helping.

Keion just shrugged. "It is the Japanese part that befuddles me. My course of study did not include Eastern warfare, other than when they invaded the West. I studied the Huns, for example. Most Earth-based military history courses divide warfare that way, between the East and the West, covering one or the other but not both, except of course for the battles within both hemispheres during the second World War."

"Well, given all that," an obviously bored Padrig interjected, "we do have a battle coming up soon. I will have the kitchen bring you one of the finest meals you have ever eaten, together with as much ale as you care to drink. Feast well, my friends, for tonight we dance with death."

GWAWDODYN

poetic meter. There are twenty-four forms in elf poetry, everything from simple couplets to very complex mid-word consonant patterns, and you'd better know them all if you're going to be queen!

A Bardd's Tale

The kitchen elves brought our dinner to my room, accompanied by one other elf. I looked closely at him while Seph went to retrieve Keion; he looked familiar. Ellga, once she'd set out the dinner plates, introduced the elf as Grand Master Dinol, the greatest bardd of the northern lands, and then I remembered–I'd seen him telling a story the night I'd gotten way too drunk. It was the bright, multicolored robe that came back to memory first. Somebody that night explained that the northern bardds sew a colored stripe to the bottom hem of their robe after their first cycle as a storyteller, and then each year after another color is added as the next stripe. They said Dinol had long ago run out of room on his cloak for any more stripes.

Other than the striped cloak, the bardd was dressed normally, with brown linen pants, beige linen shirt, and brown leather shoes. Normal height and normal weight also failed to make him into anything remarkable as a figure, so I figured the robe would be the only way to recognize his presence if you were a newcomer like me.

"The mighty bennaeth, Padrig of the Northern Reaches, sent me to tell you the tale of Medraud, the mighty king, as you eat and prepare for battle, yourselves, kind young Prince, and Crown Princess, and ladies. Once you have settled, it would be my pleasure to begin the story," Dinol chimed, his voice lilting and beautiful.

Once we'd settled, I asked, "Didn't you tell this tale the other night, after the hunt?"

"Ah, yes, Crown Princess Alyssa, Light of the Northern Sky, She Who Shall Bring the Dragon's Fury, Beautiful Daughter of the Majestic King Cadfael himself, yes, I did indeed tell the tale of Medraud, the bruin menace that our mighty bennaeth removed from our realm through his tracking and hunting acumen. Tonight's tale, though, is of a different Medraud, one more distant and equally more majestic in our lore. It is one that, I pray, you have not yet heard before, and thus will the telling be as entertaining as it may be educational."

"Well, I'm not sure whether I've heard it," I said. I looked around, and none of the others seemed to have any idea what was to come. I'd read the tales of King Arthur, and their villain Mordred, and I half-expected the bardd's tale to be a repetition of those with the *Medraud* spelling I'd seen more commonly in elf land. It was okay; I liked those stories enough to enjoy a re-telling. I wasn't certain I was in the mood, what with the battle coming our way, but I knew I could at least suffer through it while I ate.

Dinol smiled and nodded, my expression of uncertainty apparently enough to satisfy his desire. He opened his mouth and took a large, exaggerated breath in, and then the words started flowing like a melody.

Milwyr yn dod â'u cleddyfau
Nerthol yn curo drymiau

Fel gogoneddus troell nearthe brenin
I brwydr Cam'lann bell

I sat, entranced, listening to a lyrical presentation that was truly one of the most beautiful things I've ever heard. I wish I could repeat the whole thing in the elf language, but a bardd I'm not. I'll give you the story, and just hope that you'll be able to imagine the smoothest voice you've ever heard reciting the lovely round, throaty sounds in a periodically complex rhyming stanza. As I'd heard bragged about before, the glory of the northern elf bardds was that their storytelling rhymed, and in a way that was terrifically complex. I finally picked up on the pattern as Dinol went along. The pattern was laid out in stanzas of four lines, the first two of eight syllables that rhymed with each other at the end, and then two more, the first one ten syllables with its rhyme stuck in the middle and the second only six and rhyming at the end.

It's tough to explain, but the result was beautiful. Here's the story in English:

Soldiers brandished their swords,
Mightily they pounded upon their drums
Like a glorious fury about their king,
At the faraway Battle of Cam'lann.

Long pursued by the villainous dog,
The king self-proclaimed on his throne,
They met on the field near the river Allan,
On hills overlooking the land.

The rightful king stood proudly that day,
Sixty thousands of troops by his side.
The usurper come back from his other forays,
His own army sixty two-thousands.

It's strange at first; the elves count to twenty and then further by sixties, I guess to keep their six-day weeks straight.
Once they hit this point, they count by thousands and by two-
thousands. The poem said that the rightful king had sixty
thousand men, while the usurper had a hundred and twenty
thousand.

The chieftains faced off
Across the dry field,
The usurper's banner of crimson and gold
Against blue and white of the king

Medraud lifted his raven-maned head
And cried out for all to behold,
The usurper returned but his army would find
The true king would stay on the throne

Arthur the Snake sneered and replied
That the age of the Britons had come.
His army outnumbered the king's on that
    field,
And soon he would be on the throne.

The king called out for war,
And his army valiantly charged,
Ferociously into the usurper's massive horde,
Azure paint flashing against metal plate.

Arrows flew wickedly across the field,
Spearing men to the earth and below,
The moans of the dying bloomed into a chorus
That soon overwhelmed battle cries.

To the hillock above the two leaders did
　charge,
Galloping on mighty steeds,
The red-adorned form of Arthur the Snake
Squared off on King Medraud.

Two mighty men swung their swords fear-
　somely,
The clanging report heard for miles,
The good King Medraud was still best in the
　land,
Yet Arthur held onto his own.

The battle atop the hilltop did rage,
Ferocity mirroring below,
The two rival chieftains fought for the crown

While their men died down on the ground.

As sun crossed the sky above struggling men
The King knew he needed to move.
A strike at the Snake was too risky a path,
But corpses were piling below.

He swung at the Snake with a mighty attack,
Arthur leaped of the opening,
Not one king, but two, were fatally cut
In that dreadful moment on high.

Without any kings, the battle did end,
Troops came to bear them away.
Medraud the Fallen went back to honor and
    fame,
While the Snake was spirited home.

The resonance of Dinol's voice died away, leaving a reverent silence in its place. He seemed to expect it; the master bardd stood and smiled as we slowly came out of the spell his poetry had cast over us.

"Wow. Well done, Grand Master Dinol. Very well done! I have never heard the story told that way, and it was both beautiful and unsettling," I said.

"Beautiful and unsettling how, if I may ask, Highness?"

I nodded to his question as I thought about how best to answer it. I didn't want to insult him, and I certainly didn't want to insult my own people's legends, but the legend of King Arthur was one I'd spent hours studying back at home. It just didn't seem right.

"The story is told where I was raised–not nearly as well as you did, with the beautiful rhyming verse! But in the versions I've heard, Arthur the Snake is actually the good guy, while Medraud–Mordred, we called him–is the usurper."

"My mother says the same when she speaks of the story," Keion said, nodding. "I believe that the difference has to do with which side of the rift you are raised on. Arthur's forces were victorious in the end, and the victor is always the one about whom tales are written. Meanwhile, our ancestors–"

"The Picts!" I exclaimed, happy that I'd recognized something historic, at least.

"The Picts. Right. That the Picts are our ancestors is one explanation, though there are others, and I can tell from Grand Master Dinol's face that he has numerous stories to tell that elaborate on those. I wish we had time for them. Regardless, our ancestors who survived that day limped away from that battle without a leader and only a small area to run home to. It should surprise no one that our ancestors wrote the tale truthfully, while as the Saxons create the legend, King Arthur was the noble ruler."

"So what you're telling me is that if I don't win, the stories will depict me as the evil one?" I asked.

"None could ever depict your fair exploits in a negative light, Crown Princess," Dinol intoned.

"Aww, thanks," I answered, touched by his flowery words. "But the Saxons did it to King Medraud, right?"

"We're not going to lose this one, though," Seph said, giving her bow a confident pat.

"I'm not talking about this one. The prophecy says I am to lead troops in a huge battle some day, and that's the one I'm talking about. If I have to sacrifice myself on some hilltop somewhere in the name of my people, will the other guy's bardds make me out to be the antagonist?"

"It is our duty to make sure that question never comes up, Alyssa," Keion said. "Now, thank you once again for the beautiful telling in High Meter, Master Dinol. I wish that we had time to beg you for more of your poetry, but I am afraid that we must begin our preparations for battle."

The bardd bowed and took his leave. We started preparing immediately, strapping hardened leather around our fleshy bits.

"What's High Meter?" I asked Keion as Aerona finished wrapping and tightening half a cow around my upper body.

"There are twenty-four forms of poetry, separated into Low, Middle, and High Meters. Low Meter is used for short, simple poems, often either in praise of or in mockery of public figures. Middle Meter is the province of most bardds and poets. The few that count as High Meter are exceptionally complex and difficult to pull off."

"It sounded complex, with the first two lines rhyming at the ends and the next two rhyming differently," I interjected.

"That is a large part of it, yes. This was the highest of High Meter, though, with alliteration also being shared between the end of the third and beginning of the fourth lines. I should have pre-warned you to listen for it. Regardless, what you heard today was exceptionally well-done High Meter, and thus, quite a treat, Alyssa."

I nodded, the thought flashing through my head that it would be an even greater treat to get home to the castle and send a letter to Momma about the poetry I'd been treated to.

Confrontation

Early that evening Llew was sent to escort us through the secret route into Padrig's chambers. The plan, as far as we were involved, was simple: we would stay hidden until we heard Padrig bellow my name, at which point we would surprise the bens, more or less, by spilling out into the main dining-slash-battle room. Then the fight would happen, Padrig would win, and we would return home.

Easy peasy, right?

The northern tribe's tradition was pretty clear as to how the challenge should proceed. The bennaeth would be called out into the central clearing to face the four bens, who would accuse him of incompetence and request that he kindly step down, only in much stronger wording. The request only had one viable answer, of course, and that was no, since for a bennaeth to step down due to incompetence would bring him such extreme dishonor that his life would be considered forfeit. As soon as the bennaeth responded negatively, then, the challenge would be on. In a fair fight, he would face whichever ben had called him incompetent in a man-to-man brawl. Northern tradition didn't say it had to be a fair fight, though, and so all four bens and any number of their men they chose could join in to depose an incompetent bennaeth, who could, in turn, call out for any number of supporters he wanted.

What erupted, usually, amounted to a huge battle spread across the entire field of combat. We had to assume, Padrig had told me, that we'd see the same, only not on a field but rather in his dining hall.

Padrig winked at me as he strode out purposely and confidently from his chamber. He was going to meet their challenge with a bellowed no, and as soon as the bens began their attack he would fall back into the main room of the keep, which had already been prepared with upturned tables and stumps and other nasty little surprises to slow the bens' advance. He'd yell for us, and we'd all step out to greet the bens, who, if Padrig's lieutenants succeeded in their part of the plan, would be unaccompanied by their troops.

"It is a good plan," I'd told Padrig, hoping to hear him agree.

"Oh, certainly," he'd said, his tone at odds with his words.

"You don't sound confident. Should I be worried?"

"You should not be worried. It is just—you have not fought enough battles yet, Alyssa. The only thing you can say for certain about the path a battle will take is that it never, ever, follows the plan."

"You believe that this won't, either?" I'd asked, my heart rate inching upward at the thought.

He'd chuckled drily. "No, Princess. There is no belief involved. I know with certainty that it will not."

"Oh. So why did we bother planning, then?"

"Because occupying your mind with planning is better than sitting around hoping that you will eventually be victorious. Oh, cheer yourself, Alyssa. I jest, in part."

"So tonight's battle might follow our plan? It is, as you know, the first battle I've been in where I've gotten to plan anything."

"No, I say again that it will not follow the plan. But the real reason we took the time to plan is to create a body of battle knowledge as to what should happen. That way, when the fog of combat engulfs us, each of us knows our part and can execute, or make up a new plan, whichever the wind of the moment makes necessary."

The memory of that conversation flashed through my head as I heard Padrig bellow: "Come, and quickly, Alyssa! And bring the others!" It wasn't what he was supposed to have yelled according to our plan, but it was a yell, and we did have a plan, and so I figured that meant it was time for us to get our butts out into the hall and start acting on that body of battle knowledge he'd spoken of.

With no time for exchanging worried glances first, as I would've preferred to normally, we rushed out as a gaggle. Seph and Booboo darted out first, followed closely by Keion, Aerona directly on his heels. I jumped out last. I saw Padrig's personal guard, Sarah the Battle Savant in the center, arrayed across the room with the group of us from Cysegredig each sprinting toward our positions spread out just behind. I also saw our bear of a bennaeth running full-tilt back down the hall toward his own line. The huge man nimbly darted past the obstacles and surprises we'd laid, skidding to a stop in the spot from which he planned to challenge his foes.

Through the open front doors the four treasonous bens strode leisurely, black-robed Cult members pouring in beside them.

I was surprised that the bens weren't pursuing Padrig at a run as we'd assumed they would. Instead, the four clan leaders stood snarling just inside the entrance. In front stood an unmistakable Iolyn, Ben of the Pobl'yrhew. Like the ice fields he ruled over in the far north, his furs were solid white. His thick, full black beard hung in an intricate braid down across his chest, its tip brushing against the top of his gleaming brass belt buckle. He was the shortest of the four, and only medium height for an elf, but his stocky body and the way he popped his club in his hand were threatening enough. Meanwhile, his face was the most striking of the four, thanks to the malevolence I could read in it. The others wore expressions ranging from angry to resolved, but the ice fields ben was obviously the one of the four who was most viciously out for Padrig's head.

The elf I recognized as Rhodri stood to Iolyn's right hand. The northern shores ben stood both head and shoulders taller than Iolyn, and to his side he spun a wicked-looking double-bladed battle axe, both of its blades gleaming in the candle light of the room. I could just make out the expected blue gleam on the weapon. Keion had told us that this relic of an earlier age, Gylfangnan, was famed for its ability to split all the way through an ale keg, or a moose, or a bear, or even, it was rumored, a dragon. Rhodri's most defining feature, his pink scar, curled down from his cheek to make a line through his trimmed black goatee.

To Iolyn's left stood the ben I recognized as Madog, the leader of the interior clan. The elf was every bit as tall as Rhodri, and was reported to be both stronger and meaner than his northern shore colleague. He'd won every wrestling match he'd ever entered, Padrig had told me with a fair amount of respect in his voice. He wore a grim smile on his face as he stared us all down.

Madog bounced his own club in his hand. Padrig had told us that the club wasn't actually Madog's favorite weapon in a battle; when he fought by himself he typically wielded a quarterstaff or a bow and arrow. Whenever he appeared beside his fellow ben, though, or when he went on a hunt, he used the club just to show he was as brave as, and even better and stronger than, Iolyn.

Past Iolyn's shoulder, near the door, stood the fourth of the group, a tall, rangy elf with straggly grey hair leaking out of his floppy-brimmed hat. At his side he held his trademark staff that boasted a long, hooked blade at one end; Keion called it a gisarme. Prince Charming had also said the old elf was pretty good with it because he'd had a lot of practice using it as a fishing gaff over the years. Merfyn was the oldest of the four, and ben over the fishing villages far to the west. I'd asked Ellga, who'd grown up in his village, about him, and she'd told me the most wonderful things about this father figure of a ben. He was, she said, both even-keeled and steady as a leader, and as a result he'd held a title of ben for longer than the other three combined.

Looking past Iolyn into Merfyn's face, I could see that he, at least, wasn't wholly into the plan that the four bens had created. His eyes looked nervously about, quickly taking in not only Padrig's guard force but also the five of us, and a couple of times he glanced back at the door, looking for all the world like his greatest desire was to back right out of the building.

He didn't get the chance, though. The doors to the main hall closed with a solid thump. I'm not sure who shut them, but as they did, the noise of battle from outside quieted down a lot. In the relative silence I looked over the assembled battle lines and saw four bens with eight black-robed Cult members, twelve total arrayed against our bennaeth, his six guards, and the five of us.

It hadn't gone according to plan.

Still, it was twelve on twelve. It seemed pretty even. Those were okay odds, I figured. They weren't what we'd planned for, with just the four bens facing us, but with everything considered they weren't too bad. It was even better, in fact, because both Booboo and Slartibartfast waited in the shadows for their masters' calls. Fourteen against twelve, all totaled. The battle leaned quite a bit in our favor, and we still had some surprises going for us, or so I thought.

I was still thinking that when the lights went out.

Dance With Death

"Padrig!" a voice boomed across the hall through the darkness. I could recognize it as Iolyn's from the conversation I'd listened in on. I've heard voices containing malice, but Iolyn's practically dripped the stuff. "While that was a nice trick your forces played outside, you cannot escape us in here. We bring a weapon against which you have no defense. You should give yourself up now to our mercy, to spare the lives of those who stand beside you in such a futile gesture."

I heard a soft fleshy impact and a quiet grunt as the bennaeth worked his way backward in the dark to stand in line with his own forces. We'd planned on him facing his challengers in the front and center of the battle lines, but he couldn't face a dozen by himself very well in the darkness. I couldn't see him, but through Draignerthol I could sense him standing very near. I heard him draw a huge breath, and then his own deep voice boomed powerfully across the room.

"Iolyn. Madog. Rhodri. Merfyn," he named his subordinate—or, insubordinate, I guess—bens, dropping extra power into his voicing of the last name in the list. "The four of you are committing treason against your *bennaeth*, and the penalty for that is your death. I shall give you lenience, due to the lack of bloodshed up till now, should you decide to surrender to me and my guard instead of pursuing this silly and childish attack plan that you have hatched, one that we all know is certain to fail."

Iolyn's wicked laugh carried through the hall. "Don't be silly, yourself, *bennaeth*. You have grown weak in your time in this keep. You have even given your blessing, according to what I have heard, for the king's worthless whelp to become our queen, and that is a matter that has to be corrected, and now. Luckily for us, I believe that I saw the little whelp herself standing back behind you. It will be good to be able to take care of not one, but two problems this very evening. How—*efficient* of you! Now, please, just surrender to us so that your guard and hers do not have to suffer more than is necessary."

"No," Padrig's defiance rang through the room. "The king's 'whelp,' as you obscenely refer to our crown princess, is a stronger and better leader than the four of you put together could ever be. She *will* be our queen, if I have to die to see it become so."

"Well, we can certainly make *that* happen," Iolyn sneered, his disembodied voice slithering across the darkness toward us.

"I am not so certain," Padrig declared. "It may surprise you to learn that I have on my side the very defense I need against this weapon that you brought. Whereas in the current age, by honored tradition worth more than any one of us here, *our* people would not have resorted to its use," Padrig paused momentarily to let the insinuated insult slip further in, and then continued, "I believe the saying holds that I should fight fire with fire. Is that not correct, Crown Princess Alyssa?"

I *heard* Padrig with my ears, but it took me a second for my brain to catch up and realize what he was saying. Then my knees nearly buckled. He wasn't just suggesting that I use magic; he was publicly excusing it, even actively calling for it!

"That is correct, Bennaeth," I said, trying to push forcefulness into my voice for dramatic effect while my brain frantically went through various options. I vaguely remembered where everybody was and could thus use an offensive spell, but that would be spell-chucking blind. If one of my friends had moved for a better defensive position, then I might hit them accidentally with any Magic Missiles that I managed to cast at the darkness.

Believe it or not, Magic Missiles, though it wasn't called exactly that, was actually a spell in the elf spellbook.

Fire! Fight fire with fire, Padrig had said. If I went into a mage war against the Cult members, it would leave me badly outnumbered while my friends fought melee-style in the darkness. Granted, we'd trapped the room pretty thoroughly, but we'd never planned—oh, that planning thing, again!—I resolved that when the bigger battles came, and I was queen, I'd figure out a way to plan for everything. But we'd never imagined that we would need to remember where the traps were in near-total darkness, so the traps posed as big a threat to us as they did to the others. I needed to bring light back to the room, one way or another, which meant finding a way to relight the torches that had been extinguished. Luckily for us, that was actually an easy spell, and so I reached up, grabbed an already-scorching Draignerthol, pushed energy into and through the pendant, and was rewarded by the sight of the torches around the room flaring back to life.

I gleefully reveled in seeing Iolyn's dark glance at one of the Cult members, who just shrugged in reply. Obviously they hadn't planned on me being there with Draignerthol. Our plan was pretty much toast, but so was theirs now.

We needed to win this.

"No matter," Iolyn sneered. "We will still defeat you, Padrig." I glanced past the leading ben to the fishing villages leader, and was happy to see that Merfyn didn't look as sure.

And then, battle happened.

Iolyn charged first. Sarah, leading Padrig's guard as she was, met him halfway across with a muted clang as his club rang solidly against her sword. The ben staggered back slightly, leading me to wonder if Sarah actually had the hulk-like strength she bragged about. I didn't wonder long, though; he recovered quickly and then pushed back in, swinging his mighty cudgel in swift figure eights. Sarah proved herself his equal, though, as she nimbly whirled around and lashed in, over and then under, sword in one hand and spinning dagger in another. Before long the ben had built up enough momentum that he looked like a horizontal windmill, his staff supplying a whoosh-whoosh-whoosh rhythm as it cleaved the air, while Sarah's sword beat a less regular pattern in response.

It was clear after a while that Sarah was better than the ben. After several minutes he hadn't hit her once, but his arms and legs bore several bloody lines. He growled in frustration, and I nearly cheered at the sound.

In hindsight, I should've seen his growl as the command it probably was. Blue energy played out from the closest Cult member's hand, and it imprisoned Sarah just long enough for her to fall prey to one of Iolyn's mighty swings. The club came to a deadly stop against the side of her motionless head, caving it in while forcing it to the side. The mage released the spell just in time for her lifeless body to crumple to the floor, blood pooling around her corpse.

Iolyn looked up, sneering at Padrig.

"*NOOOOOOOOOOOOO!*" I heard someone yell, the word echoing through my brain and the entire room. I realized that the screamer was me, but that just fueled my rage more. Furious, I tightened my hold on Draignerthol. I figured that if they wanted spellcasting, they'd get their spellcasting, bless their little blackened hearts and soon-to-be blackened breasts. I pulled as much energy as I could grab hold of through the dragon-shaped pendant, noticing that it bathed my entire upper torso in blue light as I did so. One of the offensive spells I'd read about involved throwing electrical energy—lightning bolts, basically—at an enemy, and in my anger I could see the instructions for the spell imprinted within my eyeballs in a glowing, pulsating red.

The air crackled and sizzled and the whole room suddenly went blindingly white.

I lunged forward, bathing the room in energy. Through the withering brightness I could see the black robes moving, shuffling, trying to dart out of the way. They weren't anywhere near fast enough to stand against me, though, much less powerful enough to stand against Draignerthol. The beautiful thing about electricity, the spell book had said, was that it could be made to go around corners. Well, columns are like corners, the furious part of me ranted. Tables have corners, too, right? I didn't stop seeking corners to push electrical power around until every black robe I could see had stopped twitching in a smoking ruin of charred flesh.

"You can stop now," Seph stage-whispered, but I was coming to a stop anyway due to the lack of targets. I smiled, my lips curling up into a feral grin as my eyes refocused on the new situation at hand. Every Cult member in the hall had been turned into charcoal. Some of them were still spasming, but all of them were completely dead.

"Iolyn, maybe we should–" Merfyn's shaky voice sounded from behind a table way across the hall, but he was cut off by the roar of his leader.

"Nonsense!" Iolyn raged. "Your Crown Princess pet there just used magic against us, in direct violation of tradition. Your life, and hers, are forfeit!"

I was still trying to figure out why he thought my magic was a direct violation of tradition while his pet mage's use of the arcane, which had killed a beautifully talented warrior, was hunky-dory, when he charged Padrig. The bennaeth barked out a chuckle as he met the ben, club against axe.

I watched the two mighty warriors trade blows for a few moments, idly wondering what might have happened if I'd somehow convinced the bennaeth that an Uzi made a better weapon than an axe. Granted, I'm sure his honor would've been a little bit injured, but still—

Madog and Rhodri siezed the moment to charge, each of them going around to the side of the great hall, leaping over the charred bodies of their mages to get to either side of the bennaeth. No doubt they wanted to chop him down from the flanks, but neither had counted on the extra protection of the obstacles we'd laid. Twin snaps were heard on either side, and both bens fell hard, their faces slamming against the floor. Both groaned as they tried to rise, massive bear traps engulfing a leg of each.

Keion and Seph shared a meaningful look. Each shrugged and slowly nocked an arrow to a bowstring. Madog and Rhodri, clan chieftains, began howling as each received an arrow to the chest. The ranger and the warrior followed through by releasing another, and then another, and then another, each arrow finding a terrible mark that ensured its recipient, a once-traitorous ben, would never rise again.

Meanwhile, Padrig's axe sang through the air. He and Iolyn seemed evenly matched as their weapons flew in wide arcs, crashing against each other time and again.

"Should I help the bennaeth like Iolyn's 'pet' helped him?" I asked Aerona, who was still standing guard to my side, though she'd already put away her daggers.

"Don't you dare, Princess!" Padrig bellowed as he brought his axe around to crash against Iolyn's club once again. I looked at Aerona, and she looked at me, and we both shrugged.

The fight lasted several more long minutes. I'd describe it blow-by-blow, but really, two large men hitting each other becomes pretty boring after a while. That, and it didn't take long after Padrig yelled at me not to intervene before it became obvious who was going to win. Iolyn's swings became less vigorous, and in response Padrig's did the opposite. Padrig smelled the battle turning his way, and that apparently got him revved up.

Whack! Padrig's axe broke through Iolyn's tired defenses, bashing his shoulder. You'd think an axe would cleave a person, but when the bearer is tired, it apparently becomes more of a wide, metal-ended club. The crunch sounded like something had broken, though, and the ben's arm sagged beneath the blow. He dropped that arm, taking up his club in a purely defensive stance with the other. *Whack*! The bennaeth's axe zipped in again, this time taking the ben's remaining good wrist out and sending the club sailing across the room. It landed in another of the bear traps and set it off with a *clang*!

Iolyn sank to his knees, defeated. Padrig sidled up to him, clearly enjoying his pose as the victor. He lined his axe up for the killing blow, one that Iolyn didn't contest.

Suddenly the mighty bennaeth stopped and looked back toward me. "Highness," he said, "as Crown Princess, you are the ranking royalty here. Would you prefer I stay the blow, or would you like to take it yourself?"

He was testing me. He'd never stopped testing me. I thought about it for a moment, separating my logical mind from the emotions that were running rampant. I'd already killed eight in addition to the ones I'd burned to death, but though in my own mind the blasting of the mages was entirely justified, the thought of killing a guy who was on his knees made my stomach churn. Besides, I wasn't the one who'd beaten the ben to the ground in equal combat. No, I was certain elf honor code said the killing blow wasn't mine to take, and I was equally certain my stomach said if I tried, everything I'd eaten in the recent past would be revealed to me once again. I was done with death, so totally done with bloodshed.

I glanced over and saw Sarah's blood still staining the floor red, the pool grown even larger.

So. I could give in to my desire to avoid more bloodshed, spare the ben's life, but should I? He had rebelled—instigated and commanded a bloody rebellion, in fact—against his own bennaeth, and had gone into it with a plan to use the taboo forces of magic to gain the upper hand in what even I, the future queen of magic, felt was a disgustingly cheap and immoral manner. That seemed to call for death by any reasonable estimate.

What would my father do, I wondered. The ben couldn't be trusted, not ever again. If he were allowed to live, he'd have to be tracked like an animal. Dead, he'd never have the opportunity to attempt to regain trust.

What *would* my father do, I asked myself again, but this time I had an inkling for his answer. He wouldn't make such a big deal of the dilemma, I thought. He's a gentle ruler, one who lets traditions be traditions, and local matters be local matters.

I came to a decision.

"Bennaeth Padrig, I believe custom holds that you have won this battle on your own merit, and so the honor of the killing blow lies in your own hands as a result. I would not dream of taking it in your stead, nor would I consider standing in the way of what is rightfully yours as the bennaeth of your clans. Justice in this local matter is yours to determine, Padrig."

Bless his heart, Padrig actually smiled at me. He smiled at me before, and while, he swung his axe in its vicious curve that ended Iolyn's life.

GALAR

mourning. Elves don't generally mourn a "good death," but not all deaths are good.

Aftermath

Iolyn's lifeless body fell to the floor with a sickeningly wet thud. As much as it twisted my stomach to look at it, I couldn't help but notice the irony in the way Iolyn lay, head bashed in, right next to Sarah's resting place. It was fitting, though it was also bloody and a whole lot of disgusting, too.

The room was so silent for several long moments that I almost forgot about the other ben. Padrig didn't, though. Once he'd caught his breath from the massive weapon-swinging contest, he raised his voice and ripped out a mighty, "Traitor, come out from behind that table to face your judgment!"

Merfyn rose timidly from behind the table at the front of the room, holding his hook-bladed staff out peacefully at arm's length. "Now, Bennaeth Padrig," he pleaded, "I would remind you, Lord, that I did not attack you when the other bens did. I—"

"You did not attack me because you were too timid," Padrig interrupted, his voice fierce. "Hiding behind the work of these other traitors who at least met their fates bravely. Crown Princess, you said you overheard the bens discussing this treason-ous attack while you were in Gidreffydd?"

"I did."

"Did you hear anything that sounded like the coward over there arguing against the plan?"

"I did. As I recall, he argued that it wasn't the right time, and that their forces weren't ready–"

"Not ready, eh? So the timid Merfyn argued for delayed treason. It is still the same." The old ben's face dropped toward the floor.

"Do you have any other arguments that might convince me of a lack of treason on your part?" Padrig asked.

Merfyn shook his head, a defeated expression on his face. "No, Bennaeth, I do not. I merely beg for mercy in the name of my further leadership of my clan. This winter promises to be a very difficult one."

"It does, indeed. But surely–" Padrig started, but he was interrupted by Ellga's entrance. Suddenly I heard her gasp as she sprinted across the room, deftly avoiding all the bear traps, to put her arms around the old ben.

"Grandfather, are you okay?" she asked, looking up at the old man with tear-filled eyes. "You're not–he's not–he wouldn't–" she stammered before turning to Padrig and crying, "Bennaeth, no. Please forgive him. For all of his faults, he is all that my village, all that my clan has left."

A few things clicked into place. That was why she'd always been so graceful around me, and also why she'd been the one chosen to join Padrig's household. It was also probably why she'd been the one chosen to look after me, Padrig's primary guest.

"Would you have begged the same of him regarding me had the bens won, child?" Padrig asked, his voice not as harsh as it could have been.

"Bennaeth, I have enjoyed my time under your roof," she said. She even sounded convincing with it, slave though she was. "You have been far more kind than you needed to be, and I have not wanted for anything at your hearth. Still, this man is my grandfather, and I would die before I see him cut down. He speaks the truth that a harsh winter is coming, and my village and the rest of our people need his wisdom desperately."

"He has committed treason, though. He should have his head separated from his neck for that," Keion stated, his voice flat and angry.

I was torn. As much as I agreed that treason needed to be dealt with harshly, I didn't want to see his or any village suffer because of his bad decision. That, and I'd come to like Ellga, and I didn't want to see her hurt.

"I'd invite your guidance, Crown Princess, but you'd probably just tell me once again that local justice is in my own hands," Padrig said, his gruffness belied by a twinkle in his eyes as he looked back toward me.

Aw, dangit, I thought. The previous decision, the one I sloughed off, was easier to make than this one. Still, he was obviously giving me a second chance at a test, and it was one that I needed to pass. What to do, then? Should I go with what my head told me was the just thing to do, or with what my heart told me was best?

Then I realized that it didn't have to be one or the other. "Bennaeth, you frequently take slaves to settle debts, do you not?"

"I would argue that such practice is not best described as frequent, but yes, present company bears evidence that I have done so before. Go on."

"So why not have the best of both worlds? You cannot trust Ben Merfyn any longer. That is obvious. But he has much wisdom and knowledge from his many years. So why not take him slave and use him around your household?"

"But he is needed back in the villages," Ellga objected, and then flushed and added, "Crown Princess."

"I know that, but.... Ben Merfyn, do you love your grand-daughter as much as she obviously loves you?"

"I do," he said, gazing at her. "She is the perfect replica of her grandmother."

"Well, her time here is coming to an end, and quite soon. Bennaeth, why don't you keep her here for the winter as insurance against further rebellion, while Merfyn returns to help his clan survive, and then on whatever date you agree upon, he will return to surrender to you, or else be the cause of his granddaughter's death? That keeps your fishing villages fed and healthy, while at the same time satisfying the call of justice."

"Yes, that could work," Padrig agreed. "I would send some men to watch the ben in his village, just for the sake of making sure he does not commit any further treason against me, but— yes, indeed, Crown Princess, that would be a very wise plan."

Padrig genuinely smiled at me, an expression matched by both Merfyn and Ellga. None of the three had wanted to see the old patriarch dead.

"Nicely done," Seph stage-whispered to me. I smiled.

"Indeed," Padrig said, nodding. "Nicely done through the entire fight, Crown Princess. In fact, I have an idea of my own. An amendment, you might say, to your earlier suggestion. In order to show my appreciation for all that you have accomplished here, including tracking my son down when we didn't realize that he needed tracking, I shall give Ellga to you for the coming winter. She will return with and then serve you in Cy-segredig."

"What? Wait. I–" I started to object, but Ellga cut me off with a delighted gasp.

"Oh, Bennaeth, thank you! Thank you so very, very much! I–I do not deserve such a wonderful fate, though I have always dreamed of seeing the wonders of Cysegredig! And to be there serving Crown Princess Alyssa, too! Such a gentle and wonderful mistress. I shall pack immediately."

"Wait," I said. I couldn't bear to squash the delight she was showing, but.... "No, I–I shouldn't–I can't–I–the thing is, you'll be the only slave in Cysegredig. What on Earth–or, rather, Kiirajanna–will my father say to that?"

"Um, Alyssa," Seph started, and Keion coughed.

The prince followed Seph's interruption with his own smooth, quiet words. "She won't be the only slave in Cysegredig, Alyssa. Far from it, in fact."

"She–what?" I asked, confused. "What do you mean? Where are there slaves at my father's castle? Who keeps them there?"

"Alyssa, your father and my mother both do. The high priestess, as well. You don't think the servants just one day decided that they'd rather serve in the castle's kitchen than be free in their home villages, do you?" Keion explained, his voice smoothly gentle almost to the point of condescension.

"Well, I–no–just–they–who–it–" I found myself stammering again, trying to imagine my loving and wise father taking a *slave*. The thought horrified me. "That's horrible," I voiced.

"That is our way," Keion chided. "It is your way, also, now, yes?"

"While you kids explain our way to the crown princess, how about Merfyn and I go outside and make certain that our soldiers know that the battle is over?" Padrig said, sending me a castigating look. I flinched, but he just shrugged and then shifted his lips up into a grin. As he turned around and headed toward the door, he murmured, "I'm sure it'll disappoint the boys, but we'll need them healthy when the snow flies."

"I'm going to have to ask you to surrender that pig-sticker to my guards, Merfyn. You won't need it, and I still can't trust you with it, remember?" he asked as he neared the front. Merfyn shook his head glumly, spun the staff in a couple of rapid loops over his head, and then held it out, handle-first, to one of Padrig's guards. Then the pair of northern clan leaders walked out into a quiet courtyard. The light outside was so dim I couldn't see anything, but there didn't seem to be any fighting still going on.

"I guess one side or the other already won that battle?" I asked.

"It wasn't their battle to fight," Keion said, still gazing toward the darkened exit. "I'm sure, in spite of Padrig's bravado, that once the doors closed, the *boys* outside made peace to await the outcome of the battle in here. They probably even found a spare cask or two of ale to make that peace over."

"Your Battle of Cannae game plan seems kind of counter-productive, at least in hindsight, then," I said.

"On the contrary, it probably saved many lives by allowing the bens and their sorcerers into here quickly," Keion corrected. Aerona nodded, a move that made me flush in irritation. Sure, he was right, but her agreement felt a little treasonous. Besides, sometimes it just feels good to get angry, and I hadn't let go of all the adrenalin from the fight yet.

A few moments later Padrig entered by himself. "Useless fighters," he grumbled. "Apparently, as soon as the doors were shut and their leaders safely indoors, they sauntered off to gamble and drink together." Keion shot me an I-told-you-so look. "Well, those who don't belong in town are now heading back out toward their campsites, and Merfyn is safely among them watched over by a few of my best guardsmen." He looked around at the carnage and continued, "I'll get the servants to clean up the mess this evening. You have all earned a good night's sleep, and then first thing tomorrow you can head for the safety and warmth of your home."

"Sounds like you don't want me here any more, Bennaeth," I teased, feeling a little saucy after the interaction with Keion.

He looked at me with an eyebrow raised. "I didn't want you here any more many nights ago, Crown Princess. Don't get me wrong; I don't mind your company. But this is my home, and having another royal here, especially one who will some day soon outrank me, is jarring to my personal sensitivities, so to speak. Besides, I was–and I will admit, this was misplaced–concerned over your welfare in the battle that I knew in my gut was coming. Forgive a simple clan chieftain, but the safety of his liege lord's daughter is a matter of paramount concern."

I chortled and went up to Padrig, looking up into his eyes. While he wasn't as tall as either Madog or Rhodri had been, he still made me feel small. "There is nothing to forgive, Bennaeth Padrig, nor are you a simple clan chieftain in any sense of the term. I'll make sure to report to my father how bravely you defended not only yourself but also the group of us visitors from the capital, to the point of making sure we had an escape route if needed. I will also make sure to tell my father how you worked to ensure that we remained safe during the buildup of forces, and how it was my own decision that caused us to be in the path of trouble now–"

"Shut. Up," Keion's stage-whisper cut through my speech. Confused, I looked at him, and then back at Padrig. I was dismayed to see Padrig nodding in agreement with Prince Charming.

"...and I shall now do as you suggested and reward the efforts of this evening by going to my bed," I finished what I'd hoped would be a rousing and memorable final speech in a quiet mutter. Feeling self-conscious, I turned on my heel and walked toward the doorway leading back into the guest rooms.

"Crown Princess Alyssa," Padrig said, his voice stopping me in my tracks. I turned back, and was humbled to see him holding his arms out in an incredibly rare offer of a hug. I started moving back toward him in what I figured was a stately manner befitting a crown princess, but then I realized that my training hadn't involved situations like this and so I really didn't know what a stately manner befitting a crown princess should look like. I gave up and skipped over to Padrig to fall into his bear hug like a bee into its hive.

"You're doing fine, lass," Padrig whispered to me as he held me within the confines of his mighty arms. "Quit trying so hard. You're not expected to be the expert on diplomacy. If you were, you'd be sent by yourself. Relax, girl, and let those who have been given the task teach you something."

I looked up into the bearded man's tender face, and he brushed away the tear that had come, unbidden, to my eye.

"No elf with any sense at all wants to be you," he said in a low voice. "You come to us without having been asked, wielding powers that have been named taboo through our longest-observed and strongest traditions," he paused to send a look over toward the charred corpses of a few of the Cult members for emphasis. "Yet, now, the forces arrayed against you require the use of such powers, and prophecy suggests that it will only become worse. Your path ahead is difficult, Alyssa, but take heart that both your father and I, two of the most powerful men in the realm, stand firmly behind you with our arms and our armies prepared for the tumultuous times to come. That being said, though, it is my firm belief, based on what I have seen, that you do not need two old men and our armies. You have the strength within yourself, right in here," he tapped me on my chest, ironically touching Draignerthol through my blouse as he did, "to win whether we old warriors stand behind you or not. "

Padrig clamped his bearpaw-like hands over my shoulders and held me out at arm's length. His eyes maintained the same father-like expression as he continued in a loud growl, "Crown Princess Alyssa, you are the hope for this realm that the prophecy has foretold. Go home now—or in the morning, anyway—to Cysegredig and to your father the king with my blessings, and also with my pledge of support when the need is great, and, I should add, with my thanks as well."

He released my shoulders and kissed me right in the middle of my forehead. Feeling dazed over what had just happened, I turned and quietly trudged back to my room.

HIRAETHUS

homesickness. At times I had so many different layers of this going that I couldn't see straight.

Departure

The next morning brought a really weird mix of emotions. As excited as I was to be headed home, my mission successful in every way, I was sad to leave a mentor like Padrig, and his really awesome family also, behind. And as if that weren't enough, I also had to deal with Ellga's up-and-down mood as she rejoiced at leaving to go see Cysegredig, which is apparently a really big deal for rural elves, while at the same time despairing to leaving her homeland and kin behind for the winter.

Padrig's guards weren't any better. I'd sent all but the one of Dad's guards home, not counting poor Gerallt, so Padrig insisted on sending his own personal entourage south to see me safely into my father's hands. Technically, I could have objected, but I knew that any objection to his plan would be overruled no matter what I said. His guards seemed happy to make the trip, anyway. They'd done it with Padrig several times, but this time they were going with the king's daughter. I could tell from the chatter I overheard that escorting the crown princess somehow might end up as the penultimate achievement of their lives.

I also sensed a tremendous sadness among them, though. The loss of Sarah, after seeing her tied up in magical energy and then cut down helplessly, seemed to have had a profound effect on the way they viewed the world and their job. While she certainly wasn't all that well-liked as a peer, she'd been extremely well-respected. We had to leave before the elves of Ganolog had a chance to dig her grave, but they marked it that morning, and Padrig's team insisted on visiting the spot where Sarah would be laid to rest on their way out. I could tell from their faces that the passing of their resident savant, in the sickening manner in which she'd fallen, shook them all up.

Our departure got even more awkward when the old man in the sparkly blue wizard robes showed up at Padrig's right hand.

"Crown Princess," Grigor said, adding a respectful gesture to his greeting. "I wish that we could some day spend more time together, but I pray that your journey southward is safe. Please give my blessings to your father for me."

I looked at Grigor for a moment and then turned a suspicious look Padrig's way. "I thought—"

"You thought wrong, Alyssa," Padrig said, his voice soft. He led Grigor and me off a little way, out of earshot of everyone else, and then said, "Crown Princess, you need to work on your ability to deduce friend from foe, but then again, so do we all. Grigor has been and still is my most loyal advisor. He is also quite talented with—earth energy manipulation, so to speak, in part because he shares some of the same blood that courses through your extremely talented veins."

"What?" I asked, more to Grigor than Padrig. I'd just gone one large step beyond confused.

Grigor's response was to step up and fold me into his arms. Grigor's hug wasn't as engulfing as Padrig's had been, but it still felt warm and pleasant. He whispered into my ear, "Alyssa, very few know this, but your father's mother was my sister. He is my nephew, which makes you my great niece."

He released me, and I stepped away in shock. "I thought, from the way you had been examining me...."

"Critically, yes?" he whispered with a nod. "You are the only daughter of our king, and thus destined to be our queen, and besides that, you are a blood relative. Of course I have expected greatness from you, and I watched closely to see if you met that expectation. You did, by the way. I am proud to be your uncle."

Grigor handed me a sealed envelope and then walked away, vanishing through the door into the hall, leaving just Padrig, Esyllt, and Llew to say their farewells. Then we left the same way we'd come in, trudging through brown, muddy streets with absolutely no fanfare at all.

Thus it transpired that a tremendously excited, yet also very depressed, party rode out, southward toward the elf capital. The clip-clopping hooves of our horses made the only sounds for a while.

"Wait," I asked Seph as I saw her start out ahead of the party, ready to begin her ranger scouting duty. She turned in her saddle, surprised, to look back at me.

I pushed Awel into a canter. "So," I said once the mare had caught up to and slowed down beside Seph's horse, "where do elves–particularly those who are with us from Padrig's household–believe that someone like Sarah's soul has gone?"

"The high priestess didn't teach you this?" Seph asked, her surprised expression bending even more so.

"I never asked," I answered with a shrug, though the ill-timed gesture was lost in the up-and-down of the mare's trot. "Honestly, I don't think it's Sternyface's job to teach everything."

"Well, that's a shame. I'm sure she could have taught you far more eloquently, and more fully, than I can, cousin. To answer your question, though, Sarah's soul's energy, to be a little bit sloppy with terminology, will end up back in the land, ready to regenerate or rejuvenate as needed."

"So souls are energy to be regenerated?"

"Well—no. As I said, it's—well, it's just more complicated than that. You know, on second thought, let me just say that I can't answer your question. You need to ask the high priestess."

"Thanks, Cousin."

She rode off with a wistful smile. At least Seph was starting to get my sarcasm.

I pulled Grigor's note out of my pocket. He hadn't said who was meant to read it, and there wasn't a name on the front, so I figured that meant it must be for me. Gently I worked open the seal and read my uncle's neat handwriting.

My Dearest Alyssa,

I first must offer you my sincerest apology for the attitude that came across to you as dislike and loathing. It was never my intent to put you ill at ease. After years of being the advisor to the owner of one of the most contested leadership roles in the kingdom, my manner has become a little sharp, but I promise it was not intended that way toward you.

Some of what I write now, we spoke on the night the bennaeth's son left, but your mind was thoroughly bewitched by the alcohol that evening and so I assume you do not recall any of it. It is important that you know of it, however, so I must beg the privilege of some of your time and attention as you read what I have prepared in this note.

Very few know of the relationship between Cadfael and me, and even fewer know the details of what transpired between him and Padrig at the start of his reign. I am, to most, simply a humble advisor, well educated in the center of the continent and lucky to have entered Padrig's inner circle. In actuality, however, I am more of an ambassador, and it is your right both as my niece and as our future queen to know that.

I'd be surprised if the historians haven't already taught you some of this, but before Cadfael assumed the throne, the antagonism between Cysegredig and Ganolog nearly ripped the realm into war several times. When he was chosen to be ruler, your father came to me to ask my help in changing that. He had a tremendous personal respect for Padrig in the first place, but he knew of the prophecy, suspected rightly that you would be the one foretold, and understood strategically how important it would be in the coming years to have a solid relationship with the great white north.

Thus, he sent me. He asked me to go, I suppose, in a nice way, and I said no. What elf, after all, would want to leave the relative paradise that surrounds Cysegredig to live in the forsaken, frigid white barrenness? He argued that Padrig would give a different opinion, and I suggested that Padrig had never lived down where we did. To make the story shorter, it was an argument, but eventually he won me over.

I have never regretted the move, I must say. It was rough the first winter, but Padrig's people say that if you make it through one winter your feet freeze in the north and you will never wish to leave. That is true, though the freezing part is a little exaggerated. But I have come to love the land of the north, and its people, and its haphazard woodlands that so vibrantly blaze to life each springtime.

I have also come to love Padrig and his family, and it is for this reason that I write this letter. Dark times are coming, and to the entire realm, as you are already painfully aware. The attack by the bens was but the first in what will, I fear, be a long line of struggles for us, and for you. To that end, you must always count Padrig among your most loyal supporters, but you must also always listen carefully to what he says. The great bear-man's pride will never allow him to ask Cadfael for assistance, but I have seen in my waking dreams that the time will come when he will desperately need it. Alyssa, you must learn to listen not only to what is said, but also to what is not said.

I say all of this with every confidence that you will be our greatest Talaith ever. So saith the prophecy, and so also saith my heart and my mind. Please know that you will forever have not one, but two powerful allies up here on the northern Rim.

With love,

Your uncle

Grigor

PS: please destroy this once you have read it, as this missive contains information that can only be known by a very few. Allow no one, not even your father, your cousin, or your mutual love interest, to read it.

I crumpled the paper and put it into a pouch for burning later. Mutual love interest, hmmph.

RHAGOROL

fantastic, amazing, spectacular.

The Lights

We were really tired when we pulled up to the ranger cabin that evening. It doesn't take long in town to forget how exhausting it is to travel by horseback. It's not like taking a long trip by car; the horse actually has its own mind, its own feelings. Instead of just setting it on cruise control and putting gas in every so often, you actually have to pay attention, and even more so when you stop to "rest." Granted, the first time, when we'd left Cysegredig en route to the library, it was exciting to be on a long adventure, but I was well past that. A long ride on horseback now seemed just a chore.

Seph was waiting for us outside the cabin when we arrived. "Alyssa, your presence is eagerly awaited by someone inside," she said with a twinkle in her eye.

"What?" I asked, confused, but the question went unanswered as I raced in to the cabin. My eyes focused in the darkened interior, and then I felt both horrified and overjoyed at the same time.

The someone awaiting my presence was Little Treebeard!

The squat little potted elm was in the back corner of the cabin, her branches shaking with joy as she sensed my entrance. I ran up and—well, I checked the tree out. I'd love to say that I hugged it, but to say that would sound weird. It's not a large enough tree to hug, anyway. Instead—and yes, this is weird—certain specific branches bent outward in my direction, and I took them and—well, I stroked them in a kind, loving way.

It's—well, it's comforting to a tree. Look, if you haven't been inside a tree's head like I have, then just don't ask. It's easier that way.

Next to L.T. was a note addressed to "Her Royal Highness, the glorified and eternally forgiving Crown Princess Alyssa." I opened it immediately, curious. Inside was a rambling series of apologetic phrases that attempted to explain why His Royal Majesty's Royal Guard had just dropped L.T. off at the cabin. Noisy, I got. Demonstrative, I got, too, though I have to admit it made me giggle that a tree—the most non-demonstrative entity I'd ever seen back on Earth, short of a boulder—was being left behind for me to deal with because, here on Kiirajanna, she was *demonstrative*.

"Why are you craving my presence?" I sang, my voice doing random ups and downs in pitch. The sing-song method of communication was the only way she'd really listen to me.

In response, I received a torrent of mental images through the physical contact I maintained. Most of them were related to the tree's fear that I would go off somewhere she couldn't get to and die. Once those were under control, though, I also got a sense that L.T. had been holed up in this little cabin for several days without either daylight or water. That horrified me, considering how rapidly her little pot could dry out.

"I'm here, all is well," I sang under my breath, and repeated it several times. There really wasn't any other way I could see to calm the tree down, as hysterical as she had become. The branches I wasn't holding were quivering, quaking, and, in a few cases, whipping around through the air.

Eventually I succeeded through repetition. Ignoring Keion's exaggerated sigh of relief when I stopped singing to the tree, I rose and stepped behind the small divider in the cabin to prepare for bed.

"I'm not certain whether the tree is your pet, or vice versa," Keion's voice carried across the room.

"How about neither?" I asked through the divider. A moment later I stepped around in my night clothes and was able to give the boy a proper glare. "L.T. is a sentient being, as am I. We like being together, but we have different means of communicating that. You should know that." I ignored his shrug as I sauntered to my bed and plopped down, happy to no longer have my backside on a horse's back. "Do the guards need us to take a shift tonight? I'm particularly exhausted."

"They have it, Princess," Aerona said. "Thank you for asking, though. You and the rest of the party can sleep through the night uninterrupted."

"We hope," Keion muttered as he slid under the covers of his own bed.

We all may have hoped, but it didn't happen that way.

Sometime between the middle of the night and the butt-crack of dawn, as Momma used to say, I came awake. I'd been dreaming, and the scene was vividly implanted in my mind. It was a nighttime landscape gone terribly wrong. Bright lights joined with the cacophony of a tremendous buzzing, all in combination with a steady rhythmic whumping as the trees around us slammed their branches to the ground.

I opened my eyes in the darkness, and as my senses slowly rejoined me, I realized that at least the noise part of the dream had been real. There was a weird, constant background buzzing hum, while the tree branch whumping sound I had heard was coming from Little Treebeard. In the strange undulating light that streamed in through the window, I watched the elm sapling raising its limbs to the sky and then smashing them downward in a frantic movement. At the same time, Draignerthol connected to the strange background hum with a buzz of its own.

"What? What?" I frantically whispered to my tree companion, trying to figure out what I needed to do to make everything right once again.

"Alyssa," Keion's voice sounded from the door. Apparently he'd already awoken and slipped out. I jerked my head up; he hadn't used such an urgent, commanding voice since the run to the library. "Come. Quickly. Hurry!"

I stood up and ran, leaving L.T. there. The tree was obviously freaking out about something, raising her little limbs and shaking. Still, I had faith that Keion wouldn't pull me away from that without good reason. I paused just long enough to wrap myself in the cloak by the door, and then I launched myself out into the frigid night air.

What awaited me there was unlike anything I'd ever seen before. The cold winter night had come spectacularly alive; the darkness, what little there was of it, seemed to shift and shimmy. My eyes landed on the elves already standing outside and then darted upward in the same direction theirs faced, just in time to take in a light show more commandingly beautiful than anything I'd ever imagined.

A bright green band undulated across the sky. I figured it had to be the northern lights—the aurora borealis—that I'd heard about and seen pictures of, except that I could actually hear a matching buzz while I watched the colored band of light dance for us. The heavens above joined Draignerthol in a long, deep-throated hum, and every time the line of color shifted, there was a corresponding shift in the overture.

Before long, a red band joined its green friend. The two swaths of brilliant light moved like twin snakes, bending and flowing about in a current I couldn't see. Meanwhile, a higher-pitched hum joined in to the symphony.

A gorgeous band of white light joined in, and even stoic Aerona, who'd come up to stand behind me, gasped. Unlike the other two bands that seemed happy enough doing their jig way up in the heavens, the white curtain swayed and twisted just above the tree tops, and it even occasionally dipped down to touch the ground out away from us.

"*Croyw*," one of the guards muttered, his voice reverent. *Pure*.

"The pure light doesn't join us except on the deepest, darkest, coldest days of winter. It is a special, and highly positive, omen," another guard added for our benefit.

The light show gained another distinct hum, one that sounded like a huge power transformer, only deeper, broader, more resonant. It reminded me of the mantra chants I'd once heard at school, but instead of being vocal it sounded electrically-generated. Draignerthol joined in and amplified all three into a joyful-sounding melody that made me want to dance. Instead, I looked around a little self-consciously, wondering whether anyone else could hear it, and was relieved to see others' heads rising and falling with the tune. My attention refocused, hypnotically, on the amazing show to our front.

"Alyssa," Keion's pointed whisper cut through the symphony. He shook my hand, which I hadn't realized till that moment had clasped itself around his. "You're glowing."

The shock of finding myself gripping Prince Charming's hand caused me to miss the meaning of his words for a moment, but as I jerked the guilty appendage away, I looked down at my own body. He was right! Amazed, I held my arms out in front of my face, stretching my fingers out to take in the blue glow emanating from all along and between them. I glanced down, and even my bare toes were putting out the same beautiful azure light.

I sensed movement to my front and looked up. Around me, in a tightened semicircle, Padrig's guards had all dropped to one knee, bowing reverently. I looked to the side to smile at Seph and was shocked that she was on her knee, too! A glance backward confirmed that Aerona had, for once, apparently decided we were safe enough to allow her own gesture of respect as she joined Seph and the guards in a deep bow.

I turned in awe toward Prince Charming, the only member of our group still standing. As I did, he shocked me more than all the rest of the group put together by granting me his own gesture of respect. Granted, he didn't go all the way down on a knee, but he was the one who'd taught me that elf princes and princesses never, ever do that, not even for the king and queen of Kiirajanna. Still, the bow of his head and and the gesture toward his chest was a sign of respect far deeper than any I'd ever expected to receive from him.

"It's just—" I started, feeling self-conscious all of a sudden and wanting to suggest that maybe it was merely a case of Draignerthol acting out in the energy of the aurora. The truth was, though, that it didn't actually feel like my pendant was doing it. Instead, the energy actually seemed to be flowing from within me. It was pretty, but it felt a little creepy at the same time.

Keion quietly shushed me.

"As foretold by the most ancient of prophecy, the Dragon Queen has come down from the heavens to rule upon Kiirajanna," Keion intoned, and everyone else freaked me right out by repeating those same words.

I let them have their little honorary ceremony, despite being completely out of sorts over it. Keion had, if you ignore the one kiss, only ever wavered between neutral and acerbic toward me. Now he was leading a ceremony exalting me, *as foretold by prophecy*. It was way too weird.

After a few moments the ceremony ended with everyone silently rising and going back to watching the lights display. All they'd said was Keion's one line. I watched the aurora dance, myself, for a couple of more minutes, but the mood had been spoiled. I turned and stumped back into the cabin.

L.T. was sulking when I got back inside.

Look, I know how silly it is to accuse an elm sapling of sulking, but I've already said far sillier things about her. Besides, I could clearly feel it through the bond I'd built. The little tree was *sulking*.

Feeling sorry, I went over to the corner and started softly humming L.T.'s favorite song, *Blue Suede Shoes*. No, I don't know why that's her favorite song. I mean, it's Momma's favorite song, too, but there can't be any connection with that, can there?.

A dose of Elvis did the trick, regardless. Before long, the little tree stopped her sulking and was writhing around happily, bouncing her little elm leaves to the tune. Then Keion came in, and she quit.

She never did like Keion.

"You're still glowing," he said, his voice still kind of reverent, as he looked directly at me and ignored the elm tree that was so pointedly ignoring him back. Now, I've never had the heart to let on to L.T. that when a tree ignores you, it's a little bit hard to tell. Still, he was right; my skin was awash in a blue glow.

"Must be Draignerthol got charged up by the aurora borealis," I explained, believing that it was a lie as I said it, but nevertheless trying to defuse the weird vibe in the air. In just a few moments, Prince Charming had gone from being the most sarcastic and arrogant person on the planet to practically worshiping me, at least as much as an elf prince would ever be willing to worship anyone. Beyond being weird, it actually frightened me.

"No," he said, shaking his head. "You're not the only one here who can sense magical energy, Alyssa, though I don't tell very many people that and I'd beg of you to keep my secret to yourself. No, now don't look at me like I've just grown a second head. You know how deeply our people resent both magic and anyone who can even sense it, much less manipulate its flows. Well, I'm a prince of the realm, and one of its most favored and popular athletes and warriors, as well. Of course I've hidden my ability from everyone—everyone except for you, anyway, and for what I hope are obvious reasons." The prince looked nervously at the door, and I could read on his confused face his fear that it would open at any moment. He thrust the conversation forward awkwardly, his voice growing quieter but more intense, "No, Alyssa, I–I can tell that that glow, that power, comes from you, from within you, not from the pendant, as powerful as the relic may be. You really are an incredibly special person, Alyssa."

"I keep hearing that," I said, crossing my arms in the best show of defiance I could muster as my body glowed blue in the night air of the solitary cabin in front of Prince Charming, who was becoming by the moment more and more obviously, and awkwardly, the only other inhabitant of that cabin. "So what's that I heard about the prophecy's foretelling? Does that one involve all the king's men, too?" I asked.

Keion chortled at that, and the mood was temporarily paused. The bit of prophecy that had been thrust in all our faces at the library involved all the king's men, and all the king's horses, riding to the Dragon Queen's—my, I suppose I learned fairly definitively—defense. It had been proven true thanks to a thoughtful transmission by Sephaline to her ranger buddies before she'd gotten sick, and Dad actually had shown up astride a black charger with over a thousand warriors behind him to fight the crucial battle. So king's men–check. King's horses–check again.

You gotta love prophecy.

"No, no king's men this time," Keion purred, his deep, resonant voice ratcheting the mood right back up there. "This is a well-known refrain from the prophecy about the Dragon Queen. That verse states simply that she will return as a brilliant light of guidance for her people, glowing brightly in the night to rival even the lights in the heavens above. I always assumed, as, I think, did everyone else, that it referred to the lights of the stars, not that your beauty and radiance would actually pull our attention away from the northern lights. But you did. Your beauty shone–"

The door banged open, ending Prince Charming's sappy mood. He turned, and I glared.

"Hi," we both greeted Seph coldly.

My cousin looked at the prince with one eyebrow raised, and then at me. Her other eyebrow went up. "I can always go sleep in the trees, under the stars and the northern lights, if you two prefer," she offered, her voice tinged with sarcasm and a few other emotions as well.

"No, it's–" I started, shaking my head, but she wasn't convinced.

"No, really, Cousin, it's plenty warm out there for a ranger, and Booboo would *love* to keep me company," she said, turning to leave.

"*Seph!*" I said, the word coming out as more of a command than I'd meant it to. It worked, though. She turned around, looked me in the eyes with a wicked grin, and shrugged.

"I just thought–" she started, and then, when neither of us started to contradict her, she left the sentence unfinished and tumbled back into her bed.

"Good night, Keion," I said, wondering why I was still longing for him, and wishing I could keep it out of my words. I couldn't have him, after all. Not ever, I reminded myself for the umpteenth time, not by a tradition much, much older than all of us put together. Granted, that tradition was only as old as the one preventing me from working magic, but I didn't dare upset elf society too much. *Period.*

If I had to choose between breaking tradition in doing magic and breaking tradition in marrying my king, I thought, it was better to break tradition to teach elves that it was okay to do magic once again. That way a whole society–the entire realm, in fact–could benefit from their enhanced abilities while Keion's promised bride could have him and....

My brain stopped at that thought. According to tradition, the king had to journey back to Earth to find a human bride as my father had, yet Keion, the likely-favored king, had already been promised an elf maiden many years his junior. I wanted to laugh at how that might, or might not, turn out well, but I was tired, and so was he, and so was my cousin, and I really owed it to the entire cabin to leave the matter for other times to consider and discuss.

L.T. didn't care. She jiggled her leaves in a tittering pattern. Luckily, elm leaves shaking was a sound both warrior and ranger were used to, so nobody yelled at her. I thought it was hilarious, of course, but I mostly just thought that I needed to get some sleep.

With that, I slipped between the rough woolen sheets of my bed, closed my eyes against the glow of my own skin, and then I fell, finally, totally exhausted, to sleep.

A Triumphant Return

The next morning, my last one atop Kiirajanna's continental Rim, I got to see for myself why they say the snow flies.

Seph and I stepped out of the cabin into a winter wonderland. Overnight, half an inch or so of the fluffy white stuff had blanketed everything around us. It was still coming down, and as I looked up into it to watch I got a strange feeling of vertigo. It felt for a moment as though I were flying up into the snow rather than the snow falling down toward me.

Unlike the hardened ice crystals that the wind whipped into my face in the frozen land of the Pobl'yrhew, these huge snowflakes were soft and fluffy when they splooshed onto my cheeks. I marveled at the fact that many of them were half an inch across or larger. The big ones were less affected than their smaller brethren by the wind gusts that churned them about to create the flying effect, but they all danced sideways as they fell. Standing there with neck craned back and looking straight up into the falling, dancing, flying granular whiteness, I was mesmerized.

"Nice, isn't it, Cousin?" Seph called over her shoulder. Her voice brought me back to the reality that I still needed to visit the outhouse. I skipped to catch up.

As the party started down the long, gradual slope back toward the center of the continent, the snow let up. By noon I was left with just a memory of the beauty in a snow-flight in the great white north.

We made a little better time going down than we had coming up, in part due to the elevation change but also thanks to our shared desire to just get home. Poor L.T. was actually shivering at times and let me know through our mental link just how much she didn't enjoy the cold. She complained that her leaves were losing their vitality, and when I assured her that dropping leaves in the winter to regrow them in the spring was perfectly normal, she balked at the idea. Apparently trees don't enjoy the change of seasons as much as you might think.

Embarrassingly enough, all the king's horses and all the king's men were indeed assembled once again, sitting and waiting on me to descend from the plateau down into central Kiirajanna. The next afternoon, Seph seemed pretty proud of herself as she trotted back to the group alongside my father and his pennant bearer, who were in turn followed by the same thirty-six of my father's finest men riding two abreast in a military column formation, just exactly as they had ridden to see me off.

"Hi, Dad," I greeted the king. I really was glad to see him, but it had been a long ride, and a long trip.

He maneuvered his massive black charger close in to Awel, who didn't seem affected at all by the crowding in of the mighty steed. He pulled off his glove, and seeing that I pulled off my own, exposing my hand briefly to the cold winter air. Reaching out, he clasped my fingers inside his own in the most tender display of affection that an armored man can physically pull off from the back of a horse.

"Alyssa, it is good to see you again. We have missed you. I trust that your journey to Ganolog was successful?"

I nodded, and he turned to the rest of the party to greet them.

"Prince. Ranger. Guardian," he acknowledged my companions. "And Gelt," he said, acknowledging the guard who'd bravely managed our steeds beside the portal. "Where's Gerallt?" he asked Gelt.

"Highness, I–" the guard started, but I felt too heavy a personal weight to let him dangle with it. Guiltily I realized that it had been a couple of days since I'd thought about the guard's sacrifice.

"Father, Gerallt died–" I started and was surprised when a sob tried to slip through my facade, but I got it under control as quickly as I could and continued, "defending me. I am sorry for–"

"We shall speak of this upon our return to Cysegredig," Dad interrupted me. I was torn; I was relieved to have not had to finish the sentence, but I also felt guilty for it. He could probably tell that I was very close to sobbing, hysterical tears, though, and knew that that discussion was better suited for a private moment. "For now, I rejoice that you are back within my care, my daughter. When I saw that you had sent the bulk of my guard back to Cysegredig, I became concerned, but I remained confident in Padrig's ability to keep you safe."

I nodded. "Your confidence was well-placed, Father. He, with some input from Prince Keion, really came up with a good plan. From the–"

Dad cut me off, looking past me toward Padrig's guard force. "I am glad that the bennaeth had a plan. He is a truly admired leader. Thank you all for escorting my daughter safely back to my care. Please express my thanks to the bennaeth upon your return."

"Dad, I–" I said, hoping to explain how they'd asked to accompany me all the way back to Cysegredig in honor of the whole Dragon Queen colorful vision thing.

"I have this, Alyssa," he muttered.

"No, Dad, you don't," I said, my words drawing a look of surprise from him as well as from my own party. I pressed forward, "Your Majesty, I, the Crown Princess of Kiirajanna, would very much like to see these brave soldiers who stood by my side in the defense of Ganolog accompany me back to the palace." It was difficult, standing up to him, but I'd heard them talking about how much they wanted to see the castle. Two of them had been to my coronation, but they'd had to stay back in the northern clan's camp rather than experience the whole thing. I wanted them to have the experience, and darn it, they deserved it!

Dad leveled an unreadable gaze my way. I'd expected either hurt or anger, but I saw neither. Instead, the king glared for a moment and then suddenly popped a smile. He nodded once and then said, "Daughter, Highness, I, the King of all the land and realm of Kiirajanna, would very much like to declare your request granted. " He raised my hand to his lips and kissed my knuckles in a sign of loving respect, and then he spun his charger about and took off down the path.

I watched him and his vanguard thunder away, shocked. I'd won.

That night, just like the nights we'd spent on the trail returning from the library, we didn't stop at the ranger cabins. His Royal Majesty didn't–couldn't, Keion had explained–stay in a mere ranger's cabin due to his regal status. Nor would I, apparently, once I finally got the crown placed on my head. It wasn't like we really needed a cabin, though. The king's guard carried a whole camp with them, complete with a pavilion-sized tent and enough cots for everybody. That, and another couple of hundred men to put up and take the camp down as needed. When the queen traveled, they actually brought a full bed frame that could be lashed together, along with a set of thick rugs to keep her feet off of the ground, an actual mattress, and enough freestanding room dividers to set off a full bedroom, a dressing room, and a reception area. He could have all that too, Dad had explained, but he preferred a simple cot in memory of his military days.

Before long the two of us were relaxing, stretching our legs out near the bonfire while looking up into the clear and chilly night sky. The cook had brought us each over a roast leg of something that was layered with plenty of tasty meat, and everybody else took their food elsewhere to allow us to dine by ourselves.

Dad pulled a flask from somewhere underneath his armor, uncorked it, and handed it over. I sniffed and recoiled; it was whiskey.

"Um—no thanks. I still haven't recovered from this one night at Padrig's. I'm not sure if I'll ever drink again."

My father snorted at me and took a swig. "Did I not warn you ahead of time about that, Alyssa?"

"You did, you did. You told me so, you sure did. It was just that it was such a festive evening, us just coming back from a hunt, and everybody was dancing and drinking, and nobody would let my glass go empty."

"He took you on a hunt." Dad said. It was a question, but it really wasn't, nor did he seem surprised, so I wasn't certain how to answer it.

"Yes."

The next few seconds drew out into a very pregnant pause. I had no idea where it was going.

"Well?" he asked, finally.

"Well, what?"

"Did you get anything? You have hunted before, have you not?"

"No, I haven't, and no, I didn't. Aerona was about ready to battle Halbiorn when he came up, though. Just herself, and just with daggers."

"Halbiorn—the bear?" Dad's neck swiveled so that he was looking directly at me, a shocked look playing through the fire's flickering light.

"Is there another Halbiorn?" Since I'd survived the encounter, I felt worthy of wisecracking a little about it.

"That beast is but a whispered legend down here. So I heard the tale of my daughter's inebriated rebuff of the bennaeth's son, but nothing of her encounter with one of the most powerful creatures in the realm. That—well, that is how these matters typically work, unfortunately."

"You already knew about Llew?"

Dad chortled and handed me the flask again. "Drink, Alyssa. Those are legs that you need to pull back underneath yourself. You must learn to control it so that it does not ever control you. But yes, I have my sources for information up there."

"Grigor," I said, nodding, and then I took a swig.

The liquor burned a little, but then it started doing its job of warming my insides, and so I took another swig and then handed it back to Dad. Before, the smell of it made me feel like gagging, but once I'd taken it back in, the sick feeling went right away.

"You are aware of his position, I take it?"

I glanced around, trying to judge how isolated our discussion really was. With all the secrecy up there and in the note my uncle wrote, I figured that I had to assume the same was called for in camp, too. Instead of voicing it, I just nodded.

"Did he behave—strangely?"

I shrugged. I had no idea how to answer the question. Yes, yes, and triple yes, Grigor had behaved strangely. But he was my father's uncle, and he'd explained much of it away. The request to not even let my father in on the contents of the letter bothered me a little, but as a test it made sense. Dad and Grigor obviously corresponded, and so I was sure that letting Grigor's missive to me slip would make it back to him and be seen as a weakness.

Finally I settled on a firm non-response. "Everybody up there behaved strangely, Dad. Grigor was no stranger than the rest."

"I see," he said, but from his calculating, questioning expression, I wondered how much he actually did see.

"Dad, can I ask you a question?"

"Why do you need to ask a question to ask a question, my beloved daughter?"

"I–I don't. I guess. It's just that I've been through such a weird time of not being able to trust those I wanted to trust. Did Keion tell you that we walked right into the home of Blodwyn the Grey?"

"I was so informed," Dad said in a tone that suggested it hadn't come from Keion.

"Oh, right. Your source."

"Was that your question? It is a strange choice."

"No, no. It was just meant to illustrate how strange it's been since we left. My question was a lot simpler. Why didn't you want Padrig's guard accompanying us back to Cysegredig, and why did you react the way you did when I countered you?"

Dad snorted again. "You say your question is single, and then you ask two in one. You will make a magnificent queen, doing that."

I shrugged. "Fair enough. Two questions, then, and simple ones."

"Allow this old man the benefit of responding to them separately, please. And, I should add, in the opposite order from the asking. I reacted the way I did when you countermanded my order because I was quite proud of you, my daughter. Though I disagreed, and still do, with your decision, I recognized the growth required in you, personally, to stand up to me, and especially in the positive manner that you managed it. I am proud of you."

"Okay, thanks, but why didn't you want Padrig's men to accompany us to Cysegredig?"

Dad looked sideways at me and sighed. Several moments passed, as did several hits of the whiskey for us both, before he finally sighed again, took in a long breath, and answered my question.

"Alyssa, I wanted the bennaeth's guard to return safely to Ganolog rather than travel to Cysegredig because...," he started, and then he paused again. I was just getting ready to ask him to continue when he did, pain creeping into his voice. "Because Ganolog and Cysegredig will be at war by the time they can get back."

"War...?" I sat there, stunned silent, for a long while. Finally I was able to ask, "War with Padrig? Why?"

Dad shook his head. "No. Not with Padrig. With Ganolog."

"I fail to see the difference."

He lost the depressed tone and went back to speaking briskly, instructively. "You need to work on it, then, as this is an essential understanding for a future ruler. If you are at odds with another person, even another member of the peerage as Padrig is, then that is a fight. If you are at odds with an entire clan, then that is a war."

"But I thought you and Padrig were old friends, that you respected each other enough that—well, that nothing could bring you to war."

"You are still not getting the point, Alyssa. Padrig and I are, personally, very close, but that does not prevent his territory and mine from being in conflict."

"So you two can remain friends while still sending your armies to fight one another."

"Precisely."

I looked across the darkness, hoping to see a hint of sarcasm in the fire's flickers lighting up my father's face. When I saw none, I shook my head again and said, "Still not getting it. Maybe it would help if you told me why you believe you're probably going to war."

"It is simple. I want Blodwyn the Grey."

"You want her–to torture?"

"I want her to question. I believe that torture rarely works to obtain valid information. Whatever you call it, though, and to whatever extent that it goes, I *will* obtain the names of the leaders of the Cult of the Wyrm, and she is the most likely to have that information. Thus, war."

"Can't you just ask Padrig for her?"

"Certainly. I already have, in fact. I can also ask the horses to carry us all the way back to Cysegredig at a gallop. Neither is likely to happen, as I hope you understand by now."

I looked across the fire toward the tent where I knew that Ellga would be working to prepare my bedding for my arrival. I thought of what she had taught me regarding northern clan values, and then nodded. "No matter what Blodwyn's done, she's still a member of his clan, and you're not."

"Precisely."

"And you're not willing to trust what he tells you he obtained from her."

"It is not a matter of trust in Padrig. I cannot allow such knowledge to be kept from me. Not while my daughter's life and succession to the throne hang in the balance."

"I sure am tired of being the cause of so much angst and fighting, you know, Dad."

"I do not envy your position. And yet, if you were to abdicate, the same prophecy lays even more strife, pestilence, and suffering at your feet."

"Strife, pestilence, and suffering. Wow. All I lack is death, and I'd be the antichrist. No, never mind, it's another of those Earth stories. So, I take it you're going to signal to Padrig that you want her, and if he somehow magically agrees, war will be averted, and if not, then we'll have ourselves a clan brawl?"

"I have already been assured by my contact in Ganolog that Padrig is not receptive to any request I have made. He has, in fact, already sent forces to capture this Blodwyn. So have I." Dad was looking off into the distance, but I could sense the steel in his attitude from his voice.

"Oh. Well, then. I think I get it, finally. You've sent an armed expedition into the northlands without the permission of the clans up there, thus effectively declaring war."

"Correct."

"So, Dad, forgive me for this one remaining little sliver of ignorance, but I am drawn to ask—since you've gone and done something that is so much against the northern way of thinking—how do you know that you and Padrig will still be friends once this is all over and done?"

"I do not," Dad said, turning toward me. For the first time, I saw something that looked like uncertainty in his eyes. "I merely make the best decisions I can for those who are under my protection. I am, I confess, quite tired, though, and so I find myself needing to beg your leave, my daughter."

It had already been a weird conversation, but the king begging the princess's leave to depart took the whole cake of weird. Still trying to digest what had happened, I nodded, and to my surprise he rose. As I watched, my father unfolded his entire length upward from his sitting position, and then he slowly and with some effort donned his king facade right there in front of me. First his shoulders rolled back into the regal posture, and then his head rotated up. One deep breath was all that remained for the mask of royalty, and then he regally stepped over to the tent and entered.

It wasn't supposed to be like that, I told myself. King outranks everybody, and so he decides who goes to bed when. It suddenly occurred to me just how much stress and strain he had to be going through. He had all of the machinations that were normally part of politics, and then the cancer of the Cult to boot, and suddenly in order to protect his own daughter he had to declare war on his best friend.

No wonder he was tired. I wondered how much more weight that I didn't know about he'd been carrying on those broad shoulders.

Suddenly exhausted, too, I rose and followed him into the tent, and then allowed myself to slip into the warm cot that Ellga had prepared for me. The quiet rustling of elm leaves beside the bed provided a nice, calming effect that I sorely needed, and I softly hummed my thanks to L.T. as I drifted off to sleep.

DICTER

anger, wrath. The normal expression on the high priestess's face, in other words.

Interrogation

"So," the high priestess spat, glowering at me across her simple wooden desk. Her hands were held palms together in what would have been a prayerful position if there hadn't been so much tension in them that her fingertips turned white. Her eyes bulged, unblinking, and her nostrils flared while her lips scrawled a thin, rigid, bleak line across her drawn and flushed face.

I waited to see what the rest of her sentence would be, but finally realized that she'd intended the one word to serve by itself. She was hotter than a skillet in Hell's kitchen. High Priestess Naissa went from Sternyface to Furiousface in less than the moment I required to take the seat across from her.

"Naissa, it's—" my father started to speak. He'd come in after me and taken up a dangerous-looking pose, leaning against a bookshelf across the room with his hands on his hips and elbows out. He looked like one of those gunslingers trying to appear relaxed just before he draws and shoots.

The high priestess didn't seem to notice his posture; she apparently took his voice as a reason to continue speaking, and angrily cut him off.

"There's no need to say anything, Cadfael," she hissed, still boring through my face into my soul with the heat of her glare. I barely held back a gasp of outrage, managing to keep my face blank with some effort. I opened my mouth to object, to ask how dare she speak in such a manner to my father, the king, but she rolled right over me in a quiet voice that was sharp enough to slice through stone. "The *one* thing I asked of your daughter—begged of her!—upon her departure was that she avoid entirely, or at the very least limit the visibility of, her use of the powers that have been forbidden our kind for centuries! Your response, Alyssa? You managed, right there in the grand hall of Ganolog, to skewer a dozen men with lightning bolts, and then later you lit up the *entire* northern sky. I am willing to believe that you could, *somehow*, have found a way to do the exact opposite of what I asked you to do even more obviously and capriciously than you did, but for the life of me I cannot figure out how that might have been done." She turned her glare down to her hands for a moment, realized how much force she was putting into pressing them together, and then repositioned her palms to lie separately on the desk. She looked back up at me, and her face lost just the teensiest portion of its glare.

"Does the future of the land that you are destined to lead mean so little to you, child?"

I glared back at her silently for several long moments. It didn't take long for her manifested fury to slice through her attempt at patience. She raised her eyebrows and shot a single-word query at me.

"Well?"

"High Priestess Naissa," I answered, sitting up rod-straight and drawing my voice out to match the quality of hers. Out of the corner of my eye I noticed Dad moving toward us, probably ready to break up a fistfight if needed, though I wasn't heading that way. "I am *not* a child, nor am I a simpleton to need the same lecture more than once. I am well aware of the danger to our society of someone using magic simply to further their own needs, but that was precisely what I managed to *end* as I cut down the sorcerous dogs of the Cult. One of them, in fact, had already used his power to kill Padrig's most capable defender. The bennaeth had told us to escape if he fell, but when he saw the Cult members using magic, he *asked* me to use my own power in his defense. Would you prefer I have let him *die*?" I waited for half a second in hopes that she would shake her head. She didn't, and so I pressed forward quickly for fear of being cut off like my father had been. "Besides, I did *not* light up the northern sky; the Aurora Borealis did. All that I am guilty of is–glowing, a little. And even that wasn't intentional!"

Her mask of fury dropped cleanly off of her face, and she sent my father a shocked look. She turned back to me and asked, "You–glowed? What do you mean by that, exactly?"

I nodded, pleased with myself that I'd broken the interrogation so quickly. "Yes, I glowed. We were awoken by the guards, who were excited to see the lights so early in the winter. That is why I stepped out of the cabin in bare feet and sleeping clothes with only a cloak wrapped around me. Keion said, 'Alyssa, you're glowing,' and I looked down to see that he was right. There was a blue light coming from every inch of my body, from my feet to my fingertips. I promise you, I didn't do anything consciously to make that happen. It just did."

"Cadfael, did you know this?" Naissa asked my father, who just shrugged and slipped back into a more relaxed pose.

"No, I did not. Neither she, nor her guards, deigned to tell me of such an occurrence during the two days of our return trip. I am going to have to beat that prince, I see."

"Father," I chided, shaking my head. I hoped that I guessed right that he was only joking, and then I turned back to Sternyface. "I didn't think it was a big deal, but everyone else did, mumbling something about prophecy and glowing and Dragon Queen. And then they bowed."

"I'm going to suggest that you put some effort into getting used to dealing with that type of behavior, Alyssa," Sternyface said. She rubbed her eyes for a moment and then continued, "Not that you have demonstrated any particular propensity toward following my suggestions, of course, but you might actually find that one useful."

"How is a new high priestess selected?" I blurted out.

"What?" Naissa asked, obviously taken off guard by the question. "From what I have studied of your religious traditions on Earth, it is very similar to how a new Pope is selected. Why do you ask?"

"Oh. I don't know how a new Pope is selected, either."

"Well, it is a process in which—never mind. The High Priestess of Kiirajanna is selected from among the peerage. That is all. But why, Alyssa, do you ask such a question?"

She'd actually called me by my name twice in a row, and that brightened my day considerably. It was the first time she'd used something other than *child* to address me since I'd come to Kiirajanna. "Well, I don't know for sure, but you and Dad seem to be about the same age, and you, Dad, and the Queen make up a ruling triumvirate. It was just a guess that the transition to a new King and Queen would also call for a new High Priestess."

"Do you want to get rid of me that badly, Alyssa?" she asked.

She seemed genuinely curious, so I let down my guard and answered truthfully. "Well, yes, and no. I mean, no, I don't want to get rid of you badly at all. You are wise, and widely respected. You've taught me a great deal, even though I guess I don't seem to show that very often. We had a–a rough start, so to speak. I just don't have the connection with you that my father seems to have, and I wondered whether the transition happened across the board for that reason."

Naissa nodded, serious once again. She gazed thoughtfully at my father's face, and then her eyes focused off into a distant corner of the room as she drew a breath. She met my eyes to answer, "First, I suppose that I should be honored that you imagine your father and I to be about the same age, Alyssa. That is not the case, but I appreciate the error. I am nearly two hundred cycles old. No, really," she added; I must have looked as shocked as I felt. "That is something we are concerned about, in fact; all elves, in times long past, had lifespans similar to those of the priesthood, but these days–well, we do not, and it is puzzling to our best scholars. Those of us who serve in the priesthood still often live nice, long lives, but the remainder of our race barely live as long as the humans any more."

"There has to be a reason for that," I offered, and she smiled and nodded.

"Of course there is," she said. "We just have yet to find it. But if I may steer this conversation back to your original query, no, the high priestess does not transition at the same time as the royalty do. That serves to maintain a constancy of knowledge, if nothing else. The closeness you have observed between your father and me is a simple matter of personality meshing. Specifically, I appreciate the current Cadfael's wit and personality." She stopped and smiled at my father, who nodded mutely and smiled back. "We have bonded, and are–well, to use a term loosely, friends. I wouldn't expect such a thing during your term as queen, Alyssa, because it hasn't happened in my memory or to my knowledge before, but.... Well, let me just say that your father has been a singularly popular elf king, not just in my eyes, but in the entire realm's, and that, in turn, elevates him greatly in my opinion. You would do quite well to select a co-ruler similar in popularity, if not everything else, to your father."

Great, I thought. The old stereotype of girls trying to marry a guy just like their father was one thing, but I actually needed to find a *king* just like my father. No problem, right?

"That's going to be difficult," I said. "My father is one in a million, I'd say."

He smiled at the compliment, but Naissa exhaled a long, sad sigh. "Unfortunately for Kiirajanna, Alyssa, I believe you have judged correctly. Still, you will not be alone in your search when the time comes."

"We have plenty of time to worry about that," Dad said, shrugging off the conversation. "I am not going anywhere anytime soon. My daughter is, however, so if you are done with her, Naissa, may I take her from you in order to accompany her to her next hazing session?"

The High Priestess turned a playful glare on Dad. I couldn't help but imagine that if I hadn't been there she would have stuck her tongue out at him, the way her eyes twinkled over a barely-suppressed grin.

"Fine," she said, sending a more serious expression my way. "Get her out of my sight, Your Majesty. And Crown Princess, if I hear of you working more of your magic here in Cysegredig, I *swear* that I shall—" She didn't finish; I'd started turning around, but on hearing the threat begin I jerked my head back over my shoulder to give her a dangerous look.

Our glares crossed that way for several long seconds, until finally she shocked me. She looked away, and I actually won the mute stare-down.

"Go," she commanded, following the single word by sitting down and pulling out some papers.

TE

tea. I suppose it's really kind of a universal, ever-present word.

Afternoon Tea

The next hazing session, it turned out, was to be in the queen's private chamber, and at a very specific time.

She'd invited me to take afternoon tea with her.

Of course, *invited* is too weak of a word, though technically that's what she did. She'd asked my father to pass along her sincere *invitation*, he said. When the queen of Kiirajanna invites you to afternoon tea, though, there's really no difference between that and receiving orders from my father. It's just like in high school when the principal *invites* you into his office. Whether or not you really want tea, you go—to the queen, that is, not to the principal's office.

Not that I minded much. I'd joined her for different tea sessions a few times, and enjoyed the more formal event of afternoon tea once before, immediately after my coronation ceremony. To me it felt like playing dress-up games as a kid, but she'd been raised British, and so the ritual was no game to her.

Luckily, I still remembered all the steps to it—the cordial greeting, the guest sitting down first, the elegant way to add sugar and cream to the tea, and the order in which we took the little delectables from the sweet tray and the savory tray. Tea wasn't just something she drank. It was literally a ritual, its step-by-step process something to be adhered to no matter what.

I even remembered the bit about always leading with small talk, so I pushed my curiosity aside and smiled more or less pleasantly as we talked about the change in seasons, and how I'd been through my first truc snowfall, and how exciting it was that the boys would soon be engaged in their winter sporting events. The last bit almost made me crack a grimace from the memories of arguments with Keion, but I managed to keep a straight smile going. I was getting better at faking facial expressions.

"So, Alyssa, I am led to understand that you succeeded at your first quest," she said mildly after a while. There was just the subtlest change in her tone, but it was there, and I caught it, and it signaled that small talk time was over.

I nodded, not sure how much detail on eating moose head stew, riding weihr, and playing the northern elf games to get into over fancy tea cups and plates.

"Bennaeth Padrig gave me his blessing, Your Majesty."

"Oh, I am sure there is much more to the story than that, Alyssa. Please, do tell me. It has been so very long since I have called upon our northern cousins, a group I quite miss. When you are queen, you must make it your business to get out and see the people more often than I have. It is so difficult to do, with all the business here, but it is also so very vital. Your father is such a popular king, yet I am—well, never mind. Please, tell me a story."

I nodded as I chewed a little sweet pastry, stalling, not sure what to think about her comment about Dad. Was she— jealous? Could she, who had three incredibly beautiful and talented children, kids who were the talk of all the realm, really be jealous of my father, the man who brought only a gangly, smart aleck Mississippi girl to be queen?

Nah. It couldn't be. She was the queen, and she had nothing to be jealous over. I went on and told her the story of our arrival, followed by the hunt. She brightened up as I spoke, seeming for to be just a normal girl hearing a story for the first time.

"I've heard that they enjoy eating the marrow of animals. What was it like? Was it squishy and strange?"

"No, it was actually a little bit chewy, and the flavor was strong. I mean, it was good. I've never had anything quite like it, though. It was like a salty beef jerky with a gamey flavor and a bit of a fatty texture."

"Oh, okay," she said, her voice tentative.

"You've never had beef jerky before, either, have you, Your Highness?"

"No, I have not, but you must stop calling me Your Highness. At least, here, over tea. The term is too stuffy for a conversation with my future replacement. Just call me Talaith."

"Okay. Talaith it is, then," I said, using the elf name for the queen as she'd requested. As all kings are Cadfael, so are all queens Talaith. It hit me as odd; some day people would call me by that name. It was almost like I was talking to a future version of myself.

Talaith said, "When I went up there, it was mid-summer, which I must say is a spectacularly beautiful time in the northern reaches. I remember it being the first time I'd eaten real, wild-caught salmon, and I showed so much love for it that Padrig sends me some of the fresh harvest every year."

"Probably not any longer," I said, remembering my father's comments about war with Ganolog.

From the nod she gave me, I could tell that she knew about it already. She shrugged. "It is just salmon. A tasty treat, nothing more."

"We should worry more over the real casualties of war, shouldn't we?" I asked. It felt weird to discuss war while nibbling on sweet cakes.

The queen, apparently, agreed. "My dear Alyssa, while enjoying tea together, we should speak of more pleasant topics." She busied herself choosing another pastry; apparently the selection of a more pleasant topic was up to me.

Her comment about the fishing clan reminded me of something, though. While it was an unpleasant topic to me, I figured it probably wasn't to her. "So, Talaith, what am I supposed to do with a slave?"

Talaith stopped mid-bite and cocked her head to the side, a curious expression on her face. "A what? Where did you get a slave, Alyssa?"

"Padrig gave me one, sort of. Lent me one is probably more accurate. It's—well, it's a long, and weird, story."

"We have some time, you know."

I figured I didn't have much to lose; Sternyface already knew all about the magic, after all. It couldn't hurt to tell Talaith as well, and if I didn't tell her, that might insult her later on. So I told her the story—the whole story, starting with my rebuffing of Llew, followed by our trek through the snowy mountain pass, and then the journey back to Ganolog and our defense of Padrig. The only part I left out was Grigor.

Talaith listened, her expression delicately unreadable. "Wow," she said after I'd wound down, and then she nodded to herself and repeated the declaration. "Wow. That's quite the story, Alyssa. It is far more danger-filled than my simple tale of going up to Ganolog in the summer, eating nice meals, and being sent back a few days later with the bennaeth's blessing.

Padrig actually gave you permission—asked you, even—to use magic in his defense?"

I nodded.

"Wow," she said again.

Since this was the first English conversation I'd had with her in a while, I was surprised at her choice. "Do British people normally say wow?" I asked.

"Oh, yes," she said, smiling. "That is a fairly universal term, I would think. But, back to your story. You say that Padrig gave you Merfyn's granddaughter to keep as your own slave here in Cysegredig till the Digonol ben has done his duty for the winter?"

I nodded, having just taken a bite of a tasty piece of bread and not wanting to talk to the queen with my mouth full.

"Well, then, she's yours to use as you see fit. You could send her to the kitchens, but the castle has plenty of kitchen workers as it is. I suppose—"

"But she's a slave," I interrupted. "I don't think the British have had slaves for centuries, and neither have the Americans I grew up with. Doesn't that—I don't know, doesn't it bother you?"

Talaith's expression grew serious. "Alyssa, life here is—" she started, and then stopped. Looking up at a blank spot on the wall for a moment, she sighed, slowly and deeply. Finally, she refocused her eyes on my face. "Elves take slaves, dear. It's not a permanent matter of ownership, nor is it a trivial matter, but it is part of the society in which you and I find ourselves. If you choose to try to change that society, then by all means I wish you luck, but—well, I suppose that my own reign has not been punctuated by such brave overtures. It has, instead, been quite boring by comparison, and will likely generate absolutely no songs for our bardds. That is what I get, I suppose, for being succeeded by the Dragon Queen."

"What does that mean?" I was curious, and nobody had managed to answer the question yet.

"It means that you are the Dragon Queen, she of whom the great works of prophecy have spoken," she replied with a shrug.

"Why dragon, though? I get the queen part, and everything else in prophecy and so on, but what do dragons have to do with it, when they've been extinct for centuries?"

"Millennia, I believe, is the correct time frame. Yet, I do not know the answer to your question, Alyssa. Maybe a long conversation with the high priestess–do you really call her Sternyface?" She giggled lightly when I nodded, and then she continued, "Your father told me, and just between you and me, I think that is hilarious. Trust me, she was every bit as severe with me as she has been with you."

"I suppose I should've expected that. Did she get nicer after you became queen?"

Talaith shook her head, still grinning. "No, I cannot say that she did. That said, if you are looking for my advice, you should sit down with her and beg for her honest opinion. She keeps much to herself, and speaking with her can be like caressing a pineapple, but she will tell you what you need to know."

"Okay. I will." I didn't have a problem with the idea of asking for Sternyface's opinion. Heck, I figured that might even make her happy for once.

"Now, tell me about the Aurora Borealis. Remember, I went during the summertime."

I told her about watching the bands of light expand and shrink in the sky above, and how it had been an aural experience in addition to visual, all while trying to be as descriptive as possible. She loved it. It was obvious, from the expression on her face, that she really didn't get out much.

"Keion told me that you glowed," she said. It was a statement, not a question.

"I did. When the lights were playing their way across the sky, every bit of my skin glowed blue. That was the weirdest thing."

"They told you that that was the fulfillment of yet another prophecy, did they not?"

"They did. They bowed accordingly," I said with as much disdain as I could put into the word *bowed*.

"Good. You should probably put some effort into becoming accustomed to such horrible and inhumane treatment," she said with a sly grin, and then the grin disappeared as she looked at me much more intently. "Alyssa, it is obvious to me that you are to be the queen of whom the prophecy was written. While I do not know entirely what that means at this point, nor am I likely to ever know, I would ask you to promise that you will take care of my son through it all."

"Your—your son?" I asked, stunned into stuttering. I'd built several mental images of where her request was going while she spoke, but Keion wasn't part of any of those. "But—but Keion has taken care of me through two battles so far, to be honest. He is already a great warrior."

"Keion is a great warrior, yes. He has been trained by the best, and no doubt he has blossomed into a force to be reckoned with on the battlefield. But if what I have understood of the prophecy comes to pass, his physical prowess will matter far less than the powers that you wield with the help of your legendary amulet. Please, Princess, promise to take care of my son."

Sometimes I can be a little slow on the uptake, but I finally caught on to the inflection in her voice, her failure to mention her daughters in her request, and the fact that she darted her eyes down toward my heart when she said the word *son*. She wasn't asking me to take care of Keion's physical condition, and that realization punched me in the gut.

"I–I promise," I whispered. It was all I could do, despite my brooding doubt that I'd ever have the chance to keep it. There were so very many reasons that he and I could never–but then I wondered if that was the direction she was going. Maybe she wanted me to refrain from going down a path that we all knew was forbidden? I realized that I'd made a promise with no idea what I'd just agreed to, and I could tell from her brightening expression that the opportunity to ask for clarification was past.

"Thank you. Alyssa, it has been wonderful sharing tea with you. Please, consider yourself invited any day that your duties leave you free to attend."

"I will, Talaith," I said as I accepted her assistant's hand in rising and leaving. Dismissal by the queen was difficult to miss. As I left, I noted that her invitation had been phrased in a sneaky, sideways manner. Any time I might demonstrate that my duties left me free to attend, I'd be silently calling into question the importance of the training I still needed to get to. That would be a bad message to send.

Dad surprised me by still being out in the hallway. "Have a nice time?" he asked as we walked. I smiled; as much as I was looking forward to some alone time in the comfort of my own room, I was very happy for another chance to walk and talk with him, especially after the gut-wrenching end of the conversation over tea.

"I did." I didn't figure he needed to know about my turmoil over Keion.

"Did the two of you discuss all of the trip?" he asked, his voice tinged with meaning.

"Nearly all," I said, nodding.

"Ah," he said with his own nod. He apparently felt capable of guessing, without asking, which parts of the trip I hadn't discussed with the queen.

"Do I need to increase your guard?" he asked. We'd sent Padrig's guard home under Dad's promise of peaceful passage in spite of the diplomatic situation, and so all I had with me was Aerona. Still, I felt perfectly safe under her watch, and so I shook my head.

"Alyssa," he said as we neared my door. I stopped and turned, and he did the same. We stood facing each other in the hall for several moments, and then he spoke quietly.

"I am very proud of you."

Suddenly nothing I'd been through, and nothing I would face in the coming months, mattered.

My father had just said the most important words of my life.

About the Author

Dean by day and writer by night, Stephen H. King grew up being asked whether he was "that Stephen King." "Not the author," he'd say until his writing addiction took hold and made that into a lie. Now he writes and reads and blogs as The Other Stephen King--you know, the one who writes fantasy and science fiction. When he's not writing, he enjoys thinking about writing while going on hikes or long road trips. When he's not thinking about writing, it's usually because he's fishing.

Find other Stephen H. King works at:
http://TheOtherStephenKing.com

Read his ongoing thoughts about writing, authorpreneurship, and other key parts of life at his blog:
http://TheOtherStephenKingOnWriting.blogspot.com